By Marc Jacobs © 2020

The Hidden Coordinate
(Book 2 in *The Coordinate Series*)

It has been three years since Emma James and Logan West chased down the clues of mankind's past, leading humanity into a new era of intergalactic exploration. Happily settled into college life and working part-time at the Pentagon on top-secret projects worthy of one's wildest imagination, the future looked bright for them. All seemed well until a mysterious signal beckoned from the other side of the planet. Compelled to investigate, the United States government would once again call upon Emma and Logan to help solve the mystery. Only this time, they find themselves investigating a secret hidden in mythologies not just around the globe but across the galaxy, on a collision course with a dangerous destiny neither were prepared for... *Emma's*.

Copyright

[handwritten: G—7 Good seq. #2]

This book is a work of fiction. Names, characters, places, and events are the product of the author's imagination and are not used factiously. Any resemblance to actual persons, living or dead, events, or locales is entirely coincidental.

Printed in the United States of America

First Printing, 2020

Paperback ISBN: 978-0-578-69790-1

Publisher: Marc Jacobs

marc@marcjacobsauthor.com
www.marcjacobsauthor.com

Dedication

To My Loving Family, Friends, and Editors:
This book is dedicated with love and appreciation to my family, JJ,
MJ, and CJ; my friends; and my incredible editors – Thank you,
Edward!! Thank you, Sue!! – who have inspired me and helped me
to make this sequel become a reality.

Contents

CHAPTER 1 – MIT'AWI CHASKA   7

CHAPTER 2 – THE SEVEN SISTERS   23

CHAPTER 3 – PEGASUS EAST   32

CHAPTER 4 – BIG FOOT   50

CHAPTER 5 – AN IMPERFECT PLAN   65

CHAPTER 6 – A MESSAGE FROM CHERSKY   82

CHAPTER 7 – CRASH COURSE   97

CHAPTER 8 – OPERATION RED SNOW   102

CHAPTER 9 – ONE SMALL STEP...   113

CHAPTER 10 – SIGNAL ACQUIRED   128

CHAPTER 11 – REF. #: 137A-2D-444   143

CHAPTER 12 – BREAKER OF CODES   157

CHAPTER 13 – THE FINAL JOURNEY OF THE VANIR   167

CHAPTER 14 – A SMALL FAVOR   183

CHAPTER 15 – A LONG WAY FROM HOME   203

CHAPTER 16 – REMNANTS   227

CHAPTER 17 – THE SECRET OF EVERYTHING   245

CHAPTER 18 – MACHU PICCHU   259

CHAPTER 19 – THE TEMPLE OF THE MOON   276

CHAPTER 20 – THE FAULT IN THE STARS   284

CHAPTER 21 – THE VOYAGE HOME   297

CHAPTER 22 – THE TREE GATES OF JAANNOS   308

CHAPTER 23 – THE FROZEN SHARDS   316

CHAPTER 24 – BETTER AND BETTER   335

CHAPTER 25 – LUNDSTRÖM'S THEORY   346

CHAPTER 26 – RAIN CHECK   366

CHAPTER 27 – ONLY A MATTER OF TIME   373

CHAPTER 28 – INSERTION POINT   388

CHAPTER 29 – GLASS HOUSES   399

CHAPTER 30 – EXTRACTION POINT   416

CHAPTER 31 – REFLECTIONS   429

Chapter 1 – Mit'awi Chaska

"How many more weeks of this?" asked Harry Foote, uncomfortably sitting on top of a slow-moving, bag-laden mule. His back was killing him. They had been exploring the remote jungle west of Cusco, Peru in the Andes Mountains for weeks, and Harry was starting to have regrets.

Hiram Bingham, riding a pack mule of his own and loving every minute of it, responded, "What? Where else would you rather be, back in your chemistry lab?"

"Why, yes!" exclaimed Harry, sweating profusely from the thick humidity clinging to his skin. He had only agreed to join his long-time college friend and now Yale faculty colleague, South American history professor Hiram Bingham, on this expedition because no one else wanted to go with Hiram on his foolhardy search for the last Inca capital... except for Harry and their other college buddy, William Erving. Since the three men graduated from Yale in 1898, 13 years earlier, they had remained the best of friends.

"Wait!" hollered William from the distant rear downhill, struggling to control his mule and trailing far behind. William's mule had actually stopped in the middle of a small stream for an impromptu siesta.

"Give 'em a kick," Hiram shouted back, laughing. William was a highly-trained surgeon back at Yale, but he was no adventurer.

William tried kicking his mule in the ribs with both feet, but the mule felt nothing beneath the leather bags covering its body.

"Harder!" encouraged Hiram. "And put some heel into it!"

William tried again, kicking his mule with everything he had, but like before, the mule barely noticed. William kept kicking until eventually he lost his balance, slid off his mule, and plopped into the stream.

Hiram watched William fall into the water. He shook his head, chuckled, and privately wondered whether the challenges of this jungle adventure exceeded Harry's and William's skillsets. He thought that bringing his college friends along made sense. After all, one was now a chemistry professor and the other, a doctor. Putting together a well-rounded team with diverse skillsets was not only practical, but it was also how he justified receiving funding for all three for this expedition. Unfortunately for Harry and William, their skills borne of higher education didn't translate to the jungle as Hiram hoped. Still, Hiram was correct about one thing: he thought it would be fun for the three friends, each now in their mid-30s, to do this together, and as he watched William splash around in the stream cursing at the innocent jungle, he knew he was right.

"Stop your griping and get up, will you?" screamed Harry, tired of William constantly lagging behind, convinced they would have found the ruins by now if it wasn't for him.

William stood up in the water, and just as soon as he did, unprompted, his mule rushed forward to join the other beasts of burden uphill. "Of course," griped William.

Up ahead, the jungle's branches and leaves rustled and swayed. Someone or something approached.

"Melchor, is that you?" asked Hiram, fairly certain it was but wanting to make sure because, in these parts of the Andes, not all natives welcomed their presence.

"Ari, upiy," confirmed a high-pitched voice from the trees, speaking Quechua. Melchor Arteaga, a local farmer from Cusco who had been guiding Hiram's team for weeks, emerged from the jungle's dense foliage.

8

The short farmer, like most native Quechuans, had brown skin and long straight black hair. Melchor had gone ahead to scout the upcoming terrain and, if necessary, negotiate with locals to ensure safe passage for the Americans. Sometimes, bartering away their supplies was the only way to make that happen. And where not even bartering would do, Melchor knew which alternate routes to take. Suffice it to say, Melchor's services were invaluable.

Hiram stepped off his mule to talk to Melchor. At six foot four with a lanky build, Hiram easily stepped down to the ground. He wore tall hiking boots, beige khakis, a long-sleeved pale-yellow collared shirt, and a brown vest. A heavy brimmed hat covered his head. Being fully clothed in these parts was critical because of the insects.

Harry jumped down to the mushy ground to join Hiram. Standing only five foot eight, Harry's drop down was longer. "Does he know where he's going?" asked Harry.

"Of course, he does," assured Hiram. Hiram last visited Peru two years earlier in 1909, when Melchor guided him to the Inca ruins at Choqquequirau. Melchor proved himself indispensable on that expedition, and Hiram saw no reason to doubt him now. Hiram removed his hat, revealing soaking-wet blond hair. "We're almost there, I'm sure of it," he said, trying to reassure his friend.

"You know, we've already got more than enough to publish," Harry reminded Hiram. They had been away from home for nearly two months, and Harry was ready to return home to his family.

"I know," responded Hiram.

Since arriving in Cusco where their base camp was located, they had engaged in substantial archaeological, geological, and topographical exploration in the region. They kept journals describing the people, customs, ruins, and terrain they encountered and created annotated maps with a level of detail never before captured by the Western world. They had collected vertebrate bones believed to be evidence of a previously unknown pre-Inca race and assembled a collection of new species of insects indigenous to the region. Harry was right, they had more than enough to publish a book detailing their discoveries; publishing, after all, was a key stepping stone for their professorial careers, and something Yale, in particular, insisted on. But Hiram wanted more than journals, maps, bones, and insects; he wanted Vitcos, the last Incan capital built and used by Manco Inca to rule while hiding from Pizarro's army after the Spanish invaded. And Hiram needed Melchor to get him there.

"Melchor, how much longer do you think?" asked Hiram.

Melchor, who had a good ear for the American's English even though he could not speak the language, muttered a soft response to Hiram.

"What'd he say?" asked William, just now catching up, his clothes sopping wet.

"He said, 'Almost there, he can hear the roar,'" replied Hiram.

"The roar of what?" asked William rhetorically, trusting Melchor less than Hiram.

Using hand gestures, Melchor urged them to follow. He disappeared between the leaves. The three men remounted their mules and followed him. They climbed over a ridge through the jungle and descended a slope into the Urubamba Valley. As they made their way into a deep canyon, they began to hear the roar Melchor was referring to: the Apurímac River which wove along the canyon floor.

"Apurímac," announced Melchor, pointing at the raging torrent 250 feet wide.

"Apurímac means 'Great Speaker,'" advised Hiram, who spoke Quechua. And the name fit, too, because up close, the river's roar overpowered all other jungle sounds.

For the next few hours, they followed the rushing whitewater of the Apurímac through the valley, surrounded by the snow-capped

Urubamba and Vilcabamba mountain ranges. Looking up, green foliage and vibrant, colorful flowers covered the mountain slopes all the way up to the distant snowlines, a mix of terrain that could only be found here in the cloud-forests of the Andes, where jungle and mountain blended harmoniously.

After a half-day traveling through the jungle, they ascended a steep mountain pass that rose 500 feet above the Apurímac's turbulent waters. The narrow trail matched the river's contours. Navigating the trail up the mountainside was grueling and nerve-wracking, not just because of the sharp slope but because their mules were clumsy. They had to be careful none of their mules lost their footing and slipped off the mountainside. If they did, it was a long drop down.

Following several hours of climbing, they came upon an old-looking suspension bridge spanning the canyon over the river. Their path continued beyond the bridge.

"Mana," uttered Melchor, urging them to ignore the bridge and keep going. "Kay ñan."

"That is not our way," translated Hiram, much to the relief of Harry and William who doubted the bridge could sustain a man much less a mule. But Hiram wondered what was beyond the bridge on the other side of the river, especially because of the trouble it must have taken to construct it. That anyone took the risk to build it gave Hiram reason to believe something interesting waited on the other side.

From a distance, even in the long afternoon shadows, Hiram could see a path leading up into the higher elevations across the bridge. Curious, Hiram asked Melchor, "Where does this bridge lead?"

Melchor did not answer. He just kept walking. Melchor's uncharacteristically evasive reaction piqued Hiram's interest.

More insistently this time, Hiram asked, "Melchor, friend, what is up there?"

"You're not thinking of crossing that thing, are you?" questioned William, looking at the shaky bridge and then down at the fast-moving whitewater hundreds of feet below. "It looks like a death trap."

Hiram ignored William and asked Melchor once again, "Melchor, what is this bridge?"

Quietly, almost begrudgingly, Melchor responded, "Mit'awi Chaska."

"The 'Timeless Bridge,'" Hiram whispered to himself, thinking out loud about Melchor's response.

"Timeless? Sounds about right," said Harry. The bridge, which looked like nothing more than branches, vines, twine, and wood tied together, did not look like it had been maintained in a long time.

"Hamuy! Hamuy!" said Melchor, urging his charges to continue on their way to Vitcos.

But Hiram didn't budge. In his studies of South American history and the Incan Empire, a specialty of his, he had heard about the legend of Pachakutiq, a great Inca-emperor from the mid-fifteenth century whose name meant "he who overturns space and time." Stories say Pachakutiq earned his name during the invasion of Cusco by the warlike army of the Chanka, the Incas' traditional tribal archenemies in Peru. When others fled in fear of the massive Chanka army, Pachakutiq rallied those who remained behind in defense of his homeland. Legends tell of how Pachakutiq called upon the earth and stars and how the stones rose up to fight as soldiers on Pachakutiq's side. Pachakutiq led his people to a crushing victory over the Chankas, launching the Incan dynasty and giving rise to the godlike legend of Pachakutiq.

Unfortunately, because the Incas never developed a written language, no writings confirmed or explained the legend of Pachakutiq. Anecdotal tales often mentioned Pachakutiq hid away from mortals in the peaks of the Andes, in a hidden city concealed

12

within the clouds where the mountaintops reached the heavens, enabling him to speak directly to the stars. Looking straight up at the mountain on the other side of the river, it indeed disappeared into the clouds.

"What is this Midwi Chaksa?" asked Harry, butchering the pronunciation.

Hiram looked at Harry and responded, "To find Pachakutiq, stories say one must first find the Mit'awi Chaska, the 'Timeless Bridge' that leads to 'he who overturns space and time.'" Suddenly, in Hiram's mind, Vitcos seemed like a consolation prize. Everyone knew Vitcos was out there, and that it was only a matter of time before they found it, just another chapter in what was already shaping up to be a promising book co-authored by the three friends. But finding the mythical home of Pachakutiq? The opportunity was too much to hope for, and one Hiram wasn't willing to pass up.

"Timeless Bridge that leads to 'he who overturns space and time'? Sounds like a bedtime story if you ask me," replied Harry. As a chemistry professor, he didn't believe in legends, myths, or magic. He believed in evidence, typically the kind made up of elements on the periodic table.

William was no different. He did not believe in things he couldn't see or diagnose. Perhaps he did when he was young, but years of medical school dissecting corpses, treating patients, and performing surgeries had long since chased such notions out of him.

Hiram's mind, however, was already made up, and the words just came out. "Melchor, can you take us across the Mit'awi Chaska?"

Melchor looked hesitant, even scared. Maybe it was the thought of crossing the ancient bridge hundreds of feet above the Apurímac that worried him. Or perhaps he felt he was betraying his people. Or maybe he feared what Pachakutiq might do to him if he came face-to-face with the deity after bringing outsiders into his sanctuary. Regardless of his reason, Melchor was frightened, and it caused him to utter repeatedly, "Mánan, mánan." He didn't want to go across the bridge.

William didn't, either. "You're not serious?" blurted William. "I thought you were joking before."

"There's history to discover over there," Hiram responded, pointing across the canyon.

William quickly reminded him, "There's history in Vitcos, too, you know, the kind we actually came for: *real*."

"Do we want to write about history, or make it, gentlemen?" asked Hiram. "It will only be a small detour."

"Do we have enough food?" questioned Harry. "Our Vitcos excursion was only supposed to take three weeks round trip. We're nearly at two weeks now and aren't even there yet. If your Papakuti detour lasts for more than a short time, we won't have enough food to make it to Vitcos, much less for the way home. We may end up turning back hungry and with nothing to show for it."

"We only need to ration our food better," said Hiram, gently patting Harry's mildly plump stomach. He continued. "Vitcos will be a wonderful final chapter in our publication about our Peruvian expedition. No doubt. But the mythical home of Pachakutiq? The whole world will read about our discovery if we find it. It is *the* crown jewel of Inca history, and it is right across this bridge…"

Harry was worried. He had more on his mind than fame and fortune. "Hiram, I have Martha at home, and two little girls…" Harry paused and eyed the bridge warily. "I can't just throw caution to the river."

Trying to reassure Harry that the bridge was safe, Hiram said, "Harry, that bridge has been here 500 years—"

"That's what scares me," interrupted Harry.

"If it'll make you feel better, I'll go first, and you'll see, there's nothing to worry about," offered Hiram.

The proposal was acceptable to Harry, not that he wanted to use his best friend as a guinea pig. "Okay, fine," Harry said.

"And you, William?" asked Hiram.

William still wasn't sure. "I don't know. We have no idea if there's anything even up there."

"We'll never know if we don't look for it," responded Hiram. "Besides, look at Melchor's face. He knows something's up there. He looks terrified."

Like Harry before, William looked down at the sizable drop into the Apurímac's violent waters. "Of course, he does. And for good reason..."

"I've traveled with Melchor many times," said Hiram. "I've seen him scale jagged mountain precipices and face down the poison-tip arrows of the Adamak tribe. Melchor's not afraid of this bridge, I assure you. There's something more frightening to Melchor up there than an old bridge. A god. His god."

"And should we be frightened by what's up there?" retorted William.

"Only if you're afraid of ghosts," replied Hiram. "Are you?"

"Of course not."

"Then, shall we?" proposed Hiram.

"Mánan, mánan," said Melchor again, shaking his head *no* and stepping back.

Hiram wasn't going to make Melchor go. He could stay behind to look after their mules and supplies instead. While Hiram believed the bridge was safe, he also knew the weight of one mule could break it. They would leave the mules behind and travel light, not only because of the bridge's questionable tolerance but also because they might need to climb in the higher elevations.

"Melchor," said Hiram, "Stay here tonight and make camp. You can watch our things and we'll return tomorrow or the next day."

Melchor agreed.

The threesome prepared for the crossing. They gathered minimal supplies, two days' worth of food, and no more. Just to be safe, Hiram took a Winchester rifle for protection. He didn't know what they would encounter up in the mountains, so he strapped the weapon to his back. When ready, the men embarked.

Hiram approached the bridge first. Like one dipping a toe into the shallow end of a pool, he cautiously placed his right foot out onto the bridge and pressed down. The bridge held without so much as a creak or a crack. Slowly, Hiram shifted his body weight onto his right leg and then stepped down with his left foot until he stood completely on the bridge. The bridge was constructed with tree branches carved into uneven bumpy wood planks, twine, and tough thick liana vines spliced and tied together to make strong cables. It felt stable, so Hiram started walking. He placed his hands on the vines woven together into make-shift hand-railings and proceeded forward.

The further out he went, the more the bridge crackled and swayed. Harry and William looked on with bated breath. With each step Hiram took toward the bridge's middle, he could hear the vines pulling and stretching and feel the bridge sinking closer toward the Apurímac's turbulent waters. Even for Hiram, who thrived off the thrill of adventure, the crossing was unsettling.

The river's roar seemed to increase as he inched along, almost as if the Apurímac was hollering at him to hurry up, or perhaps calling for him to plunge into it. The rapids were so loud in the middle of the canyon that Hiram could barely hear himself think. At one point, he held on for dear life as the bridge swayed more than 30 feet back and forth.

When Hiram reached the Mit'awi Chaska's midway point, a massive brown and white feathered condor landed on the bridge 15 feet in front of him. Its razor-sharp black talons gripped the vines, and its white curved beak nosed in Hiram's direction. The menacing condor glared at the man who dared to cross over the Mit'awi Chaska. Perhaps it was conducting reconnaissance for Pachakutiq, thought Hiram. He remained still, concerned about startling the great bird, fearful of what it might do to knock him off balance, as condors could be aggressive when threatened. Fortunately, Hiram wouldn't have to wait long as the condor took flight 10 seconds later, satisfied with what it observed. The condor's 12-foot wingspan stretched out as it soared off through the canyon, its magnificence on full display.

Hiram, feeling more confident with each step, picked up his pace. He carefully navigated the wood floorboards, attentive to gaps and boards that looked fractured or weak. As he got close to the end, Harry declared, "Hiram's going to make it!"

For the final few steps, Hiram hurried to the end of the bridge at a pace just short of running. When he got there, he walked in between two massive granite boulders.

"Come!" shouted Hiram across the canyon. But over the Apurímac's roar, William and Harry couldn't hear him.

Encouraged by Hiram's success, it was time for Harry and William to go.

"Com'on, Bill," said Harry. "We can do this."

Harry went next. Like Hiram, he walked slowly, taking his time with each step. Whenever the bridge swayed, Harry gripped the vines tightly or sat down. It took him 10 minutes to go 250 feet, but he made it without incident.

William went last. Before he stepped out onto the bridge, he inhaled and mumbled to himself, "Bill, you climbed Mount Frissell when you were 30. This is nothing but a couple of hundred feet." William knew Mount Frissell was only 2,380 feet high, but it was the tallest mountain Connecticut had to offer. And right now, reminiscing about his exploits made him feel better.

William took his first steps with a shakiness that belied his normally rock-solid and steady surgical hands. Things were progressing smoothly until halfway when William's foot broke through a fractured wood plank.

"Whoa!" cried William, collapsing onto one knee while his other leg drove through the bridge. William watched the broken pieces of wood plummet toward the water below. All color drained from his face.

"Get up, William!" screamed Hiram. "Grab the vine and hold on tight. I'm coming out to get you!"

William shouted "*No*," and pulled himself back up. Suddenly, William was ready to be the adventurer he needed to be to make it across. With newfound resolve, William defiantly surged forward toward his friends, leaving self-doubt behind. If his near-fatal mishap had taught him anything, it was that he no longer had time for self-doubt. William traversed the bridge with renewed purpose, and as a result, it wasn't long before he joined his friends at the bridge's end. When he got there, Hiram had a great big proud grin on his face and patted him on the back. William coolly said, "Alright, let's go find this Pachakutiq."

The three friends followed a dirt path into the mountain. A steady rain began falling. As Hiram anticipated, occasionally they needed to climb rocks or navigate ledges with large vertical drops. The wet rock made the task more difficult, but they managed.

As they climbed steep slopes into higher elevations, the temperature dropped and low clouds rolled in. Visibility declined fast, in part because of the clouds but also because the sun was beginning to set over the mountain. Harry lit a lamp so they could see where they were going.

By nightfall, the rain gave way to a heavy mist and the incline toward the mountaintop began to level out. They came to a series of terraces with vertically-carved stone faces made from granite blocks and overgrown vegetation on top of the terraces. The terraces looked man-made. Once upon a time, Hiram surmised these terraces were probably used for farming since carving and shaping terraces into mountain slopes for agricultural purposes was a common practice in the Andes. They followed a path up, and what they found was startling.

They stood right in the middle of hidden ruins. A walkway concealed by jungle foliage continued uphill. The path led to more terraces and even more ruins. This time, long-abandoned houses hidden in between and underneath bushes, vines, and moss. The houses were made of stone and had open doorways covered by large stone lintels. Peaking their heads into the ancient dwellings, there were no visible ceilings, presumably because the bamboo, twine, leaves, or thickets that once provided cover had long since vanished.

As they continued up the mountain, the path ended in a central plaza surrounded by white granite structures. Where they stood, mist and clouds no longer enshrouded them; they had reached an elevation on the mountain above the cloud-layer, underneath a pristine, starry night sky and full moon.

In the bright moonlight, they could see the tall peaks of mountains flanking them on both sides, creating an amphitheater feel in which they stood below on center stage. In the distance, the site dropped off into the Urubamba Valley, where the Apurímac still roared.

Up ahead, nearly at the mountain's absolute peak, there was a multi-level semicircular building with its inner wall long and flat, and its outer wall sloped and curved. Hiram, Harry, and William approached it and entered through an opening. The granite stones were finely cut and worked until perfectly squared, fit together, and smoothly polished off for decorative effect. Two trapezoidal windows in the exterior curved wall looked outward, and a white granite altar rock filled the floor's center. Moonlight beamed in from above as the structure had no roof.

"What is this place?" wondered Harry.

"It looks like a temple," said William.

Hiram walked up to the altar. It had a smooth platform on top of it. The platform's northern edge pointed directly at the northeast-facing window, while the platform's southern edge lined up with the southeastern-facing trapezoid window.

"Hey, look at this," said William, who had walked over to peer through the exterior window looking northeast and angled upward at the night sky. "You can see Orion."

Harry and Hiram joined William at the window. The Orion constellation was visible dead center in the window, so much so that the window resembled a picture frame for the mythical constellation of a hunter standing in the set position, with a bow held in the hand of his outstretched left arm and his right arm cocked back and up.

"Beautiful," said Hiram, enjoying the view of the heavens.

Sarcastically, William said, "Perhaps this is where Pachakutiq spoke to the stars."

"Perhaps," replied Hiram, grinning.

Hiram walked over to the other window facing southeast. Much like the first window which framed Orion, this window captured another constellation.

"The Pleiades," said Hiram, looking at a cluster of six stars in the night sky.

"What does that mean?" asked Harry, not familiar with the term.

Hiram explained. "The Pleiades is a constellation referring to the Seven Sisters of the Heavens. Here, take a look."

Harry leaned in to look at the Pleiades, and Hiram pointed it out to him.

"Interesting that the two windows frame those two constellations tonight," remarked Hiram.

There was clearly something more behind Hiram's comment. Taking the bait, Harry asked, "And why is that?"

"Because Orion is the one who chased the Seven Sisters into the heavens," replied Hiram. "According to Greek mythology, anyway, Orion endeavored to capture the divine sisters: Maia, Electra, Taygete, Alcyone, Celaeno, Sterope, and Merope because the sisters were goddesses of love whose beauty he could not resist. But the legend was a ruse."

"A ruse for what?" asked Harry.

"For the truth. Orion didn't seek love; he sought power. The legend says that the universe bestowed upon the sisters, the knowledge of all its secrets. Not even the mighty Zeus knew what the sisters knew, for the universe restricted such knowledge even from him. The universe divided up its knowledge equally among six of the sisters and chose the seventh, Celaeno, to share *all* its knowledge with, so if anything ever happened to any of them there would always be another sister who possessed the knowledge. When Orion's hunt intensified, Zeus hid the sisters in the heavens, turning them into stars to protect them. Only, Orion outsmarted Zeus, because he also found his way into the stars, and now, Orion hunts the Pleiades in the heavens for eternity."

"If it's called the Seven Sisters, then, why are only six stars visible?" asked Harry.

"Because one of the Pleiades is missing, or so the myth goes," replied Hiram, "forever hiding from Orion... something like that."

"Which one?" asked Harry.

"Celaeno," Hiram responded, "the bearer of all the universe's secrets."

"Maybe Pachakutiq knows where she is," joked William.

"*Perhaps,* Pachakutiq watched over the sisters for Zeus, keeping an eye on Orion through these windows," added Harry, joining in on the fun.

"Or *maybe*, he watched over the sisters for Orion," suggested William.

"Maybe," said Hiram, amused by his friends' competing theories. "It's only a Greek myth and doubtful the Incas would've known about it. It's just a coincidence that Pleiades and Orion share the windows tonight," said Hiram. Without giving it another thought, Hiram gazed back out at the Pleiades, unaware how much more than a coincidence it really was.

Chapter 2 – The Seven Sisters

"The Pleiades was an important constellation in Inca culture," said Professor Albies, directing her students to an image of the constellation on the large screen built into the lecture hall wall. Emma James, sitting dead center nine rows up, diligently took notes, sketching out the constellation.

The professor continued. "The Incas used the constellation to track the seasons from an observatory at the top of Machu Picchu, the world-famous landmark in the Peruvian Andes." Using a hand-held clicker, Professor Albies switched to an aerial photo depicting the renowned tourist destination, Machu Picchu, an ancient city made up of terraces, stone buildings, and houses built into the eastern slopes of the Cordillera de Vilcabamba mountain range.

"Scholars call the observatory, the Torreón," said Professor Albies, clicking over to an image of the observatory for the class to see. "Note the Torreón's semicircular design. The Torreón was built up on top of a large white granite rock to elevate its height for viewing while incorporating the mountain's natural stone elements. As you can see, the Torreón's natural granite-rock base fades up into the smoothly carved, granite-block design of the circular observatory itself. The Incas gazed at the stars from the observatory through two trapezoidal windows in the granite-block walls which were purposefully angled toward the sky at precise degrees to guide sunlight down onto an altar in the middle of the observatory's floor. Depending on the season, sunlight would hit the altar at different angles at sunrise, enabling the Incas to track the time of year. The Solstice Window, or so it is called, points southeast at the rising point of the Pleiades in the night sky. When the constellation appeared in the window, the Incas knew the wet season had arrived.

Stargazing through the Torreón played a critical role in forecasting the seasons for their farming and agriculture."

Georgetown junior and cryptology major, Emma James, hurriedly sketched the Torreón before Professor Albies could change the image. College suited Emma, who over the last three years had gone from a high school cutie to a casual beauty. Even without makeup, or after pulling an all-nighter studying, she somehow always looked like she'd taken the time to get ready for her day. While her long sandy-blond hair, green eyes, and dimples remained the same, everything else about her had matured into a sophisticated young college student.

Within a few seconds, the professor clicked back to the prior Machu Picchu slide and continued, "When historian Hiram Bingham unexpectedly stumbled upon the hidden city of Machu Picchu in 1911, a journey he depicted in incredible detail in his famous book, *Lost City of the Incas*, it is doubtful he understood the magnitude of what it was. Pachacuti, the greatest Inca emperor, had the highly exclusive royal estate built for himself, his priests, servants, family, and select guests, so he could rule over his empire from an exclusive location high up in the Andes. His ability to predict the seasons by 'talking to the stars' only enhanced his perception among his subjects as a god or demi-god. Of course, we now know there was more than magic to Pachacuti's ability to predict the seasons."

"I can't believe I let you talk me into taking this class," whispered Kristi, sitting next to Emma. Emma's feisty red-headed friend somehow always had somewhere better to be or something better to do than what she was doing.

Emma quietly shushed her.

Kristi wasn't deterred. "Come on, it's all in the book."

"Shh," shushed Emma, starting to get embarrassed by the attention Kristi was drawing from those students seated around them.

Unaware of the commotion up above in the lecture hall, Professor Albies kept going. "The Pleiades wasn't only significant to the Inca. It played an important role in the mythology of many cultures. For example, the North American Kiowa tribe called the Pleiades, the Seven Maidens, believing the Great Spirit transported them into the sky to save them from the Giant Bear who hunted them."

Kristi mockingly growled like a bear to distract Emma, causing Emma to laugh slightly, partly amused, fully annoyed.

"Would you stop it?!" reprimanded Emma, fighting back a smile.

"Interestingly," said Professor Albies, "the Kiowa legend tracks closely with the Greek's Pleiades myth. The Greeks believed the constellation consisted of seven sisters placed into the heavens by Zeus, the most powerful of Greek gods, to protect them from the relentless pursuits of Orion the Hunter. Of course, that didn't stop Orion from following the sisters into the stars, too."

Kristi again leaned over and whispered, "Hey, do you want to go to a party tonight?"

"Someone's trying to pay attention here," snapped Emma.

"Since when has that ever mattered to me? Com'on, you told me Astronomy in Culture was going to be an easy A, so relax and have some fun. You in?"

"I can't, Logan and I are studying tonight. Now, do you mind, I'm trying to learn something here." Emma scribbled down the words she could hear in between Kristi's interruptions.

"Studying?!" blurted Kristi, thoroughly confused. "It's Friday night!"

"We're studying, and then we've got plans," replied Emma unapologetically.

"What plans?"

"We're going out to dinner."

Dumbfounded, Kristi replied. "All you guys ever do is study. You gotta live a little."

Emma shot Kristi down with an irritated look and a more definitive, "Shh."

Finally taking the hint, Kristi uttered, "Fine, but we're talking about this after class." Kristi leaned back into her own chair and turned her eyes forward or at least one of them. Her other eye looked down at her phone to stay in touch with the outside world. Emma always marveled at Kristi's ability to seamlessly take notes *and* either text or post, all at the same time.

"According to a Polynesian legend," said Professor Albies, "the Pleiades was once a single star, the brightest in all the heavens, but the god Tane disliked the star because she had bragged about her beauty. So Tane smashed her into pieces, creating the Pleiades star cluster. But Pleiades myths weren't always about mythological male figures with grudges against women…"

"I hope so," said Emma, quickly growing tired of the recurring narrative.

"The Japanese call the Pleiades, Subaru, referring to the strength of the seven sisters of the heavens. The word 'subaru' means 'unite' or 'unity' in Japanese. And yes, for those of you who are wondering, that is precisely how the automobile company Subaru chose its name and logo." Professor Albies conjured up the Subaru logo on the screen. It matched the Pleiades constellation. It consisted of a blue oval, wide from left to right, with six shiny four-pronged stars. One large star dominated the upper-left half of the logo, with five smaller stars below and bunched up to the right.

"Professor Albies," called a female voice from down in front. "If there are seven sisters, then why are there only six stars in the logo?"

"Because only six of the Pleiades are visible to the naked eye. You need a telescope to see the seventh star in the constellation."

The same student followed up with another question, "Do all the Pleiades myths revolve around the idea of the seven sisters?"

"Great question. The short answer is that many do. The odd similarity between the various Pleiades myths has long been discussed among scholars because most constellation-myths vary based on culture, geography, religion, ideology, and time frame. Rarely will different cultures see the same images in the stars or formulate the same stories, but the Pleiades is a mysterious exception to the rule. Even the Norse had a similar story for the constellation. In the Icelandic text, the *Prose Edda*, considered to be the most complete and detailed source of Norse mythology, the Pleiades is often called Frigg's Hens, referring to the daughters of gods Frigg and Odin."

Emma's ears perked up when Professor Albies mentioned the *Prose Edda*. It was a work she was familiar with. She first heard of it three years ago, when she and Logan embarked on their Copán Temple coordinates adventure. After flying to Italy and gaining access to the Vatican Secret Archives with her cousin Enyo Rossi's help, they uncovered clues which led them to Bologna. There, they discovered coordinates left behind on a coat of arms in the Archiginassio, which led them, along with then-Harvard professors, Dr. Jonas Arenot and Professor Jill Quimbey, to a secret cave in Norway. In the cave, a beaming portal of light leading to Vanirya appeared, and it was then that Dr. Arenot mentioned the *Prose Edda* because the light portal reminded him of the legend of the Light Elves referenced in the *Prose Edda*. Emma remembered that day like it was yesterday because it changed her life forever. That was when she went through the portal and encountered the Vaniryans, ushering humanity into a new era of space exploration, or at least, the select few in the top-secret Pegasus Project named after the mythical-winged horse who flew the heavens.

Unfortunately, that was the only time Emma had ever visited Vanirya because the technology that brought her, and later Logan, there, had never been able to do so again. The portals they had discovered would not let them return to Vanirya, and even the secret sphere in the subterranean alien pyramid beneath Area 51 couldn't get them back. While Vanirya was there, visible within the pyramid's holographic universe, right beside its sun and double moons, and while the Pegasus Project had been able to closely study Vanirya's solar system, for reasons unknown, the technology would not let them actually go to Vanirya's surface or make contact with the Vaniryans again. Every time they tried opening a portal on Vanirya, nothing happened.

"Ok, everybody, that's it for today," announced Professor Albies. "Read Chapters 11-13, which cover today's lecture in greater detail. Next Monday, we'll be exploring how astronomy shaped politics in different parts of the world. We're moving fast, people, so don't fall behind. Midterms are in three weeks. And with that, I'll leave you with today's 'End of Class' quote, which remember *could* be on the midterm. It's from the Greek philosopher Plato: 'Astronomy compels the soul to look upward and leads us from this world to another.' Thanks, everybody." Professor Albies turned off the screen, signaling the end of class. The students immediately began packing up.

Kristi scooped up her notes and threw them into her bag like she'd been planning her escape for hours. She stood up and said, "Ok, Emma J, you clearly need my help. You're going with me to that party tonight!"

"I told you, Logan and I are studying," replied Emma, gathering her things, "and then, we're going out to—"

"All you guys do is work at that internship and study. All work, no play."

"Kristi, you know that's not true. Just because I don't party like you doesn't mean I don't have fun."

"I'm just saying, you need to live a little. You're a junior now. There's more to life than studying and work."

Emma rose from her seat and followed Kristi toward the stairs at the end of the aisle.

"Why do you want me to go to this party so badly, anyway?" asked Emma, sensing something amiss.

"I just thought it would be fun."

Emma wasn't buying it. "Kristi, I've known you since freshmen year, and—"

"Ok, fine. The party's at Brad's."

"Oh, my god!" blurted Emma, turning down the stairs behind Kristi and the other students filing out of the lecture hall. "You just started dating Alex!" Emma knew Brad from the Cryptology Department. In fact, she had introduced Kristi to Brad a few weeks ago when they ran into him at the dining court.

"I don't like the word, 'dating,'" responded Kristi. "Sounds so formal when you put it that way. I prefer the phrase 'hanging out.'"

"You seriously go through guys like disposable straws."

Emma's dig didn't bother Kristi, though. Instead, she owned it. "As I said, you gotta live a little."

They made a right at the bottom of the stairs and exited the lecture hall through the exterior glass doors. They walked out of the science building into a small concrete plaza opposite the university bookstore, separated by a row of bushes and a pathway crammed with students.

"It'll be fun, I promise. There might even be some congressional interns there. Chance to meet some new people..."

"But Logan and—"

"Emma, I know I date a lot of guys. There, I said it, are you happy?"

With a pleased expression and a satisfied smile, Emma replied, "Yes!"

"But when I get married and settle down, I want to know what Mr. Right looks like, and I'm never going to be able to pick him out of a lineup unless I know what Mr. Wrong looks like first, you know what I mean?"

Emma did. She also knew precisely what Kristi was getting at. "Kristi, you don't know Logan like I do, he's—"

"He's great. We all like him. But how do you know for sure? He's, like, the only serious boyfriend you've ever had, right?"

Emma nodded. "Yeah, but I love Logan. Logan loves me. He's sweet... he's smart—"

"Emma, how many people marry their high school boyfriend?" asked Kristi. She paused waiting for an answer, but Emma hesitated, so Kristi answered her own question, "Not many. Are you really going to marry your high school sweetheart?"

Emma, somewhat uncomfortable with the question, fiddled with a heart-shaped pendant necklace Logan had given her on their two-year anniversary. Defensively, she responded, "Yes... I don't know... probably! I mean, we're both still so young. We've got plenty of time before we have to think about stuff like that."

Seeing Emma fiddle with the necklace Logan had given her and picking up on the uncertainty in Emma's voice, Kristi said, "Hey, Logan's awesome, but what do you two have in common besides studying and work? You need to get out and explore the world a little. The world's a big place, you know... and maybe the stars will align and lead you right back to him, but you'll never know unless—"

"Unless, what? Unless I go out on a date with a congressional intern who's just waiting to meet someone like me at the party later?"

"That's not what I meant. I'm sorry, I didn't mean to—"

"Kristi, I know it seems like all we do is work and study, study and work, but it's more than that. I wish I could explain it to you."

Kristi could tell it was time to back off. Somewhat apologetically, she said, "I just want what's best for you. Sorry, I'm being pushy. Maybe I'm just jealous."

"Jealous is one thing I know you aren't, Mrs. Right," teased Emma.

Kristi looked at her watch. "Oh crap, it's almost 11:30. I've gotta go." She started walking away but before she was totally gone, she turned around to solicit Emma one more time. "Em, think about tonight, and call me later if you change your mind, okay?"

"Okay, I will," responded Emma, although she highly doubted that she would. After all, today was a big day.

Later, the Pegasus team planned to test a portable Remote Anti-Mass Zeutyron Accelerator (*p*RAMZA) on an exoplanet orbiting a star in the Gliese 667 triple-star system. To date, the *p*RAMZA, utilizing the Vaniryan technology, had only been able to accomplish portal-to-portal transportation across the planet a couple of times, but nothing more. A successful test would be a major breakthrough because the president refused to authorize the use of the Vaniryan pyramid under Area 51 to travel the stars until scientists developed a way for the astronauts to return home without the pyramid, in case something went wrong with it. Until that happened, Pegasus was stuck in neutral.

If the *p*RAMZA test worked today and Pegasus finally reached the next phase, Emma had no plans to go to a party that evening with Kristi. If she was going to celebrate with anyone, it was going to be Logan West.

Chapter 3 – Pegasus East

Logan sat alone at a two-person table on a window at The Grind, slowly drinking his double-shot of espresso while waiting for Emma to arrive. The popular coffee shop just south of the Georgetown University Library was one of their favorite places in the city to meet. With its college students, espresso-bean infused aroma, and wood architecture blended with gray distressed stonework, The Grind's ambiance reminded them of the cafe in Bologna where, three years ago, they unraveled the hidden coordinates left behind by the Norwegian Albo in the Archiginassio. More importantly, in Logan's opinion, The Grind's coffee was the best in Georgetown, possibly all of D.C. Emma always joked it might even be the best in the entire universe, but that wasn't a theory they would be able to test until Pegasus finally took flight.

Logan lifted his espresso and took another sip, nerves flowing through his body. Today was a big day, and the infusion of caffeine into his already anxious system probably wasn't helping. To distract himself, Logan went back to reading his book, *Density: A Black Hole's Destiny*, by Dr. Francis Juliard. He'd grown more interested in reading about such topics after traveling through a portal to another world and realizing that anything is possible.

Logan was in the middle of a quote that Dr. Juliard included in her book from famed astronomer, Stephen Hawking, discussing Hawking's view on destiny: "I have noticed that even people who claim everything is predetermined and that we can do nothing to change it, look before they cross the road. Maybe it's just that those who don't look don't survive to tell the tale." Logan laughed out loud when he read it.

32

"Read something funny?" asked an outgoing young girl drinking a cappuccino, sitting at a table next to Logan, one row in from the window. She had long blond hair tied back in a tight ponytail and wore a pink Georgetown sweatshirt with light-gray sweatpants. Her friendly nature initially caught Logan off-guard.

"Just Stephen Hawking's take on destiny," he replied, noticing she was reading a book of her own called *The Fault in Our Stars*, a tragic love story by John Green also inspired by the concept of destiny. "I'm guessing Hawking's take is just a bit different than Green's," he said.

The girl pleasantly smiled at Logan, enjoying the conversation. She responded, "I'm thinking John Green's view of destiny is probably more like William Shakespeare's than Stephen Hawking's. You know, the more romantic philosophical kind, 'It is not in the stars to hold our destiny but in ourselves.'"

"Julius Caesar, Act I, Scene III," recited Logan. He knew Shakespeare well from English Lit, senior year, and remembered the quote because it mentioned the stars.

Impressed by Logan's recitation of the quote's origin, the young woman lowered her book onto the table and said, "Hi, my name's Allysa."

Logan politely replied, "Logan. Nice to meet you. You a student here?"

"Yep, a freshman. I live at Harbin Hall, 7th Floor. You?"

"Junior. I live off-campus on 34th." Just then, Logan noticed she had a bookbag full of textbooks and other materials under her chair. She looked prepared to spend several more hours at The Grind. "What's your major?" he asked.

Sheepishly, Allysa responded, "Still undecided. I came here thinking I might get into political science, you know, the whole D.C. politics thing, but now I'm leaning toward psychology, maybe. Something, like, a little more me. I don't know."

Logan grinned and reassured her, "You have time."

"And you? Judging by your book, *Density: A Black Hole's Destiny*, I'm guessing Astronomy?"

Logan looked at his book, laughed, and replied, "Yep. I started out Computer Science, but switched along the way, so, as I said, you've still got time."

"Astronomy sounds really interesting. I wish I was smart enough to do that, but it's probably crazy-hard with all the math and physics, right?"

"Some days."

"Are you reading that for one of your classes?" asked Allysa.

"No, just interested in the topic."

"Seems like we're both reading books about stars and destiny," commented Allysa with a flirty smile.

Logan, amused by her observation, responded with a slight laugh, "Looks that way."

Allysa, looking into Logan's deep hazel eyes, started to ask, "Do you want to later, maybe, grab–"

Allysa was interrupted by the sudden approach of a girl wearing a black long sleeve shirt and jeans. Emma had arrived.

"Hey there," said Emma, giving Logan a quick kiss and then plopping down at Logan's table in the seat opposite him. It was just then Emma realized she had arrived right in the middle of a conversation. "Oh, I'm sorry, I didn't mean to interrupt." Looking at Allysa, she said, "Hi, I'm Emma."

A little disappointed and slightly embarrassed, Allysa replied with a small wave, "Hi, I'm Allysa."

34

"Nice to meet you, Allysa," said Emma. "I'm sorry for interrupting. What were you guys talking about?" Emma made herself comfortable.

Logan answered, "Just chatting. Allysa's a freshman at Harbin. We were talking about the books we're both reading."

Emma glanced at Allysa's book, then Logan's. "Well, I, personally, am not sure I could get 10-pages through Logan's book before needing some espresso to wake me up. I like yours much better."

Allysa grinned, relieved. "Thanks."

"How do you like Harbin?" asked Emma.

"Love it. Everyone's so nice. Reminds me of home."

"Where's that?" probed Emma.

"Philadelphia."

"Philadelphia," repeated Emma, looking over at Logan. They shared a smile, as Philadelphia held a special shared place in their hearts.

"Well, actually a suburb just outside of Philly... Ardmore," added Allysa. "Don't know if you've ever heard of it."

"Sure, I have," Emma assured her. "In high school, I remember going shopping with my mom one weekend on the main street there, the one with all the shops and restaurants. What is it? Lancaster Avenue, I think?"

"Yep, that's it! Our pride and joy," piped Allysa.

"Did you grow up in Ardmore?" asked Emma, curious.

"For the most part. Early on we moved around a lot because my dad's a pilot, and the airline kept moving him, but for the last 10 years, we've lived in Ardmore because he's now flying private jets exclusively for a company at a local airport about an hour south."

"That's great that home's so close," said Emma.

"It's pretty cool. Every few weeks, I take the train home to visit my parents."

"Your dad doesn't just fly in and pick you up?" joked Logan.

"Yeah, I wish… it'd be a lot faster that way."

"Hey, Em, we need to get going," said Logan. It was time for them to make their way to the Pentagon.

"I know. Let me grab a drink. Be right back," replied Emma. "Allysa, again, really nice to meet you. Say hi the next time you're in here. We're here all the time."

"Absolutely, thanks!" replied Allysa.

Emma headed off to the counter to grab an espresso-to-go. Logan started packing up.

"Sorry about before," said Allysa. "Totally embarrassing. She seems really nice."

Logan immediately dispelled the notion Allysa had done anything wrong. "No need to apologize for anything." Logan stood up and added, "As freshman go, you're pretty cool, and you made two new friends today. Not a bad way to spend a morning."

"Thanks," responded Allysa, relieved she didn't make any waves, appreciative of the compliment, and genuinely pleased to hear she had made some new friends.

Emma returned with her caffeine in hand. "Alright, ready to go?" she asked Logan.

"Yep," he said.

Emma and Logan waved goodbye and walked off just before noon.

Even with the sun out, this time of year in early February, the temperature peaked in the mid-40s. Emma and Logan enjoyed a brisk walk across the Potomac River on the Francis Scott Key Bridge, heading toward Rosslyn Station in Arlington, Virginia to catch the Blue Line to Pentagon City Station.

While strolling over the bridge, Emma commented, "Allysa seemed sweet."

"Yeah, she was cool," replied Logan nonchalantly.

Emma laughed. "Adorable, actually. I think she liked you."

"Sounds like someone's jealous."

"Looked to me like Allysa was having a hard time resisting your big book of black holes."

"You know, you might have mentioned to her that you read *A Black Hole's Destiny* before I did and that it was *you* who recommended the book to *me*."

With a sly smile, Emma replied, "I could have."

Logan took her hand and they kept walking.

"Are you ready for today?" asked Logan.

"Not sure there's much we need to be ready for," replied Emma. "I mean, it'll either work or it won't, right?"

"I guess that's true," conceded Logan. "Do you think it's going to?"

"I hope so. I just… I just keep feeling like we're running out of time."

"What do you mean?" asked Logan, surprised by her comment.

"I don't know. It's just a feeling… hard to explain."

"I thought humanity had thousands of years," said Logan, recalling what Emma had told him three years ago after journeying to TYC 129-75-1, the Vaniryan home star, and about how humans had time to explore the stars.

"I know. Forget it," she said, quickly dismissing her own comment. "I think I'm just making myself crazy worrying about all this stuff and getting impatient. You and I don't have thousands of years for them to figure everything out, you know?"

"Then maybe we should walk faster," joked Logan, humoring her.

After a few more minutes, they officially left D.C. and entered Virginia when the bridge crossed over the George Washington Memorial Parkway. From there, it was only another 10-minute walk to Rosslyn Station where they picked up the Blue Line. After making a quick stop at Arlington Cemetery Station, five minutes later they arrived at Pentagon City Station just outside the United States Department of Defense's headquarters: the Pentagon.

More than 23,000 people worked at the Pentagon, a 6,500,000 square foot, 5-story, 5-sided-polygon-shaped building with 17 miles of corridors. The 23,000-person total included military, governmental, and civilian personnel, and that didn't even account for the countless visitors, contractors, meeting invitees, and other members of the public who visited daily. Scores of people came and went all day long from the Pentagon, and today was no different.

After going through security, Logan and Emma entered the Pentagon through the Metro Concourse and traveled down the Pentagon's outer hallway referred to as Ring E, heading for Corridor 9. With Ring E falling just short of a mile all the way around, it was not a short walk. When they finally reached Corridor 9, they turned left and made their way to the second innermost ring from the Pentagon's middle. They made a right and headed over to an elevator halfway down the hallway. Logan took out his access card and scanned it at the elevator doors. When the elevator opened, they went inside.

Logan placed his palm on the scanner above the keypad offering Floors 1-5 for selection. Once the scanner turned green, he waited for Emma to do the same. He waited because the Pentagon elevator's advanced technology detected two people, and so, Emma needed to scan her hand, too. She placed her hand on the screen and once it changed to green, Subterranean Floor Sub-5 appeared on the digital keypad as a selection. Logan pressed Sub-5 and down they went.

The elevator dropped rapidly, stopping at Sub-5. The doors re-opened and they entered a fully enclosed, 20 feet by 20 feet room with no windows or doors. Two armed military officers sat in the room's center behind a security desk with a retina scanner on the ledge. There were lockers on the right.

"Good afternoon, Sergeant Peterson, Sergeant Michaels," said Emma in upbeat fashion.

"Ma'am," said both men courteously and simultaneously.

"Air Force crushed it last weekend," said Logan to Sgt. Michaels, referring to the Air Force's long overdue basketball victory over rival, Navy.

"Yes, they did," said Sgt. Michaels, grinning.

Emma and Logan walked over to the lockers to store their belongings, from bags to keys, wallets to cellphones, jewelry, watches, and belts. They returned to the security desk and stood on top of two circular designs on the floor at the foot of the desk. Logan's circle lit up red and a beep went off.

"Ugh," muttered Logan. "Forgot…" He quickly made his way over to his locker, reached into his pocket, and pulled out some change. "Sorry about that," he apologized, throwing the change into his locker and returning back to the circle. "Ok, try it again."

Sgt. Peterson did and this time, Logan registered clear. "Ok," said Sgt. Peterson, "please proceed to the retina scanner."

Emma and Logan stepped forward to the raised goggle-like retina scanner on the desk. Emma leaned in for her eye-scan and then waited for Logan to do the same. He bent over for his scan, and once it ID'd him, the entire heavy door in the room's back wall unlocked and opened. They had reached Pegasus East. They walked through the door.

Lieutenant Colonel Ainsley Lain, wearing a dark navy-blue Air Force dress uniform, sat in front of a computer panel overlooking a large wall of digital screens. Lt. Col. Lain commanded Pegasus East, having been promoted to the position three years ago with Major Bryce Jameson after the president authorized the formation of Pegasus to research the Vaniryan technology and to lead the United States into a new era of intergalactic exploration. Lt. Col. Lain and Maj. Jameson had both been re-assigned to Pegasus because of their years of excellent service in the Pentagon Array Deep Space Detection Unit (the "PADS Unit") and because of their experience working with the U.S.'s top-secret high-orbit telescope, the Pentagon Astronomical Primary Array (the "PAPA"). Due to their familiarity with the PAPA and its capabilities, their transfer made sense as Pegasus relied heavily on the PAPA.

After Logan and Emma fully stepped into the room, the wall behind them zipped closed, sealing them in. Lt. Col. Lain playfully greeted them, "School let out early today?"

"Very funny," replied Emma. "Where's your boyfriend?"

The fact that Maj. Jameson and Lt. Col. Lain were dating was the worst kept secret in the Pentagon, and there were a lot of poorly kept secrets at the Pentagon. To her credit, Lt. Col. Lain continued to play her part. "Maj. Jameson had a meeting elsewhere in the Pentagon. He should have been back by now, actually."

"Maybe he got lost," said Logan sarcastically. "Are we still on schedule?"

"Yep, 1300 hours," answered Lt. Col. Lain. "You guys still have a few minutes."

"Ok, thanks," said Emma.

She and Logan turned right and walked over to an interior office on the sidewall with a long rectangular window revealing office furnishings within. They entered the office, which had a 10-foot oak conference-room table and chairs in the middle, along with cubicles, swivel-chairs, laptops, and printers in the corners for Emma, Logan, Dr. Arenot, and Professor Quimbey. The former Harvard archeology professors were busy working away in their respective corners when Logan and Emma arrived. The professors, who lost their jobs at Harvard three years ago after taking the fall for the Copán coordinates scam in order to squash the Copán rumors and clear the way for them to come work on the Pegasus Project, spun around to face them.

"You are not going to believe what they sent down for us to study this morning," said Dr. Arenot, foregoing any greetings or pleasantries.

Intrigued, Emma asked, "What?"

"The Voynich!" exclaimed Professor Quimbey.

"Really?!?!" Emma blurted, her eyes widening. She knew it well. It was cryptology lore.

"What's the Voynich?" asked Logan.

"The Voynich Manuscript. You haven't heard of it?" questioned Dr. Arenot.

"No. Should I have?"

Emma was familiar with it because she had studied it freshman year in Cryptology 101. The Voynich Manuscript was one of the greatest mysteries in modern history, a medieval text that had been confounding scholars, cryptologists, graphologists, linguists, experts, and amateurs for centuries. Emma explained, "It's a book discovered more than 100 years ago by an antique bookseller named Wilfrid Voynich, who, of all random things, purchased it at an estate sale in Italy."

"What's so amazing about this book that they'd ask us to look at it?" wondered Logan.

"It's written in a language no one can read, by an author no one can identify," Professor Quimbey explained.

"What do you mean, a language no one can read?" asked Logan.

"Whoever wrote the 250-page book wrote it in an unknown alphabet that doesn't match any known writing patterns, characters, or languages. People have been trying to decode it since its discovery," replied Professor Quimbey.

Now, Logan was sucked in. "And no one knows who wrote it?"

Dr. Arenot, looking at some material he had printed out shortly before their arrival, replied, "Right. All that is known about the manuscript is that it dates back about 800 years according to carbon-dating experts, and most believe it originates from somewhere in Europe. Beyond that, no one really knows for sure."

"Did they send us the actual manuscript to study?" asked Emma, eager to see it first-hand. She had previously only seen photographs.

"Oh no, of course not," replied Professor Quimbey. "The actual manuscript is still at Yale University's Beinecke Rare Book &

Manuscript Library, kept under lock and key. They sent us a folder containing color copies of the pages. Here, take a look."

Professor Quimbey and Dr. Arenot stood up and walked over to the conference room table. Professor Quimbey carried the folder with her. She started pulling pages out and laying them on the table.

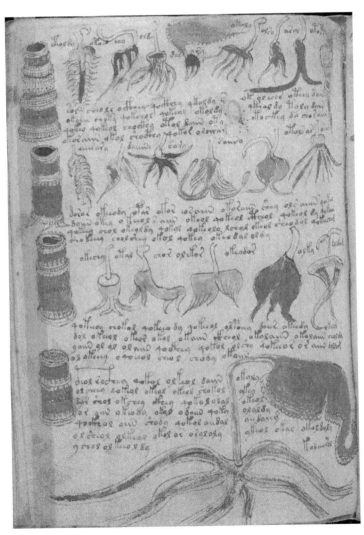

(Credit: Beinecke Rare Book and Manuscript Library, Yale University)

As described, strange lettering covered the pages, along with colorful hand-drawn illustrations of plants, roots, and other odd imagery. The text consisted of beautifully written calligraphy-like sweeping, looping, and flowing letters running left to right. There were no visible punctuation marks anywhere on the pages. To Logan, the writing looked more like J.R.R. Tolkien's made-up elvish language from one of his *Lord of the Rings* novels than it did any known alphabet.

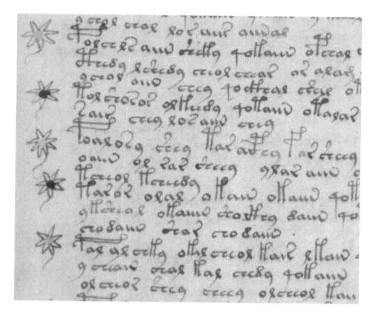

(Credit: Beinecke Rare Book and Manuscript Library, Yale University)

"That is totally wild," stated Logan. "And no one's been able to figure out what this says?"

"Nope," Dr. Arenot replied. According to the information that we looked at this morning, the manuscript consists of over 170,000 characters written in patterns similar to a natural language, with an alphabet consisting of a total of only 20 to 30 glyphs. There are a few character glyphs that appear just once throughout the entire text."

"Maybe whoever wrote it just made the whole thing up," hypothesized Logan.

"That is certainly one of the theories," confirmed Dr. Arenot. "But others have pointed out there are no errors or corrections anywhere in the entire manuscript. Graphologists say the letters were likely not fabricated for one-time use in this manuscript because, if they were, they would expect to see at least *some* variation in the lettering from word to word or page to page; variations in spacing, curvature, shape, or flow of the letters; or mistakes or other inconsistencies made throughout the manuscript. This manuscript has 170,000 characters and thousands of different words and sentences, yet, there are no mistakes or variations in the lettering, spacing, curvature, shape, or flow of the letters throughout the entire manuscript. Graphologists believe the writing system used in this manuscript was natural to whoever wrote it."

"What are the illustrations of? They look like plants," said Logan.

"Plants, roots, or herbs, something like that," Professor Quimbey answered.

"Is the whole book about plants and roots?" asked Logan.

"No," replied Dr. Arenot. "Based on the illustrations throughout the book, experts believe the manuscript falls into six categories: botanicals, biology, cosmology, pharmaceuticals, astronomy, and astrology."

"But what do they want us to do?" asked Emma. "I recall from first-year cryptology that even efforts to decode it using today's most advanced computerized cryptology technology and programs have been unsuccessful. Voynichologists have been trying to decipher this book for 100 years."

"Voynichologists?" chuckled Logan.

"That's what they call themselves, expert and amateur cryptologists who spend their time trying to decode the Voynich," replied Emma. "Some have spent their entire careers trying to do it."

Just wanting to make sure he had the assignment straight, Logan said, "So what, they think we're going to see something different in the book that experts who have spent their entire careers studying the Voynich haven't seen over the last 100 years?"

"It's not like you haven't done it before," Dr. Arenot reminded him. After all, it was Logan and Emma who solved the Copán coordinates mystery three years earlier when other experts couldn't.

"From the project's instructions, they don't want us to decode the entire manuscript, at least not yet," clarified Professor Quimbey. "They want us to focus on the astronomical and astrological pages." She pulled some more pages from the folder and laid them out on the table. Illustrations of stars arranged in a circular pattern covered the pages. "Here are a few dealing with astronomy. They just want to see what we think."

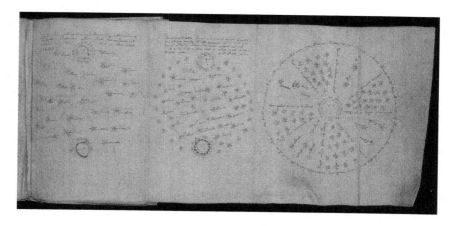

(Credit: Beinecke Rare Book and Manuscript Library,
Yale University)

Professor Quimbey continued. "Experts believe these pages are astronomical in nature because they feature illustrations of stars and even appear to have drawings of suns or moons in them. Other pages have drawings resembling spiral galaxies."

As Professor Quimbey laid out the remaining pages, Emma studied the ones in front of her. Something grabbed her attention. "That's funny," she remarked.

"What is?" asked Logan.

Emma pointed to the page on the right and said, "The one on the right that looks like a circle with a sun in the middle."

Dr. Arenot looked at the page she pointed to. "You're talking about 'F68r3?'" he said, referring to the Voynich Manuscript page number assigned at the bottom right-hand corner.

Emma leaned in to confirm and then replied, "Correct."

F68r3 consisted of a large circle with a smaller interior circle or 'sun' at its center. The sun had an orange outline and a frowning face, two eyes, and a nose. The text written in the manuscript's secret language encircled the sun, with no beginning or end. Eight lines were extending outward from the sun, each accompanied by text running parallel to the line all the way out until intersecting with the outer circle. Wrapping around the outer circle's circumference was another long contiguous line of undecipherable text, again, with no discernible beginning or end. The result was an illustration with eight equal sections that looked like pizza slices, with each slice filled with yellow stars. The number of stars varied depending on the section, from 2 to 18 stars. Lastly, in some sections, there were words written next to the stars, possibly naming them.

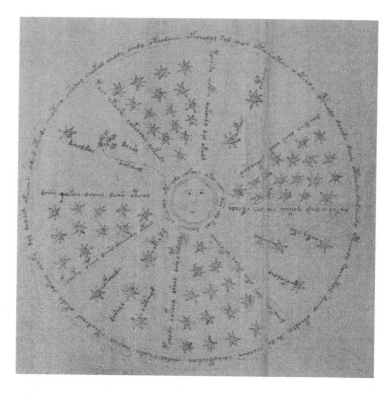

(Credit: Beinecke Rare Book and Manuscript Library,
Yale University)

"So, what's so funny about this illustration?" Logan asked
Emma.

"The section at 10 o'clock," she replied, pointing to the section
at the upper-left containing eight stars, with one large star, a group of
seven smaller stars to the larger star's right, and a meandering S-
shaped line drawn from the sun out to the group of seven stars. "That
section has a cluster of stars that resembles the Pleiades
constellation. We were just studying the Pleiades in class this
morning."

Looking at some notes discussing page f68r3, Dr. Arenot said,
"Your observation about f68r3 looking like the Pleiades has been
made by others, too. Funny, but until today, I always thought the
Pleiades consisted of six stars."

Logan corrected him. "No, it has seven, but only six are visible to the naked eye. To see the seventh, you need a telescope. Nine stars, actually, if you have a powerful telescope. Whoever wrote this book must have had access to a telescope to see that seventh star and depict it accurately... which, now that I think about it, doesn't make any sense. How old did you say this manuscript is?"

"Approximately 800 years old," replied Dr. Arenot.

"Hmmm," Logan mused to himself.

"What?" Dr. Arenot asked, wondering what Logan was thinking.

Logan replied, "It's just that the earliest known telescope wasn't invented until the 17th century." Logan was no cryptologist, nor was he familiar with the Voynich Manuscript, but as an Astronomy major, he knew telescopes. He had studied them sophomore year. "Galileo, Kepler, and other astronomers improved upon the telescope in later years, but in the 13th or 14th century when the Voynich was supposedly written, to observe the seventh star Celaeno without a telescope... *no way*."

"Ah, that *is* interesting," said Professor Quimbey. "You see? We're already making progress. And that's why they sent this down here."

The loudspeaker in the ceiling went off. "Team, it's time," announced a deep male voice. It was Maj. Jameson's.

"Why don't we pick this up later?" said Dr. Arenot.

Everyone agreed. They quickly returned the pages to the folder and made their way back to the control room. Soon, they would know whether it was time for Pegasus to finally take flight.

Chapter 4 – Big Foot

When Logan, Emma, and the two professors emerged from the office, not only had Maj. Jameson arrived but General Covington had, too. Lt. Col. Lain and Maj. Jameson sat side-by-side in front of the computers, while General Covington paced behind them.

"Good afternoon, Ms. James," said the five-star general before greeting Logan, Dr. Arenot, and Professor Quimbey next. Like always, the balding gray-haired general wore his Air Force dress uniform loaded with medals and honors. How he made it through the metal detector was unclear to Logan. The general walked over and surveyed the control panel operated by Lt. Col. Lain and Maj. Jameson. After nodding approvingly, he turned to the four civilians and said, "I hope you brought your popcorn."

The general looked at his watch and then said, "Lt. Col. Lain, please bring P-West online."

"Yes, sir," she replied.

In an instant, the large screen on the wall lit up, displaying a massive underground hangar beneath the Nevada desert, not far from the Area 51 base. Dozens of military officers and scientists were preparing for the test in the hangar. Specialized equipment, digital screens, and glass-panel maps charting the Milky Way Galaxy, and tiered-rows of desks reminiscent of a rocket launch control room filled the hangar known as 'Pegasus West,' located just a few miles away from the main base.

Pegasus West and Area 51's commanding officer, Lt. General Nemond, stepped into view on-screen. He saluted General Covington, who returned the formality.

"What's your status, General?" asked General Covington.

"Pegasus West is ready to proceed at the president's command," advised Lt. General Nemond.

"Alright, Lt. Col. Lain, can you please bring the Situation Room online and notify the Chief of Staff we're ready."

"Yes, sir," she replied. "Bringing the SIT-Room online, now." She sent the request to establish communications with the Situation Room, a state-of-the-art, highly secure conference room and intelligence management center located in the White House basement and used by the president of the United States. After a few seconds, the Situation Room appeared with Pegasus West on a divided screen. The other locations also had split screens.

"Mr. Garrison said the president will be down in two minutes, sir," reported Maj. Jameson.

"Thank you, Major," replied General Covington.

On his side of the country, General Nemond ordered all personnel to take their places and prepare for the *p*RAMZA test. When ready, Lt. General Nemond announced, "Pegasus West is a go."

"Lt. Col. Lain?" asked General Covington.

"Pegasus East is a go."

Right on time, the President of the United States, Andrew Barrett, walked into the Situation Room radiating authority in his dark navy power suit and red tie, polished black dress shoes, and finely clipped hair. The president surveyed the room with his wide-blue eyes as his team of advisors, albeit fewer than usual given the top-secret security implications of the Pegasus Project, stood and saluted him. On-screen, the generals did the same.

"At ease, everybody, if that's possible today," said President Barrett. The president sat down. Taking their seats right after him were National Security Agency Director, Sue Orson; Chief of Staff, Miles Garrison; Commander of the Air Force Space Command, General Staley; and the Director of the National Aeronautics and Space Administration, Dr. Edgar Bowling.

"General Covington, where are we?" asked the president.

"Mr. President, Pegasus is ready to proceed," he declared.

"Good. I know we're all eager to see if this thing works today. Last time, we couldn't even get a portal to open on the moon and now we're aiming for a star 23 light-years away. Quite an ambitious jump. Let me talk to Dr. Ehringer," said President Barrett, asking to speak with the science director at Pegasus West.

To the screen stepped Dr. Ehringer, a frazzled white coat scientist with brown hair, thick glasses, and a face covered in stress. His last three years' worth of work as science director was about to be put to the test, and if it didn't work, he wasn't sure how much longer he would hold the position. Nervously, Dr. Ehringer said, "Good afternoon, Mr. President."

"Dr. Ehringer, good to see you again, as always. Big day for your team. You all must be very anxious to get this test underway."

"You can say that, sir, yes," conceded Dr. Ehringer.

President Barrett always had a good sense for when his people needed a boost, and he could tell from Dr. Ehringer's voice that it was one of those times. "Doctor, you, your whole team, you are all the best of the best. I couldn't be prouder of the work your team has accomplished over the last three years, regardless of how today turns out, okay? So, take a deep breath and let your team's expertise do the talking."

"Thank you, sir," replied Dr. Ehringer, feeling a great sense of relief upon hearing the president's generous words.

The president continued. "I read the report on the way back from the treaty negotiations about the new and improved pRAMZA system. Exciting stuff. Why don't you go ahead and tell us all a little more about it and why you think it's going to work today."

"Yes, Mr. President, I would be happy to. Previously, as you recall, we attempted to charge the anti-mass zeutyrons by using an influx of oppositely charged subatomic antiparticles to repel and accelerate the z-particles. That's what the Vaniryans did in the Copán Temple, which, as you know, only generated enough z-particle acceleration for portal transportation among terrestrial locations around the globe. And when we tried it on the lunar surface, it didn't work."

"Z-particle?" asked the president.

"Sorry, that's our nickname for the zeutyron particles. We've also learned that the z-particle accelerators inside the Norwegian cave, at Stonehenge and in the pyramid beneath Area 51, use a different acceleration methodology altogether. We now believe we have been able to duplicate what the Vaniryans did to accomplish space travel."

"And how is that?" asked the president.

"Using the subsurface particle collider at the National Accelerator Laboratory in Illinois or NALI, we were able to accomplish something extraordinary. In simple terms, Mr. President, think of the power of a nuclear chain reaction caused by the splitting of an atom. In the supercollider at NALI, we succeeded in not only splitting the z-particle but also in harnessing the resulting chain reaction to charge and accelerate the z-particles to speeds billions of times faster than before. And because z-particles gain speed as they go without ever slowing down unless stopped, they reach speeds far exceeding the speed of light."

"How does this chain reaction not blow us all up, or suck us into a black hole, or something?" asked the president.

"Good question, Mr. President," said Dr. Ehringer. "In a strange way, it does. The zeutyron chain reaction is about a million times more powerful than the atomic bomb. The explosion occurs. However, because z-particles have no mass, you can't see or feel it just like nobody notices cellphone, radio, TV, and satellite signals whipping through the rooms they work, live, and breathe in, every day... in simple terms."

"Simple terms," said President Barrett with an amused laugh. "And you are certain this test poses no risk to your team in the hangar or the public?"

"Yes, Mr. President, um, we believe it is safe," replied Dr. Ehringer. "We have modeled out this test in computer simulations hundreds of times and run controlled tests in the NALI supercollider. Of course, we have never run a full-scale test into orbit, but that is what today is about."

Dr. Ehringer's answer didn't exactly allay the president's concerns. "Dr. Ehringer, with all due respect, do you believe it is safe, or do you *know* it is safe? Your response about how this plays out on your computer or in the controlled environment at NALI does not inspire my complete confidence," critiqued the president.

General Covington stepped in to help. "Mr. President, we have the sign-off of all seven appointed astrophysicists on this project, including two Nobel Laureates. All have independently confirmed their belief that the modeled test results will prevail today."

One could hear a pin drop in Pegasus West. Everyone in the hangar held their breath waiting for the president's next words.

"Thank you, all. Please give me a moment," replied the president. The audio feed to the Situation Room went mute, although the visual feed remained live. From what they could see, President Barrett was actively engaging in muted dialogue with his advisors.

"What do you think he's going to do?" Logan asked General Covington.

Without looking at Logan, General Covington calmly responded, "I don't even pretend to know but whatever he decides, it'll be the right thing to do."

When President Barrett returned, the audio feed went live, and the president said, "General Covington, General Nemond, I am authorizing Pegasus to proceed with the *p*RAMZA test. You are a go… let's see what's out there."

"Yes, sir," responded General Covington.

"And, General, if this test works, I sure hope we can come up with a better name than *p*RAMZA to fill the history books, something a little more profound to describe what may be the greatest scientific achievement in mankind's history. Good luck, gentlemen."

"Yes, Mr. President. Thank you," said General Covington.

As soon as the president authorized the test, Pegasus West erupted to a rumbling roar of activity and excitement. Dr. Ehringer took off for his post. 10 seconds later, a wall at the back of the hangar opened, revealing a mini-hangar adjacent to the main hangar.

"Mr. President," said Dr. Ehringer, "the entire hangar you see before you is the stationary part of the Zeutyron Accelerator, which we call 'Station.'

"And what is that inside *Station*?" asked the president. "Is that the *p*RAMZA?"

"Yes, Mr. President. Inside Station is the portable remote anti-mass zeutyron accelerator that the astronauts will eventually have to take with them for this to work, the *p*RAMZA."

The *p*RAMZA resembled one of NASA's Mars rovers. It sat on a titanium platform 17 inches thick, measuring 6.5 feet long by

4.8 feet wide. Sitting on the platform was a rounded, cone-shaped titanium capsule approximately 5 feet tall. An entire network of cables, wires, and technology connected the capsule to the 17-inch thick platform, with both sections housing interconnected computers. The *p*RAMZA had no exposed wires or cables to avoid exposure of its fragile interior parts to wear and tear, ripping, breaking, or other unknown environmental hazards.

Finally, to allow the *p*RAMZA to move, double-wide wheels in the corners, each measuring 20 inches in diameter, supported the whole contraption. Arranged in a rocker-bogie suspension, the wheels allowed it to maneuver over obstacles, rocks, and uneven terrain, and they had retractable cleats in-between the double-wide wheels for increased traction over steep, slippery, icy, and even muddy surfaces.

The president was somewhat stumped. "Dr. Ehringer, you call that a *portable* remote zeutyron accelerator? The thing looks like it weighs as much as my car."

"Half a car, actually, Mr. President," replied Dr. Ehringer, now wearing a headset so he could communicate with the president and his team from an elevated control-station platform in front of a computer monitor. "1,512 pounds, to be exact."

"And they're supposed to take that with them?" asked the president. "Even on wheels, I would think that is a load to push."

"The astronauts can push it if the conditions are right, but that's not the goal. The *p*RAMZA can be controlled like a remote-control car through either the computer interface, hand remote, or voice-activated controls. You'd be surprised how fast Prammy can move. She can keep up with a walking adult."

"Prammy?" asked the president.

Slightly embarrassed, Dr. Ehringer explained, "That's what we, um, call her, Mr. President… *p*RAMZA … Prammy…"

"General Covington, on second thought, let's bump the renaming process up on the priority list, could you?" requested the president. "Where is this computer interface? I don't see it."

A Pegasus-scientist walked up to the *p*RAMZA and opened a panel on the capsule's lower half, revealing an oversized extra-thick shatter-proof LCD screen, three feet in diameter. A detachable hand-remote was affixed to the right-hand side of the panel.

"Mr. President," explained Dr. Ehringer, "this computer-interface is touchscreen. If the environment doesn't allow for open skin, there's a pull-out keyboard just below the screen. And as you can see on the right, there's a remote, giving the Pegasus astronauts multiple options for operating it, depending on the situation. Best of all, the *p*RAMZA's also voice-activated, pre-programmed with nearly 3,000 voice commands. Again, we wanted to give whoever is operating the machine as many options as possible in case of unexpected circumstances."

"What if there's an emergency?" inquired the president, concerned first and foremost with the safety of the astronauts.

Dr. Ehringer responded, "The *p*RAMZA is equipped with an emergency button and has an emergency-escape-command… all an astronaut has to say within earshot is 'Fly Home,' and within seconds, the *p*RAMZA will send a z-particle signal back to Station, which will activate a portal tracked to the signal's source for the astronauts to return to Earth."

"*If* your contraption works…," the president reminded him.

"Correct," acknowledged Dr. Ehringer. "*If* it works…"

"Let's hope it does," said the president. "I'm guessing this entire hangar and your friend there cost us about $500 million in ashtrays."

"Classified defense system upgrades to Air Force One, actually," responded NSA Director Orson, failing to recognize the president's dry sense of humor.

"Right," said the president. "Let's proceed, Dr. Ehringer."

"Yes, Mr. President. Team One, please raise the metal shield," requested Dr. Ehringer.

Where once there had been a wall and then an opening to view the *p*RAMZA, there arose a clear two-foot thick panel from the floor. The transparent wall continued all the way up into the ceiling until it sealed off the *p*RAMZA in the adjacent hangar.

"*That's* metal?" asked Emma, forgetting for the moment that everyone at Pegasus West and in the Situation Room could hear her.

"Yes, it's transparent aluminum... and at two-feet thick, quite a bit stronger than your typical can of soda," answered Dr. Ehringer.

"Right out of Star Trek IV," remarked Dr. Arenot lightheartedly, remembering the famous scene from the 1980's sci-fi movie where Enterprise crew members, Mr. Scott and Dr. McCoy, taught a lowly engineer at Plexicorp how to make transparent aluminum 300 years before its time.

Dr. Ehringer had a response for Dr. Arenot. "The U.S. Naval Laboratories developed this a few years ago. It's not science-fiction, at all. By bombarding the aluminum with powerful x-rays, they succeeded in eliminating a core electron that every aluminum atom possesses which gives aluminum its color. The process leaves the aluminum nearly invisible, making it ideal for viewing and highly resistant to residual radiation. Team Two, let's open a portal," instructed Dr. Ehringer.

Team Two sent coordinates to the Stationary Zeutyron Accelerator for a planet called Gliese 667 Cb orbiting the star, Gliese 667 C. "Coordinates being sent to Station, now," replied a military officer operating Team Two's computer terminal. "Confirming: Right ascension (α) 17h 18m 57.16483s, Declination (δ) $-34°$ 59' 23.1416", Semi-major axis (a) 0.050432 ± 0.000001 AU, Orbital period (P) 7.2006 d, Inclination (i) $>30°$."

"Ok, Team Three, activate the zeutyron field," instructed Dr. Ehringer.

"Zeutyron field generated," said Team Three's representative.

"Team Three, activate the portal to Gliese 667 Cb," said Dr. Ehringer.

This was the moment they had all been waiting for. Everyone looked on, afraid to blink so as not to miss something. In a matter of seconds, a rectangular-shaped portal 20 feet wide and approximately 10 feet tall materialized in front of the *p*RAMZA. They stared at the snow and rock covered surface of Gliese 667 Cb, in the middle of a moderate snow and ice storm.

Eyes widened and jaws dropped.

"What are we looking at?" asked President Barrett.

Dr. Ehringer, himself in awe, replied, "The surface of Gliese 667 Cb, Mr. President."

"Pegasus East, can you confirm this?" asked Lt. Gen. Nemond.

Lt. Col. Lain examined data readouts from the PAPA and reported, "PAPA tracks the trajectory of the zeutyron field in orbit to the Gliese 667 C star system."

"Extraordinary," the president replied.

"Team Four, deploy the *p*RAMZA into the portal," said Dr. Ehringer, "and Prammy, have a safe trip."

The *p*RAMZA, on its high-tech wheels, rolled forward toward the portal. Its engine emitted a low hum. As it rolled closer to the portal, a voice from Team Four counted down, "Three, two, one..."

The *p*RAMZA disappeared into the portal. The moment it did, a large digital readout with bright red numbers appeared on the wall to the left of the *p*RAMZA Hangar, showing the date and a countdown clock for 10 minutes. It immediately started counting backward from 10 minutes.

As if the *p*RAMZA had done nothing more than drive over the Nevada state line, it appeared on Gliese 667 Cb's ice and snow. Because the Pegasus team did not know if they would be able to communicate with the *p*RAMZA through the portal, Dr. Ehringer's team had pre-programmed it to undertake a series of actions during the 10-minute countdown window.

First on the list, Dr. Ehringer's team had programmed the *p*RAMZA to drive around in a 15-foot loop to turn and face the portal. Due to the snowy terrain, the *p*RAMZA's cleats automatically extended out from the wheels to give it better traction. Moving cautiously on the snow, the *p*RAMZA slowly completed the loop, which took nearly two minutes. When done, the *p*RAMZA's large digital screen relayed a message in big bold blue letters: "GREETINGS FROM GLIESE 667 Cb."

Pegasus West clapped. A few laughed. The next part of the plan, once the *p*RAMZA went through the portal, was for it to visually display basic information, including the date and atmospheric conditions on the planet. The *p*RAMZA spent a few moments gathering data and then displayed the date and ten-minute countdown clock. The date was the same, and its countdown clock perfectly synced with the clock on the wall beside Station, confirming no time distortion had occurred due to Einstein's theory of relativity. The *p*RAMZA's journey to Gliese 667 Cb had, in fact, been instantaneous, thanks to the Vaniryan technology.

Next, the *p*RAMZA displayed the following message:

"IT IS MINUS 179.8°F (MINUS 117.7°C).

NO OXYGEN DETECTED. ATMOSPHERE CONSISTS OF: HYDROGEN (67.3%), HELIUM (19.5%), METHANE (8.7%), AMMONIA (3.2%), NITROGEN (2.3%), WATER (<.001%).

60

GRAVITY IS 25.44 m/s².

AWAITING FURTHER INSTRUCTIONS."

Now, it was time for the next test: could Pegasus West communicate with the *p*RAMZA through the portal?

"Team Six, please execute communication sequence alpha," said Dr. Ehringer through his headset. "Mr. President, we will now test whether we can communicate directly with Prammy through the portal. If successful, she will spin around in a circle."

"Signal sent," announced Team Six.

They waited; nothing happened. After a minute, the *p*RAMZA reported back on its digital screen: **"I CAN'T HEAR YOU."**

Dr. Ehringer wasn't surprised. "Alright, try one more time," he requested.

Team Six did. They waited a little longer. Still, no response.

"Ok, it appears Prammy is on her own out there," said a dejected Dr. Ehringer. He had anticipated the possibility, even expected it, but still, he had hoped it would be otherwise. "Mr. President, we can see her but can't communicate with her."

"So, now what?" asked the president.

Dr. Ehringer explained, "Cutting the Stationary Zeutyron Accelerator field was always the plan, sir. The portal will go dark, and Prammy will spend the next few minutes re-locating to a new location 150 feet away from where Station deposited her on Gliese 667 Cb. Before the countdown clock hits zero, the *p*RAMZA will then attempt to send a zeutyron signal back to Pegasus West. Prammy isn't powerful enough to open a portal on her own, so her technology acts more like a z-particle homing beacon to relay her location back to Station. Upon receipt of the signal, Station will attempt to open up a portal tracked to Prammy's signal to bring her home."

"Okay, let's see if you're right," replied the president.

"Team Three, shut down the portal," ordered Dr. Ehringer. For an instant, he looked pained as he realized he might never see Prammy again.

"Portal deactivated," announced Team Three, although it was obvious the moment the portal disappeared.

"Ok, Mr. President, now we wait another 4 minutes and 23 seconds," said Dr. Ehringer, reading the countdown clock on the wall.

The clock kept ticking, and still no word from the *p*RAMZA. When the clock hit one minute remaining, the tension in the control rooms became palpable. Logan reached over and took Emma's hand. She smiled back.

At T-minus 32 seconds, Team Two announced, "Dr. Ehringer, Station is receiving a signal from —"

Before Team Two could finish the announcement, a large portal displaying ice and snow materialized in the *p*RAMZA Hangar. Prammy was back, standing tall and proud for all to see from a different location than before, with ice boulders behind it. On the *p*RAMZA's digital screen, it displayed a pre-programmed message to its friends on Earth: "**I'D LIKE TO COME HOME NOW**."

Simultaneously, Pegasus West, Pegasus East, and the Situation Room exploded in simultaneous cheers. The scientists had done it, drawing a standing ovation from those witnessing the moment. Tears of joy welled up in Emma's eyes. She wiped them away and Logan hugged her. The president shook hands with his advisors.

The *p*RAMZA initiated its return sequence. It started rolling forward toward the portal. It looked like it needed to travel 10 or 15 feet based on their perception from this side of the portal. Just a few seconds before the *p*RAMZA reached the entry point, the ground beneath it shook.

"Dr. Ehringer," said Team Seven over the loudspeaker, "it looks like the *p*RAMZA may be experiencing a seismic event."

Everyone's eyes focused on the *p*RAMZA. Suddenly, a gigantic gray foot, nearly as big as the portal itself, stomped down on the *p*RAMZA, obliterating it. Some screamed, a few jumped back startled, and others simply gasped. The portal instantly disappeared. Prammy and the portal were gone, and everyone was utterly stunned at what they had just witnessed: extraterrestrial life on another planet.

"Get it back up!" shouted Lt. General Nemond.

Dr. Ehringer's team tried but was unsuccessful. His head sunk before he responded, "General, Prammy knew her job. She knew the risks, but she's gone, sir."

The president stood up. He wasn't disappointed, at all. "There can be no greater reminder of the power, wonder, and danger of space travel than what we just witnessed. Dr. Ehringer, I could not be prouder of what you all accomplished today. A great day in history. To you, to your whole team, to the entire Pegasus Project, congratulations. I have no doubt a few seconds later that your pioneering friend would have returned home. I will still want to confirm that on another test, of course. Well done."

"Thank you, sir," responded Dr. Ehringer. Just then, spurred by the president's kind words, the Pegasus West team decided to give their beloved project-leader, Dr. Ehringer, a standing ovation. Dr. Ehringer looked extremely uncomfortable with the attention, but he graciously accepted it.

"General Covington," said the president. "Please get me a full report of today's test by 9 am tomorrow and let's plan to talk about the next steps in our briefing at 11."

"Yes, Mr. President."

The Situation Room feed went dark.

"Dr. Ehringer, did you hear that?" asked General Covington.

"Yes, general, we'll get right on it."

"Thank you, Dr. Ehringer, and great work today," said General Covington.

Lt. General Nemond returned to the screen.

"Bernie," said General Covington, "sounds like some of your folks over there are already cracking open champagne bottles."

"I think that's a safe assumption," Lt. General Nemond replied.

With a smile, General Covington said, "Just make sure they don't spill on the equipment. Not sure how many more ashtrays we've got left in our budget."

Lt. Gen. Nemond laughed. "I'll talk to you in the morning once the report is finalized."

"That sounds good," said General Covington. "Lt. Col. Lain, please disconnect P-West."

Lt. Col. Lain did, and the digital screen went dark.

It was time to celebrate.

Chapter 5 – An Imperfect Plan

At 7 pm sharp, Logan walked up the distressed brick steps leading to Emma's colonial-style apartment to pick her up. Logan—who usually tossed on whatever clothes he had that were relatively clean—had tried on several outfits this evening. Tonight, he wanted to look his best, and he landed on a collared shirt, gray sports coat, jeans, and black loafers. Logan took hold of the iron door-knock on her front door and clicked it several times. Emma, excited, opened the door.

"Hi!" she exclaimed, hugging him. "Wow, you look nice. I know you said we were going out to celebrate, but I didn't think you meant—"

"You look perfect," he said. Her long sandy-blond hair was down, and she wore a black leather jacket, dark blue jeans, and low black boots. Once again, Logan thought, she looked beautiful. No matter how casual her outfit, Emma always managed to look elegant, fresh, fun, and fashionable.

"Thanks! Give me a second." Emma darted back inside and grabbed her black purse.

When she returned, she said, "Ready! Where are we going?"

"It's a surprise," he replied.

"Mysterious… I like it."

Logan had an Uber waiting for them, the same one that had brought him from his apartment seven blocks away. Gesturing to the car, he said, "Shall we?"

They took the Uber to the steps of the Lincoln Memorial, a national monument built on the National Mall's western end to honor the 16th President of the United States, Abraham Lincoln. They exited the cab, and Logan paid the driver.

Emma took in the Lincoln Memorial, impressed as always by its grandeur and history. The Memorial was built using marble in the style of a Greek Temple, with 36 massive fluted Doric columns surrounding it. A large seated sculpture of Abraham Lincoln was set back in the building's open interior, hiding behind the columns. Wondering if *this* was the surprise, Emma said, "We've been here before."

"I know," responded Logan. "I just thought we could walk through the Mall on our way to dinner. We're a little early, anyway."

"Sounds fun," said Emma. "Good thing I brought my coat."

They walked east through the grassy lawns of the National Mall, a long rectangular public park stretching from the Lincoln Memorial on the west end to the U.S. Capitol Building on the east end, totaling just under two miles. At night, the lawns were well-lit by landscape lighting. First, they walked past the Lincoln Memorial Reflecting Pool, a stroll that took more than five minutes since the rectangular pool was nearly one-third of a mile long by itself. Next, they came to the 554-foot tall obelisk-shaped Washington Monument. Visible due north from there was the White House, and due east, the Capitol Building.

Curiosity nipping away at her, Emma again asked, "Where are we going?"

Logan gave nothing away. He simply smiled slyly and replied, "Almost there."

They kept strolling through the National Mall, passing the Smithsonian National Museum of American History, the Smithsonian National Museum of Natural History, and then, the Smithsonian National Museum of African History. Finally, they reached Logan's pre-dinner destination: the Smithsonian National Air and Space Museum.

"We're going here?" asked Emma. She wasn't questioning his choice, *per se*, after all, she loved the museum. It's just that they had been there before, too.

"Think of this as an appetizer," he said, "on our way to dinner."

"Isn't the museum closed?"

"My Astro-Dynamics professor is the Academic Representative on the museum's Board of Directors. He pulled a few strings for a short after-hours tour of the new exhibit."

"What a great surprise!" said Emma, impressed by Logan's thoughtful planning.

When they reached the museum's mall-side entrance at 7:30 pm, Assistant Director Amy Reiss was waiting for them at the door, right on time.

"Logan?" she asked, just to confirm.

"Yes, hi," answered Logan, "and this is Emma."

"Hi," said Emma with a wave.

"Good evening. Nice to meet you both. I'm Amy Reiss, Assistant Director here. Please, come in."

After they went through the door, Ms. Reiss locked the entrance back up.

"Thank you so much, Ms. Reiss, for doing this," said Logan.

"Of course! Anyone studying under Professor Arden who comes with a recommendation like you received is a friend of the museum. And please, call me Amy. Did you guys walk here?"

"Yes, well, partway, from the Mall's west end, anyway," responded Logan.

"It's a nice night, a bit chilly for me, but then again, I'm from L.A. We get cold when it drops below 65 degrees. Welcome to the Smithsonian Air and Space Museum," said Amy. "Have either of you been here before?"

Both Emma and Logan answered, "*Yes.*"

"Of course, you have, probably a silly question. So, I understand from Professor Arden you're interested in seeing the new exhibit."

"Definitely!" replied Emma.

"Plenty to see along the way, too," added Amy. She guided them through the museum, explaining things and taking them slowly through a few of the exhibits including the Time and Navigation, Space Race, and Exploring the Planets displays. When they got to the Milestones of Flight section, Emma and Logan stopped in awe of the latest addition to the collection: the B-2 Stealth Bomber. The B-2 was a triangular-shaped flying wing aircraft that resembled a bat, with no fuselage or tail.

"Wow!" uttered Emma excitedly, hurrying up to the sagging red-rope barricade around the stealth bomber. "Incredible."

"How big is it?" asked Logan, shocked by its size up close. "Not sure I ever realized how huge the B-2 is."

"This one's 69 feet in length with a 172-foot wingspan. Do you want to go closer?" asked Amy.

"Yes!" exclaimed Emma.

Amy unhooked the rope so they could walk up to it.

Both put their hands on the smooth black surface of the aircraft's underside. It was made out of a carbon-graphite composite material stronger than steel, lighter than aluminum, and capable of absorbing radar energy, rendering the bomber hard to detect by enemy sensors.

"Is it still operational?" wondered Emma.

"No, definitely not. Before sending it over to the Smithsonian, the Air Force gutted it, as you can imagine. You guys want to keep going?"

"Yes!" said Emma, eager to see what was coming next.

Amy led them to the museum's east end to the new exhibit, Space Imagined. The hall was full of replicas of landmark space exploration objects, from satellites to the original Apollo Lunar-2 Module to the Jet Propulsion Laboratory's popular Mars rovers: Opportunity, Spirit, and Curiosity.

Looking at the rovers, Logan leaned over and whispered to Emma, "Notice a resemblance?"

Emma grinned, fondly thinking of their brave friend, Prammy, who gave her life earlier that day to explore Gliese 667 Cb for the Pegasus Project.

"So, welcome to Space Imagined, where the Smithsonian celebrates humanity's efforts to explore and understand its universe, and even its efforts to explain it through the millennia."

Logan and Emma spent a couple of minutes poking around. Looking at the eastern side of the exhibit hall, they saw an animated display with animals moving along the wall in a choreographed sequence. Emma asked Amy, "What's that on the wall? It's pretty."

"That is the Smithsonian's digitally animated rendition of the Chinese Zodiac, a 12-year cycle in which each year in that cycle relates to an animal sign. Up on the wall, you see moving around each other, all 12 animals of the zodiac: the rat, ox, tiger, rabbit, dragon, snake, horse, sheep, monkey, rooster, dog and pig. And on the southern wall, you will see all the Greek constellations, from Andromeda to Leo, Pegasus to Ursa Major, etc."

"How about over there?" wondered Logan, pointing at a large autumn-colored tree on the hall's western wall with branches growing out of it, autumn leaves outlined in gold and radiant colorful globes hanging at the end of each branch.

"That is the 'Yggdrasil,' depicting the mythological cosmic tree at the center of the Norse universe according to the *Prose Edda* written by Snorri Sturluson."

"It's, umm, a great big tree. Interesting view of the universe," said Logan.

"What are the globes hanging at the end of the branches?" wondered Emma.

"They represent the Nine Worlds of Norse cosmology," replied Amy.

"What are the words written in the globes?" Emma followed up.

"Those are the names of the Nine Worlds: Asgard, the world of the Æsir gods; Álfheimr, the world of the light elves; Svartálfaheimr, home of the dark elves; Midgard, home of humans; Jötunheimr, home of the giants; Vanaheimr, home of the Vanir gods; Niflheim, the primordial world of ice; Muspelheim, the primordial world of fire; and Helheim, home of the dishonorable dead."

"It's beautiful," commented Emma.

"Do you two want a picture in front of it?" asked Amy.

Logan hesitated, seeing other exhibits he thought might make for a better picture. "Uh—"

"Sure!" exclaimed Emma, smacking Logan in the arm.

Logan took out his phone, opened the camera app, and handed it to Amy. She took a photo of them, arms around each other and smiling.

"Ahh, so cute!" commented Amy.

"Thank you!" said Emma. She took back Logan's phone and changed Logan's lock screen and background image. "There! Now you'll always remember this tree!" Logan lovingly smiled back.

They walked around for a few more minutes before stopping to check out the display they had purposely saved for last, the Exhibit's biggest resident: a 43-foot-long metallic cylinder-shaped object dangling from the high museum ceiling, with two 40 feet long rectangular solar arrays on each side, 2 mirrors, and 2 antennae sticking out of it.

"Is that the Hubble?" asked Emma.

"It is," answered Amy. "It's a replica of NASA's Hubble Space Telescope named after the astronomy pioneer, Edwin Powell Hubble. Do you know a lot about the Hubble?"

"A little," replied Emma. She knew more about the Hubble's top-secret cousin, the classified PAPA telescope.

"And you?" said Amy, looking at Logan, "I'm assuming you know a whole lot about it if you're studying under Professor Arden."

"I know some," he humbly acknowledged.

In her effort to be a good tour guide, Amy said, "Let's see if I can stump you with a few questions about the Hubble. That is if you're up for it."

"Okay," he replied with a willing smile.

"How much battery power do you think the Hubble uses on a daily basis?"

Logan grinned. "That's easy. 2,800 watts, or a little more than a hair dryer on high heat," he replied.

"That's right. Pretty impressive when considering the telescope travels around the globe at 17,500 miles per hour and weighs 24,500 pounds or as much as 2 full-grown elephants. Actually, the Hubble's dual solar arrays generate most of the power it uses on a daily basis. How about this one... how much did it cost to build the Hubble?"

"$2.5 billion, I think," answered Logan.

"Reasonable guess," Amy replied. "$4.7 billion. Bonus question: what was the original estimate for the Hubble's construction?"

"$2 billion?" ventured Emma.

Amy laughed. "That would have been nice, but no. Try, $400 million."

"Wow, they went a bit over budget there," said Emma.

"Of course, no one is complaining. The Hubble's been able to make nearly 1.2 million observations since its launch in 1990."

Logan's phone beeped to remind him that they had a dinner reservation in 15 minutes. "We have to get going," he said. "We have a reservation at 8:45 pm."

"Ok, last one," said Amy. "How far away is the furthest object the Hubble has ever been able to observe?"

"Hmm," said Logan. He wasn't sure, but he knew it was far away. "Um, 9.5 billion light-years?" he guessed.

"Impressive, but a little short. How about 13.4 billion light-years away, a galaxy called MACS0647-JD."

"Now *that* is a galaxy far, far away," joked Logan.

Emma smiled, amused by Logan's Star Wars reference.

"So where are you two going for dinner?"

Logan decided to finally drop a hint. "Let's just say I'm keeping the futuristic theme going."

As soon as he said it, Amy knew exactly where Logan was taking Emma, mainly because the new hip restaurant was right across the street from the Air and Space Museum on Independence Avenue. "That should be fun," replied Amy.

"You didn't!?!?" shouted Emma, ecstatic. "Did you get reservations at Hobā?"

Logan tried not to answer, but his emerging grin gave him away, and he knew it, so he replied, "Yep."

"Logan, I can't believe you got reservations there! But how?!"

"You two should get going. I'll take you to the closest exit to the restaurant on Independence." Amy led them to an exit on the museum's Independence Avenue side, virtually across the street from the restaurant.

"Amy, thank you so much! This was awesome, really," said Logan.

"Yes, I loved it," added Emma.

"You're quite welcome. Please, come back anytime. And have fun tonight!"

They said their goodbyes and slipped across the street to an unassuming door in the floor of a multi-level building, with the name

"ホバー" set in the middle of it. Pronounced Hobā, the popular new sushi restaurant was booked all the time, so much so that Logan had to make reservations seven weeks in advance. The name ホバー or Hobā meant "Hover" in Japanese. And when they walked inside, it was easy to see why.

Hobā was the ultra-modern version of your classic sushi restaurant, accented by crisp sharp angles, neon lighting, and dancing water features. The restaurant's walkways between the tables consisted of a lit-up see-through aquarium floor full of colorful koi fish swimming below. Metal rods augmented by LCD lighting bisected the walkways every 16 inches. But most uniquely, the restaurant had no waiters. Hobā delivered all the food and drink from the kitchen or sushi bar to its patrons using Hoverers, sleek hover-trays similar to hovercrafts but smaller, smarter, silent, and smooth.

Logan walked up to check in with the hostess while Emma looked around. On a busy Friday night, dinner guests packed the restaurant, although Emma figured it was probably bursting every night of the week given its popularity.

After a short discussion, the Japanese hostess said, "Mr. West, right this way."

Logan looked back and called to Emma, "They're ready for us."

"Great."

The hostess led them through the restaurant on one of the aquarium walkways to their table. They passed by the sushi bar and watched as the sushi chef plated food on a Hoverer and sent the hovering helper on its way to a table. The hostess led them to a private two-person booth on the rear wall.

After they sat down and quickly settled in, the friendly hostess asked, "Have either of you been here before?"

"No, never," replied Emma enthusiastically.

74

"Welcome to Hobā. My name is Mei, and I will be one of your hosts tonight. Let me tell you how we work. We are, for the most part, a waiter-less restaurant. In front of each of you, beneath your glass tabletop, is a personalized touch-screen tablet. Everything you want or need can be selected off the menu with a simple touch. You can pull up images of all the food and drink items to explore options and read their descriptions, and if you have questions or want something you don't see, just type it in or dictate it, and our Kitchen Host will respond and help you within seconds. You can input special requests or instructions for any food and drink items, or ask for anything else you need. As you can see by looking around, everything here is delivered right to your table by our Hoverers."

"How do they work?" asked Emma. "I bet you get that question 1,000 times a day."

Mei laughed because Emma was right. "I'm more than happy to explain. Beneath the tray in the Hoverers' concealed underside are electromagnets generating a strong magnetic field which repel the trays from the grid of rods set into the walkways, creating a levitating effect. So, as you can see, our Hoverers only move through the network of walkways. Please, try to avoid them if you can. If you get up to go to the bathroom and see a Hoverer coming your way, just choose a different path. The Hoverers will warn you if you get too close, as they have avoidance sensors like many advanced cars do today. Of course, if you need personal assistance, either myself or my co-host, Ayane, will be around all night. We also have staff walking about to clean and clear dishes and to assist our Hoverers because there are some things the Hoverers can't handle or deliver. Tonight's special, as you will see when you start exploring the menu, is our Flaming Eel. You'll want to pull up a picture of that one, even if you aren't interested in eating it. Any questions?"

"Not for me," said Logan.

"No, I'm good, too," stated Emma.

"Great. Can I start you two off with something to drink? Alcoholic beverages are the only items on our menu the Hoverers are not permitted to deliver. It's an ABC licensing thing, and they can't check IDs, after all."

"That won't be a problem," laughed Emma. "Neither of us is 21. How about two glasses of water?"

"My pleasure," Mei replied. She walked off.

Logan and Emma watched with delight as the Hoverers departed from the sushi bar and kitchen launch stations to deliver food. A Hoverer carrying popping crackling Sizzling Shrimp floated right past their table. It smelled delicious.

"This place is so fun!" said Emma "Thank you for planning such a great evening."

Logan smiled. He knew he had done well.

"Should we order something?" asked Logan. "The sushi here's supposed to be amazing. Maybe an order of yellowtail and something else to start?"

"Perfect."

They poked through the digital menu together until they found the yellowtail. Logan pressed the digital button and it loaded into their Digital "Order Tray." They kept scanning through their options until they found the appetizer section.

"OMG, do you see the oysters?!?!" exclaimed Emma. "Listen to this… the Miyagi Sphere, with Miyagi oysters served on a bed of ice, inside an ice sphere that you crack open with a mallet. That sounds so cool."

"No pun intended?"

Emma giggled. "We have to get one of those!" Emma pressed the button and ordered the Miyagi Sphere.

Mei returned with their waters, and she also offered them mango-infused watermelon beverages in a flute, compliments of the house. After Mei left, a Hoverer delivered several small plates of wasabi and ginger to their table. They carefully removed the plates, which the Hoverer magnetically held tight to prevent them from sliding around.

"Thank you," said Emma to the automated server, laughing.

"You are welcome," responded the Hoverer, unexpectedly offering up one of its pre-programmed responses. "Enjoy your wasabi and ginger." The Hoverer floated away.

"Friendly little tray," said Emma, fully entertained.

Lifting his complimentary watermelon flute up high, Logan made a toast. "Here's to one small step for man—"

"One giant leap for humankind," chimed in Emma, finishing Logan's Neil Armstrong-quote with a slight twist.

They clinked their watermelon glasses and took a sip. They both smiled at each other, happy in the moment.

After a few more seconds, Logan looked Emma in the eyes and asked, "Do you ever think about where we're heading?"

Emma looked around and replied, "Humanity? Uh, sure, but I don't think we can really talk about that here."

Her response wasn't what he'd expected, so he clarified his question. "I'm not talking about where humanity's heading, I mean where we're —"

Emma's phone rang. She glanced down to see who it was. Because they worked at the Pentagon now, ignoring it wasn't an option. They had to keep their phones handy at all times. Looking at her phone, she saw it was Kristi, no doubt calling about the party. "Sorry, it's Kristi. I'll call her back later."

"What does Kristi want?"

"Nothing," replied Emma. "She wants me to go to a party with her later."

"Where?"

"At Brad's."

"That guy who kept sending you those cryptographic number sequences asking you out?"

"Yeah, with his number sprawled out right in the middle of every single number sequence... real cryptic," replied Emma, rolling her eyes. "So, you were saying?"

"What I was saying was: Do you ever think about what's next for *us*, you and me? It's like, work and school have been our whole lives since high school, but do you ever think there's more to life than—"

"Great, another person who thinks that all we do is work and study," interrupted Emma, thinking about a similar off-putting comment by Kristi earlier in the day.

Logan wasn't sure why he had struck a nerve. "I'm sorry, that's not what I meant. What I was trying to say was, do you ever think about *our* future beyond all this?"

"Of course, I do. I'm sorry about that, it's just something Kristi said earlier today. I –"

Emma's phone rang, again.

Logan tried to stop Emma before she answered it. "Please don't. Kristi can wait..." Logan was getting more irked with Kristi by the second.

"Logan, you know I have to look who's calling." Emma looked down, and as Logan predicted, it was Kristi, but this time, she sent an accompanying text to Emma saying: "PLEASE PLEASE CALL ME."

"It's Kristi again, and now, she's begging me to call her. I'm sorry, it'll just take a second." Emma stood up to go take the call outside.

"Em, wait—"

"Logan, she texted, 'PLEASE PLEASE CALL ME.' Maybe something's wrong, okay?" replied Emma, and Logan really couldn't argue with her, even though he wanted to. Emma took her phone and walked toward the exit, avoiding the Hoverers as she departed.

"Smooth," muttered Logan to himself, "real smooth." He looked back at Mei to motion for her to hold off, but it was already too late.

On schedule, a Hoverer sidled up next to their table carrying a plate with a silver-domed warming-lid on it. Logan uncovered the plate, revealing a small, 2" x 2" white engagement ring box. Logan looked back at Mei who had helped him set this up. Mei moved to the front door to look for Emma. She shrugged her shoulders and gestured that she couldn't see where Emma had gone.

"Alright, just another minute more," Logan reassured himself, trying to remain calm while waiting to ask the biggest question of his life. After a lifetime of self-doubt that started when his father abandoned him and his mother practically at Logan's birth, and after spending three perfect years with Emma, Logan was finally sure of one thing in his life: he wanted to spend the rest of it with the woman he loved. He had never been more certain of anything or happier than he was with Emma, and he was ready to be the man his dad never was, someone Emma could love and rely on for the rest of his life.

Over the last few weeks, Logan's friends had called him crazy for wanting to get married so young, but Logan wasn't swayed. He actually took it as a compliment. Logan kept recalling the wise words of his next-door neighbor growing up who told him, "I proposed to my Beth after our second date. I know it's crazy but I knew she was the only for me, and here we are, 50 years and six grandkids later. When you know, you know." And Logan knew.

Logan was just about ready to have Mei recall the Hoverer so he could try it again once Emma returned when another text came in, this time, for Logan. It came from a sender called "Starfleet," the Pegasus code name for the White House. The text read:

"PE-TEAM, URGENT, CAPTAIN KIRK REQUESTS U COME TO STARFLEET SIT-ROOM IMMEDIATELY. PLEASE CONFIRM. CAPTAIN KIRK ON WAY BACK TO STARFLEET NOW."

"Crap," cursed Logan, with Captain Kirk being the code name Pegasus gave to the President of the United States.

Logan slumped his head down. His proposal tonight wasn't going to happen. As soon as Emma saw the White House's text message, she was going to want to fly back to Starfleet at warp speed, assuming Ubers could travel that fast. This evening hadn't remotely turned out as Logan hoped.

Logan sighed and removed the engagement ring box from the Hoverer. Before shoving it into his coat, he opened the box to take a quick look at the ring. The shiny engagement ring had a platinum band, a single 0.75-carat princess cut diamond propped up in prongs, and two small side stones. The stone wasn't big by celebrity standards, but it was the very best that Logan could afford. He slipped the box into his inside coat pocket.

"Thanks," Logan said at the Hoverer.

"You are welcome, and congratulations," replied the Hoverer before hovering off.

Logan couldn't help but laugh at the irony and agony of the pre-programmed response. As soon as the Hoverer hovered off, Emma texted him:

"Logan, got the Starfleet text. We have to go. I called an Uber. It's arriving in 2. Can you grab my purse and jacket and meet me outside? I'm sorry about tonight. ☹ I love U. ♡ I promise we'll come back for a DO-OVER."

Logan slumped his head. He wondered how many more weeks it would take to get another reservation. He got up and gathered their things. He walked up to Mei at the hostess desk and handed her $50 to pay for the food they'd already ordered.

With a sad face, Mei asked, "What happened?"

"Something came up," Logan groaned. "We've got to go."

"I hope everything's okay…"

"Yeah, everything's fine. Thank you for your help."

"I'm so sorry it didn't work out tonight," said Mei with a pouty face. She had enjoyed helping him with his proposal plans.

"It's alright. Have a good night." Logan walked out the door.

Chapter 6 - A Message From Chersky

On the way to the White House in an Uber, they didn't speak much because of the driver, but the vague urgency of the White House's text message worried them both. Even though they worked on Pegasus, which involved top-secret subject matter, never before had they received a text like that summoning them to the Situation Room.

Their ride pulled up to the White House's Northwest Appointment Gate on Pennsylvania Avenue and dropped them off. At night, the White House beamed brightly, all lit up. They approached the guard gate and security booth.

"I'm sorry, kids, but the White House Visitor Center is closed," said the night guard, Oscar, perched in his guard booth.

"We actually have a meeting," replied Logan.

Oscar looked at both in disbelief. *"Really?"* Given that they were college students in jeans, he found Logan's claim hard to believe.

"Yes, tonight, right now," Emma responded.

Oscar presumed they were pranking him, but he had a protocol to follow for all visits. "Alright then. Your names?"

"Immaculata James," answered Emma.

"Logan West," said Logan.

"Thank you. Can I please see your IDs?"

Emma and Logan pulled out their Pentagon IDs and handed them to Oscar. They didn't have White House IDs because they weren't regulars at the White House. In fact, they had only been to the White House three times: three years ago when they met the president; two and a half years ago when they met in the Oval Office to discuss the Pegasus Project; and the last time, two years ago, when the president invited them, Dr. Arenot, and Professor Quimbey over for a private dinner with the First Lady and him.

Oscar studied their IDs closely. He saw Pentagon IDs every day and knew a real one from a fake. To his surprise, the IDs appeared authentic. He looked at the college-age visitors to confirm their photos matched their faces and then asked, "Who is your meeting with tonight?"

"The President, I think, maybe Mr. Garrison," replied Emma.

Again, Oscar didn't believe her, but he wasn't going to argue. He simply pulled up the Visitor's List on the computer, and after finding nothing, smiled smugly. He wasn't one to be made a fool of. "I'm sorry, kids, but—" He stopped himself. He found their names in the Updates Section. Mildly embarrassed, he said, "Um, I apologize... Your meeting tonight is with Mr. Garrison. I will notify the Chief of Staff that you're here."

Oscar called Mr. Garrison's office and received instructions to have them escorted to the West Wing. He buzzed open the gate. "My apologies. Officer Goff will escort you to the West Wing Lobby for your meeting." Oscar returned their IDs.

"Thank you," said Emma without any resentment. "Have a good night," she added.

"You, too," replied Oscar.

White House Security Officer Goff guided them to the West Wing Lobby entrance where, upon arrival, they went through more security. Emma checked her belongings and went through security first, followed by Logan. Logan placed his wallet, keys, and cellphone into a conveyor belt bin and carefully laid out his coat on top so as to avoid spilling out the engagement ring hidden inside. He sent his bin on its way through the scanner. As his coat went through, the White House Security Officer made eye-contact with Logan and winked. Logan's secret was safe with him.

After passing through security, two burly Secret Service agents greeted and accompanied them down to the West Wing's ground floor. They entered a secure waiting area. After a few seconds, double doors opened in front of them and the Secret Service guided them into the Situation Room. As they walked in, they got very nervous anticipating what they were about to hear.

Digital screens and flat-panel televisions covered the Situation Room's walls, with the largest concentration on the room's southern end. A 25-foot-long dark wood conference room table stretched down the middle from end to end. Dr. Arenot and Professor Quimbey were already inside, sitting on the other side of the table.

"Congratulations!" said Dr. Arenot, who hadn't bothered to look if Emma was wearing Logan's engagement ring before congratulating her.

Mortified, Logan desperately but subtly shook his head, *no*.

Confused, Emma asked, "Congratulations for what?"

Professor Quimbey, having already looked down at Emma's naked ring finger, quickly stepped in to pull Jonas' foot out of his mouth. "For... for a successful test today. Truly remarkable."

"Um, thank you," said Emma, still moderately confused.

"Mr. West, Ms. James, please take a seat next to Dr. Arenot and Professor Quimbey," said a Secret Service agent. While Emma and Logan walked around the table to sit down, Professor Quimbey kicked her husband under the table to make sure he didn't open his big mouth again.

After sitting down, Emma asked, "Does anyone know what this is about? I was minutes away from cracking open an ice sphere filled with oysters."

"Wow! Where do you get something like that?" asked Professor Quimbey, although she already knew where Logan had planned to take her for dinner.

"Hobā," replied Logan. "The place is amazing."

"*Amazing!*" added Emma with extra zeal.

The Situation Room's doors re-opened and in marched the president with the same key players from the *p*RAMZA test earlier in the day. The Secret Service closed the door behind them. Logan, Emma, Professor Quimbey, and Dr. Arenot stood up to greet the group who, one by one, sat down at the table opposite the four civilians, except for the president. He sat at the head of the conference room table.

"Thank you all for coming on short notice," said the president. "I apologize if I inconvenienced anyone tonight, but as I've learned in this office, sometimes a good day can turn into a long night. General, I'll turn it over to you."

The general stood up and walked over to the large monitor behind the president. Images of stars appeared on the monitor. Using the touch screen technology, he zoomed in on the Orion constellation and then the star Betelgeuse positioned at the back shoulder of Orion. He next focused on the stellar region slightly below and to the left of Betelgeuse, which Logan, Emma, and the professors knew was the location of TYC 129-75-1, the Vaniryan's home star. He explained, "Two hours ago, the PADS Unit notified our P-East team that TYC 129-75-1 has gone supernova." Using his index finger like a pencil, General Covington circled a blurry white ball in the screen's middle. "We believe that is or was TYC 129-75-1." Using the display's touch-sensitive controls, General Covington split the screen and pulled up a clear image of TYC 129-75-1 on the left. "On the left is a shot of the star from two weeks ago, and on the right, well, you can see it…"

"Do you mean, the star exploded?" asked Professor Quimbey.

General Covington replied, "Yes. We've had the PAPA so busy the last week charting and preparing for the pRAMZA test that we forgot to check in with the Vaniryan star."

"But how? When? Yesterday? Today?" cried Emma, suddenly feeling sick to her stomach.

NASA Director Bowling jumped in. "Hardly yesterday or today, Ms. James. That star is approximately 800 light-years away, which means it exploded 800 years ago."

"The Mauna Kea Observatory in Hawaii picked up the event two days ago," said General Covington.

"The University of Hawaii manages the Mauna Kea Observatory and relayed the information to NASA earlier today," said Dr. Bowling.

"And the PAPA confirmed two hours ago," added General Covington.

"The Vaniryans!" expressed Emma, distraught at the thought of their fate.

"It appears we now know why attempts to return to their homeworld have been unsuccessful," said General Covington. "Because it isn't there, anymore."

"Which brings us to why we're all here, tonight," said the president.

"What do you mean, sir?" asked Logan.

"General…," said the president.

General Covington switched over to a digital map of the Earth. He rotated the 3-D globe to North Asia and explained, "Dr.

Ehringer's team while incorporating the PAPA's orbital data into their post-*p*RAMZA-test report this afternoon identified something very unusual…"

"What?" asked Dr. Arenot.

"Another zeutyron signal coming from the Chersky Mountains in northeastern Siberia between the Yana River and the Indigirka River."

"In Russia?" asked Logan.

General Covington nodded, touched the screen, and zoomed in on the mountain range in northeast Russia. "The Chersky Range runs northwest to southeast through the Sakha Republic and Magadan Oblast. The signal's coming from a remote area in those mountains southeast of Chersky's highest peak, Peak Pobeda."

General Covington next displayed and ran through a series of overhead satellite images of the mountain range southeast of Pobeda from outer space. "Lt. Col. Lain and Maj. Jameson obtained these from the PAPA about 25 minutes ago."

The slew of images showed nothing but snow, ice, rocks, and mountains.

General Covington continued. "As you can see, there is no indication of activity in those mountains, but there's *something* out there. The Copán Temple, Stonehenge, Tiwanaku, the Hvit Fuge Stranda, Area 51… none of those other sites emit a z-particle signal like this one."

"Could it be the Vaniryans?" wondered the president. "Ms. James, you told us once that these Vaniryans move from planet to planet whenever it becomes necessary to do so, right?"

"Yes, sir," replied Emma, confirming the president's recollection.

"I don't see how, though," countered Dr. Bowling. "That explosion happened nearly a millennia ago. It doesn't make any sense."

"We know the Vaniryans are somehow able to travel through time, maybe that's how," said Logan.

"So, you're saying these Vaniryans could be coming here right now?" asked Dr. Bowling.

"Maybe," Logan replied.

"Are we under attack?" questioned NSA Director Orson, trained to assume the worst. Indeed, it was her job.

"The Vaniryans aren't hostile," said Emma, sensing Director Orson had an unfavorable view of the unknown.

"And why do you assume that?" retorted Director Orson. "Because they spoke to you? Because you had a polite conversation? Where I come from, we assess risk by more than—"

"It really doesn't matter now, does it?" interjected President Barrett. "There's something out there, and we need to figure out what, or *who*, it is."

"If we are going to investigate, then we need to do so fast," recommended Director Orson. "If these Vaniryans are amassing in the Chersky Mountains, do we really want them cozying up with the Russians?"

Mr. Garrison rolled his eyes at the NSA Director. "*If,* and I mean *if* it's the Vaniryans, I doubt they are coming here to play politics," said Mr. Garrison. "But the CIA's East Asia Counter-Intelligence team has picked up several recent reports of communications disruption in Russia over the last several days. Normally, that's an innocuous notation in the daily briefing that doesn't make it to the president's desk. But considering today's developments, if there's a connection, it may only be a matter of time before the RSC identifies the issue and Russian intelligence moves in on the Chersky Mountains."

"RSC?" asked Dr. Arenot.

"The Roscosmos State Corporation," responded Mr. Garrison. "It's what the Russians call their space agency, like our NASA."

"Are you suggesting an incursion into Russian territory?" asked Director Orson, concerned. "We'll need to bring in the State Department and General Sohail before we contemplate an action like that."

"For goodness sake, Sue, we're not going to war," rebuked Mr. Garrison. "No one's invading Russia. Something a little more discreet than that."

Director Orson countered, "With all due respect, Miles, we have no way of getting troops, not 10 soldiers, not 1, 1000s of miles into Russian soil discreetly. Even if we could get them in on foot unnoticed, it would be weeks before they could reach a site that deep into Russia. And, I think you are forgetting, the Chersky Mountains border the Arctic Circle. On a warm day that far north this time of year, it's 20 degrees below zero with only 5 hours of sunlight. You're talking about a complicated mission that has a better chance of starting a war than it does of succeeding."

The president understood the NSA Director's point, but he was looking for solutions, not naysayers. "If it is the Vaniryans, we need to intercept them before the Russians do. The results of a confrontational encounter between the Vaniryans and Russia could be explosive, and if Russia gets their hands on their technology, the genie will be out of the bottle."

"There's another way," said General Covington.

"How?" Orson asked the general.

"The Vaniryan technology. We could use it to portal the team into the Chersky Mountains and get them out the same way."

Director Orson didn't like the idea. "Mr. President, we've only had a few successful tests of that technology," she cautioned, "and never in conditions as severe as what the troops would be facing over there. And if we can't summon up one of those portals exactly when we need to get the troops out, or if it doesn't work, you might be sending them all on a one-way mission to Siberia."

"Thank you, Sue," said the president. "General, how many *successful* terrestrial target-to-target tests have we had of Pegasus West's Stationary Zeutyron Accelerator?"

"Four, Mr. President," responded the general.

"That's not many," said the president. "What about the Vaniryan sphere beneath Area 51?"

The general shook his head, *no*, and explained, "We've never been able to figure out how to use the sphere for transportation to coordinates around the globe. Only to stars in the heavens."

"Ms. James, do you agree?" asked the president. "You know more about that sphere than anyone."

"Yes, I have tried, Mr. President. I don't believe the sphere was meant for this. At least, I haven't been able to figure out how to do it, either."

"We could use the second *p*RAMZA unit," proposed Dr. Bowling.

"No, too risky," said the general. "The terrain in the Chersky Range, as Sue aptly pointed out a minute ago, is extremely hostile, frozen, uneven, and we don't know where the team needs to go or what they need to climb in those mountains. We all saw the *p*RAMZA. As impressive as it is, it's too clumsy for an operation like this. It'll slow them down and, if they're captured, the Russians will get their hands on the *p*RAMZA, too."

"So, what are you thinking?" asked Dr. Bowling.

General Covington replied, "Each team member will be GPS-tracked and linked to the Stationary Zeutyron Accelerator at Pegasus West and will carry a biometric 'escape button' they can press at any time to request a portal out from their current location. Upon receiving the satellite signal, P-West will generate a portal at their GPS-coordinates and get them out."

"Are you sure it'll work?" asked Mr. Garrison.

"Yes, we've tested the GPS-escape process. It works," stated the general.

"You've been testing it for intra-planetary use?" questioned Emma, concerned that the general was using the technology for the military despite the president's promise they wouldn't. She briefly glared at General Covington.

General Covington knew what Emma was alluding to. "Making safety preparations and maximizing the technology's effectiveness, Ms. James, does not mean we are war-mongering at the Pentagon. It is not, and has never been, our desire to use this technology for military gain. Only in furtherance of the Pegasus Project's mission."

Emma was skeptical, but she had also grown to trust General Covington. "Okay," she replied, letting it go for now

President Barrett had made up his mind. "Sue, Edgar, I appreciate your counsel, but I am going to go with the general's recommendation and authorize the use of the Vaniryan technology to transport troops into the Chersky Mountains to see what's there. How close to the zeutyron signal can Dr. Ehringer get us?"

"Close, sir, but not too close. We don't want them to be seen nor do we want to insert the team too close to a hot zone," responded the general. "With every hour we wait, the chances of Russian intelligence moving into the area go up as they try to diagnose the cause of their communications disruption."

"How soon can you be ready to go?" asked the president.

"Eight hours, Mr. President," answered General Covington. "I'd like to take six Special Operations Mountain SEALs and, since we may only get one shot at this, we'll need two civilian experts with us to aid our understanding of whatever we might find."

"Who?" asked Emma critically, curious who the experts might be.

"*You,*" replied the general. "You've met the Vaniryans, spoken to them. If we encounter them, we believe that will make a difference. And if we find something else, a hidden room, a secret chamber, clues... your skill in solving mysteries like that speaks for itself."

Emma's mind froze as the general spoke. After a few seconds, she responded, "What about Logan?" She wanted Logan by her side.

Logan wholeheartedly agreed. "Yeah, she's not going without me!"

"I am sorry, but we can't do that," replied the general, very matter of fact.

"Why not?" questioned Logan.

"Mr. West, Ms. James," said the president, "I understand your desire to do this mission together, but I think what the general is trying to say is, you've both spoken to the Vaniryans, deciphered the Vaniryan clues and technology, and, well... you are both irreplaceable on this project and we can't afford to lose both of you if something should happen."

"Oh," said Emma, slightly startled by the president's blunt, brutal assessment of the situation. "You said the SEALS are taking two civilian experts... so who's the other one then?" she asked.

"Professor Quimbey," responded the general.

All eyes now turned to the similarly stunned professor, who quickly responded, "What do I know about hiking through frozen mountains as part of a covert military operation?"

General Covington replied, "Professor, your expertise in cyber-technetics unlocked the mystery in the Copán Temple five years ago. If we find caves or rocks with hidden characteristics or something similar, you're one of the foremost experts in the world, and you're also already familiar with the Vaniryan tendencies, z-particles, and the Pegasus mission. You're the one we want looking at it with Ms. James."

"Ms. James, Professor Quimbey," said President Barrett, "The mission is dangerous. If you're not comfortable with the proposed plan, please let us know. I won't order either of you to do this."

Looking at her husband, Professor Quimbey put her right hand on top of his and reassured him, "I can do this."

The general hoped to comfort both by saying, "You'll be supported by the best-trained men and women in the world. The Mountain SEALs train for this terrain and these conditions all year long. They are experts at high altitude mountain reconnaissance and incursions. They will see you through this every step of the way. And if there are *any* issues, P-West will generate a portal and get you and your team out instantaneously."

"Then, take me instead," insisted Logan.

The general responded, "Ms. James's name is written on the face of the sphere beneath Area 51. We don't know how or why, but we believe... we have always believed that, for whatever reason, they chose her. If we make contact with these Vaniryans again, we believe Ms. James has the best chance of interacting with them successfully."

Logan looked at Emma...

"Logan, it's okay," said Emma.

"Emma, are you sure?" asked Logan.

"Yes." Emma, looking back at the president said, "Mr. President, I will go." She didn't know why, but somehow, she knew she had to do this.

Looking over at the general, President Barrett asked, "Eight hours for mission readiness, you said?"

"Yes, Mr. President, roughly. That is our internal estimates for mission prep if you give the green light. That accounts for the time to transport the SEALs from their training base in Colorado to Pegasus West and for them to come up to speed on mission-critical details."

"And Ms. James, Professor Quimbey?" asked the president.

"They will fly west with me immediately, with their training and mission prep commencing on the plane."

"Alright, general, you have the green light," said the president. "I want an update on mission details in three hours."

Emma's heart pounded and her pulse raced. Was she crazy to agree to this? It was all happening so fast. Professor Quimbey, on the other hand, was overcome by an eerie calm. She had a stoic look on her face.

The president stood up, and so did everyone else in the room, breaking up the formal meeting. While General Covington picked up the phone to notify his team that the Chersky Mission was a go, the president walked over to Emma and Professor Quimbey.

"Are you both sure?" he asked them one more time. "It's not too late for me to call this off or ask for a different plan or team."

"I'm scared, Mr. President, but I'm sure," replied Emma.

Likewise, Professor Quimbey responded, "Thank you, Mr. President, but I understand the importance of what we are doing here. I am willing to go."

"Okay," he replied. "You are both very brave. I promise you that the SEALs are the best at what they do. You're in good hands."

"Thank you, Mr. President," replied Emma.

President Barrett turned to shake Logan's and Dr. Arenot's hands. After doing so, he said, "Logan, Jonas, you are both welcome to stay here at the White House throughout the operation so you are nearby for all updates if you'd like. I will have the White House Director issue you some passes for the duration, and she'll have a couple of guest rooms made up for you both in the Residence. I will make it Miles's personal responsibility to keep you both informed."

"Thank you, Mr. President," said Logan, nervous beyond all words for Emma. "I would like that."

"Thank you," said Dr. Arenot.

"Okay, then, I'll have the Secret Service escort you to the Residence office and they'll take care of everything."

The president turned and exited the Situation Room, and Mr. Garrison followed him.

Professor Quimbey spoke to Dr. Arenot, while Emma turned to Logan and gave him the longest hug ever, so long that they both got lost in the embrace.

"I love you," said Emma, continuing to squeeze him tightly.

"I love you, too," responded Logan. "Are you really sure about this?"

"Logan, you know I have to. How about this: if we get in any trouble, I'll text you a secret code or something, something like, 'help us now,'" she joked.

Logan chuckled. "Very funny. And that seriously might just be the worst secret code ever."

She laughed back. "Logan, everything's going to be fine. I promise I'll be careful."

General Covington looked politely as he could at Emma and Professor Quimbey and said, "Ms. James, Professor Quimbey, it's time to go."

Chapter 7 – Crash Course

After making a quick stop at the Pentagon to retrieve some of Professor Quimbey's technical equipment, General Covington, Emma, and the professor proceeded to Joint Base Andrews where a Gulfstream C-20, with the words "United States of America" painted on the outer hull, waited for them. It would fly them across the country to Pegasus West, 13 miles northeast of Area 51 in a group of secluded low-lying mountains in the Nevada desert.

After entering the plane, Emma and Professor Quimbey followed General Covington down the center aisle toward a narrow conference room at the back of the plane no wider than the jet itself. There were couches on both sides of the aisle, a large video screen with an integrated computer panel on the back wall, and a retractable table in the floor that popped up with the push of a button. Emma and Professor Quimbey sat on one couch while General Covington sat on the other. He closed the conference room's thin sliding door for privacy.

As they settled in, the Captain's voice spilled into the conference room over the intercom. "General Covington, we are cleared for take-off. Sir, are you ready to get going?"

"Yes, Captain, proceed with departure."

"Acknowledged. Please prepare for taxing and take-off."

The three of them buckled in, and the jet began moving. After spending a few minutes taxing into position, late evening, the Gulfstream took off.

Wasting no time, the general, looking at Emma and Professor Quimbey, said, "Let's get started." He turned on the screen. A military officer in his early 40s, with a short crew-cut and wearing military fatigues, stared back at them in a live video conference feed. The officer waved.

"Ms. James, Professor Quimbey, I'd like you to meet Commander Anderson," said the general. "He heads up our Mountain SEAL Reconnaissance and Infiltration Unit, and he's going to spend the next few hours training you for the mission. If there's time at the end, we'll try to make sure you both get some sleep. But as it stands now, in a few hours, you're heading to the Chersky Mountains, so let's get to work."

"Thank you, General," said Commander Anderson, who had no idea *how* they were getting to the Chersky Mountains, only that they were. He continued. "Ms. James, Professor Quimbey, nice to meet both of you. Tonight's crash course will involve training in the areas of sub-zero terrain mountaineering, equipment readiness, covert reconnaissance, and infiltration tactics. My understanding is that all remaining mission-critical details will be provided to you and your team once you arrive at the base. We're going to move quickly to introduce you to these subjects, but if you have any questions, please stop me."

Emma immediately took Commander Anderson up on his offer. "Don't people who climb mountains into high altitudes, like we're about to do, train for months or years for a climb like that?"

"That's a great question," replied Commander Anderson, "and the short answer is, *yes*, but you must also remember, the highest peak in the Chersky range is Peak Pobeda at just under 10,000 feet, so it's not quite Mount Everest. So, while it'll be dark and cold up there, we don't anticipate altitude being an issue. I should ask though, do either of you have any climbing experience?"

"Every two or three weeks, I climb a rock wall at a Fit-N-Climb in Columbia Heights," responded Emma with an embarrassed grin, realizing just how incomparable her Fit-N-Climb class was.

Professor Quimbey's proffer wasn't much better. "A few trees when I was little. They don't really have mountains in the Ayrshire."

Commander Anderson had his work cut out for him. "Okay, how about subzero temperatures? Do either of you have experience working or operating in conditions like that?

"No," replied Professor Quimbey. She didn't mind answering his questions about her inexperience.

"How about you, Ms. James?"

"I've gone snowboarding a few times. I think it dropped below zero once or twice, maybe." With a worried-laugh and glance at Professor Quimbey, Emma remarked, "We are so unprepared for this." Professor Quimbey nodded in agreement.

"I'll get you ready for the mission, that's my job," assured the commander. "I'm just trying to get a sense of what I'm working with, that's all. How about hiking, backpacking? Ms. James?"

"Logan and I go hiking occasionally," answered Emma, "but it hardly qualifies as backpacking where we go. It's more like... sightseeing."

"And, Professor?" asked the commander.

"Sure, with a picnic basket and a bottle of wine," Professor Quimbey quipped.

Commander Anderson had heard enough. "Why don't we start by introducing you to your team. As you might expect with the Navy SEALS, each of them has gone through rigorous physical fitness, academic, psychological, and combat skills testing and training. These men and women are the best of the best, and they can *all* climb."

"Yeah, but can they carry us on their backs?" asked Emma sarcastically.

"If they need to, *yes*," said Commander Anderson in a matter-of-fact tone.

"*Oh*," said Emma, surprised and impressed.

Commander Anderson clicked a button and, on the wall behind him appeared a waist-up photo of a stern, strong-looking woman with short-cropped dark hair. To the right of her profile photo was a bullet point summary of her background.

"Meet Captain Carrie Evans, the commanding officer on the ground for the Mountain SEALs Unit. She's one of the toughest enlisted members in the entire NAVY. She's summited the tallest mountain on every continent. Once the NAVY identified her mountain climbing prowess, they moved her to the Mountain SEAL team. For her, the colder the better. Some of the SEALs claim Captain Evans likes it cold because she's cold-blooded, but I assure you, that is not the case."

Emma carefully studied Captain Evan's face and dark piercing eyes seemingly staring right back at her. Emma had never met Captain Evans, but already, what she saw and heard from Commander Anderson filled her with a sense of confidence she badly needed as they flew closer to a date with the Chersky Mountains.

Commander Anderson clicked over to the next profile, pulling up a picture of an early 30s male with no hair, light blue eyes, and a huge smile suggesting he was having too much fun for a simple profile picture. "Second in command is Lieutenant Stevens. Yeah, I know, he's jovial looking, but don't be fooled. He's also the best vertical climber in the military with particular expertise in overhanging rock faces."

"What's an overhanging rock face?" asked Emma.

"It's a rock face that is overhung or angled more than 90 degrees, forcing you, in essence, to climb partially or entirely upside down with your back angled toward or facing the ground."

"Anderson, let's run through the rest quickly," directed General Covington. "They'll all have plenty of time to get acquainted once they get to the base."

Not really, Emma thought to herself. It wasn't like they were taking a long plane ride to Russia. Emma figured they'd be stepping through the portal shortly after arriving at Pegasus West.

"Yes, General," said Commander Anderson. "I'll pick up the pace." Running through the remaining profile pictures for the 6-member team, Commander Anderson introduced them to Pacheco, Ruswell, Abrantes, and Kim, all men. As described, the entire team had a wealth of combat, tactical, and climbing experience. At least on paper, they were in good hands, just like the president said they would be.

"Ok, let's move on to something a little more challenging," announced Commander Anderson, "like those subzero conditions you'll be facing in the Chersky Mountains, frostbite, hypothermia, and how to prevent it."

To Emma, as the discussion went on, even though the Gulfstream was a perfect 72 degrees, the conference room suddenly seemed very cold.

Chapter 8 – Operation Red Snow

Their Gulfstream C-20 arrived at Pegasus West in the middle of the night, west coast time. They touched down on a simple landing strip beside a series of dimly lit one-story bungalows, one of which served as a "control tower." From above, at least during daylight, Pegasus West, or "Desert Tactical Training Base #9" as the outside world knew it, looked unremarkable, with troop barracks on the west end and ordinary training equipment strewn about, although one taking note of the base's titanium perimeter fencing and heavily secured front entrance might surmise there was more to it than meets the eye. For appearance's sake, just in case anyone was watching, the army actually conducted regular outdoor desert tactical training activities with troops at DTT #9. Then again, with a strictly enforced no-approach, no-fly zone around and above Pegasus West, no unapproved eyes ever got close enough to make that observation.

After deplaning, the ground officers escorted them all to Bungalow Mulder, a nickname selected by the base's planning team in honor of the once-popular TV show, The X-Files. Emma yawned as she walked because, despite the best-laid plans of mice, men, and generals, with all the information they had to cover on their red-eye flight, they only got about a half-hour of sleep. To make matters worse, even during that half-hour, Emma hardly slept; on information and exhaustion overload, she simply couldn't shut her brain off.

Approaching Mulder, the structure looked dilapidated, with pieces of building siding missing and a slightly ajar, partially torn screen door entrance. It was intentional, of course, consistent with DTT Base #9's low-key appearance. Emma opened the squeaky screen door which annoyingly snapped back on her rear as she walked through it.

Four armed airmen secured the bungalow's interior, with two more behind a front desk security station. There was a high-tech screening unit resembling a full-body airport security screening pod in the middle. Security did not require Emma to remove any personal belongings. Instead, they instructed her to enter and stand still inside the pod while the machine scanned her head to toe and all the way down to her bones. Once done, she exited the pod and waited for Professor Quimbey and General Covington to do the same. When they finished, the security team pressed a button to open a heavy floor door, revealing a descending staircase leading to an elevator below.

They walked down the steps to the elevator which required one final handprint scan. Already having Emma's and Professor Quimbey's scans from Pegasus East, after they provided it, the elevator shaft doors opened and in they went. General Covington pressed the down button and the elevator dropped for five seconds. When the elevator doors re-opened, General Nemond stood there ready to greet them.

"Warren," said General Nemond, saluting, and then, shaking General Covington's hand.

"Bernie," replied General Covington, saluting him back.

"Ms. James, Professor Quimbey, it's wonderful to see you again," said General Nemond politely. "We're thrilled to have you both here, at least, for a few minutes anyway..." General Nemond chuckled at his own poorly timed joke.

Professor Quimbey laughed awkwardly along with him, replying, "Not sure we're as happy to be here as you are to have us here."

"Has Captain Evans's team arrived?" asked General Covington.

"Yes, about an hour ago. They're in the briefing room with Lt. Col. Rodgers receiving logistical and intelligence details for *Operation Red Snow*. They're probably almost done, actually. Let's head over there now."

"*Operation Red Snow?* Seriously, who names everything in this place?" whispered Emma. Professor Quimbey shrugged her shoulders in a heck-if-I-know kind of way.

The general led them through the center of the hangar, stopping at Team Three's control panel. "I want to introduce you to Ian Marcus. His team's in charge of transporting you safely to and from Chersky. Marcus is a former JPL engineer with experience on a variety of missions. We're lucky to have him."

Ian Marcus, a slenderly-built young man with glasses and a bushy head of brown curly hair, rose from his round rolling chair to shake their hands. He looked starstruck. "It's an honor to meet both of you," said Ian.

"You going to get us home in one piece?" asked Professor Quimbey.

"Yes, ma'am," he confidently answered until the honest scientist in him spoke up, "unless, umm, something goes wrong."

"Well, that's not very inspiring," replied Emma.

"No, not at all," added Professor Quimbey.

General Nemond glared at Ian, unhappy with his choice of words. Ian knew he had flubbed his opportunity to make a good first impression, so he tried to clarify. "Umm, I've just never handled a portal transport for a team this size before." In truth, no one had, because they had never used the technology in this manner.

"But Mr. Marcus has never had a failure, either," stated General Nemond. "Isn't that correct, Mr. Marcus?"

"Uh, yes, sir. I have completed all three of my personnel tests without incident."

"Thank you, Mr. Marcus," said General Nemond. He led the group on their way.

"Where's Dr. Ehringer?" asked General Covington.

"In with Lt. Col. Rodgers and the Red Snow Team in the briefing room." General Nemond led them to a short staircase down to a hallway with offices and small conference rooms. In the second conference room on the left, Lt. Col. Rodgers, with the help of Dr. Ehringer, was busy briefing Captain Evans's team on the mission. Dr. Ehringer had just finished explaining to the SEAL team the mind-blowing revelation about *how* they were getting to the Chersky Mountains, although he purposely left out the part about the zeutyron transport technology being based on alien technology, or that they might encounter Vaniryans or aliens in the Chersky Mountains. The generals did not yet deem those details mission-critical.

The general walked the group straight in. Emma suddenly got nervous. Even though General Covington advised them that the SEAL team had been told why she and Professor Quimbey were tagging along on the mission, still, she wondered what the team would think of them, two untrained civilians whose very presence on the mission made it more dangerous for all. As soon as they entered the conference room, Captain Evans's entire team stood at attention and saluted the generals.

"At ease, everybody," said General Covington, but no one sat down, not with two high ranking generals in the room. General Covington made the introductions. "Ms. James, Professor Quimbey, I'd like you to meet your team commanded by Captain Evans."

Judging by the way the team looked at them, Emma knew she had to be assertive to gain any respect. She walked right up to Captain Evans, who appeared larger and more intimidating in person than on screen, to introduce herself. "Captain Evans, I'm—"

"Evans. Just call me Evans, okay, James?" Captain Evans threw her hand out to slap-shake Emma's.

"Okay."

Captain Evans looked at Professor Quimbey and acknowledged her in the same way she did Emma. She then introduced them to their new team. "Over on the far side of the table, you've got Pacheco and Kim, and on your side, Abrantes, Stevens, and Ruswell." Each raised their hand in a partial wave when Captain Evans called their names.

Emma said, "Hi," while Professor Quimbey said, "Nice to meet you all."

"Dr. Ehringer, Lt. Col. Rodgers, how much more material do you have to cover?" asked General Nemond.

"I was about to cover the Zeutyron GPS trackers that they'll all be carrying," answered Dr. Ehringer.

"Just a little more on my end, too," answered Lt. Col. Rodgers.

"Okay, we'll get out of your hair. General Covington and I will be in my office. Let us know when Red Snow Team is ready."

The SEAL team again saluted as the generals exited the room. Once the door closed behind the generals, the entire team sat back down.

"As I was saying," said Dr. Ehringer, "here is the most important piece of equipment you'll have on you – a GPS tracker linked to Pegasus West's transport technology." He handed each a small square device that resembled an old-school black pager. "They clip to the interior front pocket of the standard-issue arctic jackets y'all be wearing. They issue a location signal on the backs of muons, so they should work even through geological interference."

"What's a muon?" asked Kim.

"A subatomic particle that'll pass through most everything, stone, wood, etc.," replied Dr. Ehringer. "Should allow us to keep track of you under nearly all circumstances."

"They're like mini-LoJacks," joked Abrantes.

"What do these things do?" asked Stevens, looking at the small device which had a plastic cover over a spot designed for a thumbprint.

"The trackers don't just monitor your location. They are bio-electric activated escape buttons. If you press it with your thumb, it will send a signal that links directly to Station, and Station will immediately open up a transport portal at your current location. You press it when you're ready to return or in case of an emergency."

"All we need is a thumbprint?" asked Captain Evans.

"Right, all you need is your *own* thumbprint," clarified Dr. Ehringer. "Your *left* thumbprint, actually. Each device is synced to your personal left thumbprint. If you use any other finger or if anyone other than you tries to activate it, whether someone on your own team or anyone else, the device will automatically self-destruct. So, don't lose it, and be sure to use your left thumb."

"How will we know what this portal thing looks like, or how to find it?" asked Abrantes.

"You won't miss it. It'll open up right in front of you and will look like a very wide door," replied Dr. Ehringer.

Stevens was floored. "That's frick'n wild," he commented, laughing out loud. "Beam me up, Scotty!" Others joined in the laughter.

"I think it goes without saying, but try not to activate the thing where anyone else can see you," said Lt. Col. Rodgers.

"Like the Russians?" said Kim.

"Yes, like the Russians. This technology is top secret and we'd prefer it stay that way," responded Lt. Col. Rodgers, "which brings up a critical point. In the event you are facing capture or are captured, you are ordered to destroy your device and scuttle it, if possible. I'm sorry, guys, but if one of you is killed, another Red Snow Team member must do this for you."

Emma, concerned by Rodgers' worrisome comment, looked at Professor Quimbey for comfort. The professor half-heartedly smiled back.

"Alright, we've got a little more to cover," said Lt. Col. Rodgers, "so let's keep going."

For the next half-hour, he and Dr. Ehringer finished up discussing final details with the team, which mostly covered information Emma and Professor Quimbey had already heard on the plane. When finished, Lt. Col. Rodgers asked, "Okay, everyone ready?"

"Let's rock 'n roll," said Captain Evans.

Hearing no objection, Lt. Col. Rodgers walked over to a wall phone and lifted the receiver. He said into the phone, "Red Snow Team is ready to proceed." Rodgers listened to some instructions on the other end of the line, and then replied, "Affirmative." He hung up.

"Operation Red Snow is on the clock, starting now," declared Lt. Col. Rodgers. He turned to Emma and Professor Quimbey. "Why don't you spend a few minutes getting acquainted with your team? I'll be back in 10 to take you over to Equip to gear you up. Captain Evans, the mission is a go in t-minus 35 minutes. Have your team report back to the hangar, ready for departure, at 0345 hours."

"Yes, sir," said Captain Evans. Lt. Col. Rodgers and Dr. Ehringer left the room, leaving Emma and Professor Quimbey alone with the SEAL team.

"I understand from Commander Anderson that you bookworms are nervous," said Captain Evans.

"A little," said Emma, before conceding, "a lot, actually."

"I've sure got the collywobbles," Professor Quimbey added.

"Yeah, I would think so. Either of you ever go through that transport contraption they built?"

"No, I haven't," Emma replied, while Professor Quimbey shook her head to indicate she hadn't, either.

"Craziest thing I've ever heard," said Captain Evans.

"Like right outta Star Trek or something," Abrantes piped in.

"So, what are you guys, like zeuterion geniuses or something? Is that why we're carrying you on this mission?" asked Ruswell condescendingly.

Emma knew what Ruswell was implying, the increased danger their presence on the mission posed. "No, it's just... I'm sorry—"

"James, you don't have to explain anything to anybody," interrupted Captain Evans. "Russy, zip it! I don't exactly recall the president asking for you by name. Red Team, they're the experts on the zeutyrons and whatever it is we're looking for; they're the ones General Covington and the president want on this mission, is that understood?" No one said another word. "And James, you don't owe anybody an apology. Period. Ever."

Emma liked Captain Evans already. "What happened to Red Snow Team?"

"Stevens and I thought it sounded stupid, so before you guys arrived, we shortened it," replied Captain Evans.

Emma and Professor Quimbey grinned.

After they spent a few more minutes getting to know the team, Lt. Col. Rodgers returned to take them over to Equipment & Personnel to get ready.

ΔΔΔΔΔΔΔΔΔΔΔ

Just before 0345 hours, Emma and Professor Quimbey returned to the P-West hangar. They were no longer dressed in civilian clothing; instead, like their team, they now wore heavy white mountaineering clothing and gloves, with the entire outfit rated for - 50 degrees F. Everyone wore a gear-filled backpack, although the SEAL Team members wore heavier packs loaded with weapons and climbing equipment.

"Alright, everyone at their stations," announced Dr. Ehringer over the loudspeaker. "This is not a drill. Operation Red Snow is ready to commence."

General Covington approached Emma and Professor Quimbey. He looked them up and down. "Well, I'll be damned, you look like soldiers."

Professor Quimbey wasn't having it. "Oh, shut up, will you… we look like nitwits. Make yourself useful and help me tighten the straps on this backpack."

Her bossy tone shocked Emma. "Professor!"

"Oh, he doesn't mind. It's not like he's pushing any buttons here today to send us through that portal. He's gonna drink a cup of coffee and watch. He's got a minute to make himself useful."

General Covington chuckled. "It's alright, Ms. James. And the Professor's right, I'm pushing no buttons here today… Happy to help." He tightened the straps. "There, how's that?"

"Perfect," replied Professor Quimbey. "Thank you."

General Covington smiled. Over the last couple of years, he had gotten to know them quite well. He had grown fond of them, and

110

looking at them now was quite proud. "Are you two ready? I know you're ready mission-wise, but how are you both doing?"

"I'm sick to my stomach," said Emma. "We just need to get this started before I vomit... the waiting's killing me."

"I'm quite knackered, but ready to get on with it," chimed in Professor Quimbey. "Plus, it's bloody hot in this outfit. The sooner we get into the snow, the better."

Covington chuckled, again. "Right. Okay then, good luck to both of you." He escorted them over to their team and then walked off in General Nemond and Dr. Ehringer's direction on the Communications and Command Platform.

"Wait!" shouted Emma, stopping him in his tracks. Emma rushed up to him. "Can I please borrow your cellphone?"

"There's no—"

"I just want to send Logan a quick text. *Please...*"

"There're no cellphones allowed down here." Emma looked disappointed, so the general offered, "But I'm happy to send a text for you once I return to the surface..."

"Yes! Great! Can you please text Logan from me, saying 'I love you, see you soon'?"

"Of course. Good luck to you." The general turned and continued toward Nemond and Ehringer on the platform. Emma turned and joined the professor just as Captain Evans walked up.

"Wow, look at you two! Nice makeover!" exclaimed Captain Evans.

"Yeah, right," replied Emma.

"Hey, James, it's time for you to remember just how awesome you really are, okay? And that goes for you, too, Quimbey. I am told you are both as kick-ass with your brains as we are with our guns. This mission is going to take everyone, so you're gonna leave all that self-doubt you brought with you behind in this hangar. On the other side of that portal, you're part of Red Team now; you'll always be part of Red Team, and we look out for each other, got it?"

Emma felt inspired. "Got it!"

"Alright, then," said Captain Evans, "time to accrue some miles." Captain Evans gave Dr. Ehringer a thumbs-up.

Like the previous day with the *p*RAMZA test, Pegasus West, Pegasus East, and the Situation Room synced up on a split-screen video display in the Communications and Command Platform. Looking into the video screen at Pegasus East and Lt. Col. Lain's face, General Covington ordered, "Lt. Col. Lain, please advise the president and Mr. Garrison that Operation Red Snow is ready to proceed."

Chapter 9 – One Small Step...

Ten-year-old Logan sat on a yellow school bench with his back to Classroom #129's exterior sidewall. He opened up his brown-bag lunch to see what his mother had packed for him. She'd only been at her new restaurant job for two weeks, but long gone already were the days of peanut butter and jelly sandwiches, his favorite. Since starting her new restaurant manager job, because she had to leave so early for work every morning, his mom had taken to packing his lunch the night before with food she brought home from the restaurant.

He'd spent the first two weeks at his new school, Delaware Elementary, basically eating things he'd never heard of before that were either smothered, sautéed, puréed, braised, dredged, emulsified, infused, macerated, poached, caramelized, grilled, or reduced. He was probably the only kid in 2nd grade who needed a fork, knife, *and* spoon to eat his lunch every day, and a note from his mom to tell him what it was.

"Well, if it isn't little orphan Annie," barked Eddy, the rotund 5th-grade schoolyard bully suddenly standing right on top of Logan. Two of Eddy's cowardly friends stood behind him.

"My name's not Annie! It's—"

"Ha! Ha! He thinks we actually care!" shouted Eddy to his snickering buddies. "What'd you bring for lunch today, huh? More fancy food your mommy made you?"

Eddy and his 5th-grade cohorts had been harassing Logan all week. Yesterday, they even took his lunch, and by the look of it, aimed to do so again.

"Leave me alone!" snapped Logan while still sitting on the bench.

Eddy lunged forward and snatched Logan's lunch bag. "Thanks, Annie!" mocked Eddy.

"Hey! That's mine!" Logan leaped up from the bench and took a swipe at his bag, but Eddy held it high above and away from him so he couldn't reach it.

"Give that back!" shouted a young girl with sandy-blond hair, wearing a purple backpack much bigger than she was. She walked up behind Eddy and his friends and stopped right in the middle of the fray. Logan didn't know her name, but he had seen her around school.

Eddy looked at the pint-sized girl, laughed, and said, "Take off, pip-squeak."

"You're mean," she replied. "Give him his food back or I'm telling."

"Ooohhhh, what are you, his girlfriend?" teased Eddy.

"Girlfriend… girlfriend…," mocked another of Eddy's mean friends.

"Shut up, doofus! I'm not his girlfriend!"

Eddy's other friend, who hadn't said a word yet, joined in on the bullying. "Pip-squeak and Annie, sitting in a tree, K-I-S-S-I-N-G."

"If you don't stop, I'm gonna tell Mr. Barker," threatened Emma.

Eddy didn't seem intimidated. "We're soooo scared—"

Emma called his bluff and turned around to start walking toward the principal's office. As soon as she spun around, Eddy tossed Logan's brown-bag lunch back at him and the three bullies took off.

"Thanks," said Logan, slumping back down onto the bench, totally humiliated. His first two weeks at Delaware Elementary had not gone well. Logan badly missed his old school.

Emma sat down next to him. "Those boys are really mean."

"Yeah," said Logan, looking at the ground, dejected.

"Hi, I'm Emma. I'm in Mr. Hale's class."

Logan looked up at her. "I'm Logan. I'm in Ms. Willis' class."

"You're in 2nd grade, too?"

"Uh-huh."

"If your name's Logan, why were they calling you, Annie?"

"Because they're jerkos."

"Yeah, super-jerkos."

"I guess they were making fun of me because I don't have a dad."

Emma was confused. "Well, that's stupid... everyone has a daddy."

Logan smiled. She was totally right. "My mom and dad got divorced when I was little."

"Oh." Emma brought her legs up and crossed them underneath her body, sitting criss-cross applesauce. "Are you new at this school?"

"Uh-huh. My mom and I just moved here."

"From where?"

"Queens."

"That sounds pretty." Emma pulled a plastic bag filled with cheese and crackers out of her backpack. Without waiting for an invitation, she started eating her lunch next to Logan. He, on the other hand, didn't touch his. He had lost his appetite.

"Aren't you going to eat your lunch?"

"No."

"Why not?" asked Emma because, after all, she had just helped him get it back.

"I'm not hungry anymore."

"What'd your mom make you? Maybe we can trade."

"I don't know, some kind of mushy chicken."

"Yuk!"

Logan grinned. That's exactly how he felt!

"So, you're not going to eat it?" wondered Emma.

Logan shook his head.

Emma popped up from the bench, threw her cheese and crackers back into her backpack, and said, "Come on."

Logan stood up, stuffed his lunch back into his backpack, and followed her. She crossed the asphalt playground to the other side of the yard and guided Logan behind Classroom #4. There wasn't much there besides a few arts and crafts tables and benches, a chain-link fence, and an alley behind the school. Emma continued all the way up to the fence.

"Mr. Rufus," said Emma out loud when she got there, projecting her voice toward the alley.

From behind a trash bin, a homeless man, haggard-looking and dirty, stood up. He walked over to the fence. He had a big smile. "Hi, young lady," he said to Emma.

"We brought you some food," Emma replied. She went into her backpack and pulled out her cheese and crackers. She handed it to Rufus through the fence.

"Thank you, Emmy," said Rufus.

Logan immediately got the idea and removed his brown-bag lunch from his backpack.

"Oh, so nice of you, young man, but I can't take all that from you. You kids need your food, too, so you can grow up big and strong and not end up like me."

Logan quickly responded, "Mr. Rufus, it's okay. I don't want it."

"Are you sure?" asked Rufus.

"Yeah."

"That is mighty kind of you, son."

"Toss it over," urged Emma.

Logan gently lobbed his brown-bag lunch over the fence, and Rufus caught it. He looked inside and smiled. "Thank you, young man. You are truly kind, like your friend, Emmy... thank you, both."

"You're welcome, Mr. Rufus," Emma responded. Emma waved goodbye and off she and Logan went. As they headed back to the main yard, Emma asked, "Do you like the monkey bars?"

"Yeah, a lot."

"Okay. Let's go play! Race you!" shouted Emma, enthusiastically taking off for the main yard at full sprint.

"Emmy, wait!" Logan took off after her, running as fast as he could. It had taken him almost two full weeks to make a friend at Delaware Elementary, but today it finally happened, and he couldn't be happier...

△△△△△△△△△△△△

A loud knock on the door jarred Logan awake. He looked over at the clock which read 6:45 am. He had spent a long, restless night of sleep in the West Bedroom, one of the White House Residence's sixteen 2nd floor rooms. It had taken him nearly all night to fall asleep because he couldn't stop worrying about Emma, or Professor Quimbey, and the moment he finally dozed off, the knock came, it seemed.

In walked a Secret Service Agent while Logan was still in bed. "Son, I'm sorry to wake you, but Mr. Garrison wanted me to let you know it's time. I can escort you and Dr. Arenot down to the SIT-Room. Please get dressed and I'll take you both downstairs."

"Okay, thank you."

The Secret Service Agent left the room to go wake Dr. Arenot in the adjoining East Bedroom. Logan popped out of bed and threw his clothes back on. He brushed his teeth, washed his face, and water-shaped his messy brown hair, which always looked disheveled no matter what he did with it. He was ready. He opened his bedroom door, and Dr. Arenot was already outside waiting for him.

"Good morning," he said to Logan. "Sleep much?"

"No," Logan replied. "You?"

"Barely."

"Mr. West, Dr. Arenot, right this way," said the Secret Service Agent. Logan and Jonas followed the agent out of the Residence and down several flights of stairs until they came to the Situation Room in the White House's basement. They entered, and nearly everyone was already seated inside and ready. Logan and Dr. Arenot took the same seats they had taken the night before.

On the video screen, Logan could see Lt. Col. Lain at Pegasus East on the left, and General Covington and General Nemond at Pegasus West on the right. Portions of the P-West main hangar were visible in the background, although Logan couldn't see Emma or Professor Quimbey. Minutes later, Mr. Garrison and President Barrett arrived. Everyone took to their feet as the president entered.

"Everyone have a seat. Generals, where are we?" asked the president.

"We're ready here, Mr. President," replied General Covington. "Operation Red Snow is a go, on your command."

"Where will you be inserting the team?" asked the president.

General Nemond grabbed a tablet off the Communications and Command Platform's console, which had a topography map of the Chersky Mountains on the screen, and placed it before the camera to show the president. He explained, "There is a secluded canyon close to the target here at 65.6415 North, 144.5448 East." General Nemond used his finger to point it out. "It's remote with no roads anywhere in the vicinity, minimal risk of exposure, and has several ingress and egress points. The climb in the mountain range to the target should be short from there."

"Any update on Russian troop movement?" asked Mr. Garrison.

"There appears to be some ground-caravan activity 26 miles southwest of the proposed location along a road hugging the Chersky's southern-range," replied General Covington, "but the purpose of that activity remains unclear. It's nowhere near the mission drop-point and over two mountains away. We don't believe the activity is related or mission-compromising."

Director Orson chimed in, "Is there any air or chopper support flying with the ground caravan?"

"None," replied General Covington.

"What about Roscosmos? Any news out of the RSC?" asked Mr. Garrison.

"Nothing," said Orson.

"How about the z-particle signal? Is it still there?" asked President Barrett.

"Lt. Col. Lain, I'll let you answer that one," responded General Covington.

Lt. Col. Lain explained. "Yes, Mr. President, the z-particle signal's still transmitting. In fact, the PAPA's reporting an *increase* in the signal's intensity."

"What do you mean, an 'increase in the intensity'?" questioned the president.

"It's more than doubled is the best way I can describe it. How or why we can't tell," answered Lt. Col. Lain.

"Hmm," pondered President Barrett, considering the implications of what Lt. Col. Lain said. "Alright, can I see the team?"

"Of course," replied General Nemond.

General Nemond pressed a button to switch the view to the team gathered before the Station-hangar, all decked out in white mountaineering gear. As soon as Logan spotted Emma, his heart jumped. He was extremely nervous for her, and looking at her face, he could tell she was, too.

"Who's in charge of the team?" asked the president.

"Captain Carrie Evans is the Mountain SEAL Unit's commanding officer, Mr. President," replied General Nemond.

"Alright, let me talk to her," said the president.

"Yes, sir," answered General Nemond. He pressed a few more buttons. "You are live, now, sir."

"Captain Evans, this is the president. Can you hear me?"

Captain Evans looked up and around upon hearing the president's voice emanating from the overhead speaker system. She replied, "Yes, Mr. President, I can hear you."

"I want to wish your entire team good luck. I know what you are doing this morning may frighten you, perhaps it excites you, but today, your entire team will be making history. Your government appreciates it. I appreciate it. Thank you for your bravery."

"Thank you, Mr. President," replied Captain Evans.

"General Covington, General Nemond, you have the green-light. Send them in."

"Yes, sir," said General Covington.

Into the Pegasus West speaker system, General Nemond announced. "Operation Red Snow is a go. I repeat, Operation Red Snow is a go."

Dr. Ehringer's time had come. Using the intercom system, he ordered, "Open the Station-hangar door."

Just like the day before, a wall at the back of the hangar retreated, half to the left, half to the right, revealing a mini hangar behind it. Unlike yesterday, however, Emma and Professor Quimbey now stood right in front of it. Somehow, it appeared more intimidating up close.

"Team One, please raise the shield," requested Dr. Ehringer.

Where the wall in front of Station had once been, out of the floor rose the precautionary transparent-aluminum wall. It continued all the way up until locking into the ceiling.

"Ok, Team Three, activate the zeutyron field," instructed Dr. Ehringer.

"Zeutyron field generated," said Three's team leader, Ian Marcus.

"Activate the portal to Chersky," said Dr. Ehringer, "at, mark, +65.6415 North, +144.5448 East."

"Coordinates entered," said Marcus. He pressed a button, and almost instantaneously, a rectangular-shaped portal approximately 20 feet wide and 10 feet tall, materialized inside the mini-hangar. The snowfall in the Chersky Mountains was visible through the portal. Since it was nighttime over on the other side of the world, it was dark out there but for the scant moonlight shining down on the snow.

"Unbelievable," said Stevens. He, like his entire team, knew what the zeutyron accelerator was *supposed* to do because Dr. Ehringer had told them, but until he actually saw it in person, he didn't quite appreciate the wonder of it.

"Unreal...," mumbled Captain Evans, equally awestruck. "It actually works..."

"Team Two, how's it looking inside the Station-hangar?" asked Dr. Ehringer.

"Environment checks out," said Team Two. "Standard temperature, oxygen readings, and barometric pressure inside the hangar fit for the human condition. As anticipated, temporal parameters reflect an increase by .0134 tp."

"Pretty sure I understood what all that means," said the president, "but is it safe for them to go in?"

Dr. Ehringer quickly replied, "Yes, Mr. President. It's safe for them."

"Okay, then, have them proceed," the president replied.

"Red Snow Team, you may now enter the hangar," instructed General Nemond.

Captain Evans led her team to a heavy metal door slightly to the left of the Station-hangar. She put her hand on the handle and waited.

"Team Two, please open the door," said Dr. Ehringer.

When Captain Evans heard the buzz, she pulled the door open, revealing a smaller observation room behind it with an interior viewing window. Red Snow Team went through the door into the observation room and closed it behind them. Through the viewing window, they could see the portal just a few feet away. Dr. Ehringer's team sealed the outer door and unlocked the inner door to allow them to proceed all the way into the Station-hangar. Captain Evans opened the inner door and in they went.

Red Snow Team now stood at the foot of the portal. Behind them, the inner door locked, officially sealing them inside the Station-hangar. The moment of truth had arrived, and Emma found herself getting even more nervous, close to panic. Her breathing raced.

Captain Evans noticed her elevated stress level. "James, you need to stay calm, okay? You need to take a deep breath and focus." At this point, everything Captain Evans said could be heard through the speakers in the P-West hangar and by everyone in Washington.

"Okay, okay, okay," repeated Emma to herself, sounding out of breath because she was starting to hyperventilate.

Captain Evans walked over to Emma, put her hands on Emma's shoulders, and said, "James, I need you to relax. You've got this."

From their view in the SIT-Room, they could hear the dialogue taking place and watch the moment unfolding. Logan felt completely helpless. He stood up, unable to sit still.

"Okay, I can do this... I can do this...," Emma kept whispering to herself.

"James, look at me," instructed Captain Evans.

Emma looked directly into Captain Evans's eyes, holding onto Evans's gaze for stability in a room that suddenly felt like it was spinning around her.

"Deeper breaths," said Captain Evans. "Breathe with me James... inhale and hold it... two, three, four, exhale and stay empty." Emma listened. "Good James, let's do it one more time, okay, breathe in... two, three, four, exhale..."

As Emma went through the breathing exercise, slowly she began calming down.

"Good, James, keep—"

"Is everything alright in there?" inquired General Covington.

"Yes, sir," replied Captain Evans. "Just a few kernels popping in some of our stomachs is all." Very quietly this time so that only

Emma could hear her, Captain Evans asked softly, "James, are you okay? I need to know if you can do this."

"I'm alright...now. Thank you." The initial wave of anxiousness had passed, mostly.

With an approving smile, Evans said, "James, you're kick-ass, don't you forget it." Captain Evans looked up. "Red Snow Team is still a go," she announced.

"Okay. Continue, Captain," said General Covington.

"Here I go," said Captain Evans. She walked up to the portal, closed her eyes, and stepped through the threshold of here-to-there. Instantly, she found herself standing on the snow in the Chersky Mountains.

She looked up and around at the surrounding rocks, mountains, and trees inside the canyon where the portal had deposited her. "I can't believe it," she said, laughing out loud. "This is incredible!" She spun around to look back through the portal. Her team stood inside the Station-hangar, gazing back at her as if on the other side of a sliding glass door.

"It's freezing out here! Feels awesome! Come on in!" urged Captain Evans.

On the main computer monitor at the Communications and Command Platform, General Nemond saw a red blip pop up on a topographical satellite map of the Chersky Mountain range in Russia. He pointed it out to General Covington and Dr. Ehringer. They looked pleased. General Nemond reported, "Mr. President, we are tracking a signal from Captain Evans's GPS-tracker coming at the insertion point in the Chersky Mountain range. She's there, Mr. President." Some light clapping could be heard from the Pegasus West hangar.

Back in Russia, Captain Evans walked around the portal to see what it looked like from the back. What she saw stunned her. From behind, the portal was completely invisible, as if it wasn't there, at all. She moved back around to the front, then peaked her head to the back and then, to the front again. As her head moved back and forth, behind and to the front of the portal, it vanished and reappeared each time she moved her head one way or the other. "Freakin' bizarre…," Captain Evans said.

She looked up at the bright moon in the cloudless night sky, with the stars beaming brightly. She listened to the howling wind. For an instant, Captain Evans almost forgot where she was or what she was doing there. Then, she snapped out of it and motioned for her team to join her. One by one, they followed, cautiously stepping through the portal for the fastest trip around the world in human history. As they went through, their respective blips popped up on the topographical satellite map of the Chersky Mountains back on the console screen at Pegasus West.

As Emma approached the portal, she held her breath. Meanwhile, Logan put his hand inside his pocket where he had hidden the engagement ring. It was his personal private good luck charm, a reminder of the wonderful future ahead for them.

Once the last team member went through, all eight blips appeared on the topographical satellite map. "Mr. President," said General Nemond, "Red Snow Team has been fully delivered."

Back in the SIT-Room, NSA Director Orson, an initial critic of the proposed plan, was loath to eat her words, but she did. "Mr. President, congratulations. A new era of tactical reconnaissance and intelligence strategy is upon us."

Back in the Chersky Mountains, Captain Evans said to Emma and Professor Quimbey, who had never felt cold like this before, "Bet you're glad you brought your jackets."

Too cold to respond, Emma just nodded. She moved her outfit's warming mask over her mouth and nose to protect her face. Everyone else did the same.

Captain Evans was ready to get after it. Looking at her team, she said, "Alright, Red Team, no time for selfies. Let's move."

When the team disappeared from view, Dr. Ehringer announced, "Team Three, please shut down the zeutyron field."

Marcus shut down the portal. "Zeutyron field deactivated." The portal disappeared. Red Snow Team was gone.

"Okay, what happens next?" asked President Barrett.

General Covington explained, "They'll be hiking up the mountain for a while, and from there, Captain Evans has a satellite phone to contact us, if necessary. She has orders to keep communications to a bare minimum because using the SAT-phone risks exposure. We'll still be able to track their progress using the trackers each carries, so we'll know where they are at all times."

"Okay," said President Barrett. "Good work, everyone." The president stood up, and the SIT-Room followed. "I want updates from each of you every 30 minutes, is that clear?"

"Yes, Mr. President," said everyone in unison.

"Thank you," said the president. He exited the Situation Room with Mr. Garrison, while the Secret Service returned to the SIT-Room to escort Logan and Dr. Arenot back up to the Residence.

Chapter 10 - Signal Acquired

"I'm sorry, but I need a moment," announced Professor Quimbey, her legs cramping up and her lungs out of breath. Red Team had been hiking up the mountain for hours, taking breaks when necessary, but as they climbed into the higher elevations, breaks were getting more frequent.

"Red Team, let's rest here for a few," ordered Captain Evans.

Emma, exhausted, collapsed onto the snow next to Professor Quimbey. While on her back, she said, "Thank you!" A light snow started to fall, dropping snowflakes on her face.

Captain Evans approached them. "We can only spend a few minutes here. A storm's coming. We need to keep going. And don't lay down for too long... you'll stiffen up."

Emma looked up at the night sky. Where once she saw stars and a beaming, bright moon, now clouds had moved in. "How close are we?" she asked Captain Evans.

"We're close. According to the topo, bullseye's just over a ridge a half-mile from here on the southeast side of Peak Sahka."

"Is the ridge going to be hard to climb?" asked Professor Quimbey.

"I wouldn't try it yourselves at home if that's what you're asking. Topographics suggest some intermediate climbing, but we'll get you through it."

"The climbing's getting harder for me," said Emma. "I'm getting winded faster, and it burns to breathe."

"Some of that's the subzero temperatures," replied Captain Evans. "The air's freezing out here and you're pumping it into your lungs each time you take a breath. Remember to breathe through your warming mask if it becomes an issue. It may also be the altitude. Are you feeling dizzy?"

Emma shook her head and responded, "No."

"You, Quimbey?"

"No," answered the professor, "but I've got a small headache coming on."

"You need to drink some water, then. How about shortness of breath?"

"Other than the fact that I'm out of shape?" asked Professor Quimbey.

"Yeah… other than that," responded Evans. "I'm looking for distress beyond normal cardiovascular exhaustion. Are you having trouble breathing?"

"Just having a little trouble catching my breath," said Professor Quimbey.

"Me, too," said Emma. "It's just getting more difficult."

Captain Evans felt reassured. "Understood. Okay, rest up. Drink some water, especially you, Quimbey. Headaches can be a sign of altitude sickness, and hydration helps. We're resuming in four minutes." Captain Evans went over to check on the others.

Emma sat up and looked at Professor Quimbey. "I still can't believe we got ourselves into this."

Professor Quimbey pulled out her canteen, took a sip, and surveyed the rugged Siberian terrain around them, which consisted of ice, snow, boulders, sharp rocks, and pine trees shrouded in darkness. "I could use a warm bath and a cup of tea, right about now."

"When I was little, my dad always used to threaten to send me to Siberia if I didn't do my homework. Never thought I'd actually be sent to Siberia *because* I did my homework."

Professor Quimbey laughed. "What do you think's on the other side of that ridge? Do you think it's the Vaniryans?"

"I don't know."

"Whatever it is, I hope it's friendly," remarked Professor Quimbey.

"If not, we've got our panic button thingys," Emma reminded her.

"*If* they work…"

"They'll work," reassured Emma. "You just have to have a glass-is-half-full kind of mindset."

"My glass-is-half-*frozen*."

Her response drew a tiny smile from Emma, which was about as big a smile as she could muster in the sub-zero conditions. They spent another minute or two recovering while Captain Evans busily reviewed a small map with Stevens. It wasn't long before she informed everyone, "Snow's picking up. Let's move. Need to hit the ridge before the storm."

"Here we go, again," mumbled Emma, working hard to get back to her feet. Just as Captain Evans predicted, her muscles had already started to stiffen up, making standing a chore.

Captain Evans led the way and Stevens brought up the rear. With the bright moonlight no longer helping, the team had been using night vision goggles to aid visibility, but it also slowed them down. The final leg took the longest not just because of the visibility, but because the remaining section required bouldering, hiking up steep slopes, traversing narrow crevices, and managing tricky, icy terrain. By the time they reached the ridge that Captain Evans had mentioned earlier, Siberia's dim late-morning version of dawn had arrived and the clouds had begun to clear up. The scant light allowed Emma to see the daunting task above, and what she saw intimidated her: a combination of steep-grade hiking, bouldering, and a few near-vertical pitches, all smothered in rocks, snow, and ice.

Captain Evans kept the team moving until she found a spot in the ridge she liked. "Alright, Red Team, let's make our approach here. Get out the ice axes, anchors, and ropes for some of the upper pitches and, if we can, try to set a few bombers in there to help James and Quimbey in the trickier spots."

"What's a bomber?" Emma asked Stevens.

"It's a super-secure anchor driven into the rock for hand or footholds to help you climb," he replied.

"Got it."

Red Team went to work. Pacheco and Stevens climbed ahead. While they prepped the ascent route, Emma looked up at the ridge which appeared well in excess of 200 feet high. She said to Captain Evans, "This looks hard."

Captain Evans thought about it. "Most of it isn't bad. There are a few pitches in there that I'd grade at 5.6+, but there are also a few forgiving sections, manageable slopes, and ledges. The problem isn't the slope, it's the conditions—"

"And us," added Emma.

"James, don't you worry about that. We've got you two. This climb's going to be a cinch."

Slowly and cautiously, they hiked up the ridge. When they reached rock faces requiring short vertical climbs, Pacheco and Stevens laid the groundwork with anchors, hooks, and ropes to aid Emma's and Professor Quimbey's ascent. When they got near the top, there was a steep vertical climb requiring highly technical expertise.

"Okay, we're going to have to strap you two in from here," said Captain Evans. "Kim, Russy, assist them with their harnesses."

The two men prepped Emma's and Quimbey's gear, and when ready, Kim informed Captain Evans, "They're good to go."

Captain Evans replied, "Alright, clip them in. Stevens, lead the way. James, I'm going to shadow you on the pitch. Abrantes, you've got Quimbey. Kim, Russy, you'll carry their packs and trail right below us. Be prepared. Let's go."

Red Team's climb of the final vertical pitch began with Emma and Professor Quimbey securely roped in and Stevens offering recommendations for footholds and handholds. The amateurs listened intently to his instructions.

As expected, Emma's and Professor Quimbey's arms and legs got tired rapidly, as they weren't experienced climbers and were using muscles they didn't even know they had. Every couple of minutes, Captain Evans halted the ascent to allow them to rest on an anchor, an available ledge, or protruding rock. Other times, when the pitch offered no forgiveness, Stevens would firmly anchor himself in and hold on to Emma's and Professor Quimbey's ropes to allow them, one at a time, to hangdog for maximum rest. Then, they would continue upward for a few minutes before repeating the whole process over again. The climb to the ridge's top was going smoothly until...

"Ugh!" screamed Professor Quimbey as her gloved hand missed an anchor. She fell backward.

Stevens, who was leading the way higher up and had their ropes secured in anchors, immediately grabbed her rope from above while Abrantes instinctively snared the professor by the waist. "I've got you!" Abrantes said, tightly holding Professor Quimbey by the mid-section.

Professor Quimbey wanted to vomit. To her, it felt like she had fallen 50 feet, although, in reality, it was probably only one or two. Between the rope, anchors, Stevens, and Abrantes, her slip-up was well-handled.

"You okay?" asked Abrantes, face-to-face with Quimbey and wanting to confirm she was okay before letting go.

Normally, Professor Quimbey would have responded with a dose of wit or a sharp remark, but she couldn't muster anything other than, "Thank you."

"Quimbey, you need to keep climbing," Captain Evans reminded her. "No turning back. Don't doubt yourself. Abrantes is there. Trust it. We've got you."

Professor Quimbey pulled herself back up until she had secure footing and said, "Let's get this over with."

They continued upward. The remaining climb took place without incident. At the top, Pacheco reeled Emma and Professor Quimbey in. Emma was quite proud of herself. She'd never completed a climb like that before and, for the first time, she truly felt like an active part of Red Team, and they had a job to do: investigate the signal now just on the other side of the ridge from where they stood.

Pacheco, Kim, and Russy retracted the ropes, leaving the anchors and hooks behind. When the team gathered and repacked their things, Captain Evans said, "Okay, everyone stay sharp. We're in the target zone now."

Red Team hiked up to the ridgetop and looked over the edge at the southeast side of Peak Sahka. They saw a subtle valley in between two mountain ridges that formed a bowl slightly below their location. Pine trees blanketed the terrain. There was a clearing in the middle with a large rock formation at the center approximately 30 to 50 feet tall. Nothing obvious stood out.

"Okay, bookworms, you're on... what are we looking for?" asked Captain Evans, leaning on Emma and Professor Quimbey for guidance.

Neither Emma nor Professor Quimbey really knew the answer, but the professor had an idea of where to start. She removed a device from her bag that Emma had seen before: a portable gravitometer. The professor turned on the device.

"Hmm, that's odd," voiced Professor Quimbey.

"What is?" inquired Captain Evans.

"The gravitometer's reading 9.7687 meters per second squared," replied Professor Quimbey, "when typical minimal gravitational acceleration this far north of the equator should be closer to 9.8322 m/s^2."

"Okay, and that means what to the rest of us?" inquired Captain Evans.

"It refers to the rate at which things fall to Earth due to gravity," explained Professor Quimbey. "Gravity is stronger near the arctic poles, meaning mass falls faster at the poles than it does at the equator. But, for whatever reason, it's the opposite here... the gravitational acceleration rate is lower than the equator's rate of 9.7803 m/s^2 when it *should* be higher, closer to the 9.8322 rate at the poles."

"So, you think we're close to that z-particle signal they sent us here to investigate?" asked Captain Evans.

"I mean, there's no way to know for sure, but I can think of nothing else that could be causing this," replied Professor Quimbey.

"Stevens, hand me the TIBs," requested Captain Evans.

Stevens quickly pulled out the thermal-infrared binoculars and handed them to her. Captain Evans went to work surveilling the clearing and surrounding areas.

"Whoa!" exclaimed Captain Evans. "What's that?"

"What? What do you see?" asked Stevens.

"That rock formation in the clearing is generating a heat signature that looks like momma just took it out of the oven for dinner," replied Captain Evans. She handed the TIBs to Stevens to take a look.

"Holy Siberia! What is that thing?" echoed Stevens. "That rock's radiating energy. That can't be natural."

Professor Quimbey glanced at Emma. Had they found the Vaniryans or something else entirely?

"Quimbey, take a look," said Captain Evans. Stevens handed the professor the binoculars so she could have a turn.

Professor Quimbey looked. "Huh. The infrared energy appears to be streaming upward in proportionate distribution all the way around through the top of the rock formation..."

"So, what do you make of it?" Captain Evans asked her.

Professor Quimbey offered a theory. "I can't fully see the base because the trees are in the way, but that's not a rock. Rocks don't conduct energy like that, and if it was a natural phenomenon, you wouldn't see such a consistently proportionate distribution of energy, either. Those rocks are a façade, and my guess is they're not even made of stone."

"What is it, then?" asked Kim.

"Is it one of those zeutyron accelerators like the one back at Pegasus West, or an antenna or something?" wondered Captain Evans.

"Perhaps..." Professor Quimbey replied, but she saw something else. "Captain, there's movement. I'm seeing little infrared red lights go in and out of the trees."

"Here, let me see," said Captain Evans. She took back the TIBs and had a look. "There's definitely something moving around down there... can't tell what it is because the trees are interfering with the thermal-infrared spectral feedback."

"Could it be an animal?" asked Kim.

"Hard to say," Captain Evans responded. "Whatever it is, there's more than one. Can't tell if it's human or animal."

"I think we need to get down there to investigate," said Stevens. "We can't see anything from up here."

Captain Evans agreed. "Red Team, go get a closer look at what's down there and report back. Covert reconnaissance, only. Do not engage, whoever or whatever it is, recon and return only, is that understood?"

"Yes, ma'am," said the team in unison.

"I'll hold position here with James and Quimbey."

With a great big smile, Stevens stated, "Team, let's go see what Russia's cooking for dinner."

Stevens, Pacheco, Kim, Russy, and Abrantes descended the mountain through the pine trees. As Emma, Professor Quimbey, and Captain Evans watched the team head down the hill, Captain Evans said, "It's time to make a call..."

△△△△△△△△△△△

136

"Generals, what's going on?" asked President Barrett, looking for an update as he stormed through the Situation Room doors where everyone had re-gathered for the update.

On the left-hand side of the SIT-Room's end-wall, a digital screen displayed the GPS location of each Red Snow Team member on a topographical map, using red dots to denote their location. On the right-hand side of the end-wall, Pegasus East and Pegasus West were visible on a split-screen.

"Mr. President, we have Captain Evans on the SAT-phone, prepared to provide an update from the ground. They've found something, sir," announced General Covington from his post at the P-West Communications and Command Platform.

"Can she hear me?" asked the president.

"Yes, sir. You're live," the general responded.

The president jumped right into it. "Captain Evans, this is the president. What can you tell me?"

"Sir, we have locate---------lieve to be the source ------- signal, or at least where the ------------ originating from—"

"Can we get a better connection? I can't understand her," complained the president, struggling to make out what Captain Evans was saying.

General Nemond replied, "No, Mr. President. She's using the best SAT-phone we've got, but there appears to be some interference at the source location."

Captain Evans spoke again. "There's -------- rock formation --- ----- we think its---- zeutyron ----- transmit--- or antennae of some kind, in the mi------ clearing ------ below present location. Gravity is -------which Quimbey says------------- is not poss--le, but-----"

"Say again, Captain Evans," asked the president, frustrated.

"Red Team has --------- investigate the rock formation. Stevens leading recon----- clearing. Also, picking --- infrared signals ------ movement ---- trees -------- animal, maybe human ----------. Red Tea---- vestigating."

General Covington asked, "Captain, can you tell how many?"

Pop!! Pop!! T-t-t-t-t-t-t-chk-chk.

Logan's and Dr. Arenot's ears perked up. Everyone's did.

"Was that gunfire?" asked the president.

General Covington immediately injected himself into the conversation with Captain Evans. "Captain, this is General Covington... report..."

Before Captain Evans could answer, another round—*Pop!! Pop!! T-------chk-chk!!*—blasted through the phone.

"Wash--gton, Red Team is engaged. I repeat ------team--- engag--- Leaving audio on, Evans out. James, ---mbey, --- need --- go!"

"Can we get eyes on what's going on down there?" shouted the president.

Logan leaped out of his seat. He couldn't believe what he was hearing.

"No, sir. We've got high-orbit topographical satellite imaging only. No surveilling satellites in range," replied General Covington.

"Why can't the PAPA get a look at their location?" barked President Barrett.

Pop!! T-t-t-t-t-t-chk-chk. Pop!!

"I'm sorry, sir," answered Lt. Col. Lain from Pegasus East. "Even with maximum course correction velocity, given the speed of the Earth's rotation, PAPA fell out of range for a few seconds. It'll be back in 30 seconds, Mr. President."

"James, Quimbey, this way! Into the door!" shouted Captain Evans, her voice suddenly transmitting clear through her SAT-phone.

"A door?" the president asked. "What door?"

General Covington, looking at the monitor displaying the SAT-phone signal strength, saw that all the bars were gone. "Mr. President, the SAT-phone has dropped completely," he informed the president. "Whatever door they just went into, whatever they're inside of, for now, the SAT-signal's gone. We've still got them tracked on the GPS-tracking screen because the muons are still transmitting. Hopefully, that doesn't drop, too."

Their little red blips continued to move inside the mountain. "Where are they going?" asked Director Bowling.

The phone next to NSA Director Orson's permanent seat in the SIT-Room, patched directly into NSA Headquarters in Maryland, flashed. Orson picked it up. Logan watched her speak softly into the receiver, trying to read her lips, but he couldn't. Her face remained cold and expressionless. She hung up the phone.

"Mr. President," said Director Orson, "NSA Headquarters is reporting that a minute ago, Russia launched four Sukhoi Su-57s out of Tiksi Air Force Base, headed for the Chersky Mountains."

"How long until the jets reach the team's present location?" asked the president.

"The Su-57's max speed exceeds Mach 2.2+, so estimated intercept time is 12 minutes," answered Director Orson. Logan looked at the president who made eye contact back with Logan. Despite his calm persona, the president's eyes expressed real concern. Just when Logan didn't think things could get worse, Director Orson added, "Sir, Russian-counterintelligence is now reporting Russian Ground Forces just dispatched two Kamav Ka-50 helicopters with a full complement of troops from their Ust-Nera base in the Sakha Republic, just southwest of Red Snow Team's location. Estimated intercept time: seven minutes."

"I want options, and I want them now!" shouted President Barrett, suddenly feeling like he had sent Red Snow Team into a trap. "Orson? Covington?"

Director Orson went first. "Mr. President, we have no extraction—"

"I don't want to hear that, Sue. I want options!"

"I'm sorry, Mr. President," apologized Director Orson, "but our extraction plan was the GPS-linked-zeutyron accelerator in Nevada. They just need to press their buttons, sir."

Dr. Ehringer, who had been quiet throughout the entire exchange, jumped in, "They can't do that, sir. Not while they're moving. The accelerator's programmed to open up a zeutyron portal at a stationary GPS location. If they're all on the move like they are right now," pointing to the GPS-tracking screen, "Station's not going to be able to get a fix on their GPS position, preventing—"

"Can't we just open a portal at their GPS locations for them?" asked the president.

The phone next to the NSA Director flashed again. Orson picked it up. "Yes, thank you. Okay, direct the feed to the SIT-Room now." She hung up the phone. "Mr. President, U.S. Geological Survey Agency is reporting a seismic event in the Sakha Republic, southeastern Chersky Mountains. What are the exact coordinates of the epicenter?" she asked her Deputy Director on the phone.

"What are we talking about? An earthquake?" asked the president.

Orson kept asking her Deputy Director questions to get more specifics. "Mr. President, it's highly localized... whatever it is. The PAPA's transmitting a feed of the area now." Director Orson pressed

140

a button on a control panel from her seat and a view of the Chersky Mountains fed directly from NSA Headquarters, popped up on the screen behind Director Orson. On the phone, Director Orson asked her Deputy Director, "Can you zoom in on 65.6415 North, 144.5448 East, please?"

On the screen, the aerial satellite image zoomed in on the coordinates requested by Director Orson. They could see small rockslides and a small avalanche of snow careening down a chute on the southeast side of Peak Sahka, caused by the tremors the mountain was experiencing. Then, all of a sudden, the mountain face started collapsing in on itself. The implosion of the southeast side of Peak Sahka ejected dust and snow into the air. Everyone in the room who wasn't already standing, stood up in horror. Slowly, each of them, momentarily forgetting their places, ranks, positions, and responsibilities, walked over to the screen, wanting to get a closer look at what they were witnessing.

"It looks like the southeast side of Peak Sahka crashed in on itself," said NASA Director Bowling.

Logan's face went pale. He desperately looked for red dots and signs of life on the GPS-tracking screen, but he saw none. No red dots, not Emma's, not anyone's. All evidence of Red Snow Team was gone. He slumped into a nearby chair, crushed.

The president, looking at Logan's and Dr. Arenot's distraught faces, said, "Logan, Jonas, I am at a loss for words... I really don't know what to say. I am sorry for what you just saw..." The president, usually more eloquent than that, was stunned, confused, remorseful, devastated, and angry, like everyone else. Even before he had time to process it, another urgent phone call rang into the SIT-Room. Mr. Garrison answered it.

"Garrison... yeah. Okay, thank you. I'll let the president know." Mr. Garrison looked at President Barrett. "Mr. President, the Russian Foreign Affairs Minister is calling to speak with you. What do you want them to tell him, sir?"

"Have them tell Menputyn to hold for a minute. I'll take it up in the Oval Office." President Barrett started walking out of the Situation Room, but before he passed through the doors, he had one more instruction for his Chief of Staff, "And Miles, I want a national security briefing, and some answers from everyone in this room as to what the hell just happened, in 20 minutes."

Chapter 11 – Ref. #: 137A-2D-444

Logan laid on the sofa inside his studio apartment, staring up at the ceiling and fumbling with the engagement ring he intended for Emma. He took one more peek at the text message that had come in from Emma on General Covington's phone several hours after Logan left the Situation Room saying, 'I love you, see you soon.' Tears rolled down his cheek. He was reeling, completely sick to his stomach.

It had been 10 hours since the disaster in Chersky, and still, no word if Emma or anyone else had survived. Although they weren't included in the national security briefings following the Chersky incident, the president himself had stopped by their White House guest rooms to share some information with them before they went home. President Barrett explained Russian Foreign Affairs Minister, Viktor Menputyn, claimed Russia was conducting geological experiments in the Chersky mountains, and that something went wrong when gunfire struck sensitive equipment and triggered a chain-reaction that sparked a massive underground explosion. No one in the Oval Office believed the minister's geological experiments explanation, not that Logan cared. Politics were the last thing on his mind.

Still struggling to process what had happened, Logan heard a knock on the door. He got up to see who it was. It was Dr. Arenot. Logan let him in.

"Just checking on you," said Dr. Arenot, sounding glum in his own right.

"Who's checking on you?" responded Logan, heading back over to his couch.

"No one, I imagine." Although Dr. Arenot didn't say it, the truth was, he didn't want to be alone. He needed Logan right then just as much as Logan needed him, even if Logan didn't realize it himself. Dr. Arenot took a seat. "How are you doing?"

"Terrible. I feel like I'm living in a nightmare I can't wake up from," replied Logan, leaning forward and putting his hands over his face.

Dr. Arenot put his hand on Logan's shoulder and responded, "I know."

Logan realized he wasn't the only one hurting. "What about you? How are you doing?" he asked.

"Awful. I just keep playing it back in my head over and over, and each time I do, I feel—"

"Helpless."

The professor nodded in agreement and said, "Yeah." He noticed Logan holding Emma's engagement ring in his hand, moving it around between his fingers. "Is that the ring you picked out for her?"

"Uh-huh."

"Can I see it?"

"Sure." Logan handed it to him.

The professor examined it. "This really is a pretty ring you got her." He gave it back to Logan.

"Thanks," replied Logan. Curious, and perhaps, also looking for a distraction, Logan asked, "How'd you propose to Professor Quimbey?"

Dr. Arenot sat down beside Logan. He leaned back in the couch and responded, "Nothing as fancy as what you planned, I'm afraid. But I, umm… it was a few years after we met. We were in Brussels attending the International Archeology Symposium and were both speaking on the same afternoon panel. Jill's lecture followed mine, so I wrote on a note, 'Will You Marry Me', and when my turn was over, I left the note and ring on the podium and sat down. When Jill got up to the podium to speak, she saw my note and the ring… it left her momentarily speechless in front of an entire lecture hall of symposium attendees."

"I bet that went over well."

Dr. Arenot recalled the memory fondly. "I think she was a bit miffed with me at first, although she'd never admit it. And of course, being the true professional she is, she pulled herself together and gave her lecture. I had to wait the whole thing out. Longest 30 minutes of my life. She didn't look at me once the entire time."

"So, what happened?" asked Logan, displaying a faint smile.

"Umm, when her lecture ended, she spent a few minutes answering questions and then, after responding to the last one, said into the microphone, 'And in response to the question I received at the outset of my lecture, my answer is, 'Yes.'" For a fleeting moment, Dr. Arenot looked happy. After a few seconds, he asked Logan, "Have you told her parents yet?"

"No."

"Don't you think—"

"Mr. Garrison told me not to discuss it with anyone, not even her parents, in the interests of national security…"

"Oh."

"…at least, not until they have confirmation and figure out what to say."

"Right."

"Just three weeks ago, I asked her parents for permission to marry her, and now, I'm lying to them…"

"You're not exactly 'lying' to them…"

"Well, I doubt they're going to feel better about how I handled this once they find out, just because I did it in the interests of national security," replied Logan.

"Probably not."

"You know, the second General Covington suggested they go on the mission, I knew it was a bad idea," stated Logan.

"You couldn't have predicted this. None of us could have."

Logan shook his head. "I knew something bad would happen. I could feel it."

"You can't blame yourself."

"As soon as she left the SIT-Room, all I could think was, 'that's the last time I'm ever going to see her.' I shouldn't have let her go."

"It wasn't up to you."

"Still, I should have asked her not to."

"She wouldn't have listened."

"Maybe," conceded Logan, "but I should have tried."

"You did try."

"I should've tried harder."

"And if you had—"

"Maybe she'd still be here today, and Professor Quimbey, too!"

"*No*, they wouldn't. Emma would've told you to sit down, and had I tried to stop Jill, she would have wrapped a chair around my head. There's nothing we could have done to stop them. They both wanted to go. The Pegasus Project meant everything to them."

"And look where that got them... All we've done for three years is work on Pegasus, and for what?"

"You know the answer."

"Well, now they're never going to see the end of it."

"None of us will..."

"What does that mean?"

"The president has suspended Pegasus indefinitely."

"What?" blurted Logan, stunned.

"Bowling told me that whatever happened in the Chersky Mountains spooked the president."

"Well, of course, it did, but—"

"It didn't just level the mountain; it caused some kind of chain reaction bigger than anything Pegasus' scientists believed possible. So, until they have a chance to research it further—"

"They're just going to give up and suspend the program, just like that?"

"It's not just that. They've also revoked *all* security clearances for everyone associated with the Pegasus Project while they investigate how Russia acquired the zeutyron technology."

"Including ours?"

"Yep, *everyone*. They're certain there's an internal leak, and until they find out who, the program's suspended and we're shut out of everything, including the Pentagon."

Logan couldn't believe it. "I'm calling Covington…"

"I wouldn't waste your time. They've got bigger things to deal with, right now."

"Like what?"

"I talked to Bowling just before I left the White House, and he said before the mountain's collapse, Russian soldiers apparently killed and identified one of the Red Snow Team members as U.S. military. Now, Russia's threatened a retaliatory strike inside U.S. soil in response to the American incursion into Chersky which cost Russian lives. The president has raised the Domestic Threat Level to Severe, and he's mobilizing the Atlantic and Pacific fleets. I don't think anyone's going to answer your call today."

Logan tried anyway. He tried calling General Covington. When the prompt came up to enter the security code to complete the call, Logan entered the general's security code, and an automated voice came back saying, "CODE DENIED." Next, Logan tried sending a text to General Covington from his cellphone saying, "Do you have a minute to talk?" He hit send and when the security code request popped up, he tried the general's code again. Another message came back saying, "CODE DENIED." He next tried calling and texting Mr. Garrison and several other high-ranking members of the team, but all codes failed. He even tried the president's personal cellphone, to no avail. "You're right, we're completely shut out," bemoaned Logan.

"Yep."

"So, what then, the program's shut down and Emma and Jill may have died for nothing?"

"You know that's not true. They contributed a great deal to—"

"Stop doing that! Stop thinking like a professor, trying to rationalize everything!"

"Logan, I know you're angry—"

"And you're not?"

"Of course, I am!"

Logan's text message chime went off. He looked at his phone to see who it was. It was his mom:

> "Hi, dear. Is everything okay? You didn't respond to my text last night. How did it go? Worried. Mom"

Logan knew she was waiting on pins and needles to hear how his proposal to Emma went, but with everything that'd happened, he had forgotten to respond to her text. He knew he couldn't ignore it again; he had to say something, so he crafted a short nothing response that concealed how he was truly feeling and what was really going on at the moment:

> "Hi, Mom. Sorry for not responding sooner. Didn't propose last nite. Something came up. Will explain later. Love u."

Logan felt terrible, but he didn't know what to say or what he even *could* say. He hit send and stared at the last picture he had taken with Emma in front of the Yggdrasil tree in the Smithsonian, which Emma had saved as his background image. He smiled, then he zoomed in on Emma and his faces. He was lost in his thoughts for a moment until something caught his eye. He zoomed in closer on the tree…

"Hold on… that can't be!" he uttered.

"What?"

"We need to look at the *Prose Edda*."

"The *Prose Edda*?" The professor didn't understand. "Why? What are you talking about?"

"I know it might sound crazy, but last night when Emma and I visited the Smithsonian Air and Space Museum, we took this picture in front of the Yggdrasil tree inside the new exhibit." Logan handed the professor his phone.

Dr. Arenot looked at the photo with the mythical tree behind them. "I'm familiar with it…"

Logan sat down and said, "On the tree, it shows the Nine Worlds." Logan took back his phone and read them to Dr. Arenot. "First, we have Asgard, the world of the Æsir gods; Álfheimr, the world of the light elves; Svartálfaheimr, home of the dark elves; Midgard, home of humans; Jötunheimr, home of the giants; Niflheim, the primordial world of ice; Muspelheim, the primordial world of fire; Helheim, home of the dishonorable dead; and Vanaheimr is the home of the *Vanir* gods according to Snorri Sturluson. Do you see it?"

The professor focused his eyes on Vanaheimr, the home of the *Vanir* Gods.

"Professor, don't you see it? *Vanir… Vanir*ya… *Vanir*yans. That can't be a coincidence."

"I do…," replied the professor, intrigued and surprised. Although familiar with Norse cosmology, the *Prose Edda* and Snorri Sturluson, he hadn't made the connection before.

"Three years ago, inside the cave in the Hvit Fuge Stranda in Norway when staring at the Vaniryan light portal, you said Snorri Sturluson's *Prose Edda* talks about Light Elves, suggesting perhaps elvish mythology started in that cave."

"I remember," replied Dr. Arenot.

"Well, maybe you were right. Perhaps the *Prose Edda* actually *was* talking about the Vaniryans and Sturluson knew more about them than we realized!" Logan had an idea. "If we can find the Vaniryans, maybe there's still a way we can fix this."

"How? You've lost me."

"If we find them, maybe we can go back in time and change what happened."

Dr. Arenot's jaw nearly dropped at the suggestion. "Are you serious?"

"I'm totally serious... we can go back in time before the Chersky accident happened and stop it."

Dr. Arenot thought about Logan's idea. The idea of seeing Jill again meant everything to him, but Logan's notions were too far-fetched to take seriously. "Logan, even if we could theoretically figure out how to do it—"

"It's not just a theory, Dr. Arenot. The Vaniryans have already figured out how to do it, and we did it three years ago to save you and Professor Quimbey from the Dealer in Bologna. We can do this... we just have to find the Vaniryans."

"But how? The Vaniryan star went supernova 800 years ago. Not sure how we're supposed to do that."

"It's like the president said last night and Emma once told us... the Vaniryans move from planet to planet whenever they have to. Maybe they moved planets again before their star exploded."

"And you think Snorri Sturluson knew where?" asked Dr. Arenot, starting to understand Logan's thinking.

"It's as good a place to start as any."

"Okay, but how are we going to find the Vaniryans when we don't have access to Area 51, Pegasus West, high-powered classified telescopes, or any Vaniryan portals?"

"Just like everything else that's hard to find..."

"How?" asked Dr. Arenot.

"*Google.*"

Logan hurried over to his computer and navigated to Google. He typed in the search terms: Vanir, Vanaheimr, Sturluson, and the *Prose Edda*. Several articles came up discussing Snorri Sturluson's mythological tale in the *Prose Edda* about how the Vanir gods fled from Vanaheimr during something called the Æsir-Vanir War. "There! You see, they left Vanaheimr. Maybe there's more to Sturluson's *Prose Edda* than meets the eye."

"Does it say where the Vanir gods went?"

Logan scanned the articles. "These ones don't. Let me try searching, 'where did the Vanir gods go Norse mythology,' see if that pulls up something different." Logan did and it pulled up a ton of new search results. Logan steadily scrolled through the list. "This one looks interesting."

"Which one are you looking at?"

"The one here saying, **Vanirens Sista Resa**. Vanirens kind of looks like Vaniryans," replied Logan, directing the professor to it.

"Click on it."

Logan did, and it took them to a website called 'Uppsala Universitetsbibliotek.'

"Ah," Dr. Arenot responded, "Uppsala..."

"You know what that says?"

"Yes. Uppsala University in Sweden, just a few miles north of Stockholm. Beautiful campus."

"You've been there?"

"Many years ago, I attended a lecture there. Uppsala's one of the oldest universities in Scandinavia and is one of the world's top international universities. Highly respected."

They looked closely at the page, but couldn't read the text discussing ***Vanirens Sista Resa*** because it was in Swedish:

Uppsala Universitetsbibliotek
Plats: Specialavdelningen
Sektion: Sanuskripter
Referens #: 137A-2D-444
Titel: *Vanirens Sista Resa*
År: Tidigare-14:e Århundrade
Författare: S. Þórðarson

"Go to the bottom of the page," suggested Dr. Arenot. "International universities like this usually have an option on their webpages to select different languages to accommodate their international student population."

Logan scrolled down to the bottom, and sure enough, there was a photo of flags and language options listing numerous available languages. Logan selected the English language option, and after doing that, the page read:

Uppsala Library
Location: Special Collections Division
Segment: Manuscripts
Ref. #: 137A-2D-444
Title: *The Final Journey of the Vanir*
Year: Pre-14th Century
Author: S. Þórðarson

"There we go," said Dr. Arenot. "That title's promising."

"Pre-14th Century... wow, it's old, whatever it is," stated Logan. "I wonder what the Special Collections Division refers to?" There was an 'About the SCD' link on the left-hand side of the page, so he clicked on it and a pop-up about the "Special Collections Division" appeared:

> "Uppsala Library is the oldest and largest research library in Sweden. Its Special Collections Division contains some of Sweden's most remarkable written treasures and original documents dating back, in some cases, more than 1,000 years. The SCD is responsible for the collection, curation, preservation, and presentation of the unique collections, manuscripts, and writings under its care."

"Interesting," said Dr. Arenot. "Can we click on the document?"

Logan closed the 'About the SCD' pop-up and tried clicking on *The Final Journey of the Vanir,* but a message appeared that read: 'Uppsala Library Scholars & Affiliates Program Members only. To see the requested record, you may access it through your account on the 'ULSAP Members page.'

"Darn," said Logan.

He looked up at the top of the page. There was a blue tab for 'ULSAP Members.' Logan clicked on the tab, and it took him to a page asking for his Member ID and Password. It also provided a link to submit membership applications. Looking at the application, Uppsala required a lot of detail, academic and scholarly references, and suggested donations for membership. Either way, the approval process wasn't quick.

Logan returned to the *Final Journey of the Vanir* and asked, "Have you ever heard of 'S. Þórðarson'?"

"No."

Logan typed 'S. Þórðarson,' into Google. The first two results related to individuals in the 20th century, but the third one down was a Wikipedia page about someone by the name of Sturla Þórðarson and the Sturlungar family clan. Logan opened the page and read aloud, "Sturla Þórðarson lived in Hvammur í Dölum in Iceland and was part of the Icelandic Commonwealth's powerful Sturlungar family in the 12th century. He was the father of... of Snorri Sturluson."

"*The* Snorri Sturluson?"

Logan clicked on Snorri Sturluson's name in the article and it linked right to another Wikipedia page about the famous Icelandic historian, poet, and politician who authored the *Prose Edda*. "Wikipedia sure thinks it's the same person."

"Huh," said Dr. Arenot. "Now, *that's* interesting."

"So, the document at Uppsala Library, whatever it is, was written by Snorri Sturluson's father?" questioned Logan.

"Not necessarily. Snorri Sturluson was a famous historian, poet, politician, but he wasn't always well-liked. In fact, his life ended when a Norwegian King had him assassinated if I remember correctly. It's possible he wrote whatever this is under a pen name or even authored it under his birth name, Snorri *Þórðarson* to conceal his true identity. *The Final Journey of the Vanir*'s author might very well be Snorri Sturluson himself. Let's see if we can find this document elsewhere on the internet that isn't under the ULSAP Members' lock and key."

Logan tried searching for it by its title in English, Swedish, and Icelandic since Sturluson was Icelandic. Still, he couldn't find it anywhere. "Feels like it's three years ago all over again when Emma and I had to fly to the Vatican just to see Christopher Columbus's journal entries for his 4th voyage to the New World."

"Too bad our security clearance has been revoked. Covington or Garrison would've been able to easily get a copy of the document for us."

"Totally." Logan thought about it. "You know what, I think I've got another idea for how we might be able to get this document…"

"How?"

"We need to go visit an old friend."

"Where?"

With a sly smile, Logan replied, "In Philadelphia."

Chapter 12 – Breaker of Codes

The rush-hour commuter train from Georgetown to Philadelphia took just under three hours. By the time they reached Philly's 30th Street Station, crossed over the Market Street Bridge, and arrived at Dewey's Comic Books and Hobby Shop, it was early evening. Logan was sure Bryan Callister would still be there. He always was. Unlike the last few times Logan visited Dewey's when only a few customers milled about, the store was packed.

"This is where you hope to find help?" asked Dr. Arenot, looking upon the storefront with skepticism.

"Trust me!" responded Logan with a smirk.

Dr. Arenot and Logan approached Dewey's. A sign out front read: "FiteNite." They walked into a boisterous crowd backed up all the way to the front door. Once inside, they could see what all the commotion was about; there was an eSports gaming competition taking place. Multiple players sat at video game consoles set up on folding tables, competing against each other in a fast-paced multiplayer first-person shooter game that allowed gamers to compete against one another in player versus player combat, battling to be the last one standing.

"Hey guys, you gotta pay $5 bucks to come in. No freebies," said a male voice from behind.

They spun around, and Logan recognized the gatekeeper instantly. It was Zack, Bryan Callister's dark-haired, mid-20s faithful party companion, and sometimes, semi-competent assistant store manager.

"Hi, Zack. Remember me?" said Logan, giving him a great big smile. Emma and Logan had returned to Dewey's after Bryan helped them three years ago to thank him one more time in person. Logan always got the sense Zack didn't like him.

"Yeah, I remember you. Where's your girlfriend? She dump you yet?" asked Zack, keeping wishful tabs on Emma's availability.

"Not quite," Logan responded. "Is, uh, Bryan here?"

"Yeah, but you'll have to wait until LordSnow33 is done with his FiteNite domination." Zack pointed at Bryan smack in the middle of the video game slugfest, taking on the challengers who had invaded his lair on FiteNite.

Logan looked on as Bryan took down his competitors, eliciting cheers from his fans who watched on make-shift oversized projection-style video screens while the competitors used their own personal computer screens. LordSnow33 was dominating. The crowd hollered, yelled, shouted, and screamed, enjoying the finals where the evening's top-five remaining competitors battled it out for FiteNite supremacy. The noise from the raucous crowd overwhelmed the gameplay's audio.

In one insane, explosive melee, LordSnow33 eliminated three of the five finalists' avatars when he utilized a bomb, followed by a series of grenade and flamethrower hits. Only two avatars remained: Lordsnow33 and AvtarZlayer. Once again, Bryan employed some clever tactics to draw AvtarZlayer out into the open. Once AvtarZlayer fell for it, LordSnow33 unleashed his rocket launcher and obliterated AvtarZlayer. The crowd erupted. FiteNite had a champion! High-fives whipped around Dewey's like someone had started the wave.

As the crowd celebrated, Zack shouted to Bryan, "Hey, Lord Snow, look what FiteNite dragged in..." Bryan looked in Zack's direction and saw Logan standing there with Dr. Arenot.

Bryan recognized Logan immediately and came to say hello. Over the last three years, Bryan had matured quite a bit. Still tall and skinny, his curly-blond hair was now tightly cropped and he sported a short goatee. As always, he wore jeans and tennis shoes, but his untucked Metallica t-shirt had been replaced by a hip button-down shirt. Now in his early 20s, Bryan had definitely grown into the role of a store owner.

"Never thought I'd see you at a FiteNite throwdown," said Bryan, throwing out his hand for a fist-pump.

"Nice going, Lord Snow," said Logan, meeting Bryan's fist halfway.

"Yep, I gotta teach these kids a thing or two once in a while."

"This place is rocking," said Logan.

"Yeah, last year, I decided to start a FiteNite eSports league to help build up the store's profile, and it's totally taken off. People are coming from all over. I figured if my parents can have a bowling league once a week, why can't the rest of us have a gaming league? I'm holding FiteNite every three weeks, and they're always packed. Getting a lot of new customers, too."

"That's awesome," replied Logan.

"Who's your friend?" asked Bryan.

"Oh, yeah, sorry. Bryan, this is Dr. Jonas Arenot. He's one of the two Harvard professors who—"

"I helped save from the evil clutches of international tyranny and CIA Directors!" said Bryan. "Nice to finally meet you, Dr. Arenot."

"Likewise," replied the professor, shaking Bryan's hand.

Logan was ready to get to it. "Hey, can we talk in your office?"

"Uh, yeah, sure." Bryan led Logan and Dr. Arenot toward his back-store office. Right before going in, he yelled to Zack, "Hey dude, you can take off in a couple of minutes when everybody's out. I'll lock up."

"Yes, master." Zack bowed. Bryan rolled his eyes. He hated when Zack did that, especially in front of other people. They all went into Bryan's office and Bryan closed the door.

"So, what's up? You guys want me to break the law again?" joked Bryan.

"Umm, yeah, kind of…," replied Logan.

"Are you serious? I was kidding."

"Nothing nearly as risky as what you did for us a few years ago," assured Logan, "I promise."

"Okay, fine, what do you guys need?"

"We need you to crack into a website," replied Logan.

"Like, a government website or something super secure with multiple layers of cyber-security protection, or like, a sandwich shop website?"

"I'm thinking closer to a sandwich shop," replied Logan. "It's a university library website."

"That seems doable. So, do you have an overdue library book or something?" teased Bryan, finding their request to crack into a library website surprising.

"Something like that," replied Logan. "Actually, it's got a members-only page we need you to look at."

"Alright. Let me see the site." Bryan opened up his laptop, ready to type away.

"Okay," said Logan. "Go to Google and type in *Vanirens Sista Resa* and Uppsala Library."

"Vanirawhataresa?"

"Here, let me sit down for two seconds, it'll go faster," suggested Logan. Bryan got up and moved aside, while Logan sat down and navigated them to the page he and Dr. Arenot had viewed earlier about the *Vanirens Sista Resa* on the Uppsala Library website. Logan next navigated to the bottom of the page to choose the English language and clicked on the blue tab at the top that read: 'ULSAP Members.' He stood up and let Bryan sit back down.

Bryan, looking at the page asking for a ULSAP Member ID and Password said, "I'm guessing this is where you guys got stuck."

"Yep," acknowledged Logan. "So, is it time to summon the DarknIyT website we used three years ago to try and find a tool to crack this page?"

Bryan chuckled. "Nah… This website looks like a basic paint-by-numbers template. There's actually a free open-source software program called CodeCracker that might work on this."

Logan was surprised. "Like, free, as in, you have it and we don't have to go through the dark web to get it kind of free?"

"Yep, and *of course,* I have it," chirped Bryan. "CodeCracker's been around forever. It's a free website penetration software developed by a security training company."

"Why do you have it?" asked Dr. Arenot.

Bryan quickly put the professor's concerns about his character to rest. "Well, they put it out there for free, so why not? And it's got like 600 different website security penetration testing tools on it. It's crazy effective. I have it because I design websites on the side and it helps me test the security of the sites that I'm building. People ask me all the time for my opinion on their existing websites, and I usually use CodeCracker to explore weaknesses in the sites I'm looking at. Helps me pick up a few new clients here and there."

Bryan opened up the software program and went to one of its tools called the Penetrator.

"What's the Penetrator?" asked Logan.

"It's a CodeCracker software application designed to crack web-based login pages like the one we're stuck on now."

"How does it work?" asked Logan.

"The Penetrator's basically just a brute-force login and password cracker, but it's really effective because it incorporates a combination of CodeCracker's tools, all at once. In the simplest terms, it guesses, through trial and error, usernames, logins, passwords. But what makes it so effective is that it learns 'on-the-go' by analyzing a website's different responses on usernames, logins, and passwords to detect the site's different reactions, when the inputs reach the minimum length or character-type requirements and things like that. There's actually a lot going on behind the scenes on a website whenever you try entering usernames and passwords, and the more basic the site is, the easier it is for Penetrator to detect and track it."

"How long does it take?" asked Dr. Arenot.

"Should go quickly, I think."

"Why do you say that?" asked Logan.

"Well, in my experience, people tend to go easy on their usernames and passwords for non-personal, non-banking, and non-financial related websites, choosing easy ones to remember. Based on what I usually see with sites like this, I'm guessing half the logins or usernames are some combination of first initial and last name, and half the passwords in there use a combination of the word password with dollar signs for 's' and zeros for the letter 'o'. I don't think it will take too long."

Bryan ran the Penetrator-tool, and they watched as the program worked on the ULSAP Members page. The screen flashed with hyper-fast activity, so fast their eyes couldn't keep up. It reminded Dr. Arenot of the end-scene in one of his favorite movies, *War Games*, where Joshua busily worked on the oversized NORAD monitors on the front wall faster than the eye could follow. At five minutes and 17 seconds, they had a winner! Penetrator cracked the page with a login ID of "jlarsson" and a password of "jlarssonPa$$w0rd." They were in!

"Wow, that was fast!" blurted Logan. "Seriously, we should just call you 'LordSnow33, Breaker of Codes,'" said Logan, giving Bryan a high-five. Bryan Callister had once again proven to be the secret weapon no one knew he and Emma had.

"I aim to please," responded Bryan, flashing a proud grin. "Okay, so what now?" he asked, pulling up the ULSAP Members Page menu. It listed numerous options to choose from, including one choice at the bottom of the ULSAP Members Page called "Special Collections Division – *Members Access*."

"Can you go to the *Members Access* page?" asked Logan.

"Sure," replied Bryan, clicking on it.

It took them to another page that described the Special Collection Division's (SCD) mission, philanthropic goals and programs, exhibits, collections, research opportunities, academic articles, educational programs, and the like. It also had an option to view SCD documents... bingo!

"Hey, click on 'View SCD Documents,'" said Logan.

"Got it," replied Bryan. He did and the page produced a pop-up giving users the option to search SCD documents by Title, Author, or Reference ID.

"Okay, type in *The Final Journey of the Vanir*," said Logan.

Bryan typed it in and hit enter. Up came a page identical to the version they had viewed earlier but in English, again listing the details for *The Final Journey of the Vanir* and this time the manuscript title was clickable!

"That's one old document," commented Bryan, seeing the 'Pre-14th Century' reference in the manuscript's details.

"Yep," said Logan anxiously. "Click on the manuscript!"

Bryan did, and a new window opened up displaying the original manuscript written in Icelandic:

Óðinn, guð viskunnar, þekkingar og töfrä,
dauðlegir Midgarðs fylgja,

Sitjandi í hásæti víð hlið Frigg, synir Þór,
Baldr og Váli, og hæna Friggs, sjö í lína.

Óðínn kenndi hænum sínum að nota kraft
sinn, þekkingu og visku innan,

Og hvernig á äð lesa skrifin úr dauðlegum
Midgard kóða,

En sinni elskulëgu kenndi hann öllum
Leyandermálum alheimsins, því hún hafði
viljað að,

Því að hún sät tilbúin til að stjórna með réttu
þegar tíma Óðins lauk og þá, Frigg.

En brátt kom Guð Däuðans fyrir Vanir, Óðinn,
syni hans og hænur,

Óðinn bað Ljósálfar ög bandamenn hans um
hjálp, sama hvaðan frá,

Hann benti Æsir og Vanir, fyrir nýjä Æsir-
Vanir stríð lentu þeir í frammi andlit.

164

The Hidden Coordinate by Marc Jacobs

Ekki með hvort öðru, heldur með Dauðanum
og Dökkálfar þess, til sigurs ä Vanír, var
engum hægt að tryggja,

Ótti gerði Óðinn, komu Dauðans, að frá tóppi
Vanírs kállaði hann á kraft tímans með því að
nota stjörnurnar, tunglið og sólina,

Tíl að berjast í bardaga gat Æsir-Vanir ekki
unnið einn, því þeir skorti styrk til að,

Ënn til bardaga komu Þór, Baldr og Váli,
spurðu aðeins hvar.

Stríðið geisaði, Dauðinn grëip hús Vanirens,

Örvæntur kallaði Óðinn þann sem kollvarpar
rúmi ög tíma, svo að Vanir gætu lifað,

Hann leiddi Vanir heim að nýju og fäldi
kærust Óðins innan rýmis og tíma, að eilífu frá
bardaga.

Óðinn lamdi þá Dökkálfar en leitin að friði
hëldur áfram,

Þegar myrkur Dauðans geisär í Miðgarði, þar
sem Óðinn getur ekki lengur hjálpað,

Því hvërnig bardaga í hulinni borg lýkur er
undir komið okkur,

Æ, Óðinn örvæntír, sólin er farin, sólin er farin
og Guð Dauðans hefur hana núna.

Fortunately, the SCD's Scholars Program had the original manuscript translated into multiple languages.

"Do you guys want the English translation of this?" asked Bryan.

"What do you think?" Logan responded.

"Uh, right..." Bryan searched the page and found the English translation under 'Ref. #: 137A-2D-444 (British/English).' He selected it and an English version popped up. "Here you go... better?"

"Much," said Logan.

"I hope this is what you're looking for." Bryan moved aside to allow Logan and Dr. Arenot to get closer to the screen to read *The Final Journey of the Vanir*.

Chapter 13 – The Final Journey of the Vanir

Odin, god of wisdom, knowledge, and magic,
do mortals of Midgard follow,

Sitting on high throne beside Frigg, sons Thor,
Baldr and Váli, and Frigg's hens, seven in
line.

Odin taught his hens how to use their power,
knowledge and wisdom within,

And how to read the writings from Midgard's
mortal codex,

But to his dearest, he taught all the universe's
secrets, for she had wanted to,

For she sat ready to rule justly when Odin's
time ended and then, Frigg's.

But soon the God of Death came for the
Vanir, Odin, his sons and his hens,

Odin beckoned the Ljósálfar and his allies for
help, no matter where from,

He beckoned the Æsir and Vanir, for a new
Æsir-Vanir War did they face.

Not with each other, but with Death and its
Dökkálfar, for a victory on Vanir none could
be assured of,

Fear did Odin, the coming of Death, that from
Vanir's peak he called upon the power of time
using the stars, moons and sun,

To fight a battle the Æsir-Vanir could not win
alone, for they lacked the strength to,

Still, to battle did Thor, Baldr and Váli come,
asking only where.

The war raged on, Death seized the home of
the Vanirens,

Desperate, Odin summoned he who overturns
space and time, so the Vanir could live,

He led the Vanir to a home anew, and hid
Odin's dearest within space and time itself,
forever away from battle.

Odin then smote the Dökkálfar, but the search
for peace continues,

As the darkness of Death rages on in Midgard,
where no longer can Odin help,

For how the battle in the hidden city ends is
up to us,

Alas, Odin despair, the sun is gone, the sun is
gone, and the God of Death has her, now.

-- S. Þórðarson

It took them each a few moments to read the Icelandic poet's
tale about the flight of the Vanir, talking about Odin's rule over the

mortals of Midgard, Odin's family, and the dark forces that endeavored to conquer all. Below the English translation was an academic piece authored by Uppsala University Professor Matteus Lundström, Ph.D., for the SCD's Scholar's Program, providing an expert interpretation of the ancient work:

> "Þórðarson's, *The Final Journey of the Vanir,* is a poetic cautionary tale of darkness in the world brought on by war, a stark reminder that no war is ever really won and that no one can ever really vanquish evil. While many yearn to decipher the hidden meaning behind Þórðarson's masterpiece, Þórðarson's work is more pragmatic than that. It is a call for peace in a troubled world where there are no winners in war, only more darkness and death. -- *Professor Matteus Lundström, Ph.D., Uppsala University*"

Logan was frustrated. "It doesn't say anything about where the Vanir went."

"No, it doesn't," responded Dr. Arenot, "but maybe there's more to it. Let's go section by section," suggested the professor.

"Looks like we're the fools yearning to find the hidden meaning in Þórðarson's masterpiece that Professor Lundström was griping about."

"That we are," concurred Dr. Arenot.

Logan went first. "Okay, so the first part, 'Odin, god of wisdom, knowledge, and magic, do mortals of Midgard follow,' seems pretty straight forward to me."

"Me, too," said Dr. Arenot, adding, "According to Nordic mythology, Odin is the most powerful god."

"His character attributes in Dungeons & Dragons are pretty gnarly, too," blurted Bryan, unable to resist himself. "According to the D&D Deities & Demigods Manual, anyway…" He quietly trailed off, realizing now wasn't the time.

Logan, amused, kept going. "So, the mortals of Midgard followed Odin, who sat on his throne beside Frigg…"

"…the wife of Odin," added Dr. Arenot.

Logan continued. "Odin and Frigg sat next to their sons, Thor, Baldr and Váli, and Frigg's hens… What does 'Frigg's hens' mean?"

Bryan's fingers flew on his keyboard. "They're the daughters of Odin and Frigg, and it also says 'Frigg's Hens' refers to the Pleiades constellation, the Seven Sisters of the Heavens."

"The Pleiades," Logan echoed. Each time the Vaniryans were involved, there was always an obscure, indirect reference to the stars or constellations in there somewhere, and here it was *again*. Logan felt his brain sparking as it made all these connections.

Dr. Arenot kept going. "So, Odin taught his daughters how to think, how to read, and he taught his *dearest* daughter all the universe's secrets so she could rule one day. But then, the God of Death and Dökkálfar came to conquer all."

"What does 'Dökkálfar' mean?" asked Bryan.

"In Norse mythology, the Dökkálfar are the dark elves in Svartálfaheimr," replied Dr. Arenot, "and here, it sounds like they're the minions of the God of Death."

"And which deity is the God of Death in Norse anthologies?" asked Bryan.

"Hel, the ruler of the underworld of Helheim," responded Professor Quimbey.

"That's a fitting name," remarked Logan. He continued from there, saying, "…and after Death and its Dökkálfar tried to conquer

170

the world, Odin called upon the other deities for help. With the war going poorly, desperate, Odin summoned 'he who overturns space and time' to save his family, to lead the Vanir to a new home, and to take Odin's 'dearest' to another place and time completely where she would be safe." Looking at Dr. Arenot, Logan asked, "Which god is, 'he who overturns space and time?'"

"I don't remember," replied Dr. Arenot. "but I've definitely heard it before."

"Sounds like Odin's plan didn't work out too well," critiqued Bryan. "I mean, if the battle's still going on here in Midgard where us mortals live and the God of Death found Odin's beloved daughter anyway, that is." Bryan paused and then asked, "What is the hidden city where it says the battle is still taking place?"

"I don't know what that refers to," responded the professor.

"Me, neither," said Logan.

"What about the codex mentioned at the end of the fourth verse?" asked Bryan.

Dr. Arenot responded, "A codex is an ancient manuscript text in book form. Usually, it's constructed out of a number of sheets of paper like parchment, vellum, or papyrus, with hand-written contents."

Bryan shook his head. "I know *what* a codex is. I was wondering if you know what 'Midgard's mortal codex' refers to. Maybe it talks about the hidden city in there."

"Not sure," replied Dr. Arenot, "but between the Voynich manuscript, this one now, and the mortal codex mentioned in the fourth verse, we've been knee-deep in codices since yesterday."

"Hold on," mumbled Logan, mostly to himself. Dr. Arenot's comment had sparked a thought: *The Final Journey of the Vanir* manuscript was approximately 800 years old, just like the Voynich Manuscript, and *both* included possible references to the Pleiades constellation. A coincidence? Perhaps. Focusing on the possible references to the Pleiades in *The Final Journey* manuscript for a moment, Logan noticed something unusual, perhaps even significant: the words 'Frigg,' 'hens,' and 'codex' all came at the end of a verse…

"Bryan," said Logan, "can you print out *The Final Journey of the Vanir?*"

"Sure," replied Bryan, hitting print. As soon as the print job finished, he handed it to Logan. "Here you go."

Logan studied it and said, "Guys, look at the last word of each verse." Logan grabbed a pen off Bryan's desk and started underlining. Dr. Arenot and Bryan closely watched what he was doing…

Odin, god of wisdom, knowledge, and magic,
do mortals of Midgard <u>follow</u>,

Sitting on high throne beside Frigg, sons Thor,
Baldr and Váli, and Frigg's hens, seven in
<u>line</u>.

Odin taught his hens how to use their power,
knowledge and wisdom <u>within</u>,

And how to read the writings from Midgard's
mortal <u>codex</u>,

But to his dearest, he taught all the universe's
secrets, for she had wanted <u>to</u>,

For she sat ready to rule justly when Odin's
time ended and then, <u>Frigg's</u>.

The Hidden Coordinate by Marc Jacobs

But soon the God of Death came for the
Vanir, Odin, his sons and his <u>hens</u>,

Odin beckoned the Ljósálfar and his allies for
help, no matter where <u>from</u>,

He beckoned the Æsir and Vanir, for a new
Æsir-Vanir War did they <u>face</u>.

Not with each other, but with Death and its
Dökkálfar, for a victory on Vanir none could
be assured <u>of</u>,

Fear did Odin, the coming of Death, that from
Vanir's peak he called upon the power of time
using the stars, moons and <u>sun</u>,

To fight a battle the Æsir-Vanir could not win
alone, for they lacked the strength <u>to</u>,

Still, to battle did Thor, Baldr and Váli come,
asking only <u>where</u>.

The war raged on, Death seized the home of
the <u>Vanirens</u>,

Desperate, Odin summoned he who overturns
space and time, so the Vanir could <u>live</u>

"Do you see it?" asked Logan. "The last words of each verse,
when put together, form a sentence that says, 'Follow line within
codex to Frigg's Hens from face of sun to where Vanirens live.'"
They were both surprised, stunned actually. Could there really be a
hidden message in *The Final Journey of the Vanir*, hanging on the
last word of each verse? And Logan wasn't done...

"And if you replace 'Frigg's Hens' with the words 'the
Pleiades,' it reads, 'Follow line within codex to the Pleiades from
face of sun to where Vanirens live.' Hey Bryan, do you mind if I sit
down real quick to check something on Google?"

"Uh, no prob." Bryan stood up and stepped aside to allow Logan to sit down at the computer. He googled the words: Voynich, manuscript, stars, and sun and waited to see what came up. "There it is!" shouted Logan excitedly at the sight of one of the images of the Voynich manuscript that his search pulled up. He opened the image into a full screen and got up to let Bryan sit back down.

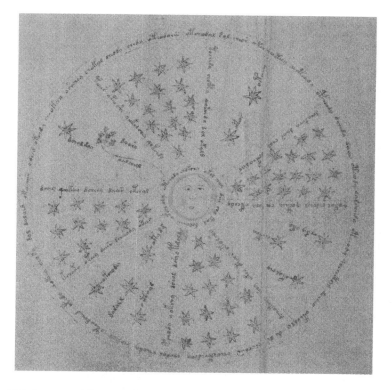

"Holy crap!" exclaimed Bryan fascinated. "There's a face on that sun just like that sentence you put together!"

"And if you notice, there's a line going out from it, too, a meandering, s-shaped line leading right to the seven stars at 10 o'clock." Logan looked at the professor. "Dr. Arenot, do you remember what you said yesterday when Emma mentioned how the seven stars in this image reminded her of the Pleiades?"

"Yes, I said others had made that observation, too."

174

"Exactly!" said Logan emphatically. "There's a line from the face of the sun to the Pleiades, and if you follow the line, it leads right to the second star in the left row…"

"Are you sure?" asked Dr. Arenot, uncertain since the line stopped short of the star Logan was referring to.

"I think so," replied Logan. "Bryan, can you print this one out also?"

"Sure." Bryan hit print, pulled it off his LaserJet and handed it to Logan. This time, using a red pen he grabbed from Bryan's desk, he finished off the line that started from the sun, extrapolating where it might end up based on where the meandering line was heading before it stopped. His line continued all the way to the second star in the left row…

"Dr. Arenot, that's where the Vanir went!" declared Logan.

"What do the words at the end of the last five verses mean?" asked Bryan.

Spurred by Bryan's question, Logan looked back down at the page and underlined the last word in the remaining verses:

> To lead the Vanir to a home anew, and to hide
> Odin's dearest within space and time itself,
> forever away from <u>battle</u>.

> Odin then smote the Dökkálfar, but the search
> for peace <u>continues</u>,

> As the darkness of Death rages on in Midgard,
> where no longer can Odin <u>help</u>,

> For how the battle in the hidden city ends is
> up to <u>us</u>,

> Alas, Odin despair, the sun is gone, the sun is
> gone, and the God of Death has her, <u>now</u>.

176

The last word of each of the final five verses formed the sentence, '*Battle continues, help us now.*' Logan's face went flush.

Oblivious to the look on Logan's face, Bryan asked, "What does 'Battle continues, help us now,' mean?"

Logan thought back to his conversation with Emma in the Situation Room right before General Covington ushered her and Professor Quimbey away. Emma had joked at the time, "If we get in any trouble, I'll text you a secret code or something, something only you'll know like, '*Help Us Now.*'" Could Emma and Professor Quimbey still be alive?

"Logan, are you okay?" asked Bryan, now noticing Logan's expression. "You look like you just saw a ghost."

"Dr. Arenot," Logan began, "right before Emma and Jill left with General Covington, Emma joked if they got into any trouble that she would text me a secret code or something that only I would know. I mean, she was only kidding at the time, but…"

"What was the secret code?" asked Dr. Arenot.

"*Help us now.*"

Now, Dr. Arenot looked like he'd seen a ghost. "But how's that possible?"

"Yeah, dude, how?" agreed Bryan. "This poem's ancient."

"Bryan, I know this will come as a shock, but Dr. Arenot and I work for a top-secret government—"

"Logan!" snapped Dr. Arenot. "You can't tell him that…"

"It's okay, we can trust him," said Logan.

"You can totally trust me!" exclaimed Bryan. "Just call me Alfred Pennyworth."

"Nice," said Logan, complimenting Bryan's comic book reference.

"Who's Alfred Pennyworth?" asked Dr. Arenot.

Bryan fired back, "You don't know Batman?"

"Well, of course, I know Batman, but—"

Bryan cut him off since the professor clearly didn't know Batman *that* well. "Alfred Pennyworth is Bruce Wayne's aka *Batman's* loyal aid and tireless butler at Wayne Manor, and most importantly, he's Batman's trusted friend, always secretly helping him behind the scenes while Batman runs around saving Gotham City from villains. That's me!"

Arenot shrugged. "Well, if Batman has a confidante, then I suppose we can clue you in."

Logan resumed explaining. "We've been working on something called the Pegasus Project that conducts research into alien-technology capable of time-travel, which is why I think that the 800-year-old message was meant for me."

Bryan grinned with glee as his wildest sci-fi dreams were coming true. "Coooolllll," he said, not doubting a word Logan said, even for a second. "And let me guess, the alien-technology you're talking about comes from the Vanir people?"

"You got it," replied Logan.

"Dude, this is sooooo awesome," uttered Bryan. "But why do you think that message is from Emma? Where is she?"

Logan explained. "Last night, the U.S. government sent Emma and Dr. Arenot's wife, Professor Jill Quimbey, and a covert military team into the mountains in Russia to investigate signals they thought might be coming from the technology I just mentioned. There was an accident, some kind of explosion, and Emma and Jill were caught up in it, or we thought they were until now."

"And that's when we lost contact with them... with their whole team," added Dr. Arenot.

Logan continued. "The explosion must have done something to send them back in time, or to another place, or to another dimension, or something, I don't know, but that message tells me they survived whatever happened in Russia. And if there's a possibility they're still alive, we have to figure out how to find them."

"And you think they're at that star in the Voynich Manuscript image you just drew your line to?" asked Bryan.

Logan responded, "I don't know where they are..."

"Or when..." added Dr. Arenot.

"Right," replied Logan. "But if that star is where the Vanir went, that's where we need to go because the Vanir will know how to find Emma and Jill. We just have to figure out how to get there."

"That's easy," said Bryan.

"It is?" asked Dr. Arenot.

"Yup, just start by finding the one who took them there, that deity Odin summoned in the poem called, 'he who overturns space and time.'" Bryan typed the phrase 'he who overturns space and time' into Google and pages of search results came up. "And there you have it... take a look," said Bryan, leaning back so they could read his laptop screen.

Nearly all the results contained the name *Pachacuti* or *Pachakutiq* in the title.

The instant Dr. Arenot saw the name, he remembered exactly where he'd come across it before: in Hiram Bingham's famous book, the *Lost City of the Incas*. "Of course!" the professor realized. "Pachacuti was an Inca emperor in the 15th century who lived in a palace hidden above the clouds."

"Where?" asked Logan.

"High up in the Andes Mountains in Peru," replied Dr. Arenot.

"The Andes Mountains?" questioned Logan. He didn't expect a deity mentioned in Norse mythology to live in Peru with the Incas.

"*Machu Picchu*," replied Dr. Arenot, "in Cusco, Peru, to be exact. The lost city of the Incas."

"Dr. Arenot, perhaps Machu Picchu is the 'hidden city' referred to in the second to last verse of *The Final Journey of the Vanir*," commented Logan.

"Maybe, but honestly, I don't understand how Snorri Sturluson or his father would have known about Machu Picchu which wasn't even built until hundreds of years after *The Final Journey of the Vanir* was written. But none of this makes sense at this point, so…"

"Only one way to find out," said Logan. "Bryan, can you look up flights from the D.C. area to Cusco… just curious what's available on short notice."

"Sure, no problem," replied Bryan. He typed it in, read, and responded, "Nothing until a day after tomorrow, but it's also got nearly two days' worth of connections. Plenty after that, though. What day are you thinking?"

Looking at Dr. Arenot, Logan said, "We can't wait two or three days to get there! Emma and Jill are in trouble! That S.O.S. for help—"

"Was sent over 800 years ago," interrupted Dr. Arenot.

"We don't know that," countered Logan. "I mean, all we know for sure is that wherever they are, whenever they are, they are in trouble and need our help. Who knows how, and even if, this time travel stuff works. I just know I can't sit around for three days waiting to find a solution."

"Don't you guys have access to private government jets and stuff?" asked Bryan.

"We did," lamented Dr. Arenot.

"Wait a minute, perhaps we still do," suggested Logan. "I know someone who might be able to help us."

"Who?" asked Dr. Arenot.

"Someone Emma and I met yesterday," responded Logan. "Her father's a charter jet pilot."

"Call her," urged Dr. Arenot. "And tell her whatever it costs, we'll pay for it. I can cover it." However expensive the private flight was, Dr. Arenot was glad that Jill's wealthy family trust could definitely afford it.

"I don't have her number," Logan replied. "Come to think of it, I don't even know her last name, but I know where she lives..."

"Well, that's a start," remarked Dr. Arenot. "Where?"

"Georgetown. If we leave now, we might be able to get there before it gets too late." Logan folded up all the pages Bryan had printed for him and put them in his back pocket.

He also grabbed a small pencil off Bryan's desk in case he needed one down the road.

"You guys want a ride?" offered Bryan. "It'll be a heck of a lot faster than taking the train at this hour."

"Bryan, we can't ask you to do that. It's easily a couple of hours away," said Logan.

"Really, it's fine. I want to help you, and my car's right out back. It'll save you a ton of time. What do you say?"

Dr. Arenot had no objection. "Okay with me."

Logan asked one more time, "Are you sure?"

"*Totally*. I *want* to help, and this is seriously the coolest thing I've ever been a part of in my entire life! Besides, I manage a comic book shop. Trust me, I live for stuff like this, and as I said before, you can count on me!"

"Dude, you're awesome!" declared Logan, giving Bryan a high-five. "Alright then, let's go."

Bryan smiled and announced, "To the Batmobile!"

And just like that, Batman, Robin, and Pennyworth were off, on their way back to Gotham City...

Chapter 14 – A Small Favor

Bryan drove up to Harbin Hall in the middle of Georgetown University's campus. The dorm was a nine-story colonial-style building with vertical sections of red-brick alternating with sections of white stucco and dorm room windows. Bryan found a spot across the street and parked. They got out, crossed the road, and entered Harbin Hall's lobby.

"You sure you don't want us to go up with you?" asked Dr. Arenot.

"I'm sure," replied Logan. "I should talk to her myself first, considering I'm asking a favor and I don't even know her last name."

"Okay, we'll be waiting down here when you're done," said Dr. Arenot.

Bryan and Dr. Arenot found a seat on a lobby couch, while Logan proceeded upstairs to the 7th floor. When the elevator doors re-opened, Logan walked out onto a floor offering three directions to go based on the building's unique three-leaf clover shape. The design allowed Harbin to have a "cluster" system with each floor divided into wings broken down by gender. Looking at the map on the wall opposite the elevator, the 7th floor had two male-student clusters and one female. Logan made a right to head down the hall to the female-student cluster, which was bustling with evening social activity.

"Hi there!" said a young woman sitting in the common area on a sofa with three dormmates. "Can we help you?"

"Uh, yeah, that'd be great," replied Logan.

"You're cute. What's your name?" asked another student.

They all rolled their eyes. "There goes Zoe, again," teased the first student. The others laughed.

"You know it!" replied Zoe proudly. "Like he's coming here to see you…"

Logan, slightly embarrassed, said, "Hi, I'm Logan. I'm looking for Allysa."

"Anders or Small?" asked a third student.

"I don't know, actually," Logan responded. "She's got long blond hair, tied back in a ponytail…"

"Anders," replied the third student. "Book girl's in the third room on the right. Have fun…"

"Thanks," said Logan, glad to escape the awkward conversation. He made his way to Allysa's room. When he got there, the door was partially ajar. He couldn't see inside but a light was on. Logan knocked.

"Come in," said a voice.

Logan pushed open the door and saw Allysa sitting on her bed, reading a book beneath a bright desk lamp. The other bed in the room was empty as Allysa's roommate was out. Just like the first time he met her, Allysa was wearing casual sweats.

"Umm, hi…," she said guardedly, surprised to see Logan.

"Hi," Logan replied back. "Can I talk to you?"

"Uh, yeah, I guess," responded Allysa, still unsure why he was there.

Logan walked all the way in and closed the door halfway. "Are you still reading that book about faulty stars?" he asked.

"Not exactly…" Allysa blushed, and then, sheepishly lowered the book she was reading to show him. It was *Density: A Black Hole's Destiny*, by Dr. Francis Juliard.

Logan was impressed. "Wow. Really?"

"Oh, my god, I'm so embarrassed right now."

"Don't be! Why would you be?"

"I'm not crushing on you, I swear, please don't think that! That's not why I'm reading it…"

"I'm not thinking that…"

"It's just, after talking to you yesterday, I feel like I want my major to be something that fascinates me. Political science, psychology, those are awesome majors, but I've always been drawn to the stars. I know I joked about how crazy-hard all the math and physics probably is, but I wanted to see if it's something I could do. So, I got the book, just to see."

"You can totally do it! Astronomy's not just about math and physics, you know. You'll figure it out. It's more important to be into what you're studying. If you are, no matter what it is, it'll come easier."

"Do you really think so? Because some of the stuff in here, I really don't get, but it's totally interesting. I don't want to give up just because of the math. I mean, I was decent in math and physics in high school…"

"Well, you got into Georgetown, so I bet you were more than decent."

"Yeah, well, I'm no Steven Hawking, let's put it that way."

"So what! Nobody is."

"Thanks," said Allysa, appreciating his encouragement. She was quiet for a moment, then, somewhat vulnerably asked, "I'm sorry, why are you here?" She didn't ask it in a harsh or defensive manner, but she was definitely wondering.

"I need a *small* favor." He sheepishly emphasized the word 'small' knowing that it would be a big one.

"A small favor? Sure. What?"

"Your dad has access to charter jets, right?"

"Well, yeah, but they're not *his* jets. They're his company's."

"Are you able to call him and see if he can arrange a charter flight for a friend of mine?"

"Sure, but you know chartering a plane is a bit more expensive than a Southwest ticket, right?"

"My friend can pay for it."

"When I say a bit more expensive, I mean it costs a *fortune*."

"He knows." Logan reached into his pocket and pulled out Dr. Arenot's black card. He handed it to Allysa.

Slightly surprised, she responded, "Oh, umm, okay, when—"

"Tonight…"

"*Tonight?*" Allysa laughed. "It's like, 10:15 pm! Your friend must really be in a hurry. Okay, where to, Mr. Short Notice? And by the way, I have no idea if this is even doable."

If she thought that was funny, Logan knew she would love his next response: "Peru."

"A *small* favor?" chuckled Allysa.

"Believe me, I wouldn't be asking if it wasn't important."

"What's so important that your friend wants to drop so much money for an ASAP charter like this?"

Logan had anticipated this question, so he and Dr. Arenot had already worked up an explanation. "His niece injured herself climbing through the Andes on a trip to Machu Picchu. He's got to get down there immediately."

"Oh, no!" said Allysa. "Is she okay?"

"I don't know, but that's why he's got to get there fast."

"Where does your friend live?"

"Actually, he's waiting downstairs in the lobby."

"Downstairs, in the lobby, right now?" questioned Allysa.

"Yep."

"Wow, when you said ASAP, you meant it. Umm, alright. I guess I can call my dad now. What's his name in case my dad asks? He'll need it to fill out the FAA passenger manifest."

"It's on the card I handed you," Logan responded.

"Oh, right, duh." She read the name on the card, "Jonas Arenot, got it."

Logan piped up, "Put me on there, too. I'm going with him… so both of us."

Allysa, somewhat embarrassed, replied, "I don't actually know your last name. What is it?"

"West."

"West... Logan West," mocked Allysa in a formal voice. "Sounds like a movie name," she teased. "And where are you guys flying to in Peru, exactly?"

"Cusco."

"Okay, give me a few minutes to call my dad. If you want, you can wait downstairs in the lobby with your friend, and I'll come down after I talk to him and let you know what he says."

"That would be awesome."

"I know," replied Allysa with a proud grin.

"Allysa, seriously, thank you," said Logan as he left the room.

Allysa smiled as Logan departed. She got up to grab her phone from her desk, and right before dialing her father, she said to herself, "Well, this is a first."

ΔΔΔΔΔΔΔΔΔΔΔΔ

About 20 minutes later, Allysa emerged from the lobby elevator, now wearing jeans, a black sweater, tennis shoes, and a bit of makeup. While Logan may have caught her looking her worst, she wasn't about to let Logan's friend see her that way. She had a great big smile on her face which, from afar, looked like good news. She approached the couch where Logan was sitting.

"Oh... there're three of you," said Allysa, not expecting to see Dr. Arenot *and* Bryan. They all stood up and Logan made introductions.

"Allysa, this is Dr. Jonas Arenot."

Allysa was caught off guard. She didn't expect Logan's friend to be a doctor, nor as old as he was. "Nice to meet you, Dr. Arenot. I'm so sorry to hear about your niece."

"Thank you," responded the professor, "and thank you for helping us. Either way, I appreciate you trying."

Logan continued. "And this is our friend, Bryan."

"Hi," said Bryan. He found himself instantly taken with Allysa's bright smile and alluring gaze.

"Hi," responded Allysa with a blushing grin. "So, are you flying down to Peru, too? Because I didn't give my dad your name."

"No, I'm just the driver tonight."

"Does that mean your dad can do it?" asked Logan.

"Yep. You guys are so lucky he can't say no to his little girl. He's already made the arrangements with scheduling and his company's logging your flight info with the FAA, right now. You've got to get to Martin State Airport in Maryland by 11:45 pm. You're flying out on Tail Number..." Allysa looked at the notes she took down on her phone. "...Tail Number N783YA. If you don't take off by midnight, you can't fly out tonight. Shouldn't be a problem though. Martin's less than an hour from here this time of night."

"Is your dad piloting the flight?" asked Logan.

"No. He's been flying several days straight. Captain Bill's handling the flight."

"This is great news... thank you!" said Dr. Arenot.

"Well, I'm not sure you'll want to thank me after you see the price tag, but because of your unfortunate emergency circumstances, he was able to get you a nice discount. Before I forget, here's your black card back." She handed him his card.

"Do you know Captain Bill?" asked Logan.

"Uh-huh. He's like family. He's been flying with my dad at SkyBlue Jets for years."

Dr. Arenot looked at his watch and said, "If we're going to make it, we better get going. Bryan, you've still got to drive us both to our apartments so we can grab our passports."

"Bryan, do you want some company?" asked Allysa. "I mean, it's a long drive. So this way, you'll have company on the way back, and I'd love the chance to surprise Captain Bill anyway."

"Sure!" responded Bryan eagerly. He decided not to mention that he lived in Philly or that Martin State Airport was on his way home. "Okay, let's go."

The four of them took off. Bryan drove by Logan's and Dr. Arenot's apartments so they could run inside and grab their passports. Neither bothered to pack anything else. There wasn't time. Then, they headed north to Maryland. Allysa sat upfront with Bryan chatting, while Dr. Arenot and Logan decompressed in the backseat.

Once they got closer to Martin State Airport, Logan perked back up and asked Allysa, "So, what do we do when we get there?"

"You check-in at SkyBlue's office in Hangar 3. The jet will be waiting for you on the tarmac when you arrive. Bryan can basically drive you right up to it after check-in."

"Sounds like you've done this before," commented Logan.

With a grin, Allysa replied, "A few times. One of the perks of having a pilot for a dad."

They reached the airport in the heart of Middle River, Maryland, at 11:42 pm with no time to spare. Hangar #3 was accessible through a private gate entrance. Pulling up to it, Bryan pressed the button on the call-in box and waited.

"May I help you?" said a female voice through the box.

Bryan replied, "We're here for a late-night flight..."

Allysa once again looked at the notes she took on her phone and, from the passenger seat, leaned over and said out Bryan's window, "On Tail Number N783Y—"

The gate buzzed open before she finished. Once the gate retracted, Bryan drove in and up a narrow road which continued to Hangar #3 until they came to SkyBlue's well-lit office. Bryan stopped in front of the double-glass door entrance to allow Logan, Dr. Arenot, and Allysa to jump out while he waited outside in the car.

They walked into the lobby where the check-in receptionist and a security guard sat behind a counter. The lobby had plush couches, a fancy automated coffee-machine, a pile of magazines on an oversized square, a glass coffee table, and lots of plants. It was the cushy lobby of the high-end, charter jet flying elite, without security checkpoints or body scanners.

"Good evening," said the young, dark-haired receptionist behind the desk to the late-night group. "I'm Kira." Looking at Allysa, she said, "You must be Captain Anders's daughter?"

Allysa hadn't met her before, but Kira obviously knew who she was. Allysa responded, "Yep, that's me. How'd you draw the short straw for tonight?"

"Someone's gotta work the late shift, so as long as they're paying overtime, that someone's me!" Kira seemed happy with it. The security guard sitting to her right, on the other hand, appeared less enthusiastic with his lot in life. His feet were lazily planted up on the reception desk while he was drinking a cup of coffee.

Kira looked at Logan and Dr. Arenot. "Didn't think you guys were going to make it. So, you two are the ones flying this evening, huh?"

"Yep," replied Logan.

"Yes, ma'am," said Dr. Arenot.

"You guys can head to the tarmac. Go to Tail Number X374TZ."

Allysa was confused. "Are you sure that's right? I thought they were flying Tail Number…" Allysa looked at her phone again. "Number N783—"

"We had to make a last-minute change," interrupted Kira, momentarily glancing at the security guard. "You gentlemen are now flying X374TZ. I see you've got a car outside… you can drive up to it." Looking at Allysa, she asked, "Do you know the way?"

"Yeah, pretty sure," said Allysa, finding the whole exchange odd.

Kira provided directions anyway. "Go around the hangar, head left, it'll be on the far end. It's the only plane out there right now. You'll see it. Captain Bill's already on board."

"You don't need to see our IDs or passports?" asked Logan.

"Are you Logan West?"

"Yeah…"

"Are you Jonas Arenot?"

"Uh-huh."

"Great, you're both cleared to go."

"You don't need anything from us?" asked Logan, having expected more scrutiny.

"Nope. This ain't the TSA. You guys are good to go."

"I don't need to sign anything for my credit card?" asked Dr. Arenot.

"Nope, it's all taken care of."

"Oh," replied Dr. Arenot.

"Have a good flight," said Kira.

They turned around and returned to the car. Bryan drove to the tarmac and made a left just beyond the hangar. He proceeded to the massive white business jet parked right where Kira said it would be, baring Tail Number X374TZ. The plane, which was far bigger than Allysa expected, sat alone on the tarmac at this late hour except for the two ground-crew members inspecting the jet's wheels. Bryan drove up to the plane, stopping 30 feet short of its retractable staircase.

"Now, that's a serious toy," commented Bryan, never having been this close to a private jet before.

"Wait 'til you see the inside," remarked Allysa.

"Really?" asked Bryan. "We can do that?"

"Totally. Things work a bit different at executive airports than they do at commercial airports," Allysa responded. "They're not taking off for a few minutes. I'm sure Captain Bill will let you look around for a second."

"Awesome," replied Bryan. He put the car in park. They all popped out, walked to the jet, and climbed the stairs.

The interior was ginormous and spectacular: leather seats, couches, tables, a bar, a kitchenette, digital monitors, and tons of space. After spending some time poking around, Bryan uttered, "Wow!"

"You like it?" asked Allysa rhetorically.

"This is what I'd like to be able to do with my money someday," said Bryan.

"You're going to have to build a few more websites," cracked Logan. "Like, a *lot* more."

The cockpit door remained closed. Presumably, Captain Bill was in the middle of flight preparation. Usually, the captain would come out to greet the passengers, but clearly, he wasn't ready yet, probably because of the flight's last-minute nature. Allysa walked up and knocked on the cockpit door anyway. No one answered. She knocked again, but still, no answer.

"Huh, that's odd," Allysa thought. She wanted to say hello, but obviously, Captain Bill was still busy. Disappointed, she decided not to interrupt him again. Because they were departing shortly, Allysa said, "Okay, I guess this is it, then."

"Allysa, Bryan, seriously, thank you both *so* much for your help," said Logan, high-fiving Bryan and giving Allysa a quick thank you hug.

Dr. Arenot shook Allysa's and Bryan's hands to say good-bye.

"Good luck," said Bryan. "Will you please let me know how everything goes?"

"Yes, please let us know how your niece is," added Allysa.

"Definitely," responded Dr. Arenot.

Bryan turned to Allysa. "You ready to drive back?"

"Yep."

"Maybe on the way back we can—"

Unexpectedly, the two ground crew members who had been working on the wheels boarded the plane, followed by a third man wearing a suit. The three men drew guns and pointed them at the foursome, motioning for them to sit.

194

"What's this all about?!" shouted Logan.

Allysa was confused. "Hey, you can't—"

"Shut up, and sit down! All of you!" ordered the man wearing the suit. He raised a mini walkie-talkie to his mouth and said in Russian, "Close the stairs. I've got them." The jet stairs retracted and one of the other men closed and locked the outer door.

"Dmitri, ready to depart?" asked a voice in Russian out of the walkie-talkie.

Dmitri responded in Russian, "Yes, let's go!"

The jet began taxing away from the hangar toward the runway.

"Where are you taking us?" demanded Dr. Arenot.

"Allysa, Bryan, they have nothing to do with this, whatever this is! Let them go!" insisted Logan.

"Nothing will happen to them *if* you cooperate," Dmitri responded.

"You're not going to get very far hijacking a SkyBlue jet," commented Allysa. "The moment the tower or FAA sees it veer off course—"

"Well, Ms. Anders, it's a good thing this is *our* plane. The plane your dad arranged for you took off a few minutes ago, and with the minor course correction we inputted remotely in a now-modified FAA flight plan, it should be landing in Buenos Aires tomorrow right as expected. So, no one will suspect a thing."

"Captain Bill?!" cried Allysa, worried for him.

"Let's just say he's no longer the captain, and he'll remain unharmed as long as you all do as you're told."

"You can't do this!" yelled Dr. Arenot, standing up in Dmitri's direction.

The 'ground crewmen' stepped in front of Dmitri, put their guns in Dr. Arenot's face, and forced him back down.

Shaking his head and waving his own gun in Dr. Arenot's direction, Dmitri said, "I suggest you make yourself comfortable, Professor, before someone gets hurt. It's a long flight to Moscow."

"Moscow!" shouted Allysa. "Logan, what's this all about?"

"I don't know…"

Allysa broke for the exit door, hoping to create an escape opportunity for them before they took off. One of Dmitri's men grabbed her body mid-stride and threw her into a chair. Angered by watching the Russian thug manhandle Allysa, Bryan lunged at the man, but he quickly struck Bryan in the side of the head with a gun, knocking Bryan to the ground, out cold. Bryan was still breathing, but he had a cut on the side of his head where the gun has struck him.

A voice blared out from the cabin speakers in Russian, saying "Dmitri… he's ready for them."

The plane straightened out on the runway and accelerated into take-off. X374TZ went airborne a few seconds later, accelerating at a steep angle.

Dmitri turned on a video monitor on the passenger cabin's front wall right where they sat. On the screen appeared a very large and burly, dark-blue-eyed man with blond hair, a menacing goatee, and a scar down his right cheek. The man wore a dark navy suit, which didn't suggest a military rank, but the men on the plane nonetheless saluted him and even appeared intimidated.

In Russian, Dmitri said, "Minister, we are now in the air, on our way, we will arrive in 10½ hours."

196

"Thank you, Dmitri," replied the minister in English. Looking directly at Logan, he said, "Mr. West, it's nice to finally meet you." Although polite, he sounded sinister.

"I wish I could say the same. Do I know you?"

The minister paused before responding, "No, but I know you. I've been watching all of you for quite some time since Bologna."

Somewhat shaken by the revelation, Logan responded, "Why would—"

"My name is Viktor Menputyn."

Logan recognized the name. "The Russian Foreign Affairs Minister?"

"And incoming Prime Minister," whispered Dr. Arenot to Logan, well-aware that Minister Menputyn had recently been nominated to the position by Russian President Vladimir Koravsky, after former-Prime Minister Teravspov's unexpected passing two weeks ago. Only Menputyn's upcoming confirmation by the Federal Assembly of Russia, a mere formality, stood in the way of his ascension to second-in-command of Russia.

The minister was impressed. "Professor, I see you've been watching CNN…"

"You didn't really kidnap us at gunpoint to discuss what we're watching on TV, did you?" questioned Logan.

Minister Menputyn liked Logan's feistiness. He expected nothing less. "Mr. West, I honestly don't know what they let you watch down in the Pentagon basement nor do I care, but I assume you watched the video feed of your comrades raiding my science outpost early this morning, no?"

"That's what you call a base with stolen U.S. technology hidden in the mountains and guarded by Russian soldiers, a 'science outpost?'"

"We have a right to protect that which is ours, Mr. West. We knew it was only a matter of time before your U.S. invaded Chersky. Your president is as predictable as a clock."

"*That which is yours?*" responded Logan, alluding to the Russian government's theft of the Vaniryan technology from the U.S.

"Do you really think that technology belongs to the United States, Mr. West? Do you honestly believe, a smart young man like yourself, that the Vaniryans left it behind for America, only?"

"Logan, Dr. Arenot, what's going on?" asked Allysa. "Stolen U.S. technology? An invasion of Russia?"

"Shut up!" snapped one of Dmitri's men.

Meanwhile, Bryan was starting to come to, sitting up, groggily rubbing the side of his head. Allysa dropped to a knee to help him.

The minister continued. "You Americans lay claim to technology left behind by extraterrestrial beings for all mankind to enjoy, and your president acts like it's his personal property to hide down in his Pegasus vault when he should be embracing his science comrades around the world in this journey of discovery."

"So, you're upset you weren't selected for the science team?" replied Logan.

"Let me remind you Mr. West who used the technology to invade another country first. Maybe you should question who the aggressors really are."

"Why are you taking us to Moscow?" asked Logan.

"I'm quite sure you know why. You and Dr. Arenot will help Russia, and Russia will help you."

Logan didn't understand. "And how, exactly, is Russia going to help us?"

Minister Menputyn replied coldly, "By not killing you."

"Now, you're blackmailing us with our lives?" replied Logan, livid.

"I like to call it doing business, Mr. West. You come to Moscow and show us how the technology works and we will make sure we don't kill you. You have my word."

"You mean, show you how to use the portal technology so you can launch a retaliatory attack inside U.S. soil?" asked Dr. Arenot.

"Doctor, you misunderstand Roscosmos' intentions, but our space program's goals are no concern of yours, especially at this very moment. I suggest you be wise, professor."

"We don't know how the z-particles work," said Logan. "Our involvement in the Pegasus Project is totally unrelated to the science and technology behind them."

The minister eyed them both. He didn't believe Logan, not with all the time they spent in the Pentagon working on the Pegasus Project. Staring back at Logan, he said, "I expected more from one of the only two people on Earth to have visited Vanirya." The minister coolly got up from the desk he sat behind and said, "I hope you're smarter when I see you in Moscow."

"Wait!" blurted Logan.

"Yes…," responded the minister, sitting back down.

"If you want us to help you, then you must help us, first," said Logan.

"I'm listening, Mr. West."

Logan explained. "We don't know how the z-particles work, but we know who does."

"Who?"

"The Vaniryans," replied Logan.

"Their star is gone, Mr. West, and so are the Vaniryans. Don't bluff me." The minister made eye contact with Dmitri, who subsequently lifted his gun and pointed it at Bryan's head. Bryan tensed up.

Logan gulped and responded, "Yes, but we believe they left the planet before their star went supernova, and we think we know where they went."

"And where is that, Mr. West?"

"We don't know for sure, but we think the answer's at Machu Picchu. That's why we were going there. You're wasting your time flying us to Russia when our best chance of understanding the z-particles is in Peru."

"And why should I believe you?"

"Because if I'm not telling you the truth, you're going to kill us. If you don't believe me, you might as well just shoot us now."

Logan's comment stunned Jonas, Bryan, and Allysa. They weren't prepared for Logan's daring bluff.

After a momentary pause and careful study of Logan's eyes, the minister said in Russian, "Dmitri, go make arrangements with Andrei to fly the plane to Peru. You will stay with them the whole time."

"Yes, minister."

Dmitri walked up to the cabin door, knocked two times, paused, and then knocked again. The door opened. Dmitri walked in.

Shortly thereafter, the plane began to change direction. They could feel it turning.

"We're changing direction," observed Dr. Arenot.

"Yes, Professor," said the minister. "You are turning to Peru. We will help you find what you are looking for at Machu Picchu, and you will share what you find with Russia. And then, we will *evaluate* your situation, again. Is that understood?"

Logan nodded.

"I know you want to believe Russia is your enemy, but we are not. We are part of humanity, just like you. I will send my men with you to make sure you hold up your end of the bargain. I expect these terms are acceptable?"

Logan agreed. It certainly beat the alternative.

"Shall I see any more trouble from any of you?"

They each shook their heads.

"Good," replied the minister. Speaking to his remaining two men, he added, "Take their phones." His men confiscated their cellphones as instructed. He had just a few more words for the Americans… "It is a long flight to Peru. I hope you will enjoy the hospitality of my airplane. And good luck to you." The video feed went dark. The minister's men put their guns away and motioned for the Americans to head to the back of the plane.

Logan immediately turned to Bryan. "Are you okay?" Logan asked him, worried about the blow he had sustained to the side of his head.

"Yeah, I'm alright," Bryan replied, wincing a little and rubbing off some blood where the gun had struck him.

Logan next looked at Allysa. She appeared confused, angry, and frightened. It was pretty obvious to him how he was going to spend the flight's first hour. He was about to say something, but Allysa spoke up first.

"Logan, you have some explaining to do, like, a lot," she said.

Regretfully, Logan replied, "I know."

Chapter 15 – A Long Way From Home

Emma removed her hands from her face to find herself laying on the soft marsh-like ground among a forest of enormous trees. Vines dangled from above. Professor Quimbey laid slightly behind her and Captain Evans a few feet in front. "Where are we?" Emma wondered, sitting up. It was so dark underneath the trees that it was hard to tell, although a purple-hue seeped through the treetops.

The last thing she remembered, the three of them had spotted a door leading into the mountain during Red Team's firefight in Chersky, and after watching Russian soldiers run out of it, they snuck in...

ΔΔΔΔΔΔΔΔΔΔΔΔ

After the Russian soldiers ran out of the door, Captain Evans led Emma and Professor Quimbey in. Captain Evans slammed the door shut and locked it from inside, leaving the gunfire behind. "Here, follow me," she said, holding her gun. They cautiously made their way down a concrete tunnel sporadically lit by flickering overhead lighting.

"Does anyone else hear a humming sound?" whispered Emma.

"I do, too," replied Professor Quimbey.

"Quiet," Captain Evans whispered. They kept going. They came to an intersection of tunnels heading left and right. There was a flight of stairs leading down in the tunnel to the right. Voices came from the left, so Captain Evans motioned right. Just as they descended the steps, they heard a muffled boom followed by a rumbling sound, and the mountain momentarily shook.

"What was that?" asked Professor Quimbey.

"Was that an explosion?" wondered Emma.

"I don't know. Let's keep going," replied Captain Evans.

The stairs led down to another hallway lined with doors set back in alcoves. The corridor continued until disappearing around a bend. After making the turn, they heard footsteps fast approaching from behind.

"Here, quick," said Captain Evans.

They ducked into an alcove and stood stiff with their backs to the inner wall on the side the footsteps were coming from. Seconds later, a group of Russian soldiers ran by without seeing the American intruders, too focused on wherever they were running to notice. Once the soldiers passed, Captain Evans, Emma, and Professor Quimbey resumed their journey down the corridor, keeping their eyes and ears out for more soldiers. They came to another descending staircase. A pulsating glow came from the bottom of the stairs, along with frantic panicked shouting.

"Something's wrong down there," said Captain Evans. "You two wait here. I'm going in for a closer look."

"Uh, no thank you… I'm going wherever you go," said Emma, uncomfortable being left alone in the Russian base.

"Me, too," said Professor Quimbey, "if you don't mind."

"Fine. Stay close, be ready."

The threesome inched down the steps which made a sharp left halfway down. Captain Evans peeked around the corner and what she saw shocked her…

The stairs spilled out into an oversized control room filled with white-coat scientists running around. Half the ceiling had collapsed and scientists, as well as soldiers, were desperately trying to free those trapped beneath fallen debris. Meanwhile, numerous other scientists were urgently trying to gain control of a randomly pulsating white light reminiscent of the portal back at Pegasus West, but without the same rectangular shape or definition. This portal, if it could be called that, appeared out of control, and the scrambling scientists looked like they didn't know what to do. They just kept shouting in Russian, "Shut it down! Turn it off! Hurry!" With so much commotion going on and no one focused on the staircase, Captain Evans motioned for Emma and Professor Quimbey to sneak a peek.

"They're trying to shut the thing down," translated Captain Evans. "What does that look like to you two?"

The mountain started rumbling and the white light pulsed again, resembling a solar flare reaching out to ensnare the scientists. Everyone in its path dove to avoid it. During the commotion, one Russian soldier saw them peeking into the room and reached for his weapon, but he never got the chance to fire it…

In that instant, another explosion rocked the room, causing additional sections of the ceiling to collapse on top of most of the remaining scientists and soldiers, including the one who had spotted them. The explosion shook the room so violently that Captain Evans, Professor Quimbey, and Emma tumbled down several steps, virtually into the control room. A split second later, one final explosive flare-up of the light portal shot out toward Emma, Professor Quimbey, and Captain Evans. Emma covered her face with her hands as the light swallowed her whole right before the mountain collapsed on the rest of the control room…

The next thing Emma knew they were in the dark forest of enormous trees. She stood up and that's when she saw a gun pointed at her head, held by a Russian scientist who was also caught up in the portal's final flare-up along with them. In fact, there were three Russian scientists with them in the unfamiliar forest. Two were male including the one holding the gun and one female, all wearing lab coats.

In a flash, Captain Evans leaped from the ground, lifted her gun and aimed it at the armed scientist. "Put your gun down!" she warned. "Now!"

"You, first!" responded the frightened scientist, his gun still fixed on Emma.

"I don't want to kill you!" yelled Captain Evans. "Please, I'm trained military, you're a scientist. I don't want to hurt you... lower your gun!"

"No," screamed the scientist. He didn't trust Captain Evans.

In a fleeting moment amid the tension, Professor Quimbey looked up at a small clearing in the treetops where something had caught her attention: two large overlapping white moons in a purple-tinted night sky. "Everyone, put your guns down!" she yelled. "There are two moons above our heads!"

"Quimbey, what are you talking about?!" questioned Captain Evans, keeping her sights locked on the Russian scientist.

"Look up," said the professor. "We're not on Earth anymore."

The unarmed Russian scientists glanced up and saw what Professor Quimbey was referring to. Immediately, they said something in Russian to their armed comrade, who still feared lowering his weapon. In one last desperate attempt to defuse the situation, Professor Quimby hollered, "Stop this nonsense! Both of you! We're trillions of miles from home... politics are irrelevant here... please *end* this!"

Slowly, the armed Russian scientist lowered his gun and Captain Evans followed suit. With tensions eased, at least temporarily, Captain Evans and Emma looked up to see what Quimbey was talking about.

"How in the world?" said Captain Evans.

After seeing the moons, Emma asked the Russian scientists, "Do you know where we are?"

Professor Quimby immediately went into her gear to pull out instruments, including a gravitometer and an O2 monitor for starters. She took measurements of the surrounding conditions and atmosphere.

An uncharacteristically frazzled Captain Evans shouted at the scientists, "She asked you a question!"

"I don't know," said the armed scientist.

Emma wasn't convinced. "Seriously, look around. This isn't the time for secrecy."

"Wherever we are, we better figure it out soon," announced Professor Quimbey. Looking at her O2 monitor, she explained, "There's less oxygen in the air here… 40.4% of normal, along with nitrogen, argon, carbon dioxide, methane, and a few other gases this monitor doesn't recognize. Who knows what we're breathing in right now. We're lucky there's oxygen at all, but our bodies can't survive in this long term."

"Is that why it feels like someone's sitting on my shoulders?" asked Captain Evans. She felt weighed down and found the act of lifting her weapon harder than expected.

"No… that's the gravity," responded the professor. Looking at her gravitometer, she continued, "Gravity here is about 2.6 times greater than Earth, which means whatever planet we're on, discounting for other possible factors, is roughly the size of Jupiter or a whole lot bigger than Earth."

"Vanirya," piped up the female scientist. Her Russian colleagues shook their heads disapprovingly at her cooperation, but given their situation, she was ready to collaborate.

"What did you say?" asked Emma.

"You asked if we know where we are, so I answer your question. This place is Vanirya, I think."

"That's not possible," responded Emma. "Vanirya doesn't exist anymore…"

"Is possible, is what I say," replied the female scientist. "Is what we were pointing at in Chersky. Particle collider portal take us here."

"Annika!" reprimanded her armed colleague, not wanting her to share any more details about Russia's highly classified project with the Americans. Annika dismissed him. She clearly didn't care about politics at the moment as her colleagues did.

"What is that?" said Emma, distracted by a pink and green glow originating from a large plant at the base of a tree a few feet away. They walked closer to it, and suddenly, dozens of additional plants started glowing, too, along with their roots which splintered outward throughout the marsh-like ground covering beneath their feet. They were surrounded by glowing plants with thick wide leaves, long stems, and colorful bulbs, standing on a network of interconnected glowing roots.

"Something certainly woke these plants up," remarked Captain Evans.

"Perhaps something coming," said Annika.

"Maybe we're the thing that's coming," suggested Professor Quimbey.

Each portion of the plants shined a slightly different color from pink to green to blue and every color in between. The plants' colors pulsed from vibrant to bright white in a cycle that ended up as a burst of white light before returning back to the plants' original colors and repeating the cycle over again. The roots in the ground followed the same color cycle as the plants they grew out from.

"Fascinating," said the gun-wielding scientist who still held his gun in hand. He took a few steps closer to observe. The closer he got, the more the plant's colors intensified as if sensing his approach. He held out his gun and, with the tip of his weapon, touched the plant's exterior green-glowing leaves. The green illumination shimmered and rippled as if the scientist had disturbed a pool of still water, but nothing else happened. "Looks like there's some type of energy moving through these plants." He reached out again with the tip of his gun, this time tapping the pink-glowing leaf. It rippled with intermittent waves of pink and white before settling back on pink again.

"So beautiful," said Emma, looking around, mesmerized by the forest, the double moons, the purple sky, and the glowing plants.

Next, the scientist reached out with the tip of his index finger to touch the pink-glowing leaf. He put his fingertip directly on the leaf and its glow surged to the area around his finger like he had touched a plasma energy ball. He ran his finger along the leaf's surface and the glow-surge followed his finger. He let go.

"What does it feel like?" asked Professor Quimbey.

"Is warm and smooth," he replied, reaching out and feeling the leaves again.

"Is it a plant?" asked Professor Quimbey.

"Yes, feels like one… the texture is the same." As he felt the pink leaf, a pink glow slowly enveloped his hand.

"Nicholai," said Annika, alarmed.

"Is okay, Annika, I feel nothing. I think it's communicating with me."

Steadily, the pink illumination made its way up his arm until covering his entire body. Nicholai's entire body glowed pink but he was still visible within the pink aura. Nicholai leaned in to get a closer look at the plant's center. The glow intensified, consistent with the glow-cycle they had observed from the plants, as did the pink aura around Nicholai.

"Nicholai, I think you should let go now," said Annika.

"Starting to feel a slight tingle," he replied. "Okay, I am letting go…" But he did not let go.

"Nicholai?!" blurted Annika urgently. Nicholai didn't respond. He couldn't move. Annika tried to grab his arm, but before she could, the glow flared into a blinding bright light and the definition of Nicholai's figure became momentarily indistinguishable within it. Annika turned her eyes away from the brightness, and when the glow re-cycled back down to the plant's base colors again, Nicholai was gone and his gun and clothing dropped to the floor. All that remained of him were a few specks of his bio-energy flickering about until evaporating into nothingness. A wave of his consumed energy flowed out to the surrounding plants, shared through their interconnected root system.

"Nicholai!" screamed Annika, stunned. "Artyom!" she called to her colleague for help, but he couldn't do anything either. He was equally devastated by what he had just witnessed.

"Everyone, back up," shouted Captain Evans. "Now!" They backed away from the plant, but all the plants around them started glowing more intensely, hungry for more energy. Even the roots in the ground pulsated brighter and faster. "Run!" shouted Captain Evans.

They ran from the plants, but the web of plants and roots extended well beyond just their immediate area, and the pulsating glow followed them through the root system as they ran. They raced through the trees, careful to avoid stepping on the roots, but Vanirya's gravity slowed them down. They felt like they were running with sandbags tied to their shoulders, waists, and legs, and it caused them to run clumsily. Emma fell down once, catching her toe on a boulder, but luckily, she didn't touch any of the roots. She bounced back up and kept running.

210

"There, up ahead, I see a clearing!" yelled Captain Evans, altering course to head that direction.

As they continued running, the next time, it was Artyom who tripped on a hole in the ground he hadn't noticed. He fell smack on top of multiple glowing tree roots. The instant his left hand touched the roots, he froze as if paralyzed by a jellyfish sting. He yelped but was otherwise unable to move. Annika turned to help him but by the time she did, he was already glowing brightly from a faster process than what doomed Nicholai. There was a look of terror on Artyom's paralyzed face, as he couldn't move but knew exactly what was happening.

"Artyom!" she screamed as she looked into his terrified eyes. The final flare-up started but Captain Evans yanked Annika's arm to keep her moving. She wasn't around to see the roots consume him.

They made it to the clearing and ran until 50 yards in. There were no more glowing plants or roots in the ground, or trees above or around them. For the moment anyway, they were safe, but also completely exposed in the middle of a hostile forest on a strange planet.

Annika fell to her knees, crying and wheezing from the lack of oxygen after sprinting in heavy gravity. It wasn't just Annika; they were *all* winded and struggling to catch their breaths. After a few minutes, Captain Evans, who recovered sooner than the others because of her superior conditioning, walked over to Annika, lowered herself onto one knee, and put her arm around the distraught scientist.

"I'm sorry," Captain Evans said.

"Thank you," Annika replied, wiping away tears. "I should have grabbed Nicholai faster…"

"Had you tried, you would have died along with him," replied Captain Evans. "There was nothing you could do." Captain Evans put her gun away and said, "Let's just work together to find a way home, okay?"

Annika nodded.

"We've got to get off this planet and not touch anything while we're at it," said Captain Evans. Turning to Annika, she asked, "How do we find one of those portals you mentioned earlier?"

"I don't know," replied Annika. "We did not plan for this. Not supposed to be here."

"Do we have a way to contact Earth?" asked Captain Evans.

Professor Quimbey shook her head. "Not that we do, but if this really is Vanirya, there'll be no one home to answer the phone. The Vaniryan star went supernova more than 800 years ago in the Middle Ages back on Earth. Somehow, we must've gone back in time."

The professor's response stunned Captain Evans. "So, how do we get home?"

"I don't know," Professor Quimbey replied. "Annika, do you have any idea what year your portal might have sent us back to?"

"No, is not like we had dial or anything. We had inadequate understanding of the Vaniryan technology, no control over the process. The whole thing was in testing in particle collider, not that that mattered to Kremlin who kept pushing us to use portal technology before we fully understood it. No matter to them. We could be thousands or millions of years in the past... no way to know."

Captain Evans bemoaned, "Well, this isn't good, lost in both space *and* time on a dangerous alien planet with an inhospitable atmosphere."

Emma walked over and sat down beside Annika and Captain Evans. "I'm sorry about your friends," she said to Annika. "I'm Emma."

212

"Annika."

"That's Professor Quimbey…"

"I think you can just call me Jill, at this point," said Professor Quimbey. "A trillion miles from home, I'm not sure titles matter anymore."

"And I'm Evans," added the captain.

"Annika, how is it possible that this is Vanirya?" asked Emma.

Annika corrected her. "I *think* this is Vanirya, I say. For 18 months, we couldn't locate Vanirya. Thought experiment incorrect, but then, in particle collider, we tested colliding z-particles with one another rather than splitting them, which generated an incredible amount of energy that sparked micro-singularities."

"What's a singularity?" inquired Captain Evans, unfamiliar with the scientific term.

Annika responded, "It is theory, in the center of a black hole is a singularity, a one-dimensional point which contains huge mass in infinitely small space, where density and gravity become infinite and space-time curves infinitely. Just theory."

"Sounds like more than theory," replied Captain Evans. "Do you mean you created mini-black holes?"

"Mini ones, perhaps. Collision generated micro-singularities with immense gravitational pull at a quantum level, which expelled even *greater* amounts of energy when singularities collapsed, which happens the instant after they form. The expelled energy altered phase of z-particles and sped them up even faster than splitting them, and then, we notice something…"

"What?" asked Professor Quimbey.

"At first, particles appeared to be doubling in mass or multiplying and disappearing just as fast. But when we analyzed, we realized particles weren't growing or multiplying, they were actually re-appearing the instant before they left."

"Like, they went back in time, as in time travel?" asked Emma.

"Yes. But outside of the particle collider, when we applied theory to the z-particle accelerator and pointed it at Vanirya, we lost control of the experiment."

"Lost control?" asked Emma.

"Even before you Americans arrived, we couldn't shut the experiment down. Something wrong. So, I think, maybe this is Vanirya based on what we were pointing at, but not know for sure."

Looking at Emma, Professor Quimbey commented, "This sure doesn't look like the Vanirya you described."

"I wasn't on the planet's surface last time—"

"I'm sorry…*what?*" blurted Captain Evans, looking at Emma. "You've been here before?"

"Once, three years ago, I went through a portal that transported me into some kind of floating pyramid in orbit over Vanirya. I'm not really sure what it was, but I never saw the ground." In retrospect, now knowing that Vanirya was destroyed approximately 800 years ago, Emma realized that the portal must have also sent her back in time, too.

Captain Evans replied, "There appear to be a few details about this science fiction movie that Lt. Col. Rodgers and Dr. Ehringer left out of the trailer. I can see now why they sent you two on this mission."

"Mission?" asked Annika.

214

"To investigate the source of the zeutyron signals in Chersky," explained Emma.

"Okay, so it sounds like to get off this planet before it kills us, we need to start by finding these Vaniryans," said Captain Evans.

A loud threatening roar echoed through the forest and into the clearing.

"Great, right on cue," remarked Captain Evans.

"Oh, bugger!" yelped Professor Quimbey.

They heard it again, a roar so loud, that they covered their ears. They looked up and around to see if they could tell where it came from.

"Let's head back into the trees," said Captain Evans. "We're sitting ducks out here."

"We're sitting ducks in there, too," Professor Quimbey retorted.

"Maybe," conceded Captain Evans, "but I'll take my chances. Whatever that roar belongs to sounds big. Let's go."

They hurried to the opposite edge of the clearing, away from where they came, hoping to avoid more trouble. When they reached the tree line, glowing plants were everywhere, although these ones looked different, lacking the same glowing root systems as the ones that killed Annika's comrades. Still, they were menacing-looking, and they chose to follow Captain Evans's earlier advice: touch nothing that glows.

They hiked deeper into the forest for hours, entirely under tree cover. All night long, the sounds of indigenous alien life warned them to stay away. Nearly every step they took, they heard growling, screeching, clucking, clicking, squealing, shuffling, gurgling, or some kind of movement nearby that made them want to turn around or change directions. Between that and the sporadic illumination of the plant life, they were all on edge, and Captain Evans held her weapon ready.

Eventually, as they got tired, when they found a secluded spot within a group of boulders, they made camp and took turns watching. At the first hint of sunrise, they resumed their travel through the forest. Even with improved visibility, there was no obvious indication of which way to go. They were lost in the middle of the forest.

"Now that the sun's up, I think we need to climb one of these trees to see where we're going," said Captain Evans. "I'll do it."

Since she was the best climber of the group, her suggestion made sense, but from Emma's perspective, that was the only part that did. "Are you serious?" questioned Emma. "The plant life on this planet has already killed two of us."

"What's the alternative? Wander aimlessly in this forest which could be larger than North America for all we know, given the size of this planet, squandering precious time?"

"The trees do not glow," pointed out Annika, "or at least, the trunks, branches, and leaves don't. The small flowers, florets, and bulbs do, so I say, don't touch those. Nicholai and Artyom weren't wearing gloves, and so I think touching plants with bare skin may be the danger."

"I've got thick gloves on and a heavy body suit rated for -50," said Captain Evans, embracing Annika's logic. "It's a risk, but I've got to. I'm already feeling the effects of this planet. We have to know. We can't just keep walking around in a forest that's getting denser by the hour."

Emma was worried. "But what if the tree does to you what it did to them?"

"Then, that'll be one more thing on this planet you'll know not to touch," replied Captain Evans. "How 'bout this... I've got some climbing cable in my bag that was meant for Chersky. Let's tie it

216

around my waist. I'll touch the tree with my gloves on, and if anything happens, you can yank me away immediately." Captain Evans removed the cable from her bag. "Here, I'll just cut off the metal clips at the end to minimize the conductivity of the cable." Captain Evans tied it around her waist, fastened a secure knot, and walked up to one of the taller trees. "Just pull me back if something looks off."

"Okay," replied Emma. She picked up the end of the cable and held it tight in her gloves.

Captain Evans reached out with her gloved hand and touched the tree trunk.

"Anything?" asked Professor Quimbey.

"Nothing," replied Captain Evans. She gave it 30 more seconds, and then reached for a low hanging tree branch and climbed six or seven feet. "Still, nothing." She kept climbing until the 50-foot-long cable held by Emma grew taut. She couldn't climb any higher until Emma let go of the rope. "Team, it looks like this is where I leave you." Captain Evans untied the rope around her waist and dropped it down. She was officially on her own.

Since mountain climbing was her specialty, and because the tree had many branches usable as hand or footholds, Captain Evans scaled it relatively easily despite the increased gravity. Once Captain Evans got up to the top, she could see over most of the surrounding trees. From up high, she could see the planet's overlapping moons in the early-morning sky, fading seamlessly into a brightening purple skyline. On this world, the moons never really fully disappeared from view, remaining faintly present even during daylight. Unfortunately, other than the alien world's sheer beauty, Captain Evans saw nothing else other than an endless blanket of trees in all directions, along with some hills and low mountains.

"Damn," she swore. The forest went on for as far as her eyes could see. When she returned to the ground, she delivered the bad news. "I don't see anything. Just more trees, small hills, and low mountains."

"No signs of civilization or intelligent life?" asked Professor Quimbey.

"Nope," Evans stated.

"Ugh," groaned Emma. "Now, what?"

"We just gotta keep going," said Captain Evans. "Stay in a straight line, and keep going straight. Nothing else we can do. At some point, we're going to hit something, or we can try stoking a fire to send up a smoke signal... but I'm not feeling that option yet since we don't know who or what that might attract. As a last resort, maybe, but not now."

As the sun rose, it got hot. Because Emma, Professor Quimbey, and Captain Evans were still wearing their heavy mountaineering gear for the Chersky Mission, to stay cool, they stripped down to the Air Force-issued tight-fitting navy blue nylon sweats they wore underneath. Likewise, Annika removed her white lab coat, revealing a red jumpsuit with a Roscosmos State Corporation insignia.

They continued on. Traveling in daylight made things easier; they could navigate the terrain better, examine their surroundings, and see where they were walking. Emma found the forest less intimidating and actually quite pretty, with its display of lush energy-infused green, pink, red, green, and blue plants and colorful flowers, all of which they carefully avoided. They traveled for an entire day, which easily lasted twice as long as a day on Earth, before finally stumbling on a small stream trickling along the forest floor.

"Water!" blurted Professor Quimbey. She leaned down to examine it. It looked like water. It sounded like water. She cupped it in her hands, brought it to her face, smelled it, and let it trickle through her fingers. "Seems like water," she said.

"We should follow the stream. Where there's water, there are people," suggested Captain Evans.

"Among other things," Professor Quimbey reminded her.

"Yeah, well, it's a start," replied Captain Evans. "That's our best hope."

Hearing no objection, Captain Evans led the way. They followed her lead upstream. As the long day continued to drag on, the stream widened into a small river, and at several points along the way, multiple rivulets poured into it or flowed out of it. They followed the stream for the rest of the day, still seeing no signs of intelligent life.

Worse, as the hours piled up, the hike through the forest grew harder. The atmosphere was starting to take its toll on their bodies. They were each experiencing the early onset of symptoms caused by the heavy gravity combined with low oxygen levels, including significant muscle fatigue, headaches, vomiting, and dizziness. Just like in the Chersky mountains, they took frequent breaks to deal with it, but rest could only get them so far. They needed to get off the planet.

After one rough two-hour stretch through a rocky hill-laden section of terrain late afternoon on day two, they stopped to rest beside the stream, more fatigued and discouraged than ever.

"Is hopeless," said Annika. "Forest is forever. I can't sustain this for much longer."

Emma felt the same way. She also felt nauseous. She stood up, walked to the stream a couple of feet away, leaned over with her hands on her knees, and vomited. Captain Evans started to get up to help her but Professor Quimbey was already on the way.

Professor Quimbey hurried up to Emma and put a hand on her back as Emma remained hunched over spitting out the remnants of vomit in her mouth. The professor grabbed Emma's long hair to pull it out of her face.

"I feel so sick," said Emma, looking up at Professor Quimbey. "Annika's right, I don't know how much longer I can do this. I feel like the air's suffocating me."

"You're stronger than you think," replied the professor, trying to lift Emma's spirits.

Emma threw her head back toward the stream and vomited again, although the second time, it was more of a dry heave. Again, Professor Quimbey held Emma's hair out of her face. When Emma finished, with tears welling up in her eyes, she looked at the rippled image of her nauseous face in the stream and cried, "I'm sorry. I'm letting everyone down."

"Nonsense… you have nothing to apologize for," said Annika, listening to their conversation from behind.

"I'm so scared that we're not going to make it," said Emma.

"Everything's going to be fine, I promise," Professor Quimbey encouraged her. "If there's one thing I've learned in my life, it's to stay positive in times like this. Things always have a way of working out."

"It's just really hard to see how," Emma replied.

"I'm sure Jonas and Logan are out there looking for us right now," said Professor Quimbey. "Do you really think those two would ever let anything happen to us? If I know our boys, they're probably trying to figure out how to turn back time to save us all as we speak."

"Well, they'll never guess where to find us, that's for sure."

The professor replied, "Won't matter. That boyfriend of yours loves you way too much to ever give up, trust me. He'll look under every rock on every planet orbiting every star in the universe before he does."

Emma smiled at the sentiment and wiped away a tear from her cheek. "You know, the other night, I think Logan was trying to propose to me."

"Really, why do you think that?" replied Professor Quimbey, playing dumb.

Emma wiped her eyes as she pulled herself together. "You know Logan, who is always dressed casually cool, showed up at my apartment wearing the nicest outfit I've ever seen him in. And he made a huge effort to plan the perfect evening, from the stroll down the Mall to the Smithsonian to Hobā. Then, at dinner, he was going on about the future and asking me if I ever thought about what else was out there for us beside the Pegasus Project. Thinking back, I realize I must have suspected something because I kind of just… panicked."

"What do you mean, 'panicked'?"

"I don't know, I gave him some lame response like I didn't understand what he was talking about. He asked me, 'Do you ever think about what else is out there for us besides this?' And I said something like, 'Sure, but I don't think we can really talk about it here.' I still can't believe I responded like that, and I think he knew it, too. Then, I took a stupid phone call from my friend Kristi that could have waited…"

"Why, though? You love him, right?"

"Of course! More than anything. I guess, in that moment, I was just scared. I'm so young, I mean, we both are… and there's so much I want to do in life, and honestly, I guess, right then and there, I just panicked. I don't know what came over me. And now we're stuck here, and I don't know if I'll ever get the chance to tell him how I feel. I'm such an idiot."

"You're not alone, love makes everyone fools… When Jonas first asked me to marry him, I said 'yes,' but then, I got this silly notion in my head I hadn't known him long enough. I told him I wanted to wait until after I finished my Cyber-Technetics Grant. I never told him the real reason why, that I was scared, but then, my mom passed away, and she never got the chance to see me walk down the aisle with the man I was meant to marry. Foolish when I look back at it, and I never finished that grant. Jonas reminded me a long time ago that time waits for no one… and he was right."

"I just wish I could go back and do it over again, tell Logan how much I love him, and—"

"You're gonna get that chance, James," chimed in Captain Evans, who'd overheard the last bit of their conversation as she approached to check on Emma. "No one's going to die out here. Not on my watch. James, you need to hydrate more," suggested Captain Evans. "It'll help with the nausea."

Emma walked back to where they were all originally sitting and reached into her bag. She grabbed her water canteen and took a drink as Captain Evans recommended. "I know we're light-years away, but I wish I could text Logan, right now," said Emma in a half-serious tone.

"Why is that?" asked Annika.

"Because right before we left on this misadventure, I promised if we got into any trouble, I'd text him, 'Help Us Now.' Sure wish I could send that text now…"

"I think we all do," said Annika.

"Hey, did anyone hear that?" Captain Evans asked.

Emma, Professor Quimbey, and Annika looked around and listened.

"Hear what?" asked Professor Quimbey.

"I heard laughter," replied Captain Evans.

"Laughter? Like, what kind of laughter?" asked Emma.

"I don't know, it sounded like—" Captain Evans heard it again. "There... there it is again!" she exclaimed, only this time, they all heard it. It sounded like giggling, like the sound of a child playing.

"It's coming from upstream," said Dr. Arenot.

They followed the stream uphill for approximately 200 more feet until they came to a large pool of water with a waterfall cascading into it from a backstop of rocks on a boulder-laden hill. The water escaped the pool at the far end, emptying into the stream they had been following. And playing in the plunge pool in front of the waterfall appeared to be a young alien girl...

"Do you see that?" uttered Professor Quimbey, her mouth agape. It wasn't like they didn't expect to see intelligent alien life... after all, they *were* marooned on an alien world and *were* looking for beings called Vaniryans, if this was Vanirya. Still, they weren't prepared for it when it actually happened.

They looked on in awe and wonder, quietly watching the girl play in the water, staying hidden behind trees. She looked like an 11-year-old girl based on her short stature, long hair, and delicate build, but who knew how old she really was or if she was female. A brown-colored outfit covered her body, leaving her arms and legs exposed. She had long golden-white hair, silver-white skin, and humanoid features, including two arms with hands, two legs, a tiny mouth, a short neck, and a circular face. She had two round white eyes with radiant blue pupils, but no nose.

The alien girl bounced around in the water chasing glowing sparrow-like creatures, laughing and giggling as she played. Each of the sparrow-creatures, which resembled small birds but glowed like fireflies, fluttered about in the air, playfully teasing the girl who was doing her best to catch them. The sparrows all radiated different colors and were interacting with the girl in her game. At one point, when she wasn't having success, the young girl began emitting prismatic-colored waves of energy nets from her fingertips to ensnare the sparrow-creatures. The radiating sparrows fluttered away from the nets, chirping back and teasing her. After the energy-nets faded, she would try again.

Crack!

Oh no, Emma muttered to herself. Her weight had inadvertently snapped the tree branch she was leaning against. The alien girl, startled, effortlessly ran through the water, almost gliding across it. She ducked into the waterfall and hid behind it. The sparrow-creatures scattered.

"Shoot. Sorry everyone," Emma apologized.

"We can't let that alien get away," said Captain Evans. "We might not see another sign of intelligent life again. One of us has to approach her, but we can't all go at once… might scare the alien away."

Emma found Captain Evans's use of the term 'alien' ironic since, on this world, *they* were the aliens. However, because she broke the branch, Emma volunteered to go. "I'll do it."

"Be careful," said Professor Quimbey. "You don't want her shooting you with her energy."

"Approach slowly," Captain Evans said. "You don't want to scare——"

"I got it, everyone," replied Emma. She stepped out from behind the trees to approach the water. "Hello…," she said out loud. No response. Emma continued to the water's edge to see if she could spot the little girl through the falls, but she couldn't. After surveying her options, Emma walked around to the side of the pool to rocks on the waterfall's right. Still unable to see the girl, she began climbing over the wet rocks to get closer to the falls. Water runoff on the surrounding rocks splashed everywhere and drenched her, but as close as she was, she still couldn't see the alien girl. Emma realized if she wanted to find her, she had to go in.

Emma removed her backpack and set it on the rocks. She climbed down into the water, which got deeper the farther in she went. The water reached her chest by the time she got to the whitewater splash at the base of the falls. Emma held her breath and went in. Water poured on her head and shoulders with a substantial force for the short moment she passed underneath the waterfall, and she re-emerged in a crescent-shaped rock-covered cove.

"Hello?" said Emma, wading through the chest-high water looking for the girl. As she got deeper into the cove and her eyes adjusted to the dim light, Emma thought she saw a pair of alien eyes staring back at her, but by the time Emma reached the back of the cove, the girl was gone and Emma realized the cove had a back exit… a crevice leading up.

Emma went into the crevice. After a minute weaving through rock, the crevice turned right toward a light. Hurrying to catch up, Emma rushed to the light, only to discover the backside of another waterfall leading outside with the late afternoon sun shining in. She ducked through the waterfall, once again finding herself outdoors in another shallow plunge pool. She swam to the edge of the water. She was soaked, but fortunately, she wasn't the only one. Wet footsteps and waterdrops continued off into the forest away from the pool.

Emma looked back, contemplating whether to go get her companions, but she didn't have time. She had to track the girl's wet footprints and water drippage before the evidence dried up. Emma took off after her.

Every few feet she saw water drops on rocks, boulders or leaves, or wet footprints on the ground. The water signs persisted in a consistent direction, ultimately leading into a dense patch of gigantic trees hundreds of feet tall with trunks 50 to 100 feet wide. As Emma continued in, she saw less evidence of water; the alien girl was clearly drying off. Eventually, she lost the girl's footprints altogether in the middle of the trees.

It was dark in there, except for a few beams of sunlight streaking through gaps between the trees up above. Emma was nervous. She felt like she was being watched. She half-expected the giant spiders of Mirkwood or something worse to leap out of the darkness and attack her. "Welcome to the Forbidden Forest, Em," she softly said to herself. She looked around and said out loud, "Now what?"

Then, she looked up…

Chapter 16 – Remnants

Emma spotted the alien girl's silhouette climbing high in the tree in front of her. She watched as the girl disappeared into a thick section of foliage a 100 feet above her head. In fact, all the trees in this part of the forest had thick foliage at about the same height up, preventing Emma from seeing any higher.

Emma studied the tree trunk, which was at least 50 feet wide at its base, wondering if she could climb it as the girl did. She walked around the trunk looking to see how the girl scaled it so fast, and sure enough, upon closer examination, she saw notches every one or two feet she hadn't noticed at first. Each was higher than the next and spiraled upward around the trunk.

Emma wasn't about to lose her now! Determined, and with renewed energy, she put her left foot in a lower notch, her right hand in an upper one, and climbed. Steadily, just like in her rock wall classes at the Fit-N-Climb, she solved the mechanics of the ascent, following a pattern of hand, foot, cross-over hand, cross-over foot. It helped that the carved notches had a slight lip, enabling Emma to fully grip them, but by no means was the climb easy. In the heavy gravity and thin oxygen, Emma labored every notch of the way, constantly resting on branches protruding from the tree. Given how slow she was climbing, Emma eventually realized the alien girl was probably long gone, but she couldn't turn back now. She was already way too high for that, plus, she saw something…

As she climbed higher, she began seeing large shadows above the foliage, and soon, it became apparent the shadows weren't shadows at all, they were structures! Emma's stomach filled with butterflies as she reached the foliage's underside that, from up close, now appeared purposefully manicured to conceal what was above it. The notches guided Emma's climb right through a gap in the foliage that wrapped around the tree inside a tunnel of leaves and branches. Emma finished her spiraling climb and emerged in an astonishing new world...

She stood on a landing overlooking an extensive network of walkways among the branches, bridges, ropes, ladders, structures, and staircases leading to more walkways and structures even higher up. The intersecting walkways and bridges linked to branches and paths from other trees, creating an interconnected tree village much larger than one tree by itself.

Looking up, the treetops formed a thick canopy that blocked out most sunlight. No matter, though. There were smaller branches growing out of the larger ones with floral bulbs blossoming outward, each emitting a soft yellow light that lit the village. No torches needed. The plant life's natural glow sufficed.

Emma stood on the landing at what seemed like the outskirts of the village, wondering what to do next. The alien girl was nowhere to be seen, but a handful of beings, similar in appearance, walked around in the distance. None had noticed Emma yet. The beings were taller than the girl, fueling Emma's intuition that she was, indeed, a child.

The moment of truth had arrived. If they had any hope of getting off the planet, Emma needed to make contact with the aliens. Her heart pounded as she stepped toward the walkway leading to the rest of the village, unsure how they would react to her. Just as she took her first step, a small round face peeked over the landing. It was the alien girl's, and her inquisitive round eyes stared back at Emma, trying to figure out what she was.

"Hi," said Emma. The alien child, standing on a branch just below the landing, stepped back. Emma stopped where she was, got down on her knees, smiled, and held her hands out, palms up. "Please, don't be afraid... I'm not going to hurt you."

The girl replied with a short response in a beautiful melodic tone that sounded like two overlapping voices came out of her mouth at once.

Emma put her hand on her chest and said, "I'm Emma..." Keeping her hand in place, she repeated her name.

The alien girl replied in her multi-layered, melodic tone, "Isa," or at least, that's how Emma's ear heard it.

Emma chuckled and teared up at the wonder of making intelligent contact with the alien girl. "Isa... such a pretty name," she remarked, shocked at herself for being so moved by the experience. After all, this wasn't her first time meeting someone from another world.

Isa didn't say anything. She just kept gazing at Emma. Then, she climbed onto the landing and approached Emma. With curiosity, Isa touched Emma's skin and explored the contours of her face. From up close, Emma saw that Isa had six slender fingers on her hands, all of equal length, and six toes on her bare feet. Isa's tiny mouth grinned, and the next thing Emma knew, Isa unexpectedly entered her mind...

Trust Isa, said a voice inside Emma's head. The voice was Emma's, but the words and thoughts weren't. It was just like how the Vaniryans communicated with Emma three years ago when she visited Vanirya, telepathically using Emma's own words and thoughts to communicate with her.

"Where am I?" asked Emma.

Forest home.

"Right, in the forest, but what planet is this?"

Vanirya.

Ugh. That confirmed it. They had definitely gone back in time.

Seeing the stress on Emma's face, Isa asked telepathically, and *out loud*, "Is being not home?"

Emma's mouth dropped. It seemed Isa could not only communicate telepathically but also could translate those thoughts into basic English. Stunned, and momentarily confused by Isa's dual communication, Emma responded, "No, unfortunately. I am far from home."

"Being looks funny. Is being a creature?" asked Isa, again communicating telepathically and verbally.

Emma replied, "No... I mean, I don't think I am."

"Then, what is Emma?"

"I am a human. At least, that's what we call ourselves back home."

"Where is Emma-being's home?"

"A place called Earth."

"Is Earth on other side of Vanirya?"

"Oh no," replied Emma. It occurred to her that Isa might not have been to the other side of her own planet before, given its size. Perhaps she didn't know what the inhabitants on Vanirya's opposite hemisphere looked like, so Emma clarified, "Earth is a planet orbiting a star in a solar system far away from here."

Isa's eyes enlarged. "Emma-being is from another world?"

Emma nodded and replied, "Yes."

"How does Emma come here, on a ship?"

"I wish it were that easy. No, we found an experiment in the mountains, there was an explosion, something happened, and the next thing we knew, we ended up here." Emma looked around at the trees and asked, "Is this place *your* home?"

"Isa home, yes. Ground unsafe."

Emma couldn't argue with that, although Isa's comment made her wonder, "Why is the ground unsafe?"

Isa began nervously pulling at her long golden-white hair before responding, "The Hunt..."

"What do you mean? Something hunts you?"

"Not just Isa. All…" Isa paused. "Does anyone hunt humans?"

"Does anyone hunt humans?" repeated Emma, struck by the odd question. "No. I mean, maybe we hunt ourselves a little bit sometimes, but no one hunts us, not really."

"Why do humans hunt humans?"

"I suppose we haven't figured out how to all get along yet," responded Emma, summarizing humankind's checkered history in a nutshell.

Isa noticed Emma's heart-shaped pendant necklace from Logan, dangling around Emma's neck and glinting in the soft yellow light of an overhead glowing floral bulb. "Pretty," remarked Isa.

Emma took hold of the necklace and replied, "Thank you. It's called a necklace. Someone I care about very much gave this to me. Do you want to touch it?"

Isa looked like she did but remained hesitant.

"Go ahead, you can touch it."

Isa reached out with her fingertip, touched the heart pendant, and smiled with the biggest possible grin her tiny mouth could give. She had never seen jewelry before. "Pretty necklace," she said.

Emma, feeling like she had made sufficient inroads with Isa, decided to ask her what she came for. "Isa, I need your help."

"How Isa help Emma?"

"My friends and I, we can't survive on your planet for very long. We need to find a way home. Can your people help us?"

"Isa not know."

"Is there someone in your village who might?"

Isa thought about it and said, "Emma, come. Tassa know what to do."

"Where are we going?"

"Home."

Isa turned and walked away, and Emma followed. Isa led them to the end of the walkway and made a sharp left down another narrow branchway to a bridge constructed of rope and wood. The bridge connected to a neighboring tree and ladder leading up to another landing. On the landing, there was a staircase winding around the tree the rest of the way up. The soft light of the scattered floral bulbs lit the way as they climbed the winding staircase until reaching a platform near the top, where a large wooden structure sat firmly on a sturdy branch.

"Isa home," announced the Vaniryan girl. Isa and Emma stepped off the staircase onto the platform where Isa lived.

"Wow, you live here?" asked Emma, amazed by the refined woodwork and solid build of the most awesome treehouse she'd ever seen. There were other houses strewn among the various branches of this and other trees at varying heights, but no more than a handful per tree.

"Follow Isa," she replied, ducking underneath a cloth dangling over the doorway.

Emma followed her into the small home. Along the right wall were chairs and a table with bowls, cups, plates, and a series of buckets, including one filled with water. On the wall directly in front of her was an open window cut into the wood, allowing a clear view of the trees outside. There was a tree branch in the home's center that poked right through the middle of the floor and disappeared into the ceiling. Trinkets, knick-knacks, and small plants sat on little notches carved into the branch, and every few feet, the same glowing floral bulbs Emma saw blossoming outside, sprouted inside, as well, conveniently lighting Isa's quaint little home. She had no intention of touching those, of course.

And finally, on the home's left-hand side was a partition wall with an opening into another room. From the other side of the partition came a high-pitched voice calling for Isa. "Issor?"

Seconds later, the voice emerged. It belonged to a much taller Vaniryan who froze at the sight of Emma. The Vaniryan had soft round facial features similar to Isa's, including the same long golden-white hair, silver-white skin, a circular face, round white eyes with radiant blue pupils, a tiny mouth, and no nose. This must be Isa's mother, Emma thought.

"Issor!" she shouted, along with some other choice words Emma didn't understand. Isa immediately relocated to the far side of the home as if she had done something wrong.

Isa, sorry, she said to Emma telepathically.

"Issor!" snapped the Vaniryan again, reprimanding Isa, or 'Issor,' for continuing to communicate with Emma. The Vaniryan stepped in between the two, suspiciously glaring at Emma. Then, unlike Isa's gentle approach to telepathy, this Vaniryan abruptly barged into Emma's mind.

"Who are you?!" she demanded, mining the words and thoughts right out of Emma's head before verbalizing them.

Emma suddenly grew uneasy. This Vaniryan wasn't nearly as friendly as Isa. Trying to remain calm, Emma replied, "My name is Emma…"

"You are not of this world. What creature are you?"

"I am a human from a planet called Earth. I—"

"How did human find Issor?"

Isa started to respond, "Tassa—"

"No, Issor!" shouted Tassa, interrupting her.

"I'm sorry, this isn't her fault, it's mine," apologized Emma. "I saw her at the waterfall and followed her here into the trees."

"Issor!" exclaimed Tassa even more harshly. She scolded Isa, an unmistakable tongue-lashing in any language. Isa responded apologetically and retreated behind the partition, leaving Emma alone with Tassa.

Looking back at Emma, Tassa said, "Issor know it is forbidden to leave trees. The Hunt will find her, then, they find us *all*. Maybe they find you. Maybe you are the Hunt," said Tassa accusingly, taking an intimidating step forward toward Emma.

Emma shook her head, trying to dissuade Tassa from whatever she was thinking. "I am not the Hunt, I promise," urged Emma, although she didn't know what 'the Hunt' meant.

"Emma say words to Tassa, but truth hides behind words," replied Tassa, stepping forward until hovering over Emma.

Emma shrunk beneath Tassa's glare. Her lips quivering slightly, Emma responded, "I come here as a friend, not enemy."

Tassa peered deep into Emma's eyes, looking for Emma's truth. Tassa could see the fear and sincerity in Emma's shivering face. Tassa broke eye contact almost immediately and said, "Emma may not be the Hunt…"

Emma exhaled, but Tassa wasn't done...

"…but maybe Emma bring Hunt here!"

"Tassa, I don't know what you are talking about. I didn't—"

"Emma may not have blood on hands and mind, but Emma not know what follows her. Emma must leave!"

"Please, I've come here for help."

"Tassa cannot help Emma."

"Issor thought perhaps you could…"

"Issor wrong."

"You tell me to leave, but I have nowhere to go. My friends and I, we're not supposed to be here. We are lost and stranded on your world. We need help to find a way back to ours."

"Issor should not have brought Emma to the trees."

"She was only trying to help me."

"Issor not help you. She is young. Issor not know. Last stranger to this place came before Issor rescued from the Hunt and brought here."

"Are you not Issor's mother?"

"No. Issor rescued from Hunt that killed her entire family and many more. I care for Issor now. Issor meant help for Emma, and so, I will help Emma by saying, *go,* before it is too late! The Remnants cannot help Emma."

"Remnants?"

A loud horn-sound blew through the trees before Emma got her answer. Tassa looked up and hurried to the window, but not before Isa bounded out from banishment, beating Tassa to the windowsill.

"What's happening?" asked Emma, as Tassa and Isa peered out.

"Invaders come," replied Tassa. "Issor, we must go!"

"What should I do?" asked Emma.

Tassa knew she was going to regret it, but she could tell Emma was a kind being which was probably why Issor, who trusted very few people, was taken with her. So Tassa replied, "Wait here and hide. If others see you, they will bring death to you. We will return. Issor, we must go!" Tassa and Isa rushed out the door.

Emma was worried. What had she done? Had she, or they, inadvertently led the Hunt, whatever that was, to this peaceful tree village, just like Tassa worried they might? Emma got low to the floor and crawled to the window to peek outside at what was going on. One way or another, she knew she was about to find out…

ΔΔΔΔΔΔΔΔΔΔΔΔ

Captain Evans returned from the waterfall where she went in search of Emma. She was drenched.

"Did you find anything?" asked Professor Quimbey, who had been anxiously awaiting Captain Evans's return. It was now dusk, with the sun setting and the planet's double moons rising into the darkening sky.

"Nothing. There's no sign of her anywhere. I found a cove and crevice behind the waterfall that leads uphill, with several possible exits. Perhaps she went out of one of those."

"Or something happened to her," said Annika, stating the alternative narrative none of them wanted to consider.

Captain Evans responded, "The sun's almost down. If we're going to find her, I think it's time to go after—"

Captain Evans collapsed to the ground without finishing her sentence, unconscious, struck by an energy beam in her back that came out of nowhere. Annika dropped to the ground next from a blast to her side.

Frightened, Professor Quimbey spun around to see who was attacking them. "Who are—" She didn't even finish asking before the energy beam blasted her in the stomach and everything went dark.

ΔΔΔΔΔΔΔΔΔΔΔΔ

When Captain Evans awoke, she was laying on the ground at the base of a wall. Her back stung badly from where the beam had struck her. She tried to rub it but couldn't because rope tightly bound her wrists and feet. She wiggled and writhed into a sitting position against the wall, with her legs outstretched.

They were being held captive in a large meeting hall made entirely of wood, carved inside a massive tree trunk, but Captain Evans didn't know that yet. The light brown wall she leaned against was edged and shaped until perfectly smooth, save for the decorative crisscross pattern etched into it. Red beams rose into the ceiling 20 feet up. There was a half-circle entrance into the hall, with trees and branches visible outside.

More than 50 Vaniryans had gathered to see the captives, with more joining by the second. Professor Quimbey and Annika remained unconscious on the floor. While the first three blows of the horn did not jar them awake, the fourth deafening horn blow finally did.

Groggily, they looked around, trying to figure out where they were and what had happened. They squirmed into a sitting position against the wall just like Captain Evans. None of them had seen or heard the Vaniryans coming in the forest while waiting for Emma to return, not even the hyper-vigilant Captain Evans, who chided herself for allowing the Vaniryans to sneak up on them like that. The Vaniryan crowd closed in, clamoring and shouting.

"Quimbey, you okay?" asked Captain Evans.

"Yeah, I'm fine," replied Professor Quimbey, wincing from the blow to her stomach. "A little sore. You?"

"Dandy," responded Captain Evans. "Just dandy. Annika, how 'bout you?"

"I am okay," replied Annika.

"Good," replied Captain Evans, scanning the room looking for Emma. Based on what happened to them, Captain Evans wondered if Emma's fate had ended up the same as theirs.

"Where are we?" asked Professor Quimbey.

"In trouble, that's where we are," replied Captain Evans.

"You said you wanted to find intelligent life…"

"Yeah… but the friendly kind."

Enough! shouted a voice inside their minds, silencing them. Judging by the confused looks on their faces, all three heard it.

The crowd quieted down and separated to make room for a Vaniryan approaching up the middle, wearing a beige tunic, pants, brown footwear that resembled boots, and an elongated laser rifle strapped to their back. The Vaniryan easily stood six feet tall and had similar features as the girl back at the waterfall, but this Vaniryan's face was rugged-looking, skin more time-worn, and hair short. The Vaniryan looked male.

"How many more invaders hide with you in the Jaans Forest?" he asked telepathically, while also speaking out loud in an entirely *different* language for the rest of the hall to hear. The Vaniryan's ability to communicate telepathically in one language and audibly in another astonished Professor Quimbey. She couldn't even begin to fathom the human brain speaking and thinking two different languages at the exact same time.

"Your highness, we have not come to your planet to invade," replied Captain Evans.

The Vaniryan glared at her with distrust. He held out his six-fingered hands and waited while another Vaniryan walked up and handed him guns and knives seized from Captain Evans's bag. The Vaniryan examined the strange-looking items and fiddled with Captain Evans's handgun.

Bam! The handgun accidentally discharged. The loud bang startled everyone. Some screamed. Professor Quimbey ducked and closed her eyes. She opened them slowly, fearing someone would be hurt. Fortunately, the bullet had only struck a plant fixture built into the wall above their heads. Pieces crashed down in between Professor Quimbey and Captain Evans.

The Vaniryan eyed and sniffed the smoke still rising out of the gun barrel. "Off-worlders say what you say, but you bring weapons." He approached Captain Evans and menacingly held the gun to her forehead. "Weapon of peace or weapon of war?" he asked her.

Alarmed but cool, Captain Evans replied, "The person holding the weapon gets to decide. But I assure you, we have not come here to harm your people."

"If you do not come here to harm my people, then why are you here?"

"We are here by accident. We did not mean to come to this world," responded Captain Evans.

"Being's words play games. Are there more of you?" questioned the Vaniryan, maintaining steadfast eye contact with Captain Evans.

"No, we are alone," she answered, not quite ready to disclose details about Emma without knowing the intentions of their captors.

The Vaniryan motioned with his right hand, calling for other Vaniryans to approach. "The twisted words and clever tongue of the Hunt never ceases to amaze me. The Hunt takes many forms, but truth is not one of them. Not for many years does a being set foot in our woods. Only the Hunt travels the deadly forest." As commanded, a Vaniryan approached carrying Emma's bag and clothes left behind at the waterfall, while another brought up the group's remaining bags. Together, the Vaniryans dropped *four* bags on the floor.

"There are four of you," said the Vaniryan leader. "You do not tell the truth."

Voices from the crowd started shouting to their leader. After listening to a few, the Vaniryan interpreted for the captives, "They want Yssil to bring death to the intruders. Perhaps I should. They do not trust you, nor should they. Your lies speak like the Hunt."

Captain Evans instantly regretted her error in judgment. She tried to apologize, "Yssil, I am sorry for my—"

Yssil wasn't interested. "I shall suffer no more lies, or you shall suffer the consequences. Now, where is your fourth off-worlder?" By the angry expression on his face, it was clear that was the first, last, and only time he intended to ask the question.

"I am right here," answered Emma from the back of the hall. The gathering of Vaniryans spun around and gasped at the sight of an off-worlder walking freely among them. Professor Quimbey and Captain Evans let out a sigh of relief that Emma was safe, although given their present predicament who knew how much longer that would be the case.

Emma walked toward the front, wearing a hooded brown cloak.

30 minutes ago, Emma had heard the horn sound and, after Tassa and Isa left, she saw the Vaniryans carrying her unconscious companions from the window. After seeing that, she searched the home for clothing to wear over her Air Force-issued sweats so she could go down for a closer look. She'd managed to enter the gathering undetected, but now that she had revealed herself, she put her hands high in the air to make it clear she was unarmed.

On the way to the front, Emma caught a brief glance of Isa, who looked like she wanted to say something, like she wanted to help Emma somehow. Emma shook her off and Tassa, sensing the girl's instincts, communicated telepathically that she should remain silent.

Several Vaniryans swarmed around Emma with laser rifles pointed at her body. They guided her to the front of the hall where Captain Evans, Professor Quimbey, and Annika sat on the ground, all bound-up.

"Hey guys," said Emma to her friends as the Vaniryans forced her to the floor beside them.

"An intruder from the forest walks among us, it appears… more lies!" declared Yssil, once again glaring at Captain Evans. "And how did this off-worlder find the trees of Jaannos?"

"Yssil, it is my wrong," announced Tassa, stepping forward to cover for Isa. "I went down to the surface for water without plan of the council. She spotted me and followed me up to Jaannos."

Yssil looked unhappy. "Tassa, you know the surface is forbidden without plan of the council. The Hunt *will* find us."

"Yssil, I am sorry for my mistake. It will not happen again."

"Yssil," interrupted Emma, "please do not punish—"

"And what is the name of the creature who invades our trees and now speaks without being asked a question?" asked Yssil.

"My name is Emma…"

"Emma," repeated Yssil. "Where do you beings come from that you would invade our forest?"

"We are humans from a planet called Earth, and we are not invaders. We are *not* the Hunt. We are lost on your world, marooned, stranded from our own. We did not mean to come here."

"You say that, but your words mean very little among the lies."

"Yssil, they are not the Hunt," said Tassa, walking up closer. "Look at her, look at them. You know it is true… look into their eyes."

"Why does Tassa protect these beings? They bring danger to us all."

Tassa responded, "We do not yet know what danger these beings bring, but death to innocents cannot always be our way."

"Please let us go. We only want to go home," said Emma.

"Let you go so you can teach the Hunt where Remnants hide? No, that is not an acceptable fate for the Remnants of Jaannos," replied Yssil.

"We won't say anything to anyone, especially the Hunt, you have our word," assured Captain Evans, having absolutely no clue what the Hunt referred to.

Yssil wasn't interested in Captain Evans's assurances. "The Hunt will find you. Whether you mean to honor your word or not, they will take the information right out of your unguarded minds, and after they kill you, they will come here. No. As Tassa suggests mercy, the off-worlders will remain here."

"What do you mean, off-worlders will remain here?!" questioned Professor Quimbey. "We can't survive if we remain here!"

"If the Hunt finds you, none of us survive. You will remain—"

"All we want is to get back to the pyramid in orbit where there's a portal to get us home!" blurted Emma.

Emma's response stunned the hall, leaving every Vaniryan speechless, including Yssil. The sound of whispers followed next. Yssil took a few more moments to regain his composure before responding, "There is no pyramid. What you say is untrue."

"But it is. I've been there," insisted Emma. "The portal in the pyramid in orbit is how I got here three years ago... it's how I got home. I've been inside it. There were dozens of glowing Vaniryans in there. Just tell us how to get back there. *Please.*"

Again, taken aback by Emma's comments, and perhaps more by her stubbornness, Yssil looked at Tassa wondering who or perhaps more importantly *what* Tassa had allowed to follow her into Jaannos. Yssil, Tassa, and the others conferred. Then, Yssil broke away and announced in Vaniryan to all gathered, "Clear the hall!"

Immediately, the crowd began dispersing. Yssil turned to two of his men and said, "Lassar, Tamos, untie the prisoners and bring them upstairs. Tassa, as you have vouched for the prisoners, you will join us. Yssil did an about-face and, together with Tassa and one other, headed for an arched doorway at the back of the hall.

"Finally! I can't feel my legs, and my knickers are twisted," griped Professor Quimbey while Lassar cut off her ropes. He next moved on to Annika's.

After Tamos cut Captain Evans loose, she stood, massaged her wrists, and asked, "What just happened?"

"I'm not sure," replied Emma. "But something I said about the pyramid sure caught his attention."

"Maybe, but I don't think he believed a word of it," remarked Professor Quimbey, her limbs now freed also.

Captain Evans disagreed. "That wasn't doubt you heard, Quimbey, it was something else..."

"Like what?" asked the professor.

"Fear."

Chapter 17 – The Secret of Everything

As instructed by Yssil, Lassar and Tamos guided the four of them to the arched doorway at the back of the hall, where a staircase wound up through the center of the tree. A light glow seeped through holes purposely cut into the bark at sporadic points to allow the tree's natural green energy to light the passageway. Eventually, they came to another arched doorway.

Lassar and Tamos opened the door and took them in. They stood inside a round sanctuary with bookshelves all the way around except for two square windows. In the middle of the sanctuary was a large circular stump growing out of the tree as if the room had been shaped around it, with a flat smooth metallic top-surface blended so perfectly into the wood stump that it was hard to tell where the stump ended and the metallic surface began. Yssil, Tassa, and an elderly wise-looking Vaniryan woman sat on benches around the stump, waiting for them to join. Lassar and Tamos closed the door from within and stood guard.

"Come, join us," said Yssil. The foursome gathered on benches around the stump.

"Emma-being, can you show us what the star system you come from looks like?" asked Yssil.

"Yes," said Emma, "but what's this all about?"

"You spoke of a myth down in the hall about stories of ages older than ages," said Yssil.

"Stories?" replied Emma. "It was all true. Every word."

"It is time to see what is true and what is not," stated Yssil. He pointed to the table and said, "Show us your star system." He touched the metallic surface and it turned on like a smart pad, changing to a very light shade of green, energized by the power of the tree. He dragged his finger along the surface to show Emma how it worked by capturing the drag of his finger. "Does Emma-being see?" he asked.

Emma nodded to show that she understood how it worked. Yssil moved his open-handed palm over the metal surface, holding it about two inches above, and erased the display with the movement of his hand. He motioned for Emma to begin.

Emma took her index finger and drew the sun. Next, she drew Mercury, Venus, Earth, Mars, Jupiter, Saturn, Uranus, Neptune, and Pluto in order, doing her best to capture the relative sizes of the planets. Still, it wasn't exact.

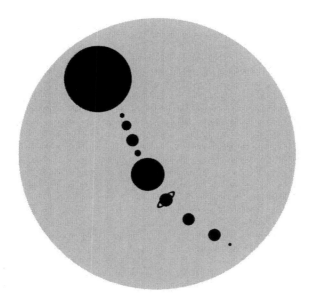

"And where is your Earth in this star system?" Yssil asked.

"It is, um, here, the third one out from our sun," replied Emma, circling Earth.

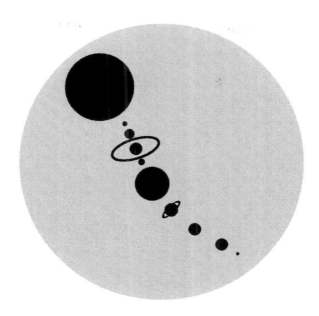

Yssil and Sorra exchanged a glance, a shocked one. Sorra closed her eyes, while Yssil stared at Emma's solar system. He rotated the drawing around by placing his finger on the screen and spinning it like a turntable.

The mood in the sanctuary had clearly changed. No one was speaking. Emma found herself getting nervous with their silence. Then, Sorra nodded to Yssil. He dismissed Lassar and Tamos from the sanctuary, leaving the three Vaniryans alone with the four humans. Yssil moved his palm over the metallic surface to erase the star system drawn by Emma.

Sorra strolled over to one of the bookshelves and removed a big old dusty book. Slowly, she made her way back to the stump and laid the book down on top of it. She opened the book to a page near the back, where there was a slightly smaller page that didn't belong, hidden between the pages. It looked like an old, brown, worn piece of parchment paper with nothing on it.

"It's blank," said Annika.

"What is it?" asked Emma.

"It is a scroll passed down through time. No one knows who scribed it," replied Sorra.

"That's probably because it's blank," remarked Captain Evans.

"Some believe the Va scribed it," said Yssil.

"The Va?" asked Professor Quimbey.

"The mythical ancestors of all Vaniryans. Ethereal beings of power and knowledge who once watched over Vanirya from pyramids hidden in the heavens," replied Sorra, echoing elements of what Emma had said moments ago in the tree hall.

Captain Evans questioned, "What happened to them?"

"One of their own overthrew them, an evil Va named Supay," replied Sorra. "It is myth but legend says the Va, after learning of Supay's evil plans for the universe, tried to expel Supay from the

248

pyramids. But he fought back behind a loyal army of followers, destroying the Va and chasing those who survived away. It is said, the few Va who escaped passed down what little power they had left to a handful of descendants so that they might be able to defend themselves before disappearing into the stars."

"Are the Remnants the descendants of the Va?" asked Emma.

"Yes," replied Yssil. "Fortunately, Supay never did find what he was after."

"What was that?" asked Professor Quimbey.

"The Leyandermál," Tassa chimed in, stating what she knew of the legend.

"The Leyandermál?" repeated Emma.

"Yes. It is the secret knowledge," said Sorra.

"The secret knowledge of what?" asked Emma.

"*Everything*," responded Sorra. "Of the universe, creation, destruction, life, death, power, the stars, dimensions, other universes, knowledge of everything that is and was… *everything*. The Va have guarded the secret since the beginning of time. When they learned Supay planned to use the Leyandermál to unmake the universe and re-create a new one in his own dark image, they tried to expel him and paid for it with their lives."

"Where is the Leyandermál now?" asked Professor Quimbey.

"It is said the Va who escaped hid the secret with a Remnant," replied Yssil. "And now, Supay's followers, the Dokalfar, hunt down Remnants for him…"

"The Dokalfar?" repeated Emma, recognizing the name.

"Is that familiar to you?" asked Annika.

"I mean, it sounds a lot like the name Dökkálfar that appears in the *Prose Edda* that Logan and Dr. Arenot are always talking about," replied Emma.

"Right, the Dökkálfar are the Dark Elves," added Professor Quimbey.

"So, are these Dokalfar, the Hunt?" Emma asked Yssil.

"Yes, and those they recruit, hunting down and killing Remnants one by one while searching for the Missing Remnant, hoping to find the Leyandermál."

"And we should hope Supay never finds it, otherwise, he will destroy all that is," said Sorra.

"Where is the Missing Remnant supposed to be?" asked Emma.

"It is myth that the Remnant hides on Vanirya, in the stars, in the past, or in the future. It is unknown," replied Yssil.

"It *was* unknown," Sorra corrected him. Sorra removed the book from the stump, put it on the floor, and placed the blank scroll flat on the metallic surface. It suddenly looked different. Where once there was nothing, now, images were visible through the parchment, faintly lit up by the green energy of the tree.

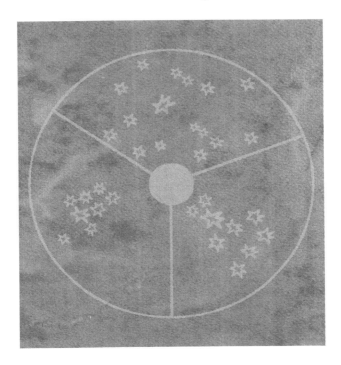

They stared at the outline of a large outer circle, with a smaller solid green circle in the middle. Three lines extended outward from the small green circle to the outer ring, dividing the whole up into three relatively equal sections like a pie-chart. Inside each section were hand-drawn stars.

The top section from 10 o'clock to 2 o'clock had 16 stars in it, seemingly randomly strewn about and drawn in different sizes with no apparent order other than that the largest of the 16 stars was located smack in the middle.

The bottom-right section from 2 o'clock to 6 o'clock had 9 stars in it, with 2 stars close to the center circle, the 3rd star – the biggest of them all – in the next row by itself, and then, 2 more outer rows of 3 stars each.

And finally, the bottom-left section from 6 o'clock to 10 o'clock contained 8 stars, with 1 star out to the left near the edge of the outer ring and a group of 7 stars to the right of it. The 7 stars were stacked on top of each other in 3 parallel rows slightly angled from the top left down to the bottom right. In the leftmost row of 3 stacked stars, the middle star was larger than all other stars in the section. In the center and right rows, there were 2 stars each, with 1 star above the other.

"What is this?" asked Emma.

"It is the *Map of the Hidden*," replied Yssil, "which only the energy of the tree lights up. It depicts where the Va hide in the stars; where the Missing Remnant hides with the Leyandermál; and where Supay hides with his armies, waiting patiently to possess the Leyandermál."

"Which section is which?" asked Professor Quimbey.

Sorra explained, "It is the myth of the *Map* that the bottom-left section of eight stars depicts where the remaining Va hide, as eight escaped, and eight stars shine on the map."

"Jill, do you know what the bottom-left section reminds me of?" said Emma. She paused to allow Professor Quimbey to study the map some more.

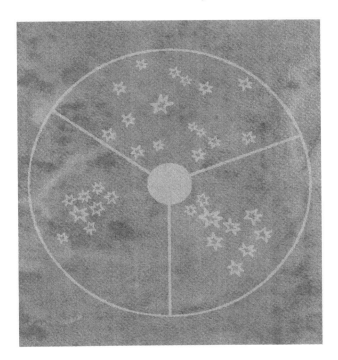

Professor Quimbey took a guess. "It kind of resembles the image in the Voynich manuscript we looked at the other day..."

"Exactly!" exclaimed Emma. "The one I said reminded me of the Pleiades." Emma thought back in her memory to visualize that Voynich image:

"You know this?" asked Yssil.

Emma replied, "The image is similar to one we've seen on Earth in a book called the Voynich manuscript. However, in the Voynich, there's a meandering line extending out from the sun in the center to the group of seven stars that I don't see here, and also, the middle star in the left row of three is enlarged in the *Map of the Hidden*, which I don't recall from the Voynich manuscript."

"Do the sixteen stars in the top section or nine stars in the bottom-right section resemble any images in this manuscript you speak of?" asked Yssil.

"The stars in the top section don't," replied Emma who knew the Voynich manuscript well given her love affair with cryptology. "But there are a lot of drawings in the Voynich manuscript containing nine stars like this one, which makes sense because we come from a solar system of nine planets..." Emma paused to study the lower-right section further. She continued, "...though none of the Voynich drawings have a star enlarged like this third one out from the middle circle is."

"It is like your star system, with Earth also three out from your sun," observed Sorra, not so subtly implying a connection.

"You think the enlarged star in this bottom-right section is meant to depict Earth?" asked Emma, surprised.

"It is what we see," replied Sorra.

Sorra's suggestion surprised Professor Quimbey. "Are you saying Earth is where the Missing Remnant hides?"

Sorra nodded and replied, "Emma-being has seen the Va and has heard of the Dokalfar, which can only be so if the Va visited your world, and you come here from a star system of nine worlds, living on three of nine just like in the *Map of the Hidden*. The Va have sent the signs."

"If the Hunt finds Emma, or any of you, they will deliver you to Supay, and if Supay learns what you know and finds the Missing Remnant, he will unmake the universe and end all worlds," warned Yssil.

Sorra chuckled, a creepy cackling sound partially attributable to her cranky old age, partially attributable to the cosmic irony. "It is too late now to conceal the knowledge! The beings' words, their very arrival, has tainted all of Jaannos. All in the open hall heard the humans speak of Earth and of the Pyramids of Va. They will cut the words right out of the minds of every Remnant in Jaannos. The secret no longer rests with the off-worlders alone. None are safe from the Hunt now."

"Were any of you ever safe?" questioned Captain Evans, doubting how that was possible. "You're talking about beings, if any of this is true, of incredible power and technology, supposedly capable of intergalactic travel, time travel, portals through the stars, and here you all are in Jaannos hiding in trees... No disrespect intended, but how have you all survived the Hunt for even this long?"

"We are not without technology here," replied Yssil, hinting there was more to Jaannos than meets the eye. "Jaannos is well-armed beyond what you see. We have harnessed the energy of the trees in the Jaans Forest to build powerful weapons and a cloaking shield that renders Jaannos invisible to the sky. The Hunt will not find us easily, no matter how many traitors or mercenaries the Hunt recruits with gifts of wealth, power, food, shelter, and other bounty."

"Traitors, mercenaries?" asked Professor Quimbey.

Yssil responded, "It is the way of the Hunt, offering promises of power or bounty to those who assist the Hunt, paying riches for information leading to Remnants. The Hunt is all around us... it is the traitorous Vaniryan, it is the mercenary off-worlder, a stranger from the stars, it is everywhere, everyone. We hide from them all."

"So, that's it then?" blurted Emma. "Your plan is to just keep hiding? It sounds like you've already given up."

"We have given up nothing," replied Yssil. "It is the way of our survival."

Emma disagreed. "Doesn't sound like much of a way of survival to me. It sounds like a way to just keep doing what Remnants have been doing for ages, running and hiding, abandoning homes, fleeing worlds, losing families to raids, hiding in far off places… and now, hiding in trees. You can't keep this up forever, you know. You'll just keep running and hiding for the rest of time until eventually, the Hunt tracks down each and every one of you, or your children, or your children's children, and finally, recovers the Leyandermál."

"What would you have us do, Emma-being?" Yssil challenged her. "We are but a few, spread out among the stars. Any other plan is a plan of doom."

"I don't know," admitted Emma, "but help us return home and we'll help you find the Missing Remnant on Earth, if he or she really does exist. And maybe, if this Remnant truly does possess the secret knowledge of *everything*, he or she will know something that will help you defeat Supay and put an end to this forever."

Yssil, Tassa, and Sorra considered what Emma said and discussed it. Never had they, or any Remnant, ever been so close to recovering the Leyandermál before, the one source of knowledge in the universe that might aid them in a fight against Supay that would otherwise be doomed without it. Their discussion went on until Yssil finally said, "It is decided and agreed. We will help you return home as you request, and in turn, you will help us find the Missing Remnant."

Professor Quimbey replied, "Thank you, but it is more complicated than simply returning us home. In coming here, we've also gone back in time before our own lives began on Earth. We don't know how far back… it could be far before the creation of the very clues we will need to help you find the Missing Remnant. If we are to help you, we must not only go home but also find a way to return to our proper place in time."

"Then, that is why you must journey to the Hidden City," replied Yssil.

"The Hidden City?" repeated Captain Evans.

"Yes, it is your best hope," said Yssil.

At that moment, Emma noticed a little face peeking through one of the outer windows. She recognized it immediately: it was Isa. Emma slightly grinned at her. As soon as Isa realized Emma saw her, she ducked down. Emma kept quiet and said nothing to anyone. She didn't want Isa to get in trouble.

"Where is the Hidden City you refer to?" asked Captain Evans.

Yssil removed the *Map of the Hidden* and handed it to Sorra. She carefully placed it back in the book. He then held his hand over the metallic surface and made a spherical fist. After the device read the shape of his hand, a translucent, holographic three-dimensional globe of the Vaniryan planet appeared right before their eyes, hovering over the stump.

The transparent sphere was tinted purple, with pockets of purple-blue oceans, hundreds of land masses of every shape and size, and even indications of terrain: a green hue against the purple backdrop for forestland, a brown-hue for desert-terrain; a white-hue for snow and ice; raised topography for mountainous regions; and so on and so forth.

"We are here," stated Yssil, pointing to a forest in the middle of a large land mass. Yssil next pointed to the center of a white land mass far northeast of their forest, with hints of sharp mountains, snow, and ice plateaus. "The Hidden City is there, in the Frozen Shards, 64.1434547 above our equator and 114.889423 to the right of Vanirya's tallest mountain. That is where you must go."

"Are those coordinates?" asked Annika, astonished.

"Yes, coordinates are how we know our way," replied Yssil.

"That is just as we do on Earth," said Annika, amazed by the commonality of mathematics.

"'Mathematics is the language in which God has written the universe,' Galileo Galilei," said Emma, quoting the famous Italian astronomer and physicist. She had just learned the quote a few weeks earlier as one of Professor Albies's "End of Class" quotes in Emma's Astronomy in Culture class.

Captain Evans still looked worried. "What is the distance to the Hidden City?" she asked, concerned about the length of the journey relative to how long they could survive in Vanirya's atmosphere.

"1,000 days," replied Yssil.

Emma yelped, "But we don't have that much time..."

"It is no worry," Yssil assured her, clearly envisioning a form of travel other than walking. "There is another way. Lassar and Tamos will guide you."

Chapter 18 – Machu Picchu

The massive white business jet carrying Logan, Dr. Arenot, Bryan, Allysa, and Minister Menputyn's henchmen began its slow descent into Cusco mid-morning the day after they left the U.S.

Shortly after takeoff, Dmitri had confiscated their cellphones, and his men, Ivan and Boris, took turns between the cockpit and passenger cabin watching the Americans. Logan and Dr. Arenot took advantage of the ten-hour flight to get some rest.

Bryan and Allysa, on the other hand, didn't sleep at all. After spending the flight's first hour grappling with their situation and getting an explanation from Logan and Dr. Arenot as to what was *really* going on, along with numerous apologies, they spent the rest of the flight talking to each other about what they had just heard, what they thought, and what they believed. While Bryan was a willing believer in the cosmic adventure that they found themselves caught up in, Allysa remained skeptical that this sci-fi narrative was actually real, although ultimately, she knew what she thought didn't matter. They were bound for Machu Picchu regardless of her opinion.

Once the plane touched down in Cusco, the former capital of the Inca Empire from the 13th until the 16th-century Spanish conquest, they had to get to Machu Picchu. Driving to Machu Picchu wasn't allowed, so their other options were a multi-day hike, a bus, or a train ride, with the latter two options taking passengers through the Urubamba Valley to Aguas Calientes, a town at the base of Machu Picchu mountain. The best Dmitri's well-funded colleagues in Moscow could arrange on short notice was a small, out-of-service shuttle bus from one of the local tour companies driven by Diego, a local villager. Diego would drive them to Machu Picchu, wait for them to explore the ruins, and bring them back to Cusco, whether later that same day or the next.

They boarded the old, creaky-looking bus, and it rumbled and puttered its way out of town on the cobblestone streets surrounded by Cusco's unique Inca-European-Spanish colonial architecture. Once they left Cusco, they traveled through the Urubamba Valley. The road had dramatic canyon walls on either side leading up into the peaks of the Andes. Along the route, they journeyed through forests, alpine tundra, and jungles, passing lush flora, streams, tunnels, and even scattered Inca ruins.

It took nearly four hours to get to Aguas Calientes. Built-up by the heavy tourism of Machu Picchu, the town was full of eateries, shops, busy streets, markets, hotels, and people. Diego took them to a local spot where they could purchase tickets to enter the ruins, and fortunately for them, there were still some tickets available for the afternoon time slot.

Tickets in hand, Diego drove them on the main road along the Urubamba River for about one mile before crossing a bridge and heading up the mountain by way of a steep, zig-zagging road named Carretera Hiram Bingham or Hiram Bingham Road. The bus carefully navigated the steep mountainside, and at one point on the way up, they could see a portion of the ruins of Machu Picchu off in the distance.

They reached the front entrance of the ruins 40 minutes after leaving Aguas Calientes. There was an entrance gate where staff collected tickets and conducted security checks. Upon seeing that, Dmitri realized their bags full of weapons wouldn't make it through security, so he pointed at Bryan and Allysa and said, "You two will stay here with Ivan and Boris." Moving closer to the Americans so Diego couldn't hear him, Dmitri muttered to Bryan and Allysa, "If either of you attempts to escape or reach out for help, or even makes so much as a sound, Ivan and Boris will shoot you both. The minister has already said you two are expendable. Do I make myself clear?"

"Uh-huh," they gulped and replied in unison. Logan gave them an apologetic look that couldn't possibly convey how badly he felt about the situation.

"Okay, West, Professor, let's go," ordered Dmitri.

They got off the bus and Dmitri escorted them up the steps to the entrance gate with a few additional words of warning. "If Ivan or Boris sees either of you walk out this entrance without me, your friends are dead, and you'll be next. No games. Now, let's go in, shall we?"

After passing through security and going through the entrance gate, the greeting staff handed out complimentary Machu Picchu brochures to incoming tourists. Logan and Dr. Arenot politely took theirs, while Dmitri rejected his. They took another zig-zagging trail made of fieldstones up the mountain and through the cloud-forest. The trail was full of tourists coming and going. When they got to the top, the forest opened up to a panoramic view of Machu Picchu from a hill slightly above the citadel, with the great peak of Huayna Picchu mountain towering behind it to the north.

The ancient Inca city looked just like it did in postcards and history books, with its architecture adapted to the eastern slope of Machu Picchu mountain. Hundreds of ruins made of fieldstones and granite blocks were constructed on top of wide parallel terraces that looked like steps built into the length of the mountainside. Stone stairways were set in between the buildings to allow access to the different terrace levels up and down the mountain. Despite their terrible situation, Logan couldn't help but remark, "This might be the most beautiful place I have ever seen."

"It's quite a sight, isn't it?" replied Dr. Arenot, himself gazing down on the ruins in wonder.

"Let's get on with it," grumbled Dmitri. "This isn't a vacation. What now, West?"

"I might've been able to answer that question had you not confiscated our phones on the plane. We could've gotten a head start researching this hours ago."

"Do you think I'm a fool, West? The only thing you would've gotten a head start on was contacting the authorities before we landed."

Logan knew the only one way out of this mess was to find what they came for: an answer hidden somewhere within the 65 square miles of ruins atop Machu Picchu mountain. With hundreds of structures, temples, palaces, tombs, staircases, plazas, homes, fountains, and more to look at, Logan and Dr. Arenot weren't quite sure where to start. They decided to at least begin with the brochure they got at the gate.

Titled the *Wonders of Machu Picchu*, the brochure contained exquisite photography of the citadel, a site map, a brief history of Machu Picchu, and a recitation of how Hiram Bingham accidentally discovered the lost city in 1911 with the help of a local guide, Melchor Arteaga. Thumbing through it, Logan stopped at a page that caught his eye called, "Fun Facts About Machu Picchu by the Numbers." He read it:

Fun Facts About Machu Picchu by the Numbers

20: The number of ruined buildings Hiram Bingham first saw when he discovered Machu Picchu in 1911. Later excavations revealed more than 500.

50: The number of tons of some of the heavier stones used to build Machu Picchu. The Inca did not use wheels to transport the rocks up the steep mountain. Men had to push the heavy rocks all the way.

74.7: The number of kilometers between Cusco and Machu Picchu. Despite its close proximity, the Spanish never discovered the citadel after conquering Cusco in 1533.

100: The number of staircases at Machu Picchu.

<u>300 to 1,000</u>: The number of people living at Machu Picchu during its peak. Those who stayed at the royal estate were the highest social class of Inca people called "llactas."

<u>700</u>: The number of terraces carved into the hillside of Machu Picchu mountain. The terraces, fortified by granite walls, were used for creating fertile land and to fight erosion and keep Machu Picchu stable.

<u>2,430</u>: The number of meters (7,970 feet) that Machu Picchu lies above sea level.

<u>1,578,030</u>: The number of tourists who visited Machu Picchu last year.

<u>3,714,256</u>: The number of Inca living in the Cusco region under Pachacuti's rule, which the Inca ruler memorialized on a gold and silver Quipu Necklace recently recovered in the Lima region.

<u>6,000,000 to 14,000,000</u>: The number of people in the Inca Empire at its peak, which continued to grow even after Pachacuti's death in 1471. Upon his death, the Inca mummified Pachacuti's body and hid him in a secret shrine in the mountains above Cusco. The Spanish discovered the shrine in 1533 and sent Pachacuti's mummified body to Lima, only it was lost in transit or destroyed on the way, along with all belongings buried with Pachacuti. Fortunately, Peru's Ministry of Culture has recovered a few of the lost items over the years.

<u>13.163333° S to 72.545556° W</u>: The GPS coordinates of Machu Picchu.

"Professor, any thoughts?" asked Logan.

"Machu Picchu means 'Old Mountain' in Quechua," said a voice in a Peruvian accent from behind. They turned around to see a skinny, short, dark-haired tour guide, one of many loitering around the entrance pitching private guided tours for a fee. With so much to get to in a short period of time, especially with the mountain closing at 5:30 pm, Logan thought a tour guide might be beneficial.

"How much?" Logan asked.

"West, what are you doing?" barked Dmitri, uninterested in bringing an outsider into their group.

"You going to guide us through the ruins, Dmitri?" queried Dr. Arenot. "This place is enormous. It's a great idea, actually."

"Fine," conceded Dmitri.

"I am Alejandro… I do tour for you for 600 soles."

Dmitri wasn't impressed by Alejandro's first offer, so he replied, "A little steep, friend, no?"

"It is the price to know Machu Picchu," responded Alejandro, sounding like a used car salesman.

Staring the guide down a bit, Dmitri countered, "You're not trying to take advantage of us, are you, Alejandro?"

"I am native, raised in Aguas Calientes. I grew up guiding visitors through the ruins. I know Machu Picchu better than your books, postcards, and maps," countered Alejandro, defending his experience and price, which equaled about $225 USD. But, bidding against himself, he compromised, nonetheless. "I do tour for 575 soles."

Still unpersuaded and trying to work a lower price, Dmitri replied, "Should I talk to another Alejandro?" He looked around.

"Don't be an ass!" exclaimed Logan, unable to keep his mouth shut after Dmitri's rudeness. "Just pay him."

"I'll be an ass to whoever I want," said Dmitri, giving Logan a dismissive smirk. Addressing Alejandro, he said, "I'll pay you $150 in American dollars, friend. You figure out the exchange rate on your own time, but that's more than enough to feed your scrawny bones for a month."

Logan shook his head at the condescending words that kept coming out of Dmitri's mouth.

Alejandro disliked Dmitri, but Dmitri wasn't the first arrogant, elitist, or racist tourist to buy his time at the mountain, and surely wouldn't be the last, so he agreed. "Sí," said Alejandro, holding his hands out to receive his money. After pocketing his fee, Alejandro escorted the three men down the steps to the ruins.

"Not a word," Dmitri threateningly reminded Logan and Dr. Arenot.

Almost instantly, Alejandro began his well-rehearsed presentation. "From here you can see the agricultural zone lower on the mountain, with Machu Picchu's famous graduated terraces of cultivation built into the mountainside. The terraces are constructed with vertical walls of granite fieldstone, which are held together by gravel and clay. The Inca cultivated the land on top of each terrace. In Quechua, we say 'Pata,' meaning 'stepped terraces' that climb the hills and mountains. There are roughly 700 terraces carved into the hillside. Higher up the hill to the left, you see the ruins of—"

Before Alejandro could continue, Logan stopped him. "What can you tell us about Pachacuti?"

Visitors frequently interrupted with questions, so Alejandro responded, "Ah, Pachakutiq Inka Yupanki, the ninth Sapa Inca of the Kingdom of Cusco who transformed Tawantinsuyu into great power. Machu Picchu was built for him… it is his royal soil we walk on."

"Can you take us to where Pachacuti lived?" asked Logan.

"Sí, sí, it is a ruin we will visit. There is much more Inca history to see on the way."

"Why don't we just go there now?" stated Dmitri abruptly, having no interest in the tour.

Alejandro was confused. Visitors rarely asked him to rush through the ruins like this. After all, they paid him for a full tour. He found the request odd. "I can tour as you like, but I assure you we will see what you seek."

"If only he knew what we were really seeking," Logan whispered to Dr. Arenot.

Dr. Arenot stepped in. "Alejandro, we have a great interest in all this, but we come here today with a particular academic interest in Pachacuti. Can we please focus on the ninth Sapa Inca for now, and if the tour takes longer this way, we'll pay more, isn't that right, Dmitri?"

Dmitri sneered but begrudgingly agreed.

"Ah, sí," said Alejandro, initially caught off guard by the request but now ready to deviate from his normal guided tour. "So, we shall tour to the Royal Palace located in the citadel's upper zone. There, in the Hanan is the residence of Pachakutiq Inka Yupanki. It is a 20-minute walk down the steps and over to the palace. Follow me."

ΔΔΔΔΔΔΔΔΔΔΔ

Bryan and Allysa sat at the back of the bus, which Diego had driven to the back of a lot slightly downhill while waiting for Dmitri, Logan, and Dr. Arenot to finish their excursion on the mountain. Ivan and Boris kept an eye on them, while Diego had gotten off the bus for a few minutes to stretch his legs.

Bryan glimpsed at Allysa. The situation they found themselves in was tense, and she looked worried.

"You okay?" he asked.

"Uh, no, not really," she replied, staring straight ahead at Ivan.

266

"Bet you didn't see this coming when Logan knocked on your door last night to ask for a small favor."

Allysa glanced back at Bryan and chuckled. "Yeah, you could say that. How'd they get you to come along on this crazy trip?"

"Well, I didn't plan to, that's for sure. I was just planning to drive them to Georgetown and then to the airport. It's not like they told me someone was after them when they came to my store, that's for sure."

"Your store?"

"Yep."

"Your store as in, 'the store you work at,' or your store as in, '*your* store'?"

"My store. I own Dewey's."

"Wow. I don't think I realized that when you mentioned on the plane you worked there. How long have you owned it?"

"A few years. The prior owner, Dewey, and I were tight. When he died, he left the store to me."

"Oh, Bryan, I'm so sorry to hear that. Was he a close friend from school or something?"

"Not quite. Dewey was in his 50s. I met him when I was 13. I was really into comic books back then. I mean, I still am today, but he always let me hang out there and read 'em for free... gave me a place to go."

"What do you mean, he 'gave you a place to go'?"

"I don't know, I guess I just meant middle school was really hard for me. I got bullied a lot. In elementary school, no one cared, but once I hit middle school... it was just hard to be the kid who likes comic books and superheroes when everyone else was growing up so fast around me, you know? Kids can be cruel, and when I needed someone, Dewey was there for me. Gave me a safe space to go, let me be me, offered me a job. Honestly, I think he was able to relate to what I was going through. He was—"

"A good friend."

"Yeah, he really was. I'm 24 years old and I still believe in heroes, because Dewey was that for me. I know it sounds stupid, but…"

Touched by the genuine sincerity of Bryan's corny comment, she replied, "It's not stupid at all. I think it's nice to still believe in heroes, and we could really use one right now to get out of this mess."

"Well, if there's one thing I've learned about Logan over the years, he's good at cleaning up messes."

"You mean, this isn't Logan's first mess?"

"Nope. Every time he comes to my store, he's hacking cellphones, messing with terrorists, saving people's lives and stuff. The guy's a do-good badass."

"Let's hope so," replied Allysa. She leaned back in her bench seat and said again, "Let's hope so."

ΔΔΔΔΔΔΔΔΔΔΔ

Logan and Dr. Arenot's trek to the Royal Palace took about 20 minutes. One of the first things they noticed when they reached it was the precise, smooth and flat white-granite-block walls, albeit with the passage of time, they were no longer white; rather, they were a dirty gray. Whereas in most other sections of Machu Picchu, the ruins consisted of fieldstones cleverly fit together based on each stone's natural shape or size, or its shape or size after being split along natural fracture lines by tools, here in the palace, all stone blocks were cut, chiseled, sanded, and worked by the Inca until

268

perfectly square or rectangular-shaped. The large, finely shaped stones were then fit together with mortar in a jigsaw-like-pattern.

The rooms where the royal family stayed, including Pachacuti himself, were actually quite small. None had ceilings like all the ruins at Machu Picchu, as the thatches that once provided roof cover were long gone.

Logan and Dr. Arenot examined the rooms for clues. The main room believed to have belonged to Pachacuti was the largest. As was common throughout the citadel, the walls had trapezoidal niches where Pachacuti and his family placed objects of adornment or belongings. Other than the dirt and grass on the ground and splendor of the stonework, they saw nothing in the rooms relating to the mystery they came for.

"What do you think?" Logan asked Dr. Arenot.

The professor replied, "I don't know. I don't see anything that stands out to me. Other than knowing the royal family stayed in these rooms, there's nothing here that tells me we've found the answer."

"Alejandro, what else is in the royal compound?" asked Logan

"Near is the Royal Mausoleum and Torreón," Alejandro responded.

"A tomb?" asked Logan. "That sounds promising. They could have hidden something in there. Are there still bodies or mummies inside it?"

"Not anymore. It is near… do you wish to look?"

"Yes, please," replied Logan.

Alejandro took them around the corner and across the steps to the Royal Mausoleum. The tomb was carved into a huge solid white granite rock which served as the foundation for a curved structure sitting on top of it. Inca stonework framed a forward-slanted sliver of an entrance leading into a natural cave in the rock. Alejandro took them into the tomb. There was a small inner enclosure of carefully carved walls with niches cut into them to hold mummified bodies, a stone shelf underneath the niches wide enough to sit or stand on, and an altar stone on the floor for bodies and rituals.

Alejandro resumed his tour guide spiel. "It is believed this mausoleum held the bodies of the elite, from the royal family, high priests, and other noble Inca of importance to Pachakutiq."

They studied the empty tomb and still saw nothing that helped them solve their Pachacuti mystery. There were no bodies or mummies in there, no constellations carved into the walls, no pattern of stones laid on the ground or carvings in the walls, or any other aggregations of stones or carvings similar to how the Vaniryans did it elsewhere where Logan and Emma found portals in the past.

Logan didn't know what to do next or where to go, or what they were looking for. He simply hadn't had enough time to research Machu Picchu. They had decided to fly there on a whim even before Minister Menputyn hijacked their journey, and Logan had assumed he would know what he was looking for when he saw it, just like what happened three years ago when he and Emma figured things out on the fly. But that strategy wasn't working so far, and Machu Picchu was far larger than the Norwegian cave and Stonehenge. It also didn't help that their lives were in danger. That only made it harder for Logan to concentrate. He could feel Dmitri breathing down his neck as they scoured the Royal Mausoleum for something relating to Pachacuti and the stars. Then, it occurred to him… why not just ask Alejandro?

"Alejandro, is there anything in these ruins relating to the stars?"

"Sí, señor," he replied, waving them back outside.

Once outside, Logan asked, "Where?"

"It is above you."

270

They glanced up at a curved stone-block structure sitting on top of the Royal Mausoleum. The tomb's natural granite rockface faded seamlessly into the stone block work of the curved structure. There were two trapezoidal windows visible on the curved structure's outer wall, one facing northeast and the other southeast.

"What's that?" asked Logan

"The Temple of the Sun or Torreón, once used as an observatory where Pachakutiq and his high priests studied the sun and stars to predict the seasons and aid with cultivation. It is said that the sacred temple is where Pachakutiq spoke to the gods and the stars, performed sacred rituals, and religious sacrifices."

As soon as Logan heard Alejandro's words, he got excited. That sounded exactly like the type of place they were looking for! Logan bound around the corner and up the steps leading to the Temple of the Sun, with the others following closely.

The Temple of the Sun was in the middle of a square courtyard, with three of the four walls intersecting at 90-degree angles, and the fourth wall on the eastern side partially open. When Logan walked into the courtyard, the round temple was on his right, and there was a stone-block wall on his left with a door leading to the High Priest's bedroom. That wall continued straight until intersecting with another wall in front of Logan. The wall then turned right and continued until meeting another wall which turned right again and led directly into the curved temple itself. The inner temple was semi-circular shaped, although the semi-circle wall did not complete the loop at the bottom, leaving an open pathway between the straight wall and curved wall for entry into the Temple of the Sun.

The Temple of the Sun was constructed of the same finely-cut white granite stones and assembled like the other expertly crafted portions of the royal compound. There were two trapezoidal windows in the exterior curved wall looking outward, and a large granite altar stone in the center of the floor in front of the windows. Unlike other areas of the royal compound, they were alone inside the Temple of the Sun, for the moment.

"What are you looking for?" Dr. Arenot asked Logan, trying to understand what he was thinking.

"You ask if there is anything in these ruins that relates to the stars, and so, I bring you in here because of the windows," suggested Alejandro.

"What do you mean?" asked Dr. Arenot.

"It is said that Pachakutiq and his priests studied the stars from the windows to forecast the seasons and foretell the time to grow and plant crops based on when the constellations rose in the windows at night and where the sun hit the altar during the day. That is how Pachakutiq predicted the seasons and spread the word across Tawantinsuyu that it was time to plant or that winter was coming."

"What does Tawantinsuyu mean?" asked Logan.

"The Inca Empire," replied Alejandro.

"Which constellations were visible in the windows?" Logan asked.

Alejandro responded, "Through Solstice window facing northeast, Pachakutiq's priests waited for the rising of the Pleiades to call the June solstice, when the Inca would celebrate with a great festival, the Inti Raymi, to celebrate the coming of season."

"The Pleiades?!" yelped Logan. He walked over and looked out the Solstice window. He still didn't see anything remarkable other than a stunning view of the Andes mountains.

"What are you looking for?" asked Alejandro, interested in helping them if he could.

Logan replied, "The Pleiades consist of seven stars. We need to find a group of seven stones, objects, or things." Logan looked around and said to Dr. Arenot, "There are eight trapezoidal niches and two windows in these walls. Maybe there's a pattern among the trapezoids that we can press or touch like what the Vaniryans did back at the cave in Norway and Stonehenge."

A brown and white feathered condor boldly landed on top of the Temple of the Sun's highest stone, surveying the tourists within its walls.

"Ah, the condor, the sacred guardians of our forest," said Alejandro, familiar with the condors of the Andes who occasionally dropped in to visit Machu Picchu and its guests, although rarely this close.

"Wow, she's magnificent," said Dr. Arenot, taken aback by the condor's sudden arrival. Almost as quickly as it arrived, the great condor took off in flight, spreading its wings, and heading north toward Huayna Picchu.

Dr. Arenot continued. "Logan, if you're looking to touch or press or make sense of a group of seven things, this Temple doesn't make sense. There are eight trapezoidal niches and two windows. The numbers don't add up."

"This has to be it," insisted Logan, wanting so badly to believe they were on the right track. "This is the sanctum of Pachacuti, he who overturns space and time, who studied constellations from these windows, including the Pleiades. It all adds up!"

At this point, after listening carefully to the conversation, Alejandro had another suggestion. "There is another sanctum of importance to Pachakutiq, where there are seven ritual niches in the stones. Perhaps that is what you seek."

"Where?" asked Dr. Arenot.

"It is known to your books as the Temple of the Moon," replied Alejandro. "It is built inside a natural cave. Very mysterious."

"In the citadel?" Logan asked, encouraged by there being seven niches and its location in a cave, which was where the Vaniryans had hidden other portals.

"No. It is on the other side of Huayna Picchu mountain to the north. You must take the trail to Huayna Picchu, and then take the pass to the left to walk around the mountain, and then descend Huayna's north face on the Stairs of the Death."

"That's what they call it, the Stairs of the Death?" asked Dmitri skeptically.

"Sí, señor, it is very steep. Then, you come across a narrow jungle path to reach the Temple of the Moon inside the great cavern. Many hours to get there."

"How many hours?" asked Logan.

"Two hours to get there, two hours to get back," answered Alejandro.

"Can you take us?" Dmitri asked him.

"It is not permitted this afternoon hour. Citadel and ruins close at 5:30 pm, and it is already late afternoon. Only persons with morning group tickets for both Machu Picchu and Huayna Picchu may go. No way now. I can take you tomorrow."

"I will pay you 600 additional soles to take us today," proposed Dmitri, ignoring everything Alejandro had just said.

"Security will not let us pass through the trail—"

"I will take care of that," assured Dmitri, although he didn't say how or what he planned to do. Logan presumed Dmitri envisioned bribing whoever stood guard at the trail from Machu Picchu to Huayna Picchu.

Alejandro was tempted but concerned. "It will grow dark as sun sets late afternoon when mountain closes."

"Alejandro, friend, you're not afraid of the dark, are you?" asked Dmitri.

"No, señor, it is just a very dangerous path for you to take in the dark, there and back. The Stairs of the Death are narrow with long drop—"

"Alejandro," interrupted Dmitri, "you said you grew up here on this mountain, giving tours. You know its paths and stones like the back of your hand, don't you?" Dmitri paused and Alejandro nodded, conceding he did. "I suspect you can do this with your eyes closed."

"Sí, señor, but—"

"800 soles," offered Dmitri, upping his initial offer.

"But the guards…" replied Alejandro.

"900 soles, and please don't make me ask again," insisted Dmitri, firmly believing everyone had a price, and sure enough, he had hit Alejandro's.

"Sí, I will take you, but we will never make it through the Huayna Picchu path from Machu Picchu. It is not just one man who stands guard. There are security cameras, and the policía will stop us if security doesn't. There is another way down at the valley floor where we can cross the Urubamba and climb up through the jungle. It is near the botanical gardens north of Aguas Calientes. It is not an easy path, but it is there."

"You see, that wasn't so hard," said Dmitri, smacking Alejandro in the back. "West, you were right, hiring a guide was an excellent idea," chirped Dmitri, proud of what his money could buy.

"We wait until after dark," said Alejandro.

Chapter 19 – The Temple of the Moon

After Alejandro agreed to guide them to the Temple of the Moon, Diego returned with the bus to pick them up at Machu Picchu's exit gates and drive them back down the winding mountain road to Aguas Calientes. With several hours to kill before dark, Dmitri had Ivan and Boris get food for everyone. He knew they all needed to eat something to have the energy to complete the mission, and there was more climbing to do.

Once the sun set, it was time to begin their clandestine journey for the Temple of the Moon. Because there were no roads in the valley, the only way to get there was on foot. So, Diego stayed behind with the bus and they walked to the botanical gardens a mile north of town. The walk took them alongside the Urubamba River, which tracked the footprint of the mountains on their left all the way around to the north side of Huayna Picchu. It was cold out, surprisingly so and at one point, seeing her shivering, Bryan insisted Allysa take his jacket.

The trail took about 50 minutes to reach the botanical gardens, and by the time they found the place in the forest Alejandro envisioned where none could see them, it was pitch-black out but for the moon and stars. They stood before the Urubamba River, at the foot of the cloud-forest covered north face of Huayna Picchu, with the moonlight shimmering off the flowing water. The section of river Alejandro chose was only 45 feet wide. There were plenty of rocks and boulders to step on to get across, and so, they proceeded with caution over the Urubamba, following Alejandro. With only a few minor missteps resulting in nothing more than wet shoes and pants, they successfully crossed the river and began their ascent up the mountain.

As Alejandro said, a little-used path wound up through the trees of the north face. The truth was, they weren't the first tourists to bribe a guide to take them up to the Temple of the Moon at night. Then again, because of the difficulty in climbing the mountain at night, it rarely happened, and so, local authorities weren't regularly looking out for such transgressions. They simply lacked the manpower to regulate all the rare instances of unauthorized hiking throughout the valley in darkness. There was seemingly an endless number of routes committed hikers could take through the mountains, and the authorities couldn't patrol them all. They didn't have the resources.

The hike up the north face of Huayna Picchu through the cloud-forest to their destination took about 2½ hours. When they reached it, Alejandro announced, "We are here."

Almost like his words caused the ruins to magically appear, they suddenly realized they were in the midst of stone-reinforced terraces with classic Inca walls sitting on top of them. The dense forest had a way of helping the ruins sneak up on hikers like that, especially in the dark. Unlike Machu Picchu, there were only a few ruins. Alejandro led them above the terraces to the Temple of the Moon.

As described, the temple was inside a natural cave. The "Great Cavern," as it was often referred to, was located below a huge, elongated overhanging rock which covered the cavern entrance. The entrance into the temple beneath the rock was 26 feet high and 20 feet wide. They passed under the rock's threshold into the sacred temple. The cavern itself was round. In the center of the Temple of the Moon was a surface like a throne.

"What was this place used for?" asked Allysa.

"It is not known for certain," replied Alejandro. "Some believe it was a lookout for intruders. Others think it was used for sacrifices or secret rituals."

"It's kinda creepy," commented Allysa, "but also cool."

"Totally," agreed Bryan.

On the left side of the cave, the Inca had constructed a white-granite-block wall reminiscent of the fine stonework back at Machu Picchu's Royal Palace. The wall fit perfectly into the eastern edge of the cave and rose up into the giant overhead rock. Just like Alejandro described, the granite-block-wall had seven niches carved into it, each equally spaced out and trapezoidal in shape. The niches resembled small doors that didn't lead anywhere.

Pointing at it, Alejandro said, "Those are what you come for."

"Those seven niches are large enough to entomb a mummy," said Dr. Arenot.

"Or serve as portal doors," stated Logan. "Now, we just need to figure out what order to press them in." Logan still assumed the Vaniryan technology he encountered previously worked the same way there. Then again, he was in the land of Pachacuti, who oversaw space and time. Perhaps Pachacuti used different technology or did things differently. There was only one way to find out.

Logan walked up, reached in, and touched the back of the first trapezoidal window on the left, then walked over and touched each one in order, and then, he walked back and touched the first window again. Nothing happened. There was no science or logic to it... he was flying blind.

"Are you serious?" blurted Dmitri.

"Just testing things out," replied Logan. "We need to figure out the combination. It was only a first guess."

Dmitri wasn't buying it. Of course, neither he nor his comrades knew about the Vaniryan technology or how it worked. They hadn't been briefed on such details by Minister Menputyn. Irritated, he responded, "This is your plan, kid? Touching rocks? The minister said you kids were the smartest the U.S. had to offer, and now this?

We traveled 20 hours by plane, bus, ground, sat on a bus all day, and hiked through these mountains in the dark for this crap?!"

"Does anyone hear that?" asked Bryan.

They all listened and sure enough, they heard something approaching outside. Ivan walked out of the cave and heard voices coming down the mountain from the Huayna Picchu trail they would have taken to the temple had it not been closed to visitors. It sounded like multiple voices and based on what he heard, Ivan quickly announced, "The police are coming!" Ivan hurried back into the cave.

"How did they know?" demanded Dmitri. He pulled a gun and pointed it at Logan. "One of you contacted the police!" Following suit, Ivan and Boris pulled their guns and pointed them at the Americans.

"Dmitri, it wasn't any of us!" exclaimed Logan, and Dr. Arenot, Alyssa, and Bryan weren't far behind in denying the accusation.

"Let's everyone calm down here," said Dr. Arenot, trying to defuse tensions.

"Shut up, professor!" snapped Ivan, further asking, "Which one of you was it?"

"Guys, think about it… You've had us in your sights all day," stated Dr. Arenot.

"Then, what about him?" rebutted Dmitri, turning his gun on Alejandro.

Alejandro had no idea what was happening. He was stunned when the Russians drew their weapons in the first place, and now that one of the guns was pointed at him, he was frightened. He shook his head and blurted, "No, señor… not me! Maybe cameras!"

The sound of the police got closer. Dmitri motioned to Ivan and Boris to head outside and prepare to defend the perimeter using the Inca walls for cover.

"None of you move," warned Dmitri. "If I see any of you attempt to leave this cave, I will shoot you where you stand. And if I lose any of my team, one of you will pay the price." Dmitri headed for the cave exit.

"What are you going to do?" Logan asked him.

"What do you think I'm going to do?" snapped Dmitri.

"Dmitri, there doesn't need to be a fight here today. No one needs to get hurt," said Dr. Arenot.

"Then, I suggest you stay where you are," replied Dmitri, ducking outside.

The authorities' voices got louder and a helicopter now circled above the area. Instructions by loudspeaker rained down from the chopper.

"The policía are telling everyone to come out with their hands up," said Alejandro.

Bam! Pop! They heard several gunshots outside.

"Logan, we don't have much time," said Dr. Arenot. "If we're going to find a way out of this, we have to do it now."

"Wait...," said Logan. He had an idea. "What about the coordinates in the brochure?" he stated, hurriedly pulling out the brochure they received upon entering Machu Picchu. Dr. Arenot pulled his out, too, while Bryan and Allysa stood next to the pair reading along with them. Logan quickly scanned the '*Fun Facts About Machu Picchu*' page where he remembered seeing something about coordinates. "There, the coordinates in the last paragraph!" exclaimed Logan, reading it aloud to everybody:

280

"<u>13.163333° S to 72.545556° W</u>: The GPS coordinates of Machu Picchu."

"Professor, do you see anything in those coordinates that might work?"

"I know what you're thinking, but I don't know… neither the longitude nor latitude are seven digits," replied Dr. Arenot.

"It has to be in there somewhere… with the Vaniryans, it's always about coordinates," insisted Logan, trying to convince himself there was a hidden clue in there. In his mind, he started playing with the numbers to come up with different variations just like he and Emma had done to decipher the Vaniryan clues three years ago.

"What about the number a few paragraphs above the coordinates, 3,714,256? That one has seven digits," suggested Bryan.

"The one referring to the population of Cusco during the rule of Pachacuti?" asked Logan, reading it over:

> "<u>3,714,256</u>: The number of Inca living in the Cusco region under Pachacuti's rule, which the Inca ruler memorialized on a gold and silver Quipu Necklace recently recovered in the Lima region."

"Yeah," replied Bryan.

"What's the Quipu Necklace?" wondered Logan.

Alejandro piped in, "Pachakutiq wore a Quipu Necklace made of gold, with silver quipu rings around it instead of strings, with each set of rings separated by a blue gem, and a larger green gem placed where the number sequence began."

"What are quipu rings?" Logan asked.

"The Inca had no system for writing numbers," explained Dr. Arenot, "so they recorded numbers on a long string made up of smaller strings knotted around it to represent numbers. If the number was 586, they placed 6 touching knots near the free end of the string in the 1's position, 8 knots in the 10's position higher up the string, then 5 touching knots in the 100's position, and so on."

"And the Quipu Necklace number, 3,714,256, represented the number of people living under Pachacuti's rule in the Cusco region?" asked Logan

"Sí, señor, at the time of Machu Picchu's completion," said Alejandro.

"Did the Quipu Necklace number ever change as his empire's population increased?" followed up Logan.

"No, señor."

"Why not?" wondered Logan. Thinking about it, he continued, "Pachacuti permanently memorialized his empire's population on a gold necklace that's oddly specific in its number, yet never once updated it over time, even as his empire grew, when all he had to do was add more silver rings to the necklace? Why didn't he update it?"

"And all the numbers are seven or below, too!" added Allysa excitedly.

"Right... seven numbers, each seven or below," said Logan. "Dr. Arenot, do you think, maybe, Pachacuti's Quipu Necklace actually memorialized the order for pressing the trapezoids, 3-7-1-4-2-5-6, instead of the population of his subjects in the Cusco region?"

There were more gunshots.

"I don't know, but if we're going to try this, we have to do it now," urged Dr. Arenot.

Logan turned to face the wall. "Okay then, let's do it now."

△△△△△△△△△△△

Outside, Dmitri, Ivan, and Boris bunkered down among the Incan ruins guarding the entrance to the cavern. The helicopter continued to fly above their heads telling them to put their hands up and surrender, and at least five officers surrounded the area. As soon as the first shots were fired, the authorities called for backup and air support. Far heavier militia was on the way, only minutes out. With Machu Picchu being the crown jewel of Peru and its tourist economy, the National Police of Peru kept a heavy complement of helicopters and trained officers close by, and all were en route.

A flash of light lit up the area. Dimitri, Ivan, and Boris spun around, wondering if the police had fired a flare or explosive into the area. For a brief moment, the Temple of the Moon cavern was brightly illuminated. Within a couple of seconds, the light dissipated.

Dmitri ran back into the cave to see what happened. He also planned to grab more ammunition from their bags, but when he got inside, everyone was gone, along with their weapons and ammunition bags.

Dmitri couldn't believe it! He cursed and ran back outside, with only two more bullets left in his gun. That was two more than Ivan and Boris had by the time he returned, and the authorities were closing fast. Their time was just about up, and somewhere, Diego was smiling smugly. He wasn't about to let the foreigners defile any part of his country's treasured ruins...

Chapter 20 – The Fault in the Stars

Logan, Bryan, Allysa, Dr. Arenot, and Alejando were inside a small hollowed-out pyramid with four walls peaking at a point above their heads. Its walls were smooth and white, and there was a metallic sphere in the middle. The pyramid and sphere were extremely similar to the one beneath Area 51.

Moments earlier, after Logan had pressed the trapezoidal niches in the right combination, the white-granite-block wall on the eastern edge of the Temple of the Moon started glowing a translucent bright white color in which they could faintly see the pyramid immediately on the other side of the wall. They all walked into it and found themselves in the pyramid they now stood in. A few seconds after entering the pyramid, the glowing wall through which they had entered closed, sealing them inside Huayna Picchu mountain.

Logan knew what to do. He approached the sphere and touched it. After placing his left hand on its surface, the sphere lit up blue and all light evaporated. The pyramid's walls disappeared and the dark sky of space and millions of stars replaced them. The other eight planets in Earth's solar system were also visible, prominently enlarged, and rotating around them.

"This is amazing," said Allysa softly, her voice weakened by wonder. "I wanted to believe, but I never actually thought it could be real…"

"Are we in outer space?" wondered Bryan, even the willing believer in him thunderstruck by what his eyes were seeing.

"I don't think so. I think we're still inside the pyramid in Huayna Picchu mountain. This place is a holographic representation of the galaxy generated by the Vaniryan technology that I told you guys about on the plane," responded Logan.

Allysa gazed around at the stars, dumbfounded. "I honestly thought you were making it all up. I'm really sorry for doubting you, Logan. So, what do we do now?"

Back at Area 51, after touching the sphere, Emma navigated the stars by pointing to where she wanted to go, and a line of blue energy extended from her finger until reaching the destination point. Logan decided to try the same thing here. Keeping his left hand on the shining blue sphere, he pointed at Jupiter with his right index finger. Logan felt the energy surge through his body, up his arm, and out his fingertip toward Jupiter. In the blink of an eye, the five of them holographically warped into Jupiter's orbit, hovering above the massive planet enshrouded in white, red, orange, brown, and yellow stripes and swirls, as if they were actually there.

"Wow, look at Jupiter's Great Red Spot," said Allysa, peering down at Jupiter's iconic churning anticyclonic storm 22 degrees south of the equator, which appeared to be right below her feet.

"And look at Earth!" exclaimed Bryan, marveling at the sight of humanity's home from afar.

"Dios mío, the world of Viracocha," uttered Alejandro, referring to the Inca god who created the Earth.

"And you can go anywhere in here?" asked Allysa out loud, recalling what Logan had said on the way to Peru.

"Yeah, I think so… that's how the pyramid under Area 51 works," said Logan.

"Like, you can go to that star right there?" she further asked, pointing at the brightest star she could see, Sirius.

"Absolutely. Watch this…" teased Logan, pointing at Sirius, but unlike with Jupiter, nothing happened this time. "Huh, that's weird," said Logan.

"What's wrong?" asked Dr. Arenot.

"I don't know," replied Logan. "The sphere's not letting me take us to the star for some reason. It's not working." Logan tried pointing at several other stars, but the results were the same. It didn't work.

"Perhaps the technology the Vaniryans left behind in Huayna Picchu has limited functionality, different from the one at Area 51," speculated Dr. Arenot. "Maybe it's only capable of going to a single star or a limited number of them or only hospitable planets or something."

"It's like a galactic escape room!" blurted Bryan.

"Yeah, and we just have to find the key that lets us out," added Allysa.

"Well, that shouldn't be hard," commented Logan. While they may have been unsure what they were looking for at Machu Picchu, he knew exactly what to look for here: the Pleiades, or more specifically, the second star in the left row as depicted in the Voynich manuscript's star page that Logan drew his red line to while back at Dewey's:

"We need to find the Pleiades," Logan announced, scanning the millions of stars in the heavens for the constellation. There were so many more stars visible in orbit than from the light-polluted surface of Earth that Logan was having a hard time finding it. There were literally millions of new stars to comb through.

"I don't know what the Pleiades looks like," said Allysa, slightly embarrassed. "I'm terrible at constellations… and math."

As the astronomy major in the group, Logan decided to describe it for everyone's benefit. "They're a group of seven stars bunched together that look like a shopping basket or baby stroller tilted slightly up on its back wheels."

"I wouldn't even know where to begin looking," said Allysa.

"They're inside the Taurus constellation. You know that one, don't you?" asked Logan, continuing to peruse the stars for the Pleiades.

"No," replied Allysa sheepishly.

"It's the one that looks like a bull."

"Oh yeah, like the zodiac sign," remarked Allysa.

"Right. You can find the Pleiades at Taurus' right hoof…," continued Logan.

"…and if it helps, Taurus is just above and to the right of Orion," Logan added, referring to the constellation depicting a hunter standing in set position, with a bow held in the hand of his outstretched left arm, and his right arm cocked back and up.

Bryan had another suggestion. "If you want to find Orion, just look for the three stars of Orion's Belt," he said.

"Exactly," responded Logan. "And actually, once you find Orion's Belt, finding the Pleiades is even easier. From there, you just follow the line of Orion's Belt to the Pleiades between 1 and 2 o'clock northeast in the night sky."

After a moment, Alyssa exclaimed, "I see it!" She pointed it out to everyone.

"Great!" said Logan. "Now, just follow the line leading from Orion's Belt until you hit the Pleiades."

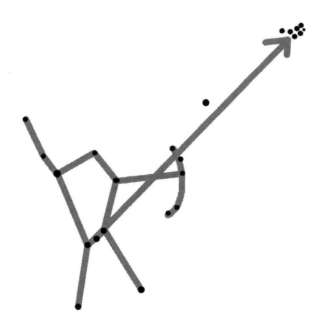

They all followed the line leading from Orion's Belt until hitting the Pleiades as Logan said.

"Now, we need to go to the second star in the left row," said Logan, referring back to what they had determined at Dewey's. When following the meandering line from the face of the sun on the Voynich manuscript star page to the Pleiades, they had deduced that the line led right to the second star in the left row:

"But which one is that?" asked Bryan. "The Pleiades we're looking at doesn't look the same as in the Voynich manuscript."

Bryan was right, the Pleiades didn't look the same. In real life, or whatever this was inside the pyramid, the configuration was different. Logan pulled the printout of the Voynich manuscript page that he had brought with him from Dewey's, along with a small pencil, from the back of his pocket. He sketched out the Pleiades constellation as they were seeing it, right beside the stars on the Voynich manuscript page so he could compare them...

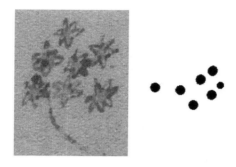

"Maybe it doesn't look the same because we're looking at it from the wrong angle," Logan considered.

"What do you mean?" asked Dr. Arenot.

"Well, it's possible the author of the Voynich manuscript drew the Pleiades from the perspective of how the constellation looked from Vanirya, not Earth. I don't know, I'm just guessing." Logan thought about it for a moment and then rotated the piece of paper with the Voynich stars on it to have a look. After trying several different angles, he saw what he was looking for. "Got it! If you rotate the Pleiades 45 degrees clockwise, it resembles how it looks in the Voynich, with two rows of three stars side by side on the left, followed by a final star dangling out there by itself on the right." Logan erased the prior Pleiades sketch, and resketched out a new 45 degree clockwise rotated version of the Pleiades on the Voynich manuscript page so they could all see it:

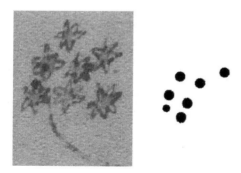

Logan kept explaining. "The only difference really is that, in the Voynich, the single star dangles alone in the middle right instead of the top right. But otherwise, the two rows of three match up."

"Okay, so which star is it, then?" asked Allysa.

"Electra," stated Logan confidently, "the middle star in the left row after reorienting our angle."

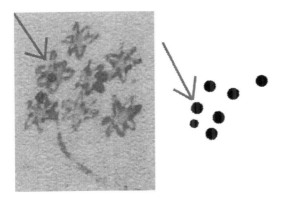

Without waiting for a consensus, Logan decided to try it. He pointed at Electra, and it worked! A blue line extended from his finger to the star and away they went. They zipped through the holographic stars until coming to a stop in Electra's solar system. Orbiting the star were two planets: a single planet, half-blue, half-green, in equal swirls, and further out, a red planet covered by large sections of white.

"That was *awesome!*" exclaimed Bryan.

"Well done, Logan!" said Dr. Arenot.

"Dios mío, Pachakutiq! Dios mío, Pachakutiq!" cried Alejandro.

"Pachakutiq," repeated Logan. "Alejandro, why do you say that?"

Alejandro pointed at the blue-green planet and responded, "The gems…"

Logan didn't quite understand what he meant. "The gems?" he asked.

"Señor, the planet is the same color as the blue and green gems on Pachakutiq's Quipu Necklace."

Logan hadn't made the connection at first. "Dr. Arenot, Alejandro's right! We have to get down there!" stated Logan.

"Do you mean, we're actually going down to the planet for real?" asked Allysa.

"Yep," replied Logan, anxious to proceed. He lifted his hand to point to the planet before Dr. Arenot stopped him.

"Logan, you need to slow down for a second. Once we go down there, we don't know if we'll be able to get back. If the technology we need to return home isn't down on that surface, we could spend the rest of our lives on the planet, and even if the technology is down there somewhere, we might spend the rest of our lives looking for it. While I'm prepared to go down there with you, the others didn't bargain for a risky interplanetary adventure."

"You're right," conceded Logan, pulling his hand back. "Listen, Dr. Arenot and I are going down there one way or another to save Emma and Jill, and whoever else is stuck with them wherever they are. And he's right, it's risky. I know none of you signed up for this, and honestly, I didn't mean to get you guys involved. I really am sorry for everything that's happened, so please, if you don't want to go or don't feel completely comfortable, I understand… just tell me, and I can lift my hand off the sphere and end this immediately. This doesn't have to be a group effort."

Bryan wasn't about to abandon Logan in his time of need. "Hey, Pennyworth isn't leaving Bruce Wayne hanging," he declared.

Allysa, however, wasn't nearly as ready to dive into the deep end as Bryan. She was conflicted. "I don't know guys… I don't know what to do."

"Allysa, it's okay," said Logan, not wanting to pressure her.

"It's not that I don't want to help you or Emma or Jill… I do! But this is a really big decision."

"Whatever you decide to do, it's okay, really, I promise. You just say the word…"

"And what happens if you let go, do we just go back to the pyramid?" she asked.

"We should, yes," replied Logan, "Theoretically, we've never left."

"What if Dmitri, Ivan, and Boris are still there? Can we just wait it out inside the pyramid, or will it kick us back out into the Temple of the Moon where Dmitri and his guys are?" asked Allysa.

"Honestly, I don't know," answered Logan.

Bryan had a thought. "Hey, didn't you say that at Area 51, the sphere let you open up a portal showing the planet's surface so you could see what was on the other side first without having to actually walk through it?"

"That's right," replied Logan.

"So, if it's the same way here, can't we just open up one of those portals, look at what's there, and make a final decision then?" asked Bryan.

"I don't see why not," said Logan. "Is everyone okay with that?"

"I guess," replied Allysa. "Are you sure that's how it works?"

Logan nodded and replied, "Positive."

"Allysa, I have seen it with my own eyes," added Dr. Arenot.

"Okay," said Allysa, agreeing to the plan.

"Alejandro?" asked Logan.

"Sí, señor, I am okay to see Pachacuti's world."

"Alright then, let's have a look," said Logan.

He pointed his index finger at the blue-green planet. After the blue line of energy extended from his finger, the Vaniryan technology kicked in, and then, unexpectedly kicked off just as fast. As if someone had flicked on a light switch, the holographic galaxy vanished, and they found themselves standing back inside the smooth white walls of a hollowed-out pyramid beside the metallic sphere.

"What happened? Where's the portal you said would open up?" asked Allysa.

"I'm not sure," replied Logan, looking around confused. "We're back in the pyramid..."

"Is it broken?" wondered Dr. Arenot.

"Maybe..." Logan responded.

Suddenly, the walls of the pyramid retracted downward into the ground at lightning speed. They stood on a triangular-shaped white platform completely exposed in the middle of a much larger, taller pyramid. Their mouths fell agape at what surrounded them. They definitely weren't inside Huayna Picchu mountain, much less on Earth, anymore...

Chapter 21 - The Voyage Home

The four-sided pyramid peaked at a point hundreds of feet over their heads. Its gigantic triangular-shaped walls were completely transparent, allowing them to see a bright green sky outside, along with dazzling metallic buildings of different shapes and sizes, some thin, some thick, and some with curvatures or angles that defied the known laws of physics on Earth. Platforms with radiant power sources floated among the buildings and erected on the hovering platforms were even more buildings and structures. Ships whooshed by outside, dashing between the buildings or rocketing up into outer space. Breezy clouds drifted past the pyramid's windowed walls, suggesting they were extremely high up.

Inside the pyramid, humanoids enveloped in light but without any visible features, were converging around them. For Logan, it was déjà vu all over again from his first visit to Vanirya three years ago. Only this time, once the beings got close, the bright glow around them melted away so Logan could see their true form: golden-white hair, silver-white skin, two arms, two hands, two legs, circular faces with tiny mouths, no noses, and round eyes. Each wore black and gold clothing from neck to toe and held a weapon of some kind in their hands. The Vaniryans surrounded the triangular white platform on which Logan and his friends stood but did not set foot on it, instead stopping at the platform's edge.

"Are those Vaniryans?" Dr. Arenot asked Logan nervously. Alejandro also looked nervous, while Allysa and Bryan anxiously stepped closer to one another without even realizing they did it.

"I think so," said Logan, not entirely sure. While the bright aura initially surrounding the Vaniryans was as he remembered from the first time he saw them, he hadn't seen them in any other form, and they certainly weren't holding weapons the last time. The beings kept their distance in a holding pattern.

"What are they waiting for?" wondered Dr. Arenot.

"I don't know," Logan replied.

"Maybe they're not waiting for anything. They look like they're guarding us," conjectured Bryan.

"We're not prisoners, Bryan," said Logan, although even he had to concede the Vaniryans' weapons were disconcerting.

"I don't know, dude, they're not exactly acting like the welcoming committee, standing at attention holding weapons."

In the far corner of the pyramid, another glowing Vaniryan arrived on a round lift that rose through a circular opening in the floor. After the lift rose fully, its edges sealed indistinguishably from the floor. The Vaniryan approached them, passing the other aliens and stopping 10 feet in front of Logan. The Vaniryan was noticeably larger than the others.

Logan stepped forward to meet the Vaniryan partway, since it appeared to be the leader, or greeter, of the group. When Logan was within arm's reach, the Vaniryan reached out to touch his face. Logan remained still. He didn't want to alarm the Vaniryan or send the wrong message by breaking away from the interaction. After the Vaniryan touched Logan's face, something unexpected happened...

The energy enveloping the alien whirled, modified, and reformed until a mirror image of Logan stood before them. The being had somehow read and replicated Logan's energy patterns to look like him. The only remaining visible differences between Logan and the Vaniryan were the specks of energy flickering in the Vaniryan's eyes which eventually dissipated to match Logan's. The Vaniryan was dressed in stark black clothing.

Logan's male-looking doppelgänger walked around the visitors, eyeing them up and down. Following a few moments of uncomfortable silence, the Vaniryan finally spoke in a voice eerily similar to Logan's.

"It is a curious fate, your arrival, through a path none knew was open," said the Vaniryan, expressing his thoughts both telepathically and verbally.

Although taken aback by the alien's appearance, Logan responded, "Are you Vaniryans?"

"It is what you see," replied the Vaniryan. "How did you come here?"

"Through a portal that you left behind on our world."

"And what world is that?" asked the Vaniryan, awaiting Logan's answer.

Emma once told Logan that the Vaniryans visited many worlds, so it wasn't surprising to Logan that the Vaniryan didn't know, so he replied, "We come from a planet called Earth. We are humans," Logan answered. "My name is Logan, and this is Jonas, Bryan, Allysa, and Alejandro." They all half-waved, too nervous to do anything more than that. "What is your name?" inquired Logan.

Logan's doppelganger paused and glared at the five visitors, then responded, "Humans come into Supay's home, a forbidden intrusion."

Uh oh... Logan's stomach tensed up. Supay's unhospitable comment caught Logan, indeed all of them, off guard, especially based on Logan's prior interaction with the Vaniryans which were amicable and inviting. Allysa took hold of Bryan's hand, while Alejandro looked absolutely terrified. He was trying to speak but he was too petrified to make a sound. He was shaking.

"Supay, I apologize if our arrival offended," said Logan. "I assure you, that wasn't our intention. We only—"

"Why have humans come?" demanded Supay, uninterested in Logan's apology.

Again, Supay's standoffish demeanor shook Logan. He swallowed hard and anxiously eeked out, "We have come here to ask for your help."

"And what makes you think I will help you?" challenged Supay, drawing coarse laughter from the other aliens surrounding them.

Logan replied, "I thought because the Vaniryans came to Earth previously and helped us once before, that you would be willing to help us again. I assumed…"

"You have not earned what you assume," howled Supay, his distrust of the humans abundantly evident.

"Please, we need your help," pleaded Logan, hoping to appeal to Supay's compassion, if Supay had compassion.

"We shall see," replied Supay. He waved his hand upward and the pyramid's four glass walls instantly turned into a dark, star-laden planetarium, albeit a pyramidal, not dome-shaped one. Where once there were transparent walls, now, every last inch of the pyramid's four walls up to the pyramid's utmost peak, portrayed a galaxy of stars like a four-sided planetarium or movie theater.

"Show me Earth," Supay instructed Logan.

Unfortunately, staring up at the millions of stars visible in the pyramidal-planetarium, Logan had no idea where Earth was in the vastness of space, nor any idea how to find it. And not that it mattered, but he had no idea what the stars in the night sky looked like from the perspective of Electra, either. Regretfully and more than a little apprehensively, Logan replied, "I'm sorry, but I don't know how."

"Do any of you?" questioned Supay. No one responded. Supay laughed at them. "Only fools travel the stars in such a lost way." He stepped forward toward the sphere in the white platform's center and said, "I will show humans."

He placed his hand on the sphere, and the stars on the pyramidal-planetarium's massive screened walls moved, activated by his touch. As if watching the flight record of their journey from Earth to Electra but in reverse, they moved away from the blue-green planet orbiting Electra, beyond the red and white planet in Electra's outer orbit and kept going, picking up speed, and leaving Electra's star system altogether. Soon, the stars were shooting by them. They zipped through an asteroid belt, and then, a pink, red, and white nebula cloud made up of dust, hydrogen, helium, and other gases.

Deep within the nebula, they witnessed the most extraordinary marvel of interstellar creation ever seen by the human eye: the wonderous belly of a nebula where stars are born, where turbulence swirls galactic clouds into knots that generate a mass so great the swirling gas and dust collapse under their own gravitational attraction and form into stars. Passing through the nebula, they observed a baby star forming, a protostar in its early hot blob stage giving off light as it wound and grew into a gravitational giant.

By the time they exited the nebula, the stars were sailing by them so fast they couldn't even see the individual stars anymore, only blurred lines. Finally, they came to an abrupt stop in Earth's orbit. The sphere had retraced their flight path, and taken them on a visual journey all the way back to the beginning.

"Is this your Earth?" asked Supay, looking up at the screens.

"Yes," responded Logan.

"It is a pretty world," said Supay, sounding both sincere and condescending. Supay waved his hand again and they resumed their voyage home, dropping into Earth's atmosphere over South America like a falling rocket. Soon, southeastern Peru came into view, then the Andes mountains, then Machu Picchu and Huayna Picchu mountains, and finally, the Temple of the Moon. Their on-screen voyage came to a screeching halt where it all started, inside Huayna Picchu mountain.

Looking around at the hidden pyramid displayed on the planetarium's four movie-screen-like-walls, Supay asked, "What is this place?"

"The hidden pyramid at the Temple of the Moon in Peru where we discovered the Vaniryan technology left behind with Pachacuti," replied Logan, hoping to earn Supay's trust and, perhaps, remind Supay that humans were once friends of the Vaniryans.

"How do you know what a Vaniryan is?" queried Supay, wanting to understand how Logan had come to know the term.

"Three years ago, Emma and I found what the Vaniryans left behind on Earth. Emma went through the portal first, traveling to the pyramid in orbit above Vanirya. She met the Vaniryans and learned about them. Then, I went through, but my visit lasted for only a few seconds before they sent me back."

Supay looked keenly interested in Logan's response. Without asking, Supay entered Logan's mind, scanning his thoughts and exploring his consciousness in search of something, although Logan knew not what. The experience was uncomfortable but short because Supay didn't find what he wanted. Supay then quickly did the same to the other visitors before returning to Logan and bluntly asking, "Where is Emma?"

"We don't know. That's why we have come," replied Logan. "We need your help to find her and others we believe are with her."

"I will find them," announced Supay, a stunningly unexpected departure from his previous combative responses.

Logan closed his eyes and exhaled, overcome with both relief and joy. As standoffish as Supay had been up until that point, his offer to find Emma and Jill could not have been more welcome.

"It is not just a place where they are lost," stated Dr. Arenot. "They are lost in time, too, somewhere in the past."

"I will find who you seek," said Supay. Supay seemed unconcerned by Dr. Arenot's revelation. After the initial lack of trust, it appeared their implausible plan to find Emma and Jill was back on track. Logan grinned. He and Dr. Arenot briefly embraced. They had done it!

"Tell me what you know," commanded Supay.

Logan promptly removed the printout of Þórðarson's *The Final Journey of the Vanir* from his back pocket where he had kept it folded since leaving Dewey's. "All we know can be found in this old manuscript writing..." Logan read it aloud for Supay:

Odin, god of wisdom, knowledge, and magic,
do mortals of Midgard follow,

Sitting on high throne beside Frigg, sons Thor,
Baldr and Váli, and Frigg's hens, seven in
line.

Odin taught his hens how to use their power,
knowledge and wisdom within,

And how to read the writings from Midgard's
mortal codex,

But to his dearest, he taught all the universe's
secrets, for she had wanted to,

For she sat ready to rule justly when Odin's
time ended and then, Frigg's.

But soon the God of Death came for the
Vanir, Odin, his sons and his hens,

Odin beckoned the Ljósálfar and his allies for
help, no matter where from,

He beckoned the Æsir and Vanir, for a new
Æsir-Vanir War did they face.

Not with each other, but with Death and its
Dökkálfar, for a victory on Vanir none could
be assured of,

Fear did Odin, the coming of Death, that from
Vanir's peak he called upon the power of time
using the stars, moons and sun,

To fight a battle the Æsir-Vanir could not win
alone, for they lacked the strength to,

Still, to battle did Thor, Baldr and Váli come,
asking only where.

The war raged on, Death seized the home of
the Vanirens,

Desperate, Odin summoned he who overturns
space and time, so the Vanir could live,

He led the Vanir to a home anew, and hid
Odin's dearest within space and time itself,
forever away from battle.

Odin then smote the Dökkálfar, but the search
for peace continues,

As the darkness of Death rages on in Midgard,
where no longer can Odin help,

For how the battle in the hidden city ends is
up to us,

Alas, Odin despair, the sun is gone, the sun is
gone, and the God of Death has her, now.

When Logan finished reading it, he folded and returned it to his back pocket and asked Supay, "Does any of this make sense to you?"

"It is understood," replied Supay with a sudden smile.

Logan followed up by asking, "Do you know where the 'hidden city' is that this writing refers to?"

"And when in time it refers to?" asked Dr. Arenot, also bursting with optimism.

Deep in thought, Supay did not respond. Instead, he began walking away from the triangular white platform, rejoining the surrounding ring of Vaniryans 30 feet away from Logan. He turned to face the humans again. "Thank you, you have given me what I need." He cackled, waved his hand, and everything disappeared! Supay, the Vaniryans, the pyramid, all of it! Somehow, Supay had transported them back to Earth inside the hidden pyramid within Huayna Picchu mountain.

"What happened?" asked Allysa.

"I think Supay just threw us out of his pyramid!" exclaimed Bryan.

"Why would he do that?" questioned Logan in complete denial. He moved over to re-touch the sphere to take them back to Electra, but nothing happened! The sphere wasn't working anymore. Instead of turning blue and bringing up a holographic map of the galaxy for them to maneuver through, the sphere did nothing. Logan touched it again and when it didn't work, he shouted, "No!" He tried several more times but to no avail.

"Logan," said Dr. Arenot, trying to settle him down. He put his hand on Logan's to calm him, but calm was not to be… the sphere started shaking, vibrating, and buzzing, and the white walls of the hidden pyramid started rumbling.

"Uh, guys, what's happening?" asked Allysa. The sound of rumbling, shaking, and buzzing increased like something was revving up to an explosion.

"We have to get out of here," shouted Dr. Arenot.

To their right, they could see the trapezoidal-niche wall flickering as if the hidden pyramid's technology was failing. They made for the wall, but before they got there, the sphere exploded, ejecting them out of the pyramid and back onto the dirt floor of the Temple of the Moon. The wall re-solidified back into solid stone the instant they cleared it.

Logan, Dr. Arenot, Alejandro, Bryan, and Allysa all laid on the ground on the dirt floor of the Temple of the Moon cave, unconscious, and they weren't alone...

Peruvian authorities were scouring the cave looking for evidence following the deadly shootout with Dmitri and his men that left two of the intruders dead, and others injured. They were also looking for clues as to what had happened to the five hikers who reportedly trekked up the north face of Huayna Picchu mountain along with the gunmen.

When the explosion occurred, it knocked the authorities backward, and some off their feet altogether. No one knew exactly where the blast had come from, especially because they couldn't see it. It was like an invisible blast or force of nature had bowled them over. Fortunately, no one was seriously hurt. While momentarily disoriented, once the authorities regained their footing, they saw the five new bodies lying on the floor of the cave.

"What the hell?" said one of the officers in Spanish upon seeing five bodies that weren't there a second earlier.

"Where'd they come from?" asked another officer.

"Were they hiding at the back of the cave, or up in a crevice somewhere?" wondered a third officer.

306

"I don't know," said the Commander, "but they match the description of the other trespassers who hiked up the north face of Huayna Picchu with the gunmen. Let's get medical on them and take them all into custody."

"Yes, sir," acknowledged the officers.

Alejandro started to wake up, and he began rambling, "Dios mío, Supay! Dios mío, Supay!"

Several officers rushed to his aid. After making sure he was okay, one of the officers asked him in Spanish, "Where'd you come from?"

Highly agitated, Alejandro replied back in Spanish, only semi-coherently, "From Supay! I have seen Supay!"

"He must have hit his head pretty good if he thinks he's seen Supay," said the officer to a second officer.

"The Inca God of Death? Yeah, right," mocked the second officer.

"Who knows, they came out of nowhere, right? Maybe he did…" joked the first officer, laughing at his own funny.

"Perhaps someone should remind him that if he'd seen the God of Death, he'd be dead right now," said the second officer.

The officers laughed together as they cuffed Alejandro and took him into custody. Logan, Dr. Arenot, Bryan, and Allysa were next.

Chapter 22 - The Tree Gates of Jaannos

Tassa shook Emma's shoulder to wake her. She had let Emma rest as long as she could, but as she explained to Emma, "It is time. The sun breaks the horizon. Soon, they will gather."

Emma cracked open her eyes and through the window saw the whispers of sunlight brightening Vanirya's pale-purple morning sky. She had managed to get a few hours of sleep in her host's home even though her body felt ravaged by an atmosphere that was slowly trying to kill it. Her muscles ached, her energy level was faltering, and taking deep breaths hurt, not that she could as her lungs lacked the strength. With some effort, she rose to her feet, fighting light-headedness. After steadying herself, she followed Tassa out to the main room.

Emma looked around. "Where is Issor?"

"Issor left early to start her village chores. She has much to do."

"Oh," replied Emma, disappointed she wouldn't have the chance to say goodbye. Isa's acceptance of Emma was the main reason why they were on their way to the Hidden City. Emma had wanted to thank her and say goodbye personally. "Will Isa be at the gathering?"

"No. The gathering is secret. Best none know where you go. How does your body feel?"

Emma eeked out an unconvincing, "Okay, I guess."

"The trees will help, you will see," said Tassa. "Are you ready to go?"

"As much as I can be." Emma reached down to grab her bag, which she had brought back with her from the tree hall.

"You do not need it," Tassa said.

"But my clothes are in there… my gear…"

"You can take nothing with you."

"Nothing at all?"

"Only that which lives may travel through the trees."

"So not even clothes?"

"Nothing. All will be left behind."

"So, what do we do when we reach the Frozen Shards? Isn't it going to be freezing there?"

"It is planned for. We must go."

Tassa led the way out the door and Emma followed. They descended the steps which wound around the tree trunk, stepping off on a branch halfway down that continued off to the right. Emma stayed close to Tassa as they traversed the network of branches from one tree to the next, navigating connections, bridges, ladders, and steps. When the gaps between branches were small enough, they hopped from one to another, although in Emma's weakened state, some of the hops proved challenging. In those instances, she simply didn't look down.

Most branchways were smooth and lined with something for Emma to hold on to. Given Emma's wobbliness, Tassa avoided the more narrow, uneven, or rougher branches that lacked handholds. After 20 minutes, they reached their destination: a tree abutting a rockface with a branch leading into a cave high up, disguised by bushes. From the ground far below, none could see the cave enshrouded in vegetation, especially because of the thick foliage that prevented anyone from seeing up into Jaannos.

They followed the branch into the opening. Inside the cave, it was pitch-black. Tassa held out her right hand, palm side up, and emitted dancing waves of energy from her palm to light up the cave. The energy waves disappeared and new ones formed every few seconds, reminiscent of what Isa was doing when they first saw her at the waterfall. Tassa guided Emma through passages leading downward and eventually out at ground level behind more plants. Tassa had taken Emma through the mountain rather than climb down a tree using notches because she didn't think Emma had the strength to safely do so in her condition, and as Emma stood at ground level, she was glad Tassa had.

"Do not touch plants," warned Tassa, referring to the plants concealing the cave entrance. There was a small path enabling them to cautiously maneuver from out behind the vegetation.

After a short walk in the forest, they entered a clearing surrounded by 12 trees, each with an arched opening carved into its trunk. Professor Quimbey, Captain Evans, Annika, Yssil, Lassar, Tamos, and Sorra waited inside the clearing. Collectively, they stood among the Tree Gates of Jaannos, 12 links to a world beyond the borders of a forest many times the size of North America.

"Nice of you to show up, James," joked Captain Evans.

"My alarm clock didn't go off," Emma dryly responded.

More seriously, Captain Evans asked, "How are you feeling this morning?"

"Like the Hidden City's going to be my last stop, one way or another."

"Yeah, Annika spent the last several hours vomiting. She's in bad shape this morning." Annika sat on a boulder a few feet away with her hands in her face.

Professor Quimby joined the conversation. "Yssil said the Tree Gate may help us, something about how it will rebuild our bodies from the subatomic level when we come out the other end. Sounds like it'll be like pressing a reset button for us."

"I hope he's right," said Captain Evans, "although the idea of having our energy absorbed by the tree and shot through the roots of the forest only to be put back together on the other end seems a lot riskier than just taking something with an engine in it to get to the other side of the forest."

Professor Quimbey shook her head. "Tamos said it is too risky to travel using artificial energy as the Hunt will track the movement. Traveling through the natural energy of the trees is the safest way."

Captain Evans grumbled, "Sure doesn't sound like it. And honestly, I still don't get how it works."

Professor Quimbey tried to explain. "Well, when you think about it, at the atomic level, every living molecule and cell in our bodies is made up of atoms which consist of protons, neutrons, and electrons. The trees are just carrying that living energy through the forest's interconnected tree root system from one place to another."

"I'm glad it makes sense to you, 'cause I saw how well it worked out for Nicholai and Artyom," responded Captain Evans.

"Yssil said these trees don't feed off living energy and can tell the difference. That's all I know," replied Professor Quimbey.

"If he's wrong, it's gonna be a really short trip," countered Captain Evans.

"How long is the trip actually going to take?" asked Emma.

"At the speed energy moves, pretty fast, I'd imagine, like the time it takes for energy to travel to a light bulb after you turn on a light switch," replied Professor Quimbey.

"What if our energy gets lost somehow in the forest's root system, how does the tree know where it's faxing us?" asked Emma.

"As it was explained to me," said Professor Quimbey, "they have maintained the root systems of the 12 trees, and each subsequent connecting tree, for the entire length of the forest in all directions, ensuring there is only one possible end-destination for each tree gate."

"What about our memories?" asked Emma. "I mean, are we going to come out on the other end knowing who we are?"

Professor Quimbey theorized, "We should. It makes sense to me because memories are just neurons stored in our brains in organized patterns primed to fire together in the same pattern that created the original experience, in the same area of the brain that initiated that experience. And since neurons are made out of cells which are made out of molecules which are made out of the same subatomic energy as everything else in our bodies, I'm assuming it works the same way..."

"Just so long as the tree puts us back together in the same pattern," added Emma. "Otherwise—"

"The circle is full," announced Yssil.

"Alright everyone, let's get ready to do this," stated Captain Evans.

Yssil approached them. "It is your time to journey. May it save you in all ways that it must," he said.

"I will do everything I can to return the favor," replied Emma.

"Yes, a kind favor between our worlds," said Sorra.

A thought occurred to Emma. "What if after we return to Earth, we find the Missing Remnant or the Leyandermál, but can't get word back to you or find a way to return the Leyandermál to you so you can use it?" asked Emma.

Sorra replied, "Then, you must destroy the Leyandermál."

"But how does that help you?"

"Our existence matters less," responded Sorra, voicing the bitter truth.

"Tamos," called Yssil. Tamos approached and stood before him. Yssil put a hand on each of Tamos's shoulders and looking face to face at Tamos said, "May the wisdom of the Va guide you." He let go of Tamos's shoulders and motioned for him to head into the tree.

Tamos bowed his head and stepped toward the tree located northeast in the circle. He walked into the trunk's arched opening, turned around, and within a few seconds, the green energy of the tree flared to a full glow and absorbed him. He was gone, with nothing but his clothes left on the ground inside the tree's base. Lassar stepped up next, and Yssil went through the same ritual with him. Afterward, Lassar walked away, entered the tree trunk, and soon, the tree's green energy absorbed him, too. Yssil looked at the four humans and said, "An off-worlder must now go."

Captain Evans volunteered. "Alrighty, I'll go first… I'm ready to be decomposed."

"I think you mean deconstructed," corrected Professor Quimbey.

"Whatever. Let's get this over with," replied Captain Evans, walking up to Yssil. He put his hands on her shoulders and said, "May the wisdom of the Va guide you." He let her go. She walked off into the tree, turned around, and gazed back at Emma and Professor Quimbey with a dignified, courageous stare. "One soldier a la carte, ready to beam out," she said just as the tree took her away. Right up until she was gone, Captain Evans's eyes oozed bravery.

"Annika, you should go next," said Professor Quimbey.

Annika looked like a ghost of herself, pale and frail, and she was too weak to argue. She simply nodded.

"Annika, are you sure you are okay to go?" asked Emma.

"I must. I have no time left for fear." Annika sluggishly ambled into the tree. Once inside, she closed her eyes to accept her fate. The bright surge of green light whisked her away.

"Emma, you go now," said Professor Quimbey.

Emma wasn't ready. "No, you go first. I'll be right behind you."

"Okay, then, I will see you on the other side." Professor Quimbey pivoted toward Yssil and said, "Thank you from the bottom of my heart."

From the look of confusion on Yssil's face, he didn't quite understand the meaning of Professor Quimbey's expression other than the words 'thank you,' but he got the gist. He put his hands on her shoulders and responded, "May the wisdom of the Va guide you."

"And you."

Professor Quimbey approached the tree, looked into its opening, and entered, and because she couldn't suppress her scientific curiosity, she had a bit of a daredevil smile. The tree absorbed her and the next phase of her never-ending journey of discovery was upon her.

Emma's turn had come. Emma walked up to Tassa and gave her a hug. "Thank you for your help, for taking me in."

"It is our way of kindness."

"I hope I can see you again," said Emma, even as she knew TYC 129-75-1 would explode someday. She had no idea when, of course, because she didn't know what year it was back on Earth. For all she knew, the supernova event was many thousands of years away.

"I would like that."

"Can you please do something for me?" asked Emma.

"Yes, you can ask," replied Tassa.

Emma removed the heart-shaped pendant necklace around her neck and gave it to Tassa. "Can you please make sure Isa gets this? I want her to have it, and tell her that a pretty necklace belongs with a special girl. Tell her goodbye from me, and thank you."

"I will."

Emma walked up to Yssil and hugged him next. She said, "I will help you if I can and return if I can. I won't let you down."

Yssil placed his hands on her shoulders and said, "I know. May the wisdom of the Va guide you."

Emma walked forward into the tree feeling ill from the effects of the gravity and atmosphere, yet excited and nervous by this next moment in her adventure. She turned around, waved goodbye, and just like that, she was gone. All that remained of Emma were her clothes.

Chapter 23 – The Frozen Shards

Emma rematerialized on the other end of the Tree Gate, standing naked and cold inside a tree at the northern edge of the Jaans Forest. She had traveled more than 50,000 miles in what seemed like, to her, an instant. She felt her skin, face, arms, and legs to confirm she was all there, but it wasn't until she touched her head that she realized she wasn't. "*OMG!*" she uttered. Her hair was completely gone, and then Emma recalled something her hairdresser once told her: that all human hair is dead once it grows out of the follicle.

Outside the tree, a light snow fell, covering the ground except in areas shielded by overhead tree cover. Professor Quimbey, Captain Evans, and Annika had all also lost their hair. They were busy getting dressed in clothes that Lassar and Tamos had retrieved for them from a supply chest buried exactly 100 paces behind the Tree Gate.

As soon as Emma stepped out from the tree, a bitter gust of wind struck her bare skin, causing her to shiver uncontrollably. "I am so cold!" she muttered, her teeth chattering. She tried wrapping herself up in her own arms. Tamos immediately tossed her a bodysuit made of a thick brown leatherlike material that stretched, allowing the outfit to easily fit her body, a one-size-fits-all kind of material. Emma put the clothes on as fast as she could, desperate to get out of the cold, and once dressed, she was amazed by how warm the bodysuit was. The brown material completely sealed in her body heat and even seemed to radiate it back toward her skin.

Next, Tamos handed her footwear made of a much thicker version of the same stretchable material. Heavy in the soles, the material provided comfortable padding and kept Emma's feet warm.

Once Emma finished dressing, Professor Quimbey remarked, "Well ladies, I guess we won't be needing a trip to the beauty salon anytime soon!" They all just looked at one another and started laughing at the unexpected, sobering surprise, a much-needed moment of levity amid a dire situation trillions of miles from home. Unlike the four of them, however, Lassar and Tamos still had their hair, indicating an obvious biological difference between humans and Vaniryans.

"Everyone always says I look like my dad, probably scarily so now," quipped Emma. "But I have to say, I feel good! Like every ache and pain is gone. Annika, you?"

"Much better, like before we arrived on this planet," replied Annika.

"Seems like we got a reprieve, for a few days anyway," said Professor Quimbey.

"We must go," Tamos said urgently. He carried a bag of supplies taken from the supply chest, as did Lassar.

"Why, what's wrong?" asked Captain Evans.

"The supply chest was uncovered when we got here. Someone has been through it recently. We may not be alone," replied Tamos.

"Do you think it's the Hunt?" asked Captain Evans.

"Could be. We should go. The North River is close." Tamos reached down and picked up a lightweight cover to insert into the Tree Gate's opening, made from the tree's original bark. He had pushed the façade out when he first arrived, and after putting it back in, it meshed seamlessly, leaving no visible evidence of the opening.

They departed to the North River. Snow continued to fall, but footing remained easy as the ground was mostly flat, and the brown leathery footwear they wore stuck surprisingly well to the snow and ice. Tamos led the way through the trees which, while still tall, were less dense in the northern part of the Jaans Forest than back near Jaannos.

As they got closer to the North River, they could hear the flow of the water and began a gentle descent. Then, all at once, the tree line stopped. They emerged on a slope, overlooking a gorge that carved its way through the forest. The North River and its cerulean blue waters flowed along the bottom of the gorge, with the tall trees of the Jaans Forest lining the snowy slopes on both sides.

They continued down to the snow-covered riverbank to a circular pattern of boulders just short of the water. Between them was a ground-colored tarp covered with snowfall, barely noticeable from more than a few feet away. The tarp wasn't secure, leaving Lassar and Tamos to wonder if the wind had pushed it around or, again, if someone had disturbed it.

Without delay, they pulled off the tarp, revealing a boat nearly 20 feet long, set in a shallow hole in the ground. It wasn't much to look at, with its outer hull made of smooth metal and no visible engine. The interior of the boat had benches, compartments in the back for storage, and a couple of elongated poles with oar-like flat blades for rowing, apparently a standard for skiff boats on any world.

Lassar and Tamos tossed their bags aboard and pushed the boat out of its hole and down the slope. It loaded into the water fairly easily. They boarded with Captain Evans sitting in the back row, Lassar in the middle row with the oars, Professor Quimbey and Annika in the row in front of him, and Emma and Tamos up front.

Once settled in, Lassar reached inside went into his bag and pulled out a metallic object approximately two feet wide and tall, and about eight inches thick. One side had vents on the bottom half. He went to the boat's rear and affixed it on the hull, partly above water and partly below, with the vent side pointing outward.

"What is that?" asked Captain Evans.

"It is a small motor. Will help us move faster," replied Lassar. He turned it on and off they went. Lassar took the first turn rowing and the boat quickly picked up speed. The motor on the back of the boat wasn't powerful like a speed boat engine but it provided some kick. The river's strong current further aided the boat's pace and, with the natural slickness of the boat's outer hull, the boat glided effortlessly through the water. Emma estimated it was traveling more than 30 miles per hour!

After approximately two hours, Tamos announced, "The Frozen Shards are not far ahead. Soon, we will leave the forest."

"How far is the Hidden City once we leave the trees behind?" asked Emma.

"One and a half, maybe two days depending on pace," he replied.

"That long?" responded Emma, concerned about relapsing to their condition before the Tree Gate.

"I know you fear the distance, but you will rest in the boat. Before Jaannos, you traveled a long way on foot, exerted much energy, hastened your demise," said Tamos, confident if they exerted minimal energy, they could extend themselves further.

"I hope so," Emma responded. "And once we get to the Hidden City, then what?"

"We seek out Qelios, the Sentinel of the Hidden City… it is believed Qelios controls a portal like you described, although none of us have ever seen it or know for sure what hides there."

"So, we're off to see the wizard, it seems," said Emma.

"Off to see the wizard?" asked Tamos, not getting the reference.

"Forget it, sorry, it's just an expression. What are the Frozen Shards, anyway?" inquired Emma.

"A massive glacier field that would take us dozens of our days in this craft to circle, with an endless web of splintered ice canyons, passages, and waterways thousands of feet high, leading in an infinite number of directions. It is a cold frozen maze where the unwary can get lost. We must be careful not to stray too far. There are dangers lurking inside the icy labyrinth."

"Why, what is in there?" queried Annika, not liking the sound of that.

"Besides the constantly falling ice rocks that can crush a boat without warning, especially in the narrow passages, there are Vaniryan inhabitants who live in the Shards that feed off life…"

"Animal life?" asked Emma.

"All life."

"Oh," replied Emma.

"But it is not just the inhabitants we must avoid. There are also creatures in the glaciers, some below water, some above in the caves, caverns, and cracks in the glacier walls. With food scarce inside the ice canyons, they are aggressive and will attack our boat if they can."

"Okay, so we're bait heading toward a feeding frenzy. How do we defend ourselves?" questioned Captain Evans.

Tamos replied, "We must keep life away from the hull, as they will try to compromise the hull or flip the boat."

"And how are we supposed to do that? Swing at them with oars?" asked Captain Evans. In response, Tamos reached into his bag and pulled out gunlike weapons. "Now that's what I'm talking about!" exclaimed Captain Evans. She took hold of one. "Is this a laser gun?"

Tamos replied, "It fires an energy blast, yes." Unfortunately, he only had three more, so he distributed one to himself, one to Lassar, and the last one to Annika who appeared to want it. Tamos continued, "We must all keep an eye out once inside the Frozen Shards."

"This place sounds terrible," commented Emma.

"It can be," replied Lassar.

"Have either of you ever sailed the Frozen Shards before?" asked Professor Quimbey.

Tamos replied, "A long time ago. The paths have changed with the movement of the glaciers. We must avoid the paths with dead ends. We don't want to find out what lives where there is no escape."

"And how do we make sure that doesn't happen?" asked Captain Evans.

"We will follow a guide," replied Tamos. He pulled a small device out of the supply bag. "We will use this device to track to the Hidden City's coordinates at 64.1434547 x 114.889423."

They heard a clunk like something had hit the back of the boat.

"What was that?" yelped Professor Quimbey, already nervous.

"It came from behind me," replied Captain Evans. She spun around, leaned over, and opened one of the storage compartments. Lassar leaped up and approached the storage compartment with his weapon at the ready.

As soon as he looked inside, he shouted, "Come out!"

First, only a head emerged, then, an entire body. It was Isa, and she was rubbing her scalp after having smacked it pretty good on the interior of the compartment.

"Issor!" snapped Tamos, angry.

"Isa?" whispered Emma, shocked like everyone.

Lassar and Tamos started in on Isa in their Vaniryan tongue. The three argued for a minute or so, with Lassar and Tamos throwing up their hands multiple times. They didn't look or sound happy with Isa, who stubbornly held on to her opinions, showing an obstinate side Emma didn't know she had. Isa made her way over to her friend Emma for comfort, sitting down beside her. Frustrated, Lassar resumed rowing and Tamos said out loud, "She comes with us. It is too late to turn back now."

"Isa...why did you come here?" Emma asked her privately.

"Isa has never seen the Hidden City. Isa has never seen anything," the little girl replied, her eyes hopeful that Emma would understand.

"But Isa, what you did is really dangerous."

"Isa wants to help Emma."

Emma took her hand and replied, "Isa, you are so sweet and I appreciate you wanting to help me, but you've already helped so much! I just wish you hadn't done what you did. You know we might not return to Jaannos, right?"

"Foolish child. You have endangered your life by coming with us," grumbled Lassar.

"Living in trees forever is not a life," Isa responded.

"It is the life of every Remnant in Jaannos," retorted Lassar. "And now, you have risked yours and theirs. The Hunt searches for us, you know this, Issor! And if they find you and learn what is in your mind, they will track your thoughts back to Jaannos, capture and kill us all, and level Jaannos to the ground."

Isa replied, "It is the same if they find any of you."

"I am prepared to end myself before that happens. Are you?" questioned Lassar. Isa didn't respond. "That is what I thought." Lassar huffed and turned around, finding the debate pointless. There was nothing he could do about it anyway.

Emma said to Isa in a low voice, "Tassa is going to be worried sick about you, you know."

"Isa left Tassa a note. Did not want to frighten her. Isa just wanted to see beyond the trees."

Emma sympathized with Isa's impulsive desire to see her world, to break free from a constricting life. After all, that was the same impulse that drove Emma to undertake the impetuous cross-continental adventure with Logan to unravel the Copán mystery three years earlier. She put her arm around Isa and replied, "I know. We'll just have to make sure you get home."

Isa leaned in and laid her head down in Emma's lap. The little Vaniryan had taken to Emma far more than Emma ever expected. Perhaps Emma was the big sister she never had.

Watching as the little girl laid her head down in Emma's lap, Captain Evans said with a smile, "Looks like you've made a new friend."

Stroking the little girl's golden-white hair, Emma grinned and replied, "So has she." The boat sailed down the river for several hours, and no one said another word on the issue. There was nothing left to say.

As the sun rose higher in the sky, Vanirya's double large moons faded into the background. The Jaans Forest came to an end and the North River spilled out into a larger body of water. After several more hours, they could finally see the Frozen Shards in the distance, spanning the entire horizon. The closer they got, the taller its imposing glacier walls became.

As Tamos had described, the glaciers rose thousands of feet above the water. Some of the glaciers were flat at the top, while others had jagged shards of ice that stuck out of the glaciers and into the sky. The shards were so tall in places that they poked through the clouds and seemingly pierced the sky's purple skin. The Frozen Shards resembled an imposing ice fortress protected by burly glacier walls and barbed wire made up of piercing-sharp ice shards.

Lassar steered them toward a crack in the ice walls. Once they rowed within shouting distance of the crack, Emma realized it wasn't a crack at all, but more of a small canyon. To enter, all they had to do was sail between the two sky-high ice shards guarding the entrance to the frozen world. As they crossed the threshold, Emma stared up at the magnificently tall guardians of the maze, wondering what secrets they protected within. After entering the ice canyon, all sound from the outside world ceased.

"Huh, even the sound is afraid to come in here," remarked Emma, who was struck by the eerie silence of the glacial canyons. "That can't be a good sign."

"Who can blame it?" said Professor Quimbey.

"It is the lonely calm of the Frozen Shards," said Tamos. Daylight now appeared only as a contoured sliver of light high above that tracked the outline and contours of the enormously tall canyon ice walls.

The waterway continued straight for a while but eventually, they came to a fork in the glacial canyon. As planned, Tamos and Lassar consulted the handheld coordinate device to help them choose which way to go. They studied the two options, decided to go left, and with that, their journey through the maze had officially begun. With each path they took, they encountered more forks, as the different paths kept splintering off in an endless number of directions.

Lassar and Tamos took turns rowing and guiding. Captain Evans offered to take a turn but they told her to conserve her energy to minimize the atmosphere's impact on her body. Captain Evans didn't argue. Plus, Lassar and Tamos didn't want to take any chances entrusting the job to someone unfamiliar with the boat's capabilities. They had to carefully navigate the icy waters to avoid floating chunks of ice and falling ice rocks, some bigger than their boat, which broke away from the glacier walls and plunged into the water. Several times, entire sections of the ice walls as large as three-story buildings would break off, thunderously crashing into the water and creating sizable waves that rocked their small boat.

To avoid finding themselves underneath falling ice, Lassar and Tamos steered the boat down the middle of the waterways, rowing equidistant from the walls, although some passages were so narrow there was nowhere for them to go if ice fell from above. In some places, Emma could actually reach out and touch protruding sections of the walls. All they could do in those circumstances was hold their breath. Although they had several near misses when ice broke away, fortunately, nothing landed on their boat just close to it, startling and soaking them only.

They spoke very little during the day as everyone watched their surroundings. Once the sun set, they slowed the boat down because they didn't want to crash into anything. Vanirya's double moons, while bright, cast very little light down into the depths of the canyons, so they had to proceed with extreme caution.

Underneath the night sky, Isa laid on her back on the boat's floor, staring up at the few stars she could see through the canyon contours high above. Emma laid down next to her.

Isa asked her, "Can Emma see her star from here?"

"No. I can hardly see any stars, but even if I could, I have no idea which is mine."

"Too bad. Isa wishes to see where Emma comes from so when Emma goes away, Isa can still see Emma."

"Well, there's a pretty heart-shaped pendant necklace waiting for you when you get back home that you can look at whenever you miss me."

"Really?" asked Isa excitedly.

"Really. How about this... after I return home, I will get another one just like it so we can both have the same necklace and, who knows, maybe sometimes we'll both look at our heart-pendants and think of each other at the exact same time. How does that sound?"

Isa smiled. "Isa likes that. Does Emma have family on her homeworld?"

"Yes, I have my mom and my dad, no brothers or sisters."

"Isa is alone. The Hunt destroyed all that I had."

"You are not alone Isa! You have Tassa."

"Tassa not family."

"Isa, if you don't mind me asking, what happened to your parents?"

"Tassa tells me that the Hunt murdered them."

"Do you remember them at all?"

"Sometimes in night stories, Isa sees them and hears them sing to Isa, but Isa does not really remember."

"There's something I don't understand... how does the Hunt tell the difference between Vaniryans and Remnants? Do Remnants look different from other Vaniryans?"

Lassar chimed in. "No, we are all Vaniryans. We look the same, but Remnants have a different, stronger energy signature and can control the energy in their bodies in ways non-Remnants can't."

"Then how do the hunters tell?"

326

Lassar replied, "If you hold a flame close to a Remnant's eyes, the heat energy of the flame will stir up the unseen energy hidden in their eyes."

"What do you mean, a Remnant's eyes will start glowing or something?"

"Kind of like those eyes staring down at us right now from the ice shelf we're approaching?" asked Captain Evans. She pointed towards a glacier wall several hundred feet up and to the left.

Everyone looked where Captain Evans was pointing. Dozens of glowing eyes were gathering on an ice shelf, waiting for them to get closer. Looking around at the surrounding canyon walls, more eyes were emerging from the dark crevices.

"Are these the Vaniryan inhabitants you told us about earlier?" asked Captain Evans.

"Definitely not," replied Tamos, taking his gun out.

"Any chance they're friendly?" Captain Evans followed up.

Tamos shook his head and responded, "No chance. They are ice creatures, partially humanoid in shape but predators of the ice. Their eyes are the only part of them you can see."

Captain Evans kept peering closer at the creatures, trying to see what she could of them. The creatures' bodies, with two long arms and two legs each possessing sharp claws, were translucent like the immortal or moon jellyfish species on Earth, enabling them to camouflage within the ice. Their translucence rendered them virtually impossible to see, especially in the dark.

As Professor Quimbey saw more eyes crawling down the glacier walls, she cursed, "Bloody hell."

Captain Evans grabbed her gun and said, "Everyone get ready for company."

In a coordinated attack triggered by a shrill cry, the creatures leaped off the walls and into the water in droves, some from very high up. Still more scurried down the ice walls. The creatures, which were extremely difficult to see in the dark and even more invisible underwater charged the boat, with their glowing eyes the only part of their bodies giving them away.

Lassar, Tamos, Captain Evans, and Annika fired their weapons wherever they saw eyes, shooting laser blasts into the water and at the creatures scaling down the walls. The creatures squealed and swam to avoid the blasts, but they kept coming back for more. It took Captain Evans a few seconds to acclimate to her new weapon, but once she did, she began picking off the ice creatures with a high degree of accuracy and at a rapid pace. Still, it wasn't fast enough to slow down the onslaught.

Two creatures took hold of the side of the boat and tried pulling it over. Emma and Professor Quimbey grabbed oars and began swinging for the creature's hands once they spotted them, which wasn't easy. After a few clear oar strikes, the creatures let go, but they weren't done, not by a long shot. The ice creatures were everywhere, beside and below the boat, trying to capsize it to knock them into the water where the creatures would have a decided advantage. The creatures bumped the bottom of the boat.

"Did you feel that?" Emma shouted.

Another blow struck the hull's bottom. The boat shook and jumped, nearly tipping over. A sharp jagged tool broke through the floor, followed by a clawed hand and incoming water. The hand grabbed Professor Quimbey's leg and tried to yank her through the opening. She didn't fit, of course, but that didn't stop the creature from trying to pull her through. Professor Quimbey screamed.

Emma went to her aid, striking the creature's hand as hard as she could with her oar but the creature just sank its claws deeper into the professor's skin. The professor shrieked as the creature yanked her leg even harder. Captain Evans turned, and without any hesitation, fired an on-target laser blast right into the creature's arm, severing it off and freeing Professor Quimbey. Professor Quimbey managed a shell-shocked, "Thank you."

Despite their best efforts, the attacking hordes were increasing in number faster than they could fight them off. All of a sudden, a creature sprung out of the water and landed on the back of the boat. It began swiping at Isa, clawing her face and neck, and then, it grabbed her! The creature lifted her up and began diving back into the water with her. Isa let out a terrified scream and released a blue energy blast from her hands that blew the creature backward away from her and off the boat, killing it instantly. Isa surprised even herself.

"Holy crap, kid!" shouted Captain Evans, caught off guard by Isa's awesome display of raw power. "More of that, please!"

The creatures congregated under the boat and started rocking the hull. The boat lifted off the water and nearly tipped over.

"This isn't working!" yelled Annika. "We can't hold them off for much longer!"

Tamos had an idea. He turned his gun to maximum power and set it to the "Self-Destruct" setting which turned the gun into an explosive device. Upon doing so, the gun made a high-pitch sound as its energy began cycling on itself and building toward an explosion. Tamos grabbed Annika's gun and did the same thing. He threw both overboard, one bowside and the other sternside.

"Get ready! Hold on tight to the side of the boat!" he yelled.

First, his gun exploded, then, Annika's. The explosions released a bright white light that lit up the water and sent a powerful energy blast in a 300-foot radius. The boat bounced off the water's surface and flew several feet forward from the explosive force, and the glacier walls shook. Ice broke away, crashing into the water. All the creatures caught in the water within the blast radius sunk, incapacitated, or died. The creatures climbing down the glacier walls stopped in their tracks, screamed and retreated, afraid. None of them dared jump back into the water.

Lassar turned the motor back on and Tamos rowed, accelerating to top speed to get away from the ice creatures as fast as possible. Meanwhile, Captain Evans worked to plug the hole in the hull left behind by the jagged tool used by the creature that attacked Professor Quimbey. She didn't have much to work with. First, she tried stuffing the hole with rags while Annika and Emma tried hand cupping the water out of the boat. Nothing worked.

"Do we have anything that can stop this leak?" asked Captain Evans as Lassar and Tamos worked to put distance between their boat and the ice creatures.

Tamos, who hadn't noticed the hole in the boat in the commotion, replied, "In the supply bag, there is a soft rock to seal the hole."

"A soft rock?" repeated Captain Evans, confused. She quickly went into Tamos's bag and found what he was referring to, a soft puttylike glob. It was malleable but hard at the same time. She stuffed it into the hole and kept pushing it in until it filled and sealed the entire hole. "It worked!" she shouted.

"It should hold until we get there tomorrow," said Tamos.

Captain Evans sat down to catch her breath.

"Isa, that was incredible what you did before!" said Emma.

Appearing almost embarrassed by her explosive power, Isa replied, "Thanks."

"Can all Remnants do that?" asked Captain Evans.

"Do not know," said Isa.

"Isa has an extraordinarily strong energy signature," interjected Tamos. "All Remnants can manipulate their energy in different ways, but few like Isa. The girl is just beginning to learn how to control it."

As they got farther away from the attack, Captain Evans looked around at her companions. Each of them had varying degrees of claw marks and ripped clothing. Professor Quimbey and Isa had suffered the worst of it, with the professor's leg badly thrashed and Isa's neck and face bleeding profusely.

"Do you have any medical supplies?" Captain Evans asked Lassar and Tamos.

"Yes, in my bag," replied Lassar.

Emma retrieved a box of supplies for Captain Evans to use while Tamos continued to guide the boat through the Frozen Shards. Meanwhile, Captain Evans, with Lassar's and Emma's assistance, spent the remainder of the evening tending to all of their respective wounds, one at a time.

When the morning sun finally began to rise on day two, they were all relieved to still be alive. If they had to endure another encounter while down two weapons, with a broken hull and recovering from injuries, Emma doubted they would have been as fortunate. She decided not to think about it anymore.

Once the sun fully took over the morning sky, although they could only see a sliver of it, day two looked and felt very much the same as day one: more waterways, glacial ice canyons, and a never-ending maze of forks to choose from. Just as they did the first day, Lassar and Tamos continued to use the coordinate device to guide them each time they came to a fork in the canyons.

Around midday on day two, Professor Quimbey noticed something… sunlight, which was never bright in the canyon depths, to begin with, was fading faster than the day before. Curious, she commented, "It's getting darker earlier today. Why?"

"It is because the darkness comes," explained Lassar.

"What darkness comes? Is that a metaphor for something?" asked Captain Evans, perplexed.

"The moons of Vanirya near the sun. Today is a rare day, happens every 6,000 of your years. Soon, both moons of Vanirya will cover the sun for a half-day of darkness," responded Lassar.

Tamos added, "Once that happens, it will be pitch-black down here on the water."

"That sounds like prime time for another ambush," remarked Captain Evans, concerned after the attack from the night before. "The sun's already dimming."

"It will not be a concern," replied Lassar. "The device reads 64.1434399 x 114.889275, not far from where we need to go. The Hidden City is very close."

"If we are that close, shouldn't we be able to see it, then?" asked Captain Evans.

"It is called the Hidden City for good reason," Tamos replied.

Emma looked around, trying to find it, and all she saw was another massive glacier ahead of the boat, thousands of feet tall and who knew how many miles wide. The waterway turned 90 degrees to the left and 90 degrees to the right before the glacier. "Tamos, is the Hidden city to the left, or right?" asked Emma.

Tamos didn't respond. Instead, he grinned.

Worried, Captain Evans said, "Tamos, seriously, you are rowing right for that glacier."

"Trust me, the Hidden City is there," he replied.

"Okay… I trust you, but where? Because you're gonna crash right into it if you don't turn soon."

"It is a false façade," Tamos said, next asking Lassar, "Are we centered?"

332

"The coordinates read 64.1434546 x 114.889422. You are on course," responded Lassar.

Tamos turned off the motor to slow the boat down to a drift. He kept the oars in the water to help steer on an accurate line right up to the glacier wall. Once they got close, looking straight up, Emma couldn't even see the top of the glacier anymore. Steadily, Tamos guided them into the glacier wall.

At the moment of impact, the boat passed through a holographic wall concealing a tunnel through the glacier ice, hundreds of feet thick. They proceeded down the passage for a minute or so before finally coming out on the other side…

"Behold, the Hidden City," declared Tamos.

Inside the glacier was a city made of ice. They floated on a waterway toward the Hidden City's dock, viewing homes, structures, towers, and city walkways that made up the small city. A white glow reflected throughout the interior of the glacier, caused by the radiance of the solar and lunar energy that powered the Hidden City and coursed through the ice itself.

"Look at this place!" exclaimed Professor Quimbey, never having seen anything so astonishing before. "It's like being inside a snow globe."

"This is incredible. How long has this been here?" asked Emma.

"Almost 10,000 of our years," responded Tamos.

"How has it avoided discovery for that long?" wondered Captain Evans.

Tamos explained, "The thickness of the glacier's fortified ice walls prevents sensors from detecting the city inside, which is itself made of ice and only uses natural energy, which helps. The glacial walls also incorporate a shielding technology that cloaks the city from scans and probes. Perhaps, though, the sworn secrecy of the Remnants is its greatest asset."

"What is that up ahead?" asked Emma, pointing to a terraced hill smack in the middle of the Hidden City, upon which sat a large ice structure, with simple, clean horizontal, vertical, and diagonal lines, basic geometric shapes and forms.

"That is where your destiny awaits," said Tamos, "Qelios, the Sentinel of the Hidden City."

Chapter 24 – Better and Better

After being taken into custody at the Temple of the Moon, Logan, Dr. Arenot, Bryan, and Allysa had spent a rough night and most of the day sitting in jail at the Instituto Nacional Penitenciario del Perú in Quillabamba, 23 miles northwest of Aguas Calientes. The authorities had released Alejandro after interviewing him and determining he was coerced, although he still faced a fine for his role in the transgression equal to the 900 soles the Russians paid him. They were all held in cells on the 2nd floor except for Allysa who was on the 3rd floor. Their 8-foot by 8-foot cells consisted of solitary concrete walls, thick steel bars, steel cots, no widows, tiny metal sinks, and low-to-the-floor porcelain toilets that were scarcely more than holes in the ground.

Logan stood up from his hard cot and paced back and forth to stretch his legs. He was getting restless, and the cramped space only made matters worse. He hadn't left his cell since the guards escorted him to an interrogation session with the police the day before. It went predictably poorly, of course, because he couldn't give the police what they wanted: a believable truth. From what he gathered in his short conversations with Bryan and Dr. Arenot, their interviews went just about the same.

As he bounced between walls, Logan wondered where the U.S. Embassy was. The Peruvians told him they had notified the U.S. agencies after they arrived at the detention facility, but here they were languishing in their jail cells, and still, no one had come to see them.

Just then, two guards approached his cell. "Come with us," one said, unlocking the bars.

"Where are we going?"

"A representative from the U.S. Embassy is here to see you," responded the guard. Logan smiled; someone's ears must have been burning. The guards unlocked Dr. Arenot's cell, too, and instructed the professor to follow.

"What about Bryan?" Logan asked the guard, pointing to Bryan's cell.

"Just you two," replied the guard.

The men escorted Logan and Dr. Arenot through the prison, flanking them closely on both sides.

Walking beside Logan, Dr. Arenot asked, "Do you know what this is about?"

"They said—"

"Stop talking!" snapped the guards in unison.

The guards led them to the same interrogation room where Logan and Dr. Arenot were interviewed previously, a 10-foot by 14-foot solitary room with run-down white walls and a dilapidated wooden table with a few chairs around it. Florescent light bulb tubes flickered overhead. The guards guided them inside, closed the door, and Logan and Dr. Arenot once again found themselves confined in a windowless room.

"What do you think's going on?" asked Dr. Arenot.

"Someone from the U.S. Embassy's here to see us," replied Logan.

"Finally!" exclaimed Dr. Arenot. "Did they say who?"

"No."

"I guess it doesn't matter. Anyone's better than no one," remarked Dr. Arenot.

"You sure about that?" probed Logan, having met his fair share of governmental officials with personal agendas over the years.

The door opened and in walked a gruff, balding man wearing beige slacks, a brown sports coat, a white collared shirt, and dark-brown loafers. It was General Covington in civilian clothing.

"General, please let us know when you are finished," said one of the guards.

"Thank you," Covington replied. The guards closed the door and stood watch outside. Looking at Logan and Dr. Arenot, the general said, "I've got to hand it to you both, you've got a real knack for finding trouble."

"We wouldn't *be* in trouble had you not shut everything down," criticized Logan. "We couldn't even call or text you. You left us with no choice."

"And now, what choice have you left me? The CIA's footage of you four boarding a plane at Martin and prancing around the globe with Russian operatives who shot up police officers at Machu Picchu doesn't look good. For heaven's sake, guys, we're in the middle of an investigation over how Russia got the Vaniryan technology, and it looks like you're working hand in hand with them! Do you know what the CIA wants to do with you right now?"

Dr. Arenot assured the general, "It's just a misunderstanding."

"General," Logan added, "You know none of it's true. They took us hostage."

"Who?"

"Minister Menputyn," replied Logan.

"The incoming Russian Prime Minister?" asked the general, concerned and skeptical.

"Yes," replied Logan. "Somehow, his men switched the planes at Martin and took us hostage at gunpoint."

"That's a pretty damn serious accusation to make against a world leader. Minister Menputyn's been a champion of the recently adopted *U.S.-Russia Science & Technology Sharing Treaty.* What makes you think he's behind this?"

"Because we talked to him," revealed Logan.

General Covington did a double-take. "You spoke to the minister on the phone? And you just happen to know what his voice sounds like?"

"On video feed, actually. I saw his face."

Dr. Arenot added, "It was him for sure. I know what the minister looks like."

"But why would he do that?" Covington asked. "He's one of the more cooperative players on the world stage."

"Obviously, it has to do with the technology the U.S. *isn't* sharing pursuant to the so-called *Science & Technology Sharing Treaty,*" Logan responded.

"I don't need a lecture from you on U.S. foreign policy, Mr. West, especially while you're sitting in a Peruvian prison."

"General, I'm not trying to offend you, but Menputyn was flying us to Moscow because he wanted us to show them how the z-particle technology works. Stolen or not, it sounded like something was wrong with their technology, and he threatened to kill us all if we didn't cooperate."

"What were…" Covington paused to look down at his notes before continuing, "What were Ms. Anders and Mr. Callister doing on that plane with you, and who are they?"

"They're friends of mine," replied Logan. "They did us a favor and drove us from D.C. to Martin. They were just in the wrong place at the wrong time."

"*Very* wrong place, I would say," concurred General Covington. "But why you two?"

"Menputyn said he's been watching us all for years," replied Logan.

Dr. Arenot further added, "I suppose it's possible the Dealer sold information about us, and about our Copán research from Bologna three years ago, and that's why he's been watching us."

Logan chimed back in, "I don't know how he knew what he knew, and he didn't say, but he seemed to know a lot about the Pegasus program, General. The minister may be a champion of the technology sharing treaty, but he's not what he seems."

General Covington nodded, reluctantly acknowledging the possibility that Logan was correct. Still, though, something confused him. "If the minister was flying you to Moscow, how'd you end up in Peru?"

"Because I told him what we needed to know could only be found in Peru, and that flying us to Moscow was a waste of time."

"A brash bluff, Mr. West," said the general. Dr. Arenot titled his head in agreement, even though Logan's tactic had worked.

"I wasn't bluffing. I told him if he truly wanted to understand how his zeutyron technology worked, he needed to find the Vaniryans."

"So, you told him there were Vaniryans in Peru?" asked General Covington. After thinking about it some more, the general followed up, "Wait, *are* there Vaniryans in Peru?"

"No, but I told Menputyn there might be a clue at Machu Picchu telling us where the Vaniryans went before their star exploded."

"Was that true?" asked General Covington.

"Every word" replied Logan.

Dr. Arenot interjected, "Logan and I discovered a manuscript called *The Final Journey of the Vanir* written more than 800 years ago with a hidden message in it that we think tells us where the Vaniryans went."

"What does it say?"

Dr. Arenot replied, "It says, 'Follow line within codex to Frigg's Hens from face of sun to where Vanirens live,' with Frigg's Hens referring to the Pleiades constellation. And if you follow the line, it leads to a star in the Pleiades called Electra."

Logan removed from his back pocket the folded pages of *The Final Journey of the Vanir* and the Voynich manuscript to show the general what they were talking about.

After looking it over, the general said, "But what's the connection with Machu Picchu?"

Logan again showed him *The Final Journey of the Vanir*. "Look at the 15th and 16th verses, General. It says that Odin summoned a being called 'he who overturns space and time' to help the Vanirens escape to Frigg's Hens."

"Okay, I see that."

Logan continued. "General, the Incan ruler who built Machu Picchu is a ruler by the name of Pachakutiq, an Incan word that means, 'he who overturns space and time.'"

"Astonishing. Who do you think put all these hidden messages in this manuscript?" asked the general.

"Emma," replied Logan.

"What are you talking about?"

"They're alive, General!" blurted Logan.

"Who?"

"Emma, Jill, maybe all of them," replied Logan.

General Covington remained silent for several seconds as he considered what Logan had just said. "No one could have survived what we saw on the screen. Are you saying the Russians are holding them hostage?"

"No, that's not what I'm saying."

"Then, what?"

Logan explained, "There was an accident at Chersky, General. Something must've gone wrong with Russia's z-particle technology, and I don't know how, but Emma and Jill must've been transported out of the mountain before it collapsed. Maybe the Russian technology formed a zeutyron field that portaled them away before it happened, I'm not sure... all I know is they're alive, and we have to find them."

"If it transported them out of there, surely we would have picked up their GPS-signals from the trackers they were wearing."

"It's not just a matter of where they were transported to, but *when*," interrupted Dr. Arenot.

Logan added, "General, before you escorted Emma and Jill from the White House to fly to P-West, Emma told me if they got into any trouble, she would text me a secret message…"

"And what was that?" asked the general.

"Help us now," replied Logan. Once again, Logan showed General Covington the poem and pointed to the words at the end of the last five verses that, when put together read, "battle continues, *help us now*." The general studied it for a few more seconds putting all the dots together before Logan said, "General, I know it sounds crazy."

"Very," replied the general. "Then again, I've learned to accept a little bit of crazy when working with the four of you on the Pegasus Project over the last few years. Let me ask you, the local who was with you—"

"Alejandro," interjected Logan.

"—he kept telling the authorities that you all saw death, or encountered the Inca God of Death, or something like that. The Peruvians expressed serious doubts about his sanity. He was evidently very frightened by whatever you saw. What did you guys find?"

"There's another portal in the Temple of the Moon, north of Machu Picchu," Dr. Arenot answered.

"Where the shootout happened?" asked the general.

"Yes, the portal's there… or at least, it was," replied Logan. "We went through it trying to find Emma and Jill."

"But you didn't find them… you found something else, something that frightened Alejandro."

"Yes," said Logan.

"Please tell me you didn't find the Inca God of Death?"

342

"No, we didn't… we found the Vaniryans," said Logan.

"You *think* they were Vaniryans," Dr. Arenot corrected him.

"Right, I *thought* they were. That's what the one who called himself Supay, told us," replied Logan.

Dr. Arenot's eyes lit up as he suddenly realized what frightened Alejandro. "Oh, no… the Inca God of Death and ruler of the Ukhu Pacha is a deity named Supay!" he said, chiding himself for not making the connection sooner.

"Ukhu Pacha?" repeated Logan.

"The Incan underworld. To the Inca, the word 'Ukhu' referred to a race of demons that tormented the living, and the word pacha meant 'world,' although it had a broader context than the word 'world' as we understand it."

"How so?" the general asked.

Dr. Arenot replied, "To the Inca, the word pacha refers to the whole cosmos as part of their world, not just the soil and dirt on Earth. And the Inca also believed that the whole cosmos belonged to the Ukhu Pacha, not just the underworld."

General Covington didn't like the sound of any of it. He asked, "Is this Supay the same God of Death who is mentioned in the *Final Journey of the Vanir* that tried to destroy the Vanirens?"

Logan wasn't sure. Could all of these sources be referring to the same villain, and could that villain possibly have been Supay, the Vaniryan they encountered? "Oh no," Logan said. "Dr. Arenot, we told Supay exactly where to find Emma and Jill, *and* how to find Earth."

"Well, this just keeps getting better and better," replied the general, now sensing a national, indeed intergalactic security issue brewing, if everything about Supay was true. "If you don't know where Emma and Jill are, how could you have told Supay, or whoever it was you encountered, how to find them?"

"Because I read Supay *The Final Journey of the Vanir*. He knew exactly what it meant and where to go after hearing my words... that's when he ejected us from his pyramid, sent us back to the Temple of the Moon, and destroyed the portal behind us," said Logan.

"General Covington, you need to get us out of here immediately," pleaded Dr. Arenot. "Emma, Jill, and possibly others are lost in time in a place called the Hidden City, and they're all in grave danger. We need to figure out where the Hidden City is and fast!"

"I'll do the best I can. These things take time with international channels and——"

Dr. Arenot urged, "We can't wait that long because once we figure out where the Hidden City is, and when, we will still need to find a way to get there."

Logan piped up, "We could go back to the Vaniryan pyramid beneath Area 51."

"I don't think the president's prepared to authorize that yet. The Pegasus program remains indefinitely suspended."

"Screw the suspension, General!" cursed Logan. "If there's even the slightest chance that they're still alive, how can he leave it suspended?"

"If national security demands it, then yes, Mr. West, he can, and should. I'm sorry, but everything I've heard tells me this issue is bigger than just Emma and Jill. If what you've said about Supay is true, then the situation demands we proceed with more caution, not less."

"We can't just give up on them!" exclaimed Logan. "Emma and Jill are only in this position in the first place because *you* asked

344

them to go on the Chersky Mission… but it's not just them: the entire Red Snow Team might be trapped with them, too. We have to help them. We can't just let them all die."

"Even if the president agreed, how are you going to do that? You said you don't know where this Hidden City is…"

"That's true, General, we don't," conceded Dr. Arenot. "But Supay knew exactly where it was as soon as he heard *The Final Journey of the Vanir* poem. Obviously, the clues are all in there, and I think I might just know who can help us solve them…"

"Who?" General Covington asked.

Dr. Arenot replied, "General, you've got to get us on a flight to Uppsala, Sweden. I'll explain on the way."

Chapter 25 – Lundström's Theory

Until General Covington met Emma and Logan, he was a by-the-book skeptic of all things paranormal. Sometimes he was amazed at how dramatically his view of the universe, of what was possible, had expanded since that fateful day three years ago beneath Area 51 when Emma and Logan showed them how to use the sphere. Now, after watching them unfold ancient mysteries time and time again over the years, General Covington had learned to trust their instincts, and that's what he told the president when he called to explain the situation in Peru, including Logan and Dr. Arenot's recommendations.

After listening to General Covington, the president gave him the go-ahead to make a deal with the Peruvian government to get the foursome out of prison and to fly them to Sweden. With a generous contribution towards site improvements at Machu Picchu and Huayna Picchu, the Peruvians were willing to let the incident pass without further punishment.

Once Covington secured their release, a security team escorted them to a nearby helicopter to fly back to the airport in Cusco. Logan, Allysa, and Bryan sat at the back of the chopper while Dr. Arenot and the general sat nearer to the pilot.

"So why are we headed to Sweden?" Allysa asked Logan over the chopper noise.

"There's a professor at Uppsala University who's an expert on *The Final Journey of the Vanir*."

"And where do we go after that?" shouted Bryan.

"You don't want to go home?" replied Logan, slightly surprised.

"Are you kidding?!?" replied Bryan, having the time of his life. "Why would I want to rush home to sell comic books about awesome adventures just like the one we're already on? What kind of comic book store owner would I be if I did that?"

"I guess that's true," said Logan.

"No way I'm leaving you guys to save the day all by yourselves, and besides, you guys need me!" declared Bryan. Logan didn't argue with him, or respond at all, for that matter. Rather, he indifferently shrugged his shoulders, causing Bryan to follow up, "Right?" Logan remained quiet, eating away at Bryan's insecurity. More urgently, Bryan asked, "Logan?!?"

After waiting a bit longer, Logan finally cracked a smile and gave Bryan a solid fist pump to make sure Bryan knew he was part of the team for as long as he wanted to be, and perhaps more importantly, to make sure Bryan knew Logan considered him a good friend. "And what about you, Allysa?" asked Logan. "You've been lied to, kidnapped at gunpoint, dragged around the universe against your will, and thrown in jail. I'm guessing this is the last time you'll ever do a 'small favor' for anyone the rest of your life."

"I'll get over it," replied Allysa with a grin, who privately, like Bryan, was enjoying herself, too. "Besides, I think I can handle one more posh flight across the pond on a fancy private jet with a general. I've always wanted to go to Sweden anyway, not to mention that meeting with a university professor sounds a lot less dangerous than what we've already been through."

Worried Allysa's words might jinx them all, Logan desperately searched for wood to knock on. Unfortunately, he couldn't find any before the helicopter started its descent into Cusco's Alejandro Velasco Astete International Airport. Their short helicopter ride from Aguas Calientes was coming to an end.

At the airport, they boarded General Covington's Gulfstream's G650ER, an "ER - extended range" jet equipped with amenities fit for Heads of State and high-ranking governmental officials traveling long distances between political destinations. Allysa was the first to notice some of its more exceptional features, including a small business center with onboard computers, faxes, and printers, and...

"Is that a shower?" she shouted.

"It is," replied General Covington. "I thought you four might enjoy that feature. After all, we have an 11½ hour flight to Stockholm ahead of us."

"Yes!" exclaimed Logan, unable to remember the last time he showered.

"I've also arranged for some clean clothes and toiletries. We did our best on guessing sizes. You'll find those in the rear closet. Let's get ready for take-off."

They found seats and General Covington told the captain to go. Once they took off and hit cruising altitude, they each took turns browsing the clothing options and taking showers while the plane flew over the rest of Peru, portions of Brazil, and Venezuela on its way northeast to the Atlantic Ocean. During the long flight, in addition to cleaning up, they passed the time resting, eating, discussing more about their findings with General Covington, and preparing for their upcoming meeting with Professor Lundström. When the plane finally touched down at Stockholm Arlanda Airport 23-miles southeast of Uppsala, all were well-rested.

They took a pre-arranged shuttle for the half-hour ride to the historic medieval city of Uppsala, best known for its world-famous university founded in the 15th century. Despite the university's prominence, Uppsala hardly qualified as a "college town." Situated on fertile flatlands, the Scandinavian city prominently featured Uppsala Castle, a 16th-century royal estate originally built for Sweden's most powerful medieval archbishop, and later remodeled into a Renaissance palace that served as the home for numerous Swedish Kings.

The Fyris River flowed right through the city center, dividing it up into two parts: the historic quarter to the west of the river where the centuries-old university was located, and the modern administrative, residential, and commercial part of the city to the east. Their shuttle headed west to the university, driving right past the Domkyrka, Scandinavia's largest cathedral, reaching nearly 400-feet or 30-stories high. Uppsala Castle and the Domkyrka dominated the skyline, with either the castle or cathedral, and sometimes both, visible from nearly everywhere in the city.

Their shuttle dropped them off at Uppsala University's English Park Campus, where the Department of Archaeology and Ancient History occupied the third floor of the Thunbergsvägen building. They walked up a medieval cobblestone pathway through a grove of trees and entered the building just after lunch.

The halls were teeming with students and professors scurrying to and from classes and offices. Professor Lundström's office was on the 3rd floor. They made their way to his office with ease, standing inside a waiting room with books and archeological trinkets in front of a receptionist whose name placard identified her as Agnes.

"May I help you?" she asked in Swedish. No one responded. By the uncertain looks on their faces, Agnes knew who they were. Switching to English, she said, "You must be the Americans."

Dr. Arenot responded in as charming a tone as possible, "You are quite correct, Agnes. We have an appointment with the professor."

"Professor Lundström is just finishing up with his prior conference. He'll just be another moment," Agnes replied.

Passing the time, Logan walked around and looked at the photographs hanging on the walls. After 15 minutes, the general impatiently asked, "How much longer do you think he will be?"

Agnes responded in kind. "The professor is a very busy man. He has many important matters to attend to. If you would like to reschedule, I can view his calendar, otherwise, he will be done when he is done."

"No, no... no need to reschedule. We'll wait," replied Dr. Arenot, giving Agnes a great big smile that confused her.

After a few more minutes, Professor Lundström's office door finally opened and out walked three young female students carrying backpacks and notepads. "If any of you have more questions, please don't hesitate to call or email me," shouted Professor Lundström in Swedish from inside his office to the blushing group of female students who were giggling on their way out to the hallway. Professor Lundström emerged immediately after.

Although he was in his late 40s, he looked younger. After seeing him, Allysa understood what all the fuss was about: he was handsome. Over six feet tall, he had light brown hair, strong cheekbones, a chiseled chin, and sea-blue Swedish eyes. Looking at the five visitors waiting for him, he said, "Good, you're here. I am so sorry to have kept you waiting. Please accept my apologies, and by all means, come in." He retreated back into his private office.

They followed him into his small study, which was far less tidy than the outer waiting room, with papers scattered everywhere, books stacked up in the corners, and piles of folders beside the stacks. Maps, photographs, and illustrations of Nordic mythology and history covered the walls.

"Please excuse the mess," said Professor Lundström. "The Chancellor's Office delivered news of your arrival on short notice. I didn't have much time to straighten up and, well, Agnes does not do what Agnes does not want to do. Have a seat." There were only two chairs in front of the professor's desk. After conferring, Logan and Dr. Arenot sat down and everyone else remained standing.

"I wasn't expecting five of you, otherwise, I would have had more chairs brought in," explained the professor.

Dr. Arenot went first. "Professor Lundström, my name is Jonas Arenot, and sitting next to me is Logan West. Behind me, you have Warren Covington, Allysa Anders, and Bryan Callister."

"Nice to meet all of you. I must admit, Chancellor Olsson does not often request that I meet with visitors. Come to think of it, he never has, so naturally, I am curious. He said you wanted to discuss one of my research projects, although he did not say which one."

Dr. Arenot responded, "Yes, we'd like to discuss an annotation you wrote for a manuscript in Uppsala Library's Special Collections Division titled, *The Final Journey of the Vanir*, written by 'S. Þórðarson.'"

Guardedly, Professor Lundström said, "Yes, I know the one…"

Dr. Arenot continued. "You wrote:

> "Þórðarson's, *The Final Journey of the Vanir,* is a poetic cautionary tale of darkness in the world brought on by war… While many yearn to decipher the hidden meaning behind Þórðarson's masterpiece, Þórðarson's work is more pragmatic than that. It is a call for peace in a troubled world…
> -- *Professor Matteus Lundström, Ph.D.*"

"It's been a few years, but I remember it. I suggest you get on with your question, as I do have a lecture to give in 25 minutes."

At Professor Lundström's urging, Logan jumped right into it, "What is the 'hidden meaning' behind Þórðarson's masterpiece that you refer to here?"

Professor Lundström smirked. "Who put you up to this?"

"I'm sorry, what?" asked Logan in return.

"It's not like Chancellor Olsson to join in on the fun like this. He usually stays far from the fray, so someone else must have—"

"No one put us up to this," interrupted Dr. Arenot. "We are interested in hearing what prompted you to write, 'many yearn to decipher the hidden meaning behind Þórðarson's masterpiece.'"

"You want to know what prompted me? Impetuousness. Writing that comment in my annotation of Þórðarson's work was one of the more imprudent things I've ever done."

"I'm not sure I understand what you mean," replied Dr. Arenot. "The hidden message—"

Professor Lundström stopped him again, appearing more agitated. "I don't mean to interrupt you, and I understand what you are asking, but a much younger, inexperienced version of me wrote that annotation years ago when I was so desperate to publish provocative pieces that I put that out there... the pressure to publish, you know, being what it is, especially at a university like this." Dr. Arenot understood exactly where he was coming from.

"So, there's no hidden meaning?" asked Logan, sounding disappointed.

"I'm sorry. I know you have traveled a long way to speak with me about this, but I haven't heard the end of it from my colleagues since publishing this academically irresponsible annotation without any evidence to support it. Over the years, I've learned to steer clear of... how shall I put this... unprovable theoretical conjecture. Respectfully, if the lessons of our past are meant to help us avoid repeating the same mistakes in our future, then Lundström's Theory shall remain a thing of the past."

"Lundström's Theory?" repeated Logan, intrigued by the title.

"That's the name one of my nitwit colleagues put to it. Never did figure out which one. Do you have any other questions for me?"

Letting it go, for now, Logan asked the next question on his list: "Do you know what the reference to 'hidden city' in the second to last verse of *The Final Journey of the Vanir,* refers to?"

"Just the poetic prose of an Icelandic poet," replied Professor Lundström.

"Snorri Sturluson?" said Logan.

"Some believe that."

"Do you?"

"Yes," replied Professor Lundström, confirming a theory Logan and Dr. Arenot had deduced when they first stumbled upon Þórðarson's work.

Logan continued. "Does the line within the codex that is referenced in *The Final Journey of the Vanir* lead to the 'Hidden City'?"

"Ha, okay, so the joke is on me, after all. You have read Lundström's Theory! Who gave a copy to you and put you all up to this? Liam? Nils?"

"No one put us up to this, professor," said Logan. "We followed the line within the codex to Frigg's Hens from the face of the sun to where the Vanirens live, a line that leads right to the star, Electra. If you want to verify it for yourself, all you need to do is look at the Voynich Manuscript."

That was the cue… General Covington, who had been carrying a small folder with him, handed Logan a picture of the astronomical page in the Voynich Manuscript depicting the Pleiades constellation, which they had printed out on the plane while flying to Sweden. Logan put the printout on the desk in front of Professor Lundström, grabbed a pen, and explained, "Here… you follow the line in the Voynich codex from the sun with a face on it, all the way to Frigg's Hens, the Pleiades constellation here with its seven stars… and you follow the line until it leads right to the second star in the left row… Electra." Logan used the pen to finish off the line to the second star in the left row, just as he had done in Bryan's office back at Dewey's days earlier. The professor now stared at Logan, his thoughts churning.

The general stepped up. "Professor, my full name is General Warren Thomas Covington. I am a five-star general in the U.S. Armed Forces and Special Advisor to the President of the United States. I personally spoke with your chancellor to arrange this meeting." He handed Professor Lundström a card and kept talking. "We come here in earnest, not to mock you. That is the last thing we would do."

"Please... *help us now*," urged Logan, cleverly referencing the last words in the final three verses of *The Final Journey of the Vanir* to pique Professor Lundström's interest. The professor remained quiet, still trying to think things through. Seeing that he almost had the professor, Logan added, "We also know who it is that is asking for help."

"And who might that be?" asked Professor Lundström.

"My girlfriend, Emma James, and Dr. Arenot's wife, Professor Jill Quimbey. We need your help. *They* need your help."

"Professor Lundström, this is not a joke, and neither was your theory," said Dr. Arenot.

The professor's face reflected that he now believed they were serious. He picked up his office phone and buzzed Agnes. "Agnes, please tell the students that today's lecture is canceled." She blurted something into the phone and the professor responded, "No, I don't need a reason!" She said something more, and he replied, "Would you just do it?" She must have begrudgingly agreed because he hung up the phone, shaking his head in obvious frustration.

Without saying anything, he reached into his desk and pulled out a printed picture displaying the Pleiades constellation with all the stars named. The picture had a title at the top that read, *Frigg's Hens*. Notes were scribbled on it, as Professor Lundström had clearly spent some time trying to work out the meaning of *The Final Journey of the Vanir*'s reference to Frigg's Hens to no avail. He tried comparing the Pleiades on his picture to Logan's printed Voynich manuscript page, trying to understand why Logan had concluded the second star in the left row was Electra, as the stars didn't line up.

Logan leaned over and rotated the Voynich manuscript page 45 degrees clockwise for him until the Voynich's seven stars, after re-orientation by Logan, resembled the Pleiades constellation on the professor's page, with two rows of three stars side by side on the left, followed by a final star dangling out by itself on the right. After Logan did that, Professor Lundström saw how Electra lined up with the Voynich's line to the second star in the left row.

Professor Lundström whispered to himself, "I was right." He almost couldn't believe it, and his face displayed relief and gratification. In a louder tone, he said, "I apologize for earlier, it's just that you opened up an old wound of ridicule."

"Is this Lundström's Theory?" inquired Dr. Arenot.

"Yes, well, part of it, anyway. You've obviously taken it a bit further than I ever discerned."

"Is there more?" asked Logan.

"Yes… a far crazier theory I never shared with anyone because I always imagined my colleagues would roast me until I was unrecognizable if it ever got out. So, I kept this one to myself after the mockery of my initial theory."

"What is the theory?" asked Logan.

"I must warn you that I spent several late nights after many fine bottles of wine thinking this last one up. And on the fateful night where I came up with the theory, quite a few shots of brännvin, too."

"Brännvin?" mumbled Logan.

"Think vodka," Dr. Arenot said.

"Yes, vodka, indeed, a favorite of mine," said Professor Lundström. "After Lundström's Theory, I named this one,

'Brännvin's Theory.' Seemed only fitting at the time." Professor Lundström chuckled to himself, maybe at himself.

"What is 'Brännvin's Theory'?" asked Logan.

"On one of my more indulgent nights of brännvin years ago, I noticed a pattern in the old Icelandic prose of *The Final Journey of the Vanir*."

"A pattern of what?" asked Logan.

"Of mistakes," replied Professor Lundström.

"I don't get it," said Logan.

The professor tried to explain better, first asking, "Have any of you ever read Shakespeare?" They all nodded or said *yes*. "Of course, you all have. Good, and what do you remember about reading it?"

"Its metrical patterns, the rhythm and meter of the prose," answered Allysa.

"Sure," said the professor, although that wasn't quite what he was looking for.

"Counting the syllables of Shakespeare's lines of iambic pentameter," tried Logan.

"How impossible it is to read!" joked Bryan. Somewhat embarrassed, he course-corrected by clarifying, "I mean, I know it's supposed to be a brilliant example of playwriting, but I never could get into it. Too hard to understand. No one writes like that anymore."

After some mild laughter by the others, Professor Lundström weighed in, "Exactly! Well done, Bryan!" The response surprised Bryan. Lundström continued, "It's written in old English, employing a style of spelling, grammar, and sentence structure unused today. Sturluson's *Final Journey of the Vanir* is no different. He wrote it in an old style of Icelandic unused today. There are numerous mistakes in the work, but because it's written in old Icelandic, Sturluson's mistakes go entirely unexplored by scholars who assume them to be a mere product of written language variations from a time long since passed."

"But you don't assume that... why?" asked Dr. Arenot.

"Because the mistakes aren't typical of Sturluson's other writings. Sure, there are some here and there in his other works, but Sturluson generally took pride in his writing and tried to correct his mistakes. Even in his seminal work, the *Prose Edda*, you can see scratch marks in the original manuscripts where he etched out the ink from the pages to correct mistaken letters, accents, or punctuation. Occasionally, a mistake would slip through but that was the exception, not the rule. That is not the case with *The Final Journey of the Vanir*, where it is the rule, not the exception."

"How do you mean?" asked Logan.

"Around 2 am in the morning on that fateful night, Brännvin's Theory was born. I noticed a pattern of mistakes so consistent in their occurrence that my tipsy self speculated Sturluson did it intentionally."

"And your sober self, now?" inquired Dr. Arenot.

Staring at Dr. Arenot and without a hint of doubt, he replied, "There's a pattern there, I am sure of it. Do you have a copy with you?"

"Umm, yeah," said Logan. He retrieved *The Final Journey of the Vanir* printout he'd transferred from his old jeans to the pocket of his new beige slacks. He unfolded the page and showed it to Professor Lundström.

"This will not do. You need a copy of the original Icelandic manuscript, not the translations which don't capture Sturluson's mistakes." Professor Lundström reached into his desk and pulled out a copy he once made of the original manuscript kept in Uppsala Library's Special Collections Division. He leaned back to make a photocopy on the copy machine behind him. He then laid it out on his desk for everyone to see and said, "I assume none of you can read the original Icelandic, so let me underline the mistakes for you and you will see what I mean…"

Óðinn, guð viskunnar, þekkingar og töfr<u>ä</u>,
  dauðlegir Midgarðs fylgja,

Sitjandi í hásæti v<u>íð</u> hlið Frigg, synir Þór,
Baldr og Váli, og hæna Friggs, sjö í lína.

Óð<u>í</u>nn kenndi hænum sínum að nota kraft
  sinn, þekkingu og visku innan,

Og hvernig á <u>äð</u> lesa skrifin úr dauðlegum
  Midgard kóða,

En sinni elskul<u>ë</u>gu kenndi hann öllum
Leyandermálum alheimsins, því hún hafði
  viljað að,

Því að hún s<u>ät</u> tilbúin til að stjórna með réttu
  þegar tíma Óðins lauk og þá, Frigg.

En brátt kom Guð D<u>äu</u>ðans fyrir Vanir,
  Óðinn, syni hans og hænur,

Óðinn bað Ljósálfar <u>ög</u> bandamenn hans um
  hjálp, sama hvaðan frá,

Hann benti Æsir og Vanir, fyrir nýj<u>ä</u> Æsir-
Vanir stríð lentu þeir í frammi andlit.

Ekki með hvort öðru, heldur með Dauðanum
og Dökkálfar þess, til sigurs <u>ä</u> Van<u>í</u>r, var
  engum hægt að tryggja,

Ótti gerði Óðinn, komu Dauðans, að frá t<u>ó</u>ppi
Van<u>í</u>rs k<u>á</u>llaði hann á kraft tímans með því að
  nota stjörnurnar, tunglið og sólina,

358

The Hidden Coordinate by Marc Jacobs

Tíl að berjast í bardaga gat Æsir-Vanir ekki
unnið einn, því þeir skorti styrk til að,

Enn til bardaga komu Þór, Baldr og Váli,
spurðu aðeins hvar.

Stríðið geisaði, Dauðinn greip hús Vanirens,

Örvæntur kallaði Óðinn þann sem kollvarpar
rúmi ög tíma, svo að Vanir gætu lifað,

Hann leiddi Vanir heim að nýju og fäldi
kærust Óðins innan rýmis og tíma, að eilífu frá
bardaga.

Óðinn lamdi þá Dökkálfar en leitin að friði
hëldur áfram,

Þegar myrkur Dauðans geisär í Miðgarði, þar
sem Óðinn getur ekki lengur hjálpað,

Því hvërnig bardaga í hulinni borg lýkur er
undir komið okkur,

Æ, Óðinn örvæntír, sólin er farin, sólin er farin
og Guð Dauðans hefur hana núna.

After the professor finished marking up the manuscript, he explained, "Now, all the letters I underlined have acute accents marks above them that should not be there. There is exactly one mistake, no more, no less, in each of the first nine verses, and one mistake in each of the last nine verses… but there is a break in the pattern with two misplaced accents in the tenth verse and three in the eleventh."

"Do the mistakenly-accented letters spell any words when put together?" asked Logan.

"Good question, but no." He quickly scribbled down the letters for them to see and said, "Here are the letters listed in order by verse, after eliminating the improper acute accent marks: aiiaeaaoaaioiaieeoaeaei. No matter what combinations you try to make with these letters, there are no words to be cobbled together there, just vowels."

"What about the words themselves in which the mistakes occur? Did Sturluson mistakenly accent those words because he wanted to point them out in some way? Maybe they form a sentence," theorized Dr. Arenot.

"I tried that, too. Written in order, the mistakenly-accented words read 'töfrä, víð Óðínn äð elskulëgu sät däuðans ög nýjä ä Vanír tóppi Vanírs kállaði Tíl Ënn grëip ög fäldi hëldur geisär hvërnig örvæntír.' In English, this translates to 'magic high Odin to dearest sat Death and new on Vanir from Vanir's peak To Still seized and hid but rages how despair.' There is no discernable sentence there."

"What if you move the words around?" asked General Covington.

"Sure, we can play word scramble," acknowledged Professor Lundström, "but how will we really know if we got it correct? We can probably form 1,000 sentences, maybe more, with the broad selection of words available. It'd end up being pure guesswork. I even tried counting which number word in each verse had the misplaced acute accents."

"What did that end up looking like?" asked Logan.

"I don't have my notes handy, but we can quickly recreate it…" Professor Lundström went through it, writing the results down. "Okay, so the first acute accent error in the first verse occurs in the sixth word of the verse; the accent error in the second verse occurs in word number four…" He kept going. When finished, he summarized it: "Here's the tally, folks: the mistakes in the first nine verses occur in order of verse, in word numbers 6, 4, 1, 4, 3, 4, 5, 4, 7. The mistakes in the tenth verse occur in words 13, 14. The mistakes in the eleventh verse occur in word numbers 8, 9, and 10. And finally, the mistakes in the last nine verses occur in word numbers 1, 1, 4, 8, 8, 9, 4, 2, 3."

Logan took hold of Professor Lundström's paper and studied it closer:

Verses 1-9: 6, 4, 1, 4, 3, 4, 5, 4, 7

Verse 10: 13, 14

Verse 11: 8, 9, 10

Verses 12-20: 1, 1, 4, 8, 8, 9, 4, 2, 3

Logan had an idea. "Dr. Arenot, I know I just tried this at the Temple of the Moon, probably because my head always automatically goes there, but do you know what those numbers look like to me from the first and last nine verses... coordinates! The numbers are all nine or below, which is required for a coordinate system."

"Interesting hypothesis," said Professor Lundström, who hadn't considered that before.

"There are a lot of potential variations of those numbers for a coordinate plotting system," said Logan. He wrote down all the possible variations, moving the decimal points around while making sure the number variations stayed below 360 degrees or 360.000000. He showed everyone the results. The latitudinal number could either be 6.41434547, 64.1434547, or .641434547, and the longitudinal number could be .114889423, 1.14889423, or 11.4889423, or even 114.889423. So, in all, 12 possible coordinate variations."

"Okay, should we plug all the options into a map to see where they plot out?" asked General Covington.

"In a moment," said Dr. Arenot, pondering, "What do we do with verses 10 and 11, which have incorrect accents over words 13, 14 and 8, 9, 10, respectively? Three of the five numbers are higher than nine, which don't work in a coordinate system. And why do those verses break up the pattern of one mistake per line?"

Logan wracked his brain trying to come up with answers, then he noticed *which* words in the tenth and eleventh verses Sturluson incorrectly accented. Specifically, in the tenth verse, the words "ä Vanír" were wrongly accented, and in the eleventh verse, the words "tóppi Vanírs kállaði" were mistakenly accented, in both cases mentioning the word 'Vanir'. "Professor Lundström, remind me again what 'ä Vanír' and 'tóppi Vanírs kállaði' mean in English…"

Professor Lundström responded, "Ignoring the mistaken acute accents, they mean 'on Vanir' and 'from Vanir's peak.'"

Logan practically jumped out of his chair. "That's it! The first and last nine verses give us the coordinates for Vanirya, not Earth!"

"Could they be coordinates for the Hidden City?" wondered Bryan.

Professor Lundström was enthralled by the dialogue his silly brännvin-inspired theory had triggered and fully entertained. "It appears that I am not the only one cursed with imprudence. Well done, lads."

General Covington asked, "Logan, how do you know these coordinates relate to Vanirya—"

"Because the incorrect acute accents in the tenth verse occur over the words 'on Vanir,'" replied Logan. "It's telling us where the coordinates are for: 'on Vanirya.'"

"Okay," said Dr. Arenot, "but even if true, there's no way to compute them without an absolute zero or Prime Meridian point. How do we determine what absolute zero is on Vanirya so we have a fixed point from which to plot out the coordinates?"

Logan replied, "Well, on Earth, the absolute zero point or Prime Meridian is where the Earth's equator meets the latitudinal north-south line of the Royal Observatory in Greenwich, England. In astronomy, astronomers always arbitrarily designate a Prime Meridian on foreign moons and planets by picking a recognizable landmark. From there, astronomers follow the designated landmark's latitudinal north-south line until it intersects with the equator, and that's how astronomers determine a moon's or planet's Prime Meridian. For example, our moon's Prime Meridian is the intersection of its equator with the north-south line determined by the lunar crater called *Mösting A*, and Mars's Prime Meridian is the intersection of its equator with the north-south line of the *Airy-0* crater."

"And what hypothetical landmark do you propose we use on Vanirya, assuming for sake of argument that you could go back in time to a planet that exploded over 800 years ago?" asked General Covington.

Logan responded, "That's where the eleventh verse comes in. The improper acute accent marks in that verse appear over the words 'from Vanir's peak.' Verse 11 is telling us to calculate our latitudinal north-south landmark from Vanirya's peak, probably its tallest peak, which is an objectively verifiable landmark."

"So, let's say you're correct about all this," started Dr. Arenot. "We have a planet; we have coordinates, possibly even for the Hidden City; we have a Prime Meridian from which to compute the coordinates… but we still don't know when in time Jill, Emma, and the others are lost. When does the battle in the Hidden City this poem speaks of, take place? And even if we could find a way to go back in time, if we arrive too early or too late, we'll miss them, by hours, days, years, centuries, or more. Who knows? We need to know the *when*."

"If I might jump back in for a moment," said Professor Lundström. "Ignoring the lunacy of what you're all discussing, I have a thought. And we're all in agreement to keep this to ourselves, yes?" Everyone nodded. "Because, if this ever got out, I'm quite certain my colleagues would chase me out into the streets, leaving me no choice but to look for a new job with you, Dr. Arenot."

"You know who I am?"

With a head nod, the professor responded, "I saw you speak at the International Archeology Symposium in Edinburgh, Scotland, almost a decade ago. Your lecture on the Copán Temple mystery was fascinating. I was sad to learn of your accused forgery at the Copán Ruins and subsequent dismissal from Harvard. I don't know if any of it was true, of course, but I think now, as I see you sitting here with a five-star general and advisor to your U.S. president discussing what we are, that perhaps there was more to your Copán story."

Dr. Arenot looked at General Covington who shook his head to make sure Dr. Arenot said nothing further.

"There is," said Dr. Arenot, "but that's a story for another time."

"Yes, I'm sure it is. Let me just say, it's good to see you working again and doing what you do best. So, what I had started to say was, if it helps, there's a reference in the final verse of this poem that says, 'the sun is gone, the sun is gone'. I have always found that phrase interesting and thought perhaps it refers to an eclipse. Maybe that will help you determine when the battle in the Hidden City occurs."

"Any idea why Sturluson repeated the phrase 'the sun is gone,' twice?" asked Logan.

"I'd only be guessing, but maybe your Vanirya has two moons or two suns, making a double eclipse."

"Wait!" exclaimed Logan. "Vanirya has two moons!" He knew that from the Pegasus Project's study of TYC 129-75-1's solar system using the Vaniryan technology beneath Area 51.

Dr. Arenot asked Professor Lundström, "Is there anything else you can tell us about *The Final Journey of the Vanir*?"

"No, I think you've heard everything I have to offer."

"Professor Lundström, thank you, you have been a tremendous help," said General Covington.

"You are welcome, General. It has been an unexpected pleasure."

Dr. Arenot wrote his cell number down on a piece of paper and handed it to Professor Lundström. "If you think of anything else, please call me."

"Of course," replied the professor.

They all said their goodbyes and departed. They had a long flight ahead of them now. Even General Covington knew it was time to head west to the Vaniryan pyramid beneath Area 51. Once he got back to the plane, he had several calls to make, starting with the president to convince him to reinstate the Pegasus Project immediately.

Meanwhile, Professor Lundström sat alone in his study, processing what had just happened. He reached to his left to open the third desk drawer down. He pulled out a glass tumbler and bottle of premium brännvin. The professor poured the clear beverage into his tumbler, leaned back, and kicked his feet up onto his desk. He brought the tumbler to his lips and chuckled. "Brännvin's Theory, huh? Gotta come up with a better name next time." He took a sip and smiled, delighted with the outcome of the most unexpected meeting of his life.

Chapter 26 – Rain Check

Major Bryce Jameson walked through the door to Pegasus East five floors below ground, carrying beverages and display case sandwiches from the Pentagon's Courtyard Cafe. The door closed behind him after he entered. Lt. Col. Ainsley Lain was waiting for him at the computer panel in front of the wall of digital monitors in the background. He set the food and drinks down on a flat portion of the computer station beside Lt. Col. Lain and said, "Alright, Ains, here you go, an iced tea and sun-dried tomato pesto chicken sandwich for you, and one iced tea and turkey sandwich for me."

"Thanks," replied Lt. Col. Lain, unenthusiastically taking hold of her plastic-wrapped sandwich.

"Sorry, our plans got ruined tonight. Rain check?"

"Sure," said Lt. Col. Lain, rotating her pre-made sandwich around to check it out from all sides before unwrapping it.

Maj. Jameson, having no such hesitation, opened his. "You see, this isn't so bad... we got the best food the Courtyard Café's display case had to offer."

"Yeah, as of about 14 hours ago when they made it. And by the way, don't think you're off the hook, here, Bryce. The Courtyard Café was probably where you were taking me anyway."

"Ains, you've seriously got no faith in me."

"You're right, I don't."

"You honestly think I was planning to take you out to dinner at the cafeteria?"

"Okay, fine… where were we going then?"

"Um, it was going to be a surprise…"

"Yeah, sure it was."

"I had several places in mind, actually."

"Name one…"

"Uh—"

"Places that take reservations?"

"Well, no, not those kinds of places, but some really great spots."

"Crazy Chicken or Fiery Fred's walk-up counters aren't my ideas of great spots."

"I would never—"

"You so would! Do you remember my birthday last year?"

"How was I supposed to know the place had been shut down by the health department?"

"Oh, I don't know, call ahead maybe… Bryce, next time, I want to go somewhere that takes reservations, and no, going to a place where the host writes your name down on a waiting list doesn't count."

"Okay, I get it. I'll—"

"And I want to go into the city for once, somewhere more than five minutes away, if that's not too far out of the way of your curmudgeon zone."

"Deal. I promise next time, we'll go somewhere in the city rated at least four stars." Maj. Jameson paused and then changed the subject. "So, what's going on here that we're missing out on Fiery Fred's Feeding Frenzy, anyway?"

Lt. Col. Lain shot him a look and smacked him in the shoulder. "I knew it! Bryce, you suck! You totally owe me."

Laughing out loud, he replied, "I know, I totally do. Really, though, what are we doing here so late?"

"Don't know. Covington told me we'd receive instructions around 7:30 pm."

"Did he say why?" asked Maj. Jameson. He looked at his watch and it was 7:30 pm on the dot.

"It has something to do with the kid and prof." Just then, the phone rang.

"Right on time," remarked Maj. Jameson.

Lt. Col. Lain picked up the phone. "Lain here…" She grabbed a pad and pen and started jotting down notes. "Yes, sir," she said as she kept writing everything down. After a minute, she hung up and said, "Alright Bryce, it's showtime."

"What's going on?" asked Maj. Jameson, putting down his sandwich without having taken a bite.

"Looks like we need to access some cartographic and topographical survey data for Vanirya, analyze it, and send the info their way," Lt. Col. Lain replied.

"And they need this tonight, on a priority basis, as opposed to a full report tomorrow?"

"I guess Covington's flying to the Pyramid with West and Arenot as we speak, and they need it ASAP," Lt. Col. Lain responded.

"Interesting… I wonder what's up."

"We'll soon find out. Let's get cracking," said Lt. Col. Lain, sliding into a senior-officer mode.

Maj. Jameson punched instructions into his keyboard to pull up the data files and various images captured of Vanirya from inside the "Pyramid" hidden underneath Area 51.

"Data files accessed and ready," he reported.

"Okay, first, they want us to identify the tallest mountain peak on the planet," said Lt. Col. Lain.

"Pulling up the topography study for Vanirya now," replied Maj. Jameson.

Lt. Col. Lain, whose computer screen now mirrored Maj. Jameson's as part of a shared file system began reviewing the data he retrieved, moving aside windows as she browsed through the information on her screen. After a few minutes, she said, "Hey, pull up the Pegasus V-Topo Study."

"Okay." Maj. Jameson accessed the study Lt. Col. Lain requested and pulled it up on his screen, with the various topographical studies visible in different windows side by side.

"Alright, now let's do a topo-comparison with the cartographic survey done two years ago."

"Got it." He ran the comparison and projected the results up on the center wall screen. Maj. Jameson remarked, "Looks like we have a winner, the peak on the eastern portion of the mountain cluster over to the left, there. Do you see it?"

"Yeah, that's one big mountain," Lt. Col. Lain replied, surveying a peak identified by a red dot smack in the middle of a cluster of mountains. "How tall is that sucker?" she asked, curious.

Maj. Jameson looked at the data column on his screen and answered, "Estimate is over 65,000 feet, assuming the info provided by the holographic imagery inside the Pyramid is accurate. Since no one's actually been to Vanirya's surface to verify this data, the computer's spitting out estimates."

"Still, that's quite the peak. Even visually, the thing looks massive. 65,000 feet is more than twice as high as Mount Everest," said Lt. Col. Lain.

"Now what?" asked Maj. Jameson.

"Now, they want us to plot out the coordinates, 64.1434547 by 114.889423, using that peak to define the north-south line of intersection with the equator in order to determine the planet's Prime Meridian," she responded.

Maj. Jameson immediately entered the coordinates into the computer and, on the large wall screen in front of them, a location popped up on the cartographic map of Vanirya's surface, again denoted by a red dot.

"What is that?" asked Maj. Jameson, staring at what looked, to him, like an ice field with interspersed waterways.

"Looks like the Norwegian fjords on steroids from here. Can we zoom in?" asked Lt Col. Lain.

"A little but it'll get blurry pretty fast." He zoomed in closer and said, "That's one hell of a big glacier field. Look at all the waterways going through those glaciers. Crazy. I wonder what they want all this info for?" said Maj. Jameson.

"Covington said they're looking for data points to execute a C-SAR operation."

"A *combat, search and rescue* operation?"

"Yep."

Maj. Jameson didn't get it. "That doesn't make any sense. The star went supernova more than 800 years ago. There's no one left there to rescue."

"Well, then this last question is really going to stump you: they want to know how often based on the orbital precessions of Vanirya's two moons, that those moons would have both passed between TYC 129-75-1 and Vanirya, resulting in a double solar eclipse, and the last time it happened."

"We're going to need the astrographic data for that," said Maj. Jameson. He accessed the data in the lunar trajectory and orbital path computer files. He uploaded numerous spreadsheets into the Pegasus computer's stellar cartography program, and a computer simulation of Vanirya, its two moons, and its sun appeared on the large oversized screen on the center wall. The computer simulation started rotating Vanirya around its sun, and the moons around Vanirya, in reverse orbit to simulate going backward in time. The planet and moons rotated slowly at first, but shortly after accelerated to a computer speed faster than the eyes could see.

On the right wall screen was a digital counter displaying the days passing by with each full rotation of the planet. As the planet and moons rotated in reverse, the counter increased until everything suddenly stopped. Vanirya's two moons were perfectly aligned between TYC 129-75-1 and Vanirya, resulting in a simulated double eclipse.

"There it is!" announced Maj. Jameson, pointing to the results on the right wall screen. "Vanirya experienced a double solar eclipse event 816.37 years ago and once every 6,247.23 years."

"Wow, literally right before TYC 129-75-1 exploded," commented Lt. Col. Lain.

"They don't think the double eclipse caused that, do they?" asked Maj. Jameson.

"I don't see how it could have, but you got me," replied Lt. Col. Lain. "Send all the info we've obtained to Covington."

Maj. Jameson sent everything to Covington. While they were waiting for further instructions, both worked on their respective computer stations for a few minutes. Eventually, a response came back that said: "RETURN TO PEGASUS EAST AT 0100 HOURS FOR C-SAR OPERATION."

"Who could that C-SAR operation possibly be for?" Maj. Jameson asked. "Unless they're planning to go back in time, this doesn't make any sense."

"Maybe you hit the nail on the head. I guess we're gonna find out at 0100," replied Lt. Col. Lain.

Maj. Jameson sat quietly for a moment before casually saying, "You know, Ains, we've got some time to kill before 0100 hours. Not too late to catch Fiery Fred's Feeding Frenzy, my treat..."

Lt. Col. Lain eyed him contemplatively for a moment, then, she shrugged her shoulders and replied, "Fine. Let's make it fast."

Maj. Jameson leaped out of his chair, excited. "Awesome, you can rip up that rain check! Looks like we don't need to reschedule our date, after all."

Lt. Col. Lain rolled her eyes. "Bryce, you kill me sometimes, you really do."

"Yeah, I know. Just make sure you ask for three Saturday nights from now, off."

"Why?"

"I got us reservations at Hobā."

Chapter 27 – Only a Matter of Time

Logan ran his hands through his hair in frustration. After the plane took off from Stockholm on their cross-continental flight back west to Area 51, he had spent the last several hours scouring *The Final Journey of the Vanir* and the internet looking for writings by Snorri Sturluson discussing the concept of time. He firmly believed there was a clue somewhere in Sturluson's works telling them how to travel back in time to Vanirya because, for reasons unknown, Sturluson appeared to be the one entrusted with leaving behind the breadcrumbs.

If they couldn't find a way to manipulate the Vaniryan pyramid underneath Area 51 to travel back in time to Vanirya, the alternative was to return to Supay's homeworld orbiting Electra where Logan assumed the time travel technology could be found. Since Supay responded "I will find who you seek," after Dr. Arenot told him their friends were lost in time, he presumed the technology to do so existed on Supay's planet. At least, that was his logic.

Even so, returning to Supay's world was risky since they didn't yet have a full understanding of Supay's capabilities, weapons, technology or army, or where on Supay's planet the time travel technology was or how it worked, or the size of Supay's planet or about its atmosphere or how they would get around it. Any return to Supay's homeworld orbiting Electra was perilous, but no more so than traveling back in time to the Hidden City on Vanirya where a "battle" was supposedly taking place.

For that reason, President Barrett authorized General Covington to assemble a combat, search and rescue ("C-SAR") team to go with them. As the president and General Covington both agreed, sending a C-SAR team would help accomplish two goals: gathering intel on Supay to see who or what they were really dealing with, and rescuing those left behind by the Chersky Mission.

While General Covington coordinated the mission, Alyssa walked down the center aisle of the plane to where Logan was sitting. He was busy conducting computer research on the plane's computer station. She sat down in the chair next to him and asked, "Can't sleep either?"

"Nope, my body's literally got no idea what time it is anymore after everywhere we've been. Just looking a few things up. How about you?"

"Dr. Arenot snores too loud. So, what are you researching?"

"I'm probably just wasting my time, but I feel like we're missing something, some clue telling us how to go back in time to Vanirya. Think about it... Emma, Jill, or whoever left all these clues behind did so because they wanted to be found, right?" Allysa agreed, so Logan kept explaining, "So it makes sense then that they would've also left the final piece of the puzzle behind, too, don't you think?"

"What I don't get though is if you're right and they did leave all these clues behind so you could find them, why not be more direct about it? Why all the hidden clues and riddles?"

"You mean, why not just write a note 800 years ago, saying, 'To Logan West, future U.S. citizen to be born May 3, 1999, in Queens, NY: here is where you can find us and how you can use the technology in the secret pyramid underneath Area 51 to travel back in time?"

"Well, like, maybe something a little more subtle than that, but yeah..."

"I thought about that. Obviously, they wanted to put the information somewhere they knew it wouldn't get lost, destroyed, or discarded for centuries, and hiding it in the words of a famous author like Snorri Sturluson, whose writings they knew survived into the 21st century and Jonas and I were familiar with, definitely increased the likelihood of all this info getting back to us. And maybe they resorted to clues because they didn't want the whole world or the wrong person to know or the information falling into the wrong hands or the wrong person finding *them*…"

"Like Supay?" interjected Allysa.

"Exactly! I don't have all the answers, and maybe I'm just convincing myself of this because the idea of going back to Electra and seeing Supay again, scares me, but I really think there's more for us to find."

"Yeah, I get that," said Allysa.

"You should be glad you're getting off the plane when it lands in D.C.," replied Logan.

"Oh, Covington didn't tell you?"

"Tell me what?"

"I'm sure he meant to. He told us the plane isn't stopping in D.C. anymore. He apologized but said because of time constraints, it's heading straight to Nevada. I thought you knew."

"No, he hadn't mentioned it yet. The hits just keep on coming for you guys, huh? Sorry…"

"Maybe it's a good thing, you know? Bryan and I were actually just talking about how we wanted to go with you."

"Are you crazy? Allysa, you know how dangerous this is going to be, right? Not to mention Covington's never going to let you below ground at Area 51."

"Why? It's not like we don't know what's down there. Like, you've already told us everything, and we've already traveled through the stars in one of those pyramids. What difference are two more people who already know everything anyway, going to make?"

"I guess that's true. Still, even if Covington lets you go, why would you want to? What we're proposing to do is really dangerous, Alyssa. I have no idea how this is going to turn out or if we'll even be coming back."

"It's like Bryan says, friends don't abandon friends in a time of need. What kind of friends would we be if we did that?"

"Alive ones."

"Bryan and I want to help you."

"Allysa, seriously… one week ago, you had no idea who we were or what any of this was about. And now, one week later, you're willing to risk your life for this, for us? Why?"

"Because I believe in what's right, and I know this is going to sound crazy, but I've known you guys for a week, and already, I feel connected with all of you. I know it's corny, but I feel like I've finally found my people."

"It's not crazy." Logan paused for a second, then asked, "This wouldn't have anything to do with Bryan, too, would it?"

Allysa blushed. "What do you mean?"

"I'm just saying, you and Bryan seem to be getting along pretty well…"

"I know. I like him. He's so easy to talk to and he's not caught up in all the BS everyone else is, not worried about what others think. I wish I could be more like him sometimes. I spend so much time being insecure about everything that I'm constantly second-guessing myself. I can't even pick a major without asking a complete stranger I just met in a coffee shop to help me…"

With a slight grin, Logan replied, "Well, The Grind is no ordinary coffee shop, and I promise you, you would have found your way with or without my help. It takes everyone time to figure things out."

"Not Bryan," replied Allysa. "He's just happy being himself, owning a store, consulting, living on his own, doing his thing. I'm kind of jealous, actually. I spend most of my time trying to impress people I don't know or care about on Instagram, and then, there's Bryan who isn't trying to impress anybody, and he's just, like, happy. Makes me really rethink what success looks like, and right now, spending time with Bryan, and all of you guys really makes me happy."

"Well, I wouldn't be so sure Bryan isn't trying to impress somebody..."

Allysa turned a slight shade of red. "So, what are you looking at right now, maybe I can help?"

"I'm reading *The Final Journey of the Vanir* for the umpteenth time. There've been so many clues hidden in there that I figured it was only a matter of time before I stumbled upon the secret to time travel, too. Wishful thinking, right?"

"At this point, anything's possible. Slide over, maybe I can help." Logan slid over to make room for Allysa. She nudged her chair closer to the screen. "What do you have so far?"

"Well, I've tried a lot of things, reversing words, looking for patterns, counting words, scrambling the whole thing like an egg. But right now, I'm actually focusing on the verses in the poem that mention 'time'... there're four of them, the sixth, eleventh, fifteenth, and sixteenth verses." He showed Allysa the verses he had written down on a piece of paper:

> For she sat ready to rule justly when Odin's
> **time** ended and then, Frigg's...

Fear did Odin, the coming of Death, that from
Vanir's peak he called upon the power of **time**
using the stars, moons and sun…

Desperate, Odin summoned he who overturns
space and **time**, so the Vanir could live…

He led the Vanir to a home anew, and hid
Odin's dearest within space and **time** itself,
forever away from battle…

Allysa looked at the four verses and commented, "The first one
seems to use the phrase 'when Odin's time ended' to refer to the
time of Odin's inevitable death, or the end of his rule, possibly. Not
sure if that helps or not."

Logan replied, "No, I agree with you, not much there. And the
third and fourth ones only talk about the name of the god who Odin
called for help – 'he who overturns space and time' – and how that
god hid Odin's daughter 'within space and time itself.' The one that
appears most promising to me, and which I've been thinking about
ever since leaving Uppsala, is the second one."

Allysa re-read the second one: *Fear did Odin, the coming of
Death, that from Vanir's peak he called upon the power of time
using the stars, moons and sun…* Once she finished reading it, she
commented, "Yeah, I see what you're saying. It implies time is a
power that Odin can use by using the stars, moons, and sun to do it."

"Right, but it doesn't merely imply it, it says exactly that. I just
can't figure out *how* to use the stars, moons, and sun, or what we're
supposed to do with them to 'call upon the power of time.' It's like
the answer is right there, staring at us in the face." Logan again ran
his hands through his hair, frustrated.

"I don't know, but you're definitely on to something. We've
still got a bunch of hours before we land. Maybe it's time to wake
Dr. Arenot and Bryan," suggested Allysa.

"Yeah, you're right. Let's wake them."

378

△△△△△△△△△△△

When the plane finally landed in Nevada, it was night and the newcomers to the base – Bryan and Allysa – couldn't see it. Their imaginations had to fill in the gaps of what the most mysterious military base in U.S. history looked like because all they saw upon deplaning were armed airmen standing on the runway strip and buildings shrouded in the evening darkness. For Logan, it was a familiar return, especially when Area 51's highest-ranking officer, General Nemond, came up to greet them.

"Warren," said General Nemond to General Covington with his usual greeting, reaching out to shake hands.

General Covington responded, "Bernie. Is Commander Anderson's team all set?"

"Yes, they arrived a few hours ago and have been in mission prep ever since. We've put together a combat, search and rescue team with an emphasis on combat, a little different than Captain Evans's climbers." Looking at Logan and Dr. Arenot, the general extended his hand to them, as well, and asked, "How are you gentlemen doing? Ready to see if we can turn back the history books?"

"Yes, sir," said Logan.

Now looking at Bryan and Allysa, General Nemond joked, "And are these the stowaways?"

"We're hardly stowaways," Allysa replied, not quite picking up on the general's humor.

"Bernie, the president has cleared them for reasons we can discuss later," said General Covington.

"I know, I spoke to him about a half-hour ago. He explained it and sent over the emergency paperwork with an executive order." As he did with everyone else, the general reached out to shake Bryan's and Allysa's hands and added, "I gotta tell you both, getting top-secret clearance to Area 51 used to be a lot harder. Let's head inside."

General Nemond led them into Homey Research Building #2. Logan had forewarned Bryan and Allysa that the building's interior was plain and boring with no windows for security reasons, and just as he said, they couldn't see a thing. They proceeded to the elevator which took them down to Basement Level 4. The elevator doors re-opened to a subterranean mission control-style command center with digital screens on the walls and stadium-seating rows of computer stations and panels. Unlike most nights, the Control Room was full in anticipation of the imminent operation.

"This is awesome!" blurted Bryan, eliciting a grin from Logan who liked Bryan's enthusiasm.

"The Pyramid is this way," said General Nemond, guiding them through the command center. General Nemond led them down the hall to a new entrance for the Vaniryan Pyramid. When Emma and Logan first came to Area 51 three years earlier, there was only a small hidden trapdoor in General Nemond's office leading down a pathway in the ground rock. Three years later, General Nemond's office had been relocated, and a heavily secured door where his office used to be had replaced it. With General Nemond's handprint, the door opened and behind it was a staircase leading down. They took the stairs several flights to a newly constructed hallway.

About 100 feet down the hallway, General Nemond stopped at a door labeled 'Equipment' and said, "We need to get you folks fitted for the mission. Right this way." They followed the general into a large room with multiple side rooms and hallways. Pegasus personnel were waiting for their arrival and took them back to dress each in a close-fitting navy-blue jumpsuit with an airtight lightweight gray outer suit over it, designed to seal them in from a hostile atmosphere. The suits weren't heavy spacesuits like astronauts wore, but they were similar.

The general had supervised the Pegasus Project's efforts to create an alternative spacesuit for the last three years in anticipation of intergalactic travel when Pegasus reached that next phase. The suits were lightweight, flexible, and regulated the wearer's body temperature, as needed. With the C-SAR operation accelerating the timeframe, the president had authorized Pegasus to put the suits, which were still in the final stages of testing, into action.

Logan was the first to emerge wearing his suit and holding an aerodynamic-looking helmet in hand. General Nemond, waiting in the main room with General Covington, looked at him and asked, "How does the Pegasuit feel?"

"Pegasuit?" regurgitated Logan.

"Pegasuit… that's what the Pegasus West team is calling it. So, what do you think?"

"I think everything Pegasus West names should go through a new approval process. But other than that, it feels comfortable, not bulky or heavy at all."

"And they showed you how to use the com-system linking all the helmets together?" asked General Nemond.

"Yep, they gave us the full tutorial back there."

Bryan, Allysa, and Dr. Arenot came out next wearing their own Pegasuits. When asked, each indicated they felt good.

General Nemond reminded them, "Your helmets and suits contain air filters to cleanse and oxygenize any unbalanced atmospheres you may encounter for an extended period of time, and enough isolated oxygen to last for eight hours if you encounter a completely inhospitable one."

General Covington chimed in, "The hope is that the planet you journey to will have a tolerable atmosphere, given that, if the intel you've provided is accurate, Ms. James was able to survive on Vanirya, and Supay's homeworld had air for the four of you inside his pyramid. Just to be safe though, we've brought over a *p*RAMZA rover from P-West to go through the portal first, to survey the environment on the other side."

"Is everyone ready to head over to Personnel?" asked General Nemond. Hearing no objection, he continued, "Good, let's go meet your new team."

ΔΔΔΔΔΔΔΔΔΔΔΔ

When Logan, Dr. Arenot, Bryan, and Allysa entered the Personnel office, General Nemond introduced them to 10 highly trained NAVY SEALS also dressed in Pegasuits. The introductions didn't last long because neither of the generals knew the NAVY SEALS particularly well. Seeing the SEALS in person was both exciting and intimidating for Logan, as he had never met one before as far as he knew. The SEALS were extremely fit, with their bulging muscles visible even through their suits.

After the introductions, Captain Santiago Velasquez, a bulky, dark-haired combat veteran and the commander of the newly assembled C-SAR unit, was ready to return to preparing for the highly unusual mission. They *all* were.

The meeting with the SEALs lasted for nearly two hours as they discussed the mission, contingencies, reunification plans, mission goals, structure, combat, and other topics, most notably, the Vaniryan technology in the Pyramid. When done, General Covington and General Nemond led the group down the last leg of the hallway to the Pyramid. The hallway stopped about 50 feet short, as Pegasus engineers had opted not to construct it any closer than that. Thus, the last 50 feet of the tunnel took them through the original low-tech passageway in the ground rock that had always been there.

"Here we are, again," said Lt. General Nemond. He pushed open the door and led them into the giant hollowed-out pyramid with smooth white walls. Only, the hollow space was now quite full of cameras, monitors, personnel, and the second *p*RAMZA rover in the corner with its operator, a Pegasus team member Ian Marcus. His job was to send Prammy's cousin, Rammy, through the portal for atmospheric feedback, while environmental specialist, Dr. Jamie Adams, was also there to analyze the readings.

Logan's eyes immediately gravitated to the five-foot-tall white metallic sphere in the Pyramid's center. Logan, Dr. Arenot, Allysa, and Bryan approached it, leaving their SEAL team behind, while the generals walked off to speak with others. As Logan did each time that he visited the Pyramid, he read the inscription on its surface: "*It is time for mankind to travel the stars – Emma J.*" Each time he read it, it gave him chills. Logan smiled as the words reminded him of what he cared about most in life: Emma. For a few seconds, all the fears swirling in his mind about what they were about to do took a backseat to his memories of Emma.

After a minute, General Covington and General Nemond returned. "Alright, are you ready?" asked General Covington, interrupting Logan's fleeting moment of mental solitude.

Logan snapped out of it and responded, "Yes."

"How about the rest of you?" asked General Covington. They all nodded. An officer hurried over to give General Covington a folder. The general thanked the runner and waved over the SEAL team.

"Captain Velasquez, does your team have any more questions?"

"No, sir. Let's go kick some alien ass and bring our friends home!" exclaimed Captain Velasquez. He gave Logan and Bryan an exuberant fist bump.

Covington gave Nemond a head nod, and General Nemond made the announcement: "Alright everyone, let's bring P-West, P-East, the Control Room, and SIT-Room online."

There were multiple display monitors erected on non-permanent stands along the southern wall of the Pyramid, and within short order, all locations popped up on the various screens with the Situation Room appearing last. The usual crew waited for President Barrett in the SIT-Room. A minute later, the president arrived and everyone stood up.

"Good evening everyone," said President Barrett, sitting down in his chair. The entire SIT-Room sat back down after him. "Generals, are you ready to proceed?"

"Yes, sir," said General Covington.

The president began. "Alright, as I understand it, you're going to activate the sphere, trying first to return to Vanirya."

"Correct, Mr. President," replied the general.

"And you believe that if you can find a way to use the Vaniryan technology to travel back in time to before TYC 129-75-1 exploded, that you'll be able to go down to Vanirya's surface and rescue our people?"

General Covington nodded. "That is the idea, Mr. President. As you know, we believe the star's explosion is why we can't return to Vanirya, because the planet isn't there anymore. But if we can go back in time to a point before the star exploded, when the planet still existed, the theory, or at least the hope, is that we should be able to."

"We've tried this before, studying the technology to see how the Vaniryans were able to go back and forth through time. We've never been able to figure it out."

"That's right, Mr. President, but the team has a few new ideas," said General Covington.

384

"And if you succeed, is the team ready for the battle you've all told me is taking place in the Hidden City that you're trying to get to?"

"Yes, sir. If we can figure out how to travel back in time, and if the coordinates P-East mapped out are accurate, and if the double eclipse dates P-East identified are correct, and if there is, indeed, a battle taking place, the team will be ready."

"That's a whole lot of ifs, general."

"Yes, sir. Rest assured, Captain Velasquez's team is locked, loaded, and ready for battle. There are no ifs about that." Indeed, all the SEALS had weapons strapped to their backs and belts, and stuffed into their backpacks, along with other equipment.

"Of course, general. And plan B, which sounds more like Plan A to me, is returning to Supay's planet where our four wily civilians toured while vacationing in Peru this week." President Barrett eyed Logan, Dr. Arenot, Bryan, and Allysa as he said it.

"Yes, Mr. President. If our efforts to go back in time to Vanirya are unsuccessful, we will turn to the world orbiting Electra in the present day, where they will try to find the technology to travel back in time, proceed to Vanirya, and find the Hidden City. As a reminder, Mr. President, once we activate the sphere, we will not be able to communicate with you until the sphere deactivates."

"Are you planning to use another rover for atmospheric feedback to make sure the environment is safe before sending the team in?"

"Yes, Mr. President. We've brought the second *p*RAMZA unit over from P-West. We'll send it in to survey the atmosphere on the other side of the portal, and if there's any doubt as to safety, we will abort and reconvene."

"And once they are in there, what is the plan to bring the team home?"

"Assuming it is in the present day, the second *p*RAMZA rover will send a z-particle signal back to P-West as we did on the *p*RAMZA test last week, so we can activate a portal tracked to the *p*RAMZA's source for the team to return to Earth. And regardless of where they go, past or present, we will be manually opening up rendezvous portals at the exact same insertion point, at regular intervals on a timed schedule that has been given to each member of the team."

"Understood. General Covington, the operation is a go at your command."

General Covington shouted loud enough for all to hear, "Pegasus, we are a go."

General Nemond announced, "Pegasus West, Pegasus East, Control Room, stand-by for initiation. All non-essential personnel, please exit the Pyramid at this time." As ordered, nearly everyone inside the Pyramid exited. That included General Nemond, the commanding officer of Area 51. He departed for the Control Room.

Once everyone was gone, General Covington said to Logan, "Mr. West, do you want to do the honors?"

"Sure..." Logan walked up to the sphere and touched it, his heart racing with feelings of excitement, anxiousness, and dread. In a matter of minutes, if they could solve the latest riddle woven into *The Final Journey of the Vanir*, it was possible he would see Emma again!

Upon touching it, the sphere lit up in blue energy outlining the continents and land masses of Earth like a globe. Next, using the tip of his left index finger, he touched all the geographic locations associated with the Copán Temple mystery he and Emma had solved three years earlier, which he had to touch in the following order to activate the sphere: Falaise, France; Storfjorden, Norway; Stonehenge in the UK; Giza in Egypt; Tiwanaku in Bolivia; Copán in Honduras; Area 51 in Nevada; and lastly, Falaise, again. He did not remove his index finger from the sphere after touching Falaise the second time. Instead, he allowed it to remain in place and watched as the mechanism activated.

The walls and floor of the Pyramid disappeared and the galaxy and its billions of stars holographically appeared around them, hovering like fireflies. Their mission was officially underway…

Chapter 28 - Insertion Point

"Wow!" voiced Captain Velasquez, echoing the sentiments of his whole team as they gazed into the dark vastness of space, hovering over Earth. In mission prep, scientists had described what to expect and played videos of the technology in action, but until they were inside it, they didn't appreciate the awesome power of the Pyramid. "Are we actually in outer space?" he asked.

"No, we're still inside the Pyramid," replied Logan. "We won't leave Earth until we open up and walk through a portal."

"Flippin' insane," replied Velasquez.

"Okay, Mr. West, what next?" asked General Covington.

"Logan scanned the Pyramid's holographic universe in search of TYC 129-75-1 and found it just below and to the left of Betelgeuse, the back shoulder of Orion. He pointed at the star with his right index finger and a blue line extended from his fingertip to it. In an instant, they surged through the stars into TYC 129-75-1's solar system where there was only one orbiting planet: Vanirya, along with its two moons.

Keeping his left index finger on the sphere as he had to do in order to prevent it from deactivating, Logan pointed his right index finger at Vanirya, and another blue line extended from his fingertip to the planet. They jumped into Vanirya's orbit and he pointed one more time at Vanirya. A blue line extended from his finger to the planet's surface, but as always, no portal opened up because the planet wasn't actually there anymore. They had gone as far as they could go.

"Alright, so we've again reached our familiar obstacle," said Covington. "Okay, gentlemen, now it's time to get creative," he said to Logan and Dr. Arenot.

Logan responded, "Okay, Sturluson's *Final Journey of the Vanir* says Odin 'called upon the power of time *using* the stars, moons and sun.'"

"What does *that* mean?" asked Velasquez.

"It's a metaphor for using the celestial bodies somehow," replied Logan. "We have to figure out what Sturluson wants us to do…"

"This… all of it… it's like a program," observed Bryan.

"What do you mean by that?" probed General Covington.

"I mean, it's not programmed in JavaScript, Python, C++, C Sharp, Java, or anything like that. It seems to me this holographic universe, these stars, these planets, they're all just part of one big incredibly complex computerized virtual reality simulation, programmed in VaniryanScript or whatever. And like any program, we just have to figure out how to use it."

"That's an interesting way of looking at it… we control the universe in here rather than the other way around," replied Logan. He started working things through, saying, "Okay, so if this is a computer program, programs have instructions, and Sturluson has given us the instructions: use the stars, moons, and sun. And if the stars, moons, and sun are usable, then perhaps they're like buttons or icons on a computer or tablet screen that can be used, and what do we do with buttons and icons on a screen, we—"

"Click on them!" interjected Allysa.

"Right, we can click on them," said Logan.

"And double-click on them!" added Allysa excitedly.

"You can delete them," said Dr. Arenot.

"Or move and drag them," said Bryan.

All of those suggestions were possibilities. Perhaps he could 'use' the planets, stars, and moons by moving, dragging, or clicking them. Logan pointed at Vanirya, waited for the blue line to extend from his fingertip to the planet, and moved his finger, hoping to 'drag' the planet along like moving an icon on a screen. Unfortunately, it didn't work.

"Maybe you need to 'double-click' on it," said Bryan.

Logan tried again, pointing at the planet, waiting for the blue line, collapsing his right hand into a fist so the blue line disappeared, re-opening his fist, re-pointing again. Still nothing.

"Do it faster," said Dr. Arenot. "You know how if you don't double-click on an icon fast enough, it doesn't open?"

"Okay," said Logan. He did the whole process faster to simulate 'double-clicking,' but got the same result. "Hmm," Logan murmured.

"This is literally like an escape room, and I'm terrible at escape rooms!" complained Allysa.

"That's it!" shouted Logan. "Allysa, you're brilliant!"

"I am?"

"I can't believe I didn't think of that," said Logan.

"What'd I say?"

"The clue is obvious. We're making a classic escape room mistake, totally overthinking this! We just have to follow Sturluson's instructions *literally*, just like you said, meaning to call upon the power of time, maybe we need to use the stars, moons, and sun in that exact order, like a keypad combination."

Testing his theory, Logan pointed his right index finger at TYC 129-75-1. A blue line extended to the star and no portal opened up. He then closed his hand to release the blue line, pointed at one of Vanirya's moons, waited for the blue line to extend, collapsed his fist, and pointed back at TYC 129-75-1 again. The blue line extended to the star, but the result was the same. Nothing activated. He tried dragging or moving his finger to see if the star would follow, but it didn't.

"I guess if we really want to follow Sturluson's instructions literally, what about using the star, moons, and the star again at the *same* time?" suggested Dr. Arenot.

"But he's going to have to let go of the sphere to do that, and that'll deactivate everything," commented the general.

Logan thought about what Covington said. If he used the star, moons, and sun in order at the *same* time, he would need his left hand, but if he removed his left hand from the sphere as the general said, the sphere would deactivate. The only exception to that as they had learned over time was after opening a portal when the sphere stayed active for approximately one minute to allow whoever opened the portal a chance to walk through it.

"I guess it's time to find out if there's another exception," said Logan. Logan pointed his right index finger at TYC 129-75-1 and waited for the blue line to extend to the star. Once it did, he removed his left index finger from the sphere and it didn't deactivate!

"That's new," commented General Covington.

"It definitely is," replied Logan. Next, Logan pointed at Vanirya's moons using both his left index and middle fingers. Blue lines extended from his fingers to both moons. With each of his hands engaged now, he wondered, "Okay, now what? How am I supposed to use the 'sun' again to complete Sturluson's three-step process? I only have two hands."

"Can you drag or move the sun with your right hand?" asked Allysa.

Logan tried moving the star slightly, but it didn't budge.

"Okay, what about the moons?" asked Dr. Arenot.

With the blue lines extending from his fingers, Logan tried dragging the moons left. The moons followed the movement of his fingers and Vanirya did, too, as if he was dragging the whole planetary system in one fluid motion! Even more, Vanirya kept rotating and the moons kept orbiting around it.

"Now we're talking!" exclaimed Logan. Using the moons, he moved the planetary system to the left even faster, and Vanirya and its moons rotated and orbited faster, matching Logan's velocity. One thing quickly became apparent to Logan: he couldn't just randomly move the planetary system about, but only along Vanirya's fixed orbital axis around its sun, like the whole planetary system was stuck on an invisible track around the star. By moving the planetary system left, they followed Vanirya's normal clockwise orbit. Next, Logan tried moving the planetary system in reverse, counterclockwise. When he did that, the planet rotated in reverse, and the moons orbited Vanirya in reverse order, like a video being played backward.

"Okay, so you can move the planet and its moons, but how do you 'use' the sun again to complete Sturluson's steps?" questioned General Covington.

"You know what I think?" asked Dr. Arenot rhetorically. "If you were to take Vanirya one full clockwise orbit around its sun, hypothetically, that would equal one year, right? And since we're talking about going back in time, I presume the reverse is also true: one full counterclockwise orbit around TYC 129-75-1 equals minus one year."

"So, you're suggesting the way we 'use' the sun again is to use it as a measurement of time?" replied Logan.

"Right!" said Dr. Arenot. "We just have to decide how far back in time to go to find the double eclipse... 816.37 years, or 6,247.23 years before that, or to a double eclipse even before that, based on P-East's double eclipse calculations."

"Well, if *The Final Journey of the Vanir* poem is approximately 800 years old, and if the Voynich is about that old, I think we should start with the double eclipse that happened in that same time frame 816.37 years ago, don't you?" responded Logan.

Dr. Arenot agreed. "Let's take Vanirya counterclockwise around the star 816.37 times, which will equal, theoretically, minus 816.37 years, if Pegasus East got it right."

"Okay, then you guys are going to have to count the number of full counterclockwise rotations I make around TYC 129-75-1 so I don't lose count," said Logan, asking, "Is everyone ready?" With a few yesses and head nods, he started moving the planetary system in a counterclockwise orbit around the sun. He picked up his pace to about one second per full counterclockwise rotation. While Logan assumed there was probably a faster if not instantaneous way to do it, he just kept methodically rotating the planet counterclockwise around the sun while the others counted.

It took a little more than 10 minutes for Logan to reach counterclockwise rotation number 800. As he got closer to 816.37, he slowed down so he didn't pass up the double eclipse, and somewhere in the middle of rotation number 816, it happened! They all watched as Vanirya's two moons aligned between Vanirya and TYC 129-75-1, resulting in a perfect double eclipse!

"You did it!" yelped Allysa.

"Now the big question is, did it work, or did we just play 'Ring Around the Rosie' for 15 minutes for nothing," said General Covington.

"Only one way to know," replied Logan. He moved his right index finger away from TYC 129-75-1 and re-touched the sphere.

He then pointed his left index finger at Vanirya, and after the blue line extended to the planet, a portal opened up on Vanirya's surface showing a forest of tall trees.

"Son of a gun! It worked!" declared General Covington. Logan's face beamed as General Covington patted him on the back. "Now kid, we just need to go to the coordinates P-West identified for the Hidden City at 64.1434547 by 114.889423."

Logan lowered his left hand, and the forest portal closed, but the double eclipse remained frozen. Again, overlooking the planet, Logan asked, "Where to next?"

The general pulled images out from the folder the runner had handed him earlier. They consisted of cartographic imaging and mapping schematics, pinpointing the exact location on Vanirya's surface they needed to go to, along with the various landmarks they could use to get there, starting with Vanirya's tallest peak. The mapping images guided them to a massive mountain on the surface of Vanirya that was hard to miss, located within an L-shaped mountain range to the left of their location in orbit and slightly above the equator.

After finding that landmark, the images guided them to the northeast edge of the mountain range to a continent-sized forest. From there, the images took them to an enormous river on the northeastern edge of the forest. From the northern mouth of the river, the image directed them to head straight north into a sea of white until they found the glacier field. From there, the visual cues provided by Pegasus East, including arrows, led them from glacier to glacier. It wasn't long before they identified the spot on Vanirya's surface in the middle of a glacier that Pegasus East had identified as their 'insertion point.'

"Okay Mr. West, you're on, again," said General Covington.

Logan pointed his left index finger at Vanirya's surface to the precise spot they had identified. A blue line extended to the planet's surface and a 10-foot-tall and 20-foot-wide rectangular portal materialized in front of them. And that's when they saw it and heard it…

Explosions! Laser blasts! Screaming! The portal opened up to chaos, a beautiful city with buildings and structures sculpted of ice being obliterated right before their very eyes. It was the battle *The Final Journey of the Vanir* forewarned them about, and yet, when they finally saw the battle, it was horrifying...

Dark fighter ships, smooth and triangular in shape, were blasting through the city at lightning speed, firing laser cannons, blowing up buildings, and leaving holes in the pathways. Vaniryans desperately ran for cover but fighter ships kept picking them off on the run. Building-sized chunks of ice came crashing down from above as fighter ships blasted apart what appeared to be an ice ceiling, flattening structures and killing those caught underneath the falling ice. The crashing ice sounded like detonations.

Logan closed his left hand to make the portal disappear. He couldn't bear to watch or listen to the ongoing death and destruction taking place anymore. He didn't know who was attacking whom, or who the heroes and villains were, but it didn't matter. The thought that Emma or Jill might have been underneath one of those blocks of falling ice, sickened him. Once Logan let go and took a breath, he said, "We have to go back before this battle started to save Emma, Jill, Captain Evans, and the others!"

"But we can't go back in time too far," responded Dr. Arenot. "If we do, we risk not finding who we came for or something else might happen to us before we find them, or we might do something that alters the course of events, preventing them from ending up where they are supposed to be. We have to minimize our exposure."

Logan replied, "The only place and time we know for sure where they are is in the Hidden City during the double eclipse, so we should try to go as close to that as we can, or we might never get the chance to save them."

General Covington agreed. "Let's drop-in slightly before the double eclipse begins, and we'll open up a portal every half-hour to make sure you can get out before that battle takes place. If you don't find them in the first hour, return and we can regroup, assess the intel gathered on the mission, and try again."

"Yes, sir," replied Captain Velasquez.

General Covington continued, "Mr. West, can you take us back in time to a point slightly before the double eclipse? I'd tell you to shoot for an hour or two before, but do your best."

Logan nodded and did what he did before, adjusting the moons a little. When done, Logan opened another portal on Vanirya's surface, sending them to the same spot. A rectangular portal materialized in front of them, this time revealing a much more serene view of the Hidden City. They were looking at an icy embankment behind two buildings made of ice. The buildings had clean lines complemented with decorative ice patterns. The insertion point appeared secluded. Everything looked quiet, eerily so.

"Looking now at this place, it's astonishing to think what's going to happen," remarked Dr. Arenot.

"We'll be long gone by the time that all happens," said Captain Velasquez.

"Mr. Marcus, please send in the rover," ordered the general.

Marcus activated the second *p*RAMZA rover, Rammy. Marcus guided Rammy from the background into the portal. As soon as it crossed the threshold, Rammy turned around to face them, relying on its rocker-bogie suspension and retractable cleats in its double-wide wheels to grip the ice and manage the embankment's slope. Rammy's large digital screen relayed a message in big, bold, blue letters: "**GREETINGS**." Rammy next displayed the atmospheric conditions on the planet:

"**TEMPERATURE: MINUS 16.2° F (MINUS 26.78°C).**

ATMOSPHERE CONSISTS OF: OXYGEN (NITROGEN (82.1%), OXYGEN (13.6%), ARGON (1.3%), CARBON DIOXIDE (1.1%), UNKNOWN (1%), UNKNOWN (.9%), METHANE (.002%), UNKNOWN (<.001%), WATER (<.001%), UNKNOWN (<.001%).

GRAVITY IS 25.49 m/s^2.

AWAITING FURTHER INSTRUCTIONS."

"Dr. Adams, is that atmosphere suitable for human life?" asked General Covington.

"Hard to say, General. Those numbers are not ideal. It's awfully cold there, and Rammy doesn't recognize some of the gases in the air. The gravity is heavy, too," Dr. Adams replied.

"Dr. Adams, can our team tolerate the environment or not?" Covington asked again.

"Yes, sir, the environmental and atmospheric assist provided by their suits will sustain them in those conditions for a short period of time, and we know Ms. James survived down there. The suits will do nothing, however, to address any difficulties posed by the gravity. I'd recommend short bursts of time on the surface."

"Doctor, will having them return every hour suffice?" asked the General.

"Yes, I am okay with that, but no longer."

Satisfied, General Covington said, "Alright team, you're a go. Sync your watches the moment the final member of your team arrives on Vanirya. We'll have a portal waiting for you at the 30 and 60 minute marks. I don't want to hold it open for long to avoid attracting eyes or visitors we don't want, not until I get more intel from you about what we're dealing with there."

"Alright team, let's head out," said Velasquez.

Logan let the sphere go, and all 14 of them approached the portal. They had approximately one minute to walk through it.

"Alright, here goes nothing." Velasquez put his helmet on, clicked it into place, saluted the general, and marched through the portal. He came out on the other end, standing on the icy embankment. Velasquez looked around to confirm the coast was clear. Seeing no one, he waved for the others to join him. One by one, they put their helmets on and went through the portal. Bryan took Allysa's hand when their turn came up, and they walked through the portal together.

Finally, it was Dr. Arenot and Logan's turn to go. With a half-smile, General Covington said to them, "Alright gentlemen, go find your better halves... and if you have a chance on your way back, try bringing Rammy home. That rover cost more than a few million ashtrays. Good luck."

Logan and Dr. Arenot put their helmets on and walked through the portal. A few seconds later, the sphere deactivated, the holographic galaxy disappeared, and the lights inside the Pyramid turned back on. The C-SAR Team was on its own.

Chapter 29 – Glass Houses

Upon arriving in the Hidden City, Emma felt as if time had stopped. There was no wind inside the glacier, no sunlight, or outside weather changes. The environment was as frozen as the Hidden City itself, a cold hard city forged out of its circumstances.

Lassar and Tamos guided them through the secret city on paths carved in the glacier, made out of a combination of ice and stone and with fanciful grooves for better footing. The paths snaked between homes and buildings themselves made of ice, under ice bridges leading from one short building to another, and through tunnels in glacial ice. The lunar and solar energy harvested by the Hidden City coursed through the frames of the structures, giving the homes, buildings, bridges, and tunnels a luminescent glow emanating from within the ice itself.

While many of the structures they saw were homes, others appeared to be stores where Remnants could obtain food or supplies. As Tamos explained, everything in the Hidden City was free – no money exchanged hands – but everyone in the city had a different role to play and the shops lining the pathways reflected some of those jobs.

"This place is like a winter wonderland times a million over," remarked Professor Quimbey, marveling at the structures' incandescent glow sparkling off the icy surfaces.

"More like a billion," said Emma.

The view didn't just amaze Emma and Professor Quimbey. Isa was also blown away by the view that she had risked nearly everything to see.

"How did this place get here?" asked Emma.

Tamos explained, "It started with a small group of Remnants who sought refuge from the Hunt somewhere no one would find them, lost within the maze of the Frozen Shards. They found a crevice large enough to hide in and that is where it began. They hunted the Shards for food and built a life, and over time, expanded the crevice, digging deeper and deeper into the ice as their families and needs grew. As their children aged, the Remnants realized isolation could not be their only destiny and what they had built could save others. Many braved a return to land to bring other Remnants back, and as their needs beckoned, they brought in even more with the resources, technology, and skills to help build the city into what it is today – a fortress."

"But how is it possible something like this has remained hidden for so long?" asked Emma.

"The unwavering trust among Remnants, a bond born out of persecution and resilience... that is what guards the secret," Tamos responded.

"And Qelios, is he—"

"Qelios is an original child of the ice, and now, the Sentinel of the Hidden City."

"If this place is so secret, how do you know about it?"

"Yssil is also a child of the ice."

"Really?" replied Emma. "Why did he leave?"

"He chose not to live in the frozen city forever..." replied Tamos, trailing off, holding something back.

"Was there more to it?" probed Emma.

"Yssil and Qelios did not always see the same future for the city."

As they traversed the frozen paths, Remnants walking to and from warily stared at them, wondering who they were, why they were there, what they wanted. It was rare for strangers to visit the Hidden City, especially off-worlders.

Emma commented, "They look at us so suspiciously."

"Did you expect otherwise?" replied Tamos.

"No… maybe… I just thought because we were traveling with Remnants, it wouldn't be so bad."

"They are afraid of you and wonder why you come," said Tamos.

"For help, and to help *them* if we can."

"They do not know that. They do not trust unfamiliar faces, especially off-worlders."

"Have they ever seen off-worlders before?"

"Yes, but it is rare… this is a place *few* dare come."

Listening to their conversation, Captain Evans asked, "And why is that? This city seems safer than everywhere else we've been on this planet so far."

"Because once non-Remnants enter the Hidden City, they cannot leave."

"What does that mean?" demanded Captain Evans.

"Either Qelios helps you… or he does not. It is how it has always been and how the Hidden City's secret remains to be."

"You said nothing about this!" asserted Captain Evans.

"Would you have made a different choice?" responded Tamos.

"Had you offered us one? Maybe!" replied Captain Evans.

Lassar intervened to end the debate. "There is no other choice. The only known portal on our world is here. The Hunt have destroyed all other technology on this planet except for what they have taken for themselves."

"And what happens if Qelios can't help, is he just going to kill us?" questioned Emma.

"It'll be a colder day in hell than it is in here before I let that happen!" declared Captain Evans.

Tamos replied, "If Qelios cannot help you, death on this world is your destiny regardless."

"We'll see about that," replied Emma, far from resigned to that fate. "How much longer until we get there?"

"Not long," replied Lassar. "After we leave the living quarter, we will enter the technology row. Once we pass that, we reach Qelios."

ΔΔΔΔΔΔΔΔΔΔΔΔ

When they arrived at Qelios's compound, they found a 20-foot-tall wall of ice surrounding it. Given the family ties and unwavering bond among Remnants that Tamos spoke of earlier, Emma wondered why this imposing wall was necessary. Still, there it was, a tall wall designed to keep others out.

There was an entrance gate with thick, horizontally laid ice bars reaching from side to side, fortified by a blue energy running through them, and two guards stationed at the gate. Tamos walked right up to them.

Tamos spoke in Vaniryan to the guards clad in dark uniforms, holding weapons that resembled laser guns. Lassar translated the conversation for his off-world friends: "Tamos asks to see Qelios. They have told him Qelios cannot be disturbed."

"Well, tell Tamos to disturb him!" insisted Emma.

"Tamos tries. He explains we come with message from Yssil."

The guards backed away from Tamos to discuss and relay the message through a wrist device to someone on the inside, possibly Qelios. The guards returned with more questions.

"They now ask what the message is and who the off-worlders are," translated Lassar.

"I would think friends of Yssil who are accompanied by Remnants, would be more welcome here," commented Emma.

"I'm starting to feel like this was a huge mistake," said Annika.

"You're just feeling that now?" replied Captain Evans.

"Tamos has told them the message," Lassar announced.

"What did he say?" Emma asked.

"He told them the scroll of the Va has been read and the Missing Remnant's location found on your planet. He asks Qelios for help."

"If that doesn't do it, we should turn around fast," said Captain Evans.

"And go where?" questioned Professor Quimbey.

The guards paused, genuinely surprised by Tamos's response. They withdrew to confer further before finally communicating

Tamos's message to someone on the inside. Whatever they said worked because the gate opened.

The guards motioned them in. The group walked up an ice path leading to a large round door in the oddly shaped structure. Blue, green, and purple-glowing foliage lined the walkway's edges, followed by manicured gardens filled with more of the same glowing plants.

"Incredible," uttered Professor Quimbey as they strolled past the gardens. "Look at the roots of the plants, they grow straight into the ice. It's remarkable."

Emma looked and the professor was right, the plant roots grew down into the ice just like plant roots on Earth grew into the soil. "How do the roots have the strength to push through solid ice like that?" she wondered.

"It must have something to do with the energy in them," deduced Professor Quimbey.

Before they could discuss it further, they reached the front entrance where another group of seven guards waited for them.

"I'm surprised this is the welcome friends of Yssil get," remarked Captain Evans, looking at Tamos and Lassar.

The guards said something to Tamos, who advised, "They ask for our weapons." Having no choice, they all pulled out their weapons and handed them over.

The guards moved aside and the round door swung open. All seven guards ushered them in. After they crossed the threshold, the door slammed shut behind them. The guards escorted them down a hallway decorated with rugs and floating pieces of ice art hovering along the walls every few feet. The floating art pieces consisted of ice fragments elegantly carved into randomly angled geometric and non-geometric shapes.

At the end of the hallway, the guards turned left into a cylinder-shaped tunnel of ice far less elaborate than the entry hallway, and much darker. The tunnel had only a dim glow, just bright enough to see. Every footstep and noise they made while walking through the tunnel, from the dragging of feet to the crunching of ice, echoed. The tunnel emptied into a tall five-sided pentagonal-shaped pyramid constructed of metal and ice. There were large abstract-shaped ice statues in front of each wall and a metallic sphere in the center reminiscent of Area 51. Emma's heart leaped! She felt closer than ever to returning home.

"Jill, do you see that?!" she blurted to Professor Quimbey. The professor nodded.

"What? What do you guys see?" asked Captain Evans.

"This pyramid, the sphere... this place is our way home!" exclaimed Emma. Emma could hardly contain her excitement about seeing Logan again, and of course her mom and dad and all her friends. A journey home that had once seemed hopeless suddenly seemed only minutes away from coming to an end.

Through an open archway in one of the pentagonal walls behind a statue entered three extremely tall Vaniryan guards carrying laser guns. An even taller Vaniryan dressed in a black body length garment trailed behind them...

"Qelios," said Tamos in Vaniryan, noticeably uneasy addressing the Sentinel of the Hidden City.

Qelios, whose face was drawn and darker than most other Vaniryans, perhaps due to his age and the icy conditions he had been living in for 10,000 years, glared with interest at the off-worlders.

"So, Yssil dared not come himself," said Qelios in Vaniryan.

Lassar, sticking up for Yssil, replied back in the alien tongue, "It is not due to avoidance that Yssil has sent us."

"No, it is his abandonment of his people and fear of seeing those he left behind that he avoids."

Although Emma, Captain Evans, Annika, and Professor Quimbey couldn't understand the words being said, they could hear the tension in the Vaniryans' conversation.

"Yssil has no such fear. He has saved lives, accomplishing what he set out to do," replied Tamos. "Seeing the walls you surround yourself in confirms what he feared. Yssil does not distinguish himself from others the way you do."

"Why do you judge what I have built here, and how I choose to protect my people?" questioned Qelios.

"Your people?" replied Tamos. "Yssil owns no one in Jaannos."

"But does he keep them safe? I keep my people safe from the Hunt and they revere me because of it."

"What Yssil has built in the Jaans—"

"Do the Remnants of Jaannos really think the trees protect them from the Hunt? Is that what Yssil tells those who rely on him, to hide behind leaves?" Qelios cackled and the others around him followed suit.

Isa, frightened as she was, couldn't help herself from sticking up for Yssil. She snapped at Qelios in Vaniryan, forcefully so. Whatever she said angered him. He approached her, towering over her small frame. Isa, standing next to Emma, nervously took her hand.

Qelios stopped inches before her face, bent over, and put his hand on her head. "You are brave to say what you say, little girl, not what I would expect to hear from the deserters hiding in the trees with Yssil. Trust me, girl, you have not seen what terror Vanirya holds for you, and Yssil cannot protect you from it." He pushed Isa's head backward and walked away. Isa clutched Emma's hip.

406

Qelios then entered the off-worlders' minds to read their words and use them to speak in sentences they could understand. He whirled his finger in the air. The guards in the room lifted their weapons and pointed them at the visitors. Qelios, now gazing directly at Emma, Professor Quimbey, Annika, and Captain Evans, said to them, "I would end you all right now if my brother had not sent you. Despite his unforgivable sin, I will hear your request. Foolish of Yssil to send you here, for he knows the Hidden City's law. If your tale about the scroll of the Va is false—"

"It is not," stated Tamos. "We need to return these off-worlders to their world, a planet called Earth. They come from a star system of nine planets. Their Earth is the third planet shown in the nine worlds of the scroll. The Va have visited their world and the off-worlders have seen them! The Missing Remnant hides there. Qelios, we need to act fast."

"We?"

"Lassar and I will go with them to help find the Missing Remnant, recover the Leyandermál, bring it back here, and with it, we can defeat Supay together and end this nightmare once and for all!"

It was a stunning declaration by Tamos, one that offered hope to Remnants everywhere, a chance for freedom, yet Qelios said nothing. Whether he was shocked or uncertain what to do next or just thinking things through, he very deliberatively contemplated Tamos's words. Then, he approached the sphere and touched it...

The ice pyramid's five walls disappeared and a universe of stars appeared in their place. Emma got very excited as it seemed they were getting closer and closer to a way home.

"Let us see this Earth where you say the Missing Remnant hides," said Qelios. He spoke instructions in Vaniryan into the sphere.

"What's he saying?" Emma asked Isa.

"He instructs the sphere to eliminate all of the stars not orbited by nine worlds."

It's voice-activated and operated, Emma realized. Humans didn't speak Vaniryan nor could they make the multi-layered sounds required to do so, explaining why the Pegasus program had never figured out that sound could activate or instruct the sphere.

Following Qelios's instructions, the sphere narrowed down the choices, eliminating hundreds of billions of stars in the holographic heavens – the majority of them, in fact. Still, billions remained. Continuing with the process of elimination, Qelios asked the off-worlders, "Which planet is the largest in your star system?"

Annika replied, "The fifth out from our sun."

Qelios instructed the sphere to limit the stars to those in which the fifth planet was the largest, and billions of more stars disappeared. Next, he asked, "How many worlds in your star system have rings?"

Annika, an astronomer in Russia's space program, quickly responded, "Four."

"Really?" asked Captain Evans. "Which other than Saturn?"

"Jupiter, Uranus, and Neptune also have ring systems," replied Annika.

"And which planets from your sun are those?"

Annika responded, "The fifth, sixth, seventh, and eighth planets."

Using the multiple additional pieces of information, Qelios narrowed down the stars even further. "How many moons does your Earth have?" asked Qelios. After hearing the answer – one – he instructed the sphere to again narrow the choices, and very few stars remained in the holographic galaxy.

"How many full rotations of your world does it take to orbit your sun?" asked Qelios.

"How many rotations of our world?" responded Emma, not quite sure what he was asking.

"He asks how many days it takes for Earth to orbit our sun, with each day on Earth being a full 'rotation' of our world," replied Annika.

"365 days," said Emma.

"365.256 to be exact," corrected Annika, the Roscosmos State Corporation astronomy expert.

With the information provided, Qelios instructed the sphere one final time, and only one star remained. Qelios pointed his finger at the star, and after the blue line extended, they warped into Earth's solar system of nine planets. Qelios quickly pointed to the third planet out from the sun and they surged into Earth's orbit. Their breathtaking blue planet with its white swirls, blue oceans, and land masses colored brown, green, and white spun in rotation before their very eyes.

"I can't believe we made it!" said Professor Quimbey who, until that moment, doubted they'd ever return home despite her never sharing those feelings.

"Is this your Earth?" asked Qelios.

Emma responded, "Yes, we're home..."

Qelios remarked, "That which was hidden in space and time, now so nearly found. Such a small world on which to hide such a big thing," he commented, referring to the Leyandermál. Without asking, Qelios randomly pointed at Earth's surface just to see what it looked like. Specifically, at a brown and white land mass in the North Atlantic Ocean, just below the Arctic Circle: *Iceland.*

A portal opened up to Iceland's beautiful wintery countryside, a mix of green foliage, gravel, ice, and snow. There were no structures or humans visible, only a stunning view of one of Earth's most spectacular landscapes before humanity intruded upon its serenity. Isa pulled on Emma's hand, wanting to go over for a closer look at Emma's homeworld. Emma let her go.

Hurrying to the portal's threshold, Isa marveled at Iceland's scenery and looked on in wonder as a bird – with a white stomach, black back and head, and orange beak and feet – flew by. Isa had seen everything she ever dreamed of on her adventure away from the trees and knowing her adventure was almost over, telepathically said to Emma, "Thank you." Emma smiled. It took everything she had not to walk over and join Isa one last time, but there was more work to do.

"Qelios, this is not our time," she said. "If we are to help you find the Leyandermál, we need to return to our own time first. What you see is many years in the past for us. Our future is where we have the technology to help you find what you're looking for. Can your sphere return us to our future?"

"Yes, using your moon and sun and rotating your world around its star, or by speaking the words of the Va. How many rotations around your sun to find your future?"

"I don't know… we don't know how far back in time we went," replied Emma.

"Plesetsk!" shouted Annika.

"What is it you say?" asked Qelios.

"The Plesetsk state testing cosmodrome where Roscosmos creates, develops, constructs, and launches rockets, spacecraft, and space complexes. It's in the town of Mirny in Russia. There is a large digital monitor on top of the largest launching complex that displays the date and time. If we open a portal in Mirny countryside, gradually moving forward in time until Plesetsk is built, we can then view the monitor and know when we reach our date."

410

"Yes," said Captain Evans, adding, "All we need to do is observe that location until we reach our time, February 26, 2020."

Qelios let go of the sphere and lowered his hand. The portal to Iceland remained open, as it would for a little while longer. He took a step toward it and while staring into the portal, shouted in Vaniryan, "Supay shall have you all now!"

Isa screamed and the guards started firing their weapons. The moment Isa screamed and the guards moved, Captain Evans lunged for Emma and Professor Quimbey to take them down to the ground. Laser fire shot by overhead, although not at Emma. In a gut-shattering moment, one of the blasts struck Lassar mid-chest, disintegrating two-thirds of his torso and killing him, ending his life in an instant. It was an awful sight, and what little Emma saw of it as she hit the ground, sickened her.

Captain Evans launched into combat mode, leaping to her feet and charging one of the guards. The guard fired back at her, but she ducked and avoided the blast. She grabbed and wrestled the guard to the ground using her right leg to sweep his ankles. As he fell, Evans dropped onto his neck with her elbow, injuring him just enough to shake his laser gun loose. She grabbed it and shot him in the stomach, killing him. She next fired at the guards chasing Emma and Jill, causing those guards to scramble for cover.

Tamos, meanwhile, having no time to mourn, released a blue charge of his internal Remnant energy from his hands at two other guards. The charge didn't kill either of them but knocked both off their feet. Tamos pounced on one and fought to gain his weapon, while the other looked for an opening to shoot Tamos. Tamos rolled the guard on top of him just as the other guard tried shooting him. The shot killed the guard right on top of Tamos, who immediately took hold of the guard's weapon and fired it at the other guard, blowing his midsection apart. Tamos ran for cover behind a statue.

While all of that was going on, Annika had taken off after Isa to rescue her from blasts being fired her way. Her heroism was rewarded with good fortune, as the laser blasts missed her while she sprang for Isa. Her momentum knocked them both into the portal just as lasers passed through where Isa had been standing.

From the other side of the portal in Iceland, Isa and Annika were safe. The laser blasts couldn't penetrate the portal. Seeing that, one of the guards took off after them, but before he got there, the portal vanished. Isa and Annika were gone, lost in Iceland. Emma screamed "No!" as she saw the portal close up on Isa and Annika. As soon as the portal disappeared, the sphere deactivated and the ice pyramid re-appeared.

Captain Evans and Tamos continued to fight, running, rolling, leaping, ducking, diving, and shooting, killing five more guards but it wasn't enough. In another tragic instant, a red laser blast from a large gun held by Qelios, which started small but expanded into an unescapable cone of red energy 20 feet wide, ripped through Tamos's body, shredding him into nothingness.

Captain Evans started to charge Qelios, but she stopped mid-stride upon seeing Qelios's powerful weapon pointed at her forehead and his two personal guards holding Emma and Professor Quimbey hostage with guns jammed into their heads. Qelios stepped toward Captain Evans with his weapon fixed on her, smirking. With the tip of his gun, Qelios motioned for her to toss her weapon aside. Although she played out multiple escape scenarios in her mind, at Qelios's insistence, she dropped her gun.

"You are cunning, but not enough to save them," taunted Qelios, unconcerned by the loss of life that had just taken place in his pyramid. After all, his guards were commodities to him.

Defiantly, Captain Evans retorted, "Emma and Jill are no one's prisoners. I think you should worry more about who is going to save you."

"We shall see."

The sphere flashed, a portal appeared, and through it walked Supay with two of his Dokalfar wearing black and gold clothing and carrying weapons. The portal disappeared behind them. Supay, also

412

wearing black clothing, surveyed the humans, pleased at their capture.

"Supay," said Qelios, bowing. "I offer the gift you asked for," he said in Vaniryan, pointing at Emma.

Supay walked up to Emma and grabbed her face. He forcefully turned it from side to side to look at her, and then pushed his way into her mind, searching her thoughts. She tried to resist but Supay easily overcame any mental barriers she put up. The experience was painful for Emma, like an acute migraine moving around in her mind as Supay searched through it.

When done, Supay let go of her face, turned to Qelios, and said in Vaniryan, "This is the one... she knows the Va's secret. You offer me nothing that was not already coming your way, walking freely on your world while you did nothing about it. Had I not prepared you for their arrival, based on the stank of death in here, they would have overwhelmed your complacency completely."

"I could not have known that they walked these lands, Supay. The off-worlders had help in Jaannos."

"Then you couldn't even control the trees. I granted you what you asked for: power, wealth, and technology. I left your pitiful glacier city alone, too, always waiting for you to find what I seek, listening to your empty promises. I let you guide my Hunt in search of the clues you said only a Remnant could understand, always assuring me the answer would come to you. Yet, after 10,000 years, even with my help, your sorry brother hiding in the leaves outsmarted you. You have wasted my time with excuses."

"But Supay—"

To his Dokalfar, Supay said, "This city has no more use to me. Destroy it, every last memory of it. It reminds me of the vile existence that has lived here too long. I should have killed the Ice Remnants long ago. Start the invasion now!"

Supay's Dokalfar nodded, bowed, and spoke into a hand-held device. Almost instantly, they heard Supay's army of fighter ships – which had been lying in wait outside the glacier – blasting away at the Hidden City's outer glacier walls.

"No!" cried Qelios.

Unmoved, Supay cocked his head in pity, and then coldly said to his Dokalfar, "I have no more use for this Sentinel either." Supay's Dokalfar took aim at Qelios and fired, killing him.

In that moment of distraction, Captain Evans grabbed her weapon from the floor and ran out of sight behind a statue before the Dokalfar realized what was happening. Then, she fired two laser blasts at the heads of the guards holding Emma and Professor Quimbey. She hit both on the mark, killing them and freeing her friends.

The Dokalfar fired back at the statue where Captain Evans was hiding, breaking it apart. Captain Evans narrowly escaped and threw herself behind another statue.

Emma and Professor Quimbey started running away, too but Supay trapped Emma in a prismatic energy net that emerged from his hand, similar to the energy net Isa had been using to capture the birds the first day they saw her at the waterfall. Only, Supay's net was bigger and stronger, and he easily yanked Emma back in his direction. Fortunately, Professor Quimbey got away, joining Captain Evans behind the statue.

"Forget the humans!" shouted Supay to his Dokalfar. "They are of no consequence and will die underneath the crumbling ice just like every other Remnant in this city. We have the one I want. Let's go!"

Supay turned and walked back toward the sphere, dragging Emma along. Captain Evans took several shots at him, but he was cloaked in an energy barrier that absorbed her laser blasts. Captain Evans next fired at the Dokalfar but they, too, appeared insulated in a protective energy forcefield.

"Crap, they're all protected by some kind of shield!" uttered Captain Evans.

"Shoot the sphere!" exclaimed Professor Quimbey.

"But it's our only way back!" shouted Evans.

"We have to protect Emma. We'll find another way."

Captain Evans tried shooting the sphere. Unfortunately, the Dokalfar had anticipated that and were body blocking Captain Evans's line-of-sight to the sphere so she couldn't shoot it, either.

There was nothing more they could do. Captain Evans and Professor Quimbey were completely helpless. If they were to save Emma and get out of the city alive, they needed a miracle and they needed it right then.

Then, seemingly out of nowhere, a grenade flew over the heads of the Dokalfar, blowing the sphere off its base and knocking Supay and his Dokalfar to the ground. Perhaps there was hope after all...

Chapter 30 – Extraction Point

25 minutes earlier…

After Logan stepped through the portal, Captain Velasquez announced, "Alright, that's everyone! Timers starting now! Remember, there will be a portal at the 30-minute and 1-hour marks. Let's get the infrared and audio surveillance devices ready."

Logan looked around. They were in the middle of the frozen city looking up at remarkable ice structures. Nobody was around as far as he could tell. Glancing up, Logan saw a ceiling of ice and the whole city glowed a soft white luminescent color. Extraordinary, he thought. The Hidden City appeared, indeed, hidden inside a giant glacier in the ice field.

Using the teamwide communication system in their helmets which, like most high-grade walkie talkies, had a range of several miles, Captain Velasquez said, "Extraction Team, as we discussed, hide Rammy and secure the perimeter. We need to keep the area clear at all times. Try and stay out of sight. If you need to interact with any indigenous life, call in for instructions and remember your mission objectives: guard the extraction point, surveil the area for intel and bogies, and keep us informed of what's going on around the extraction point. Do *not* engage hostilely unless absolutely necessary, is that clear?"

"Yes, sir!" replied SEALS Chalmers and Allen.

Bryan and Allysa more causally said, "Yes, sir," although because they weren't military, their response lacked the same zeal. Since Bryan and Allysa weren't combat trained, General Covington and Captain Velasquez had decided they could best help the team by surveilling the perimeter and providing intel to help ensure a safe return for the field teams. It was a decision Logan supported and his friends agreed with, as they wanted to help but didn't want to get in the way. The assignment allowed them to assist in a manner that maximized their non-combat skillsets.

"Alright, teams, let's head out," ordered Captain Velasquez. Team Strong, led by Commander Strong, consisted of five SEALS and they departed uphill to the left. Team Velasquez, consisting of Captain Velasquez, Logan, Dr. Arenot, and two other SEALS, Commanders Davis and McGee, took off in the other direction. Commander Davis carried their audio and infrared surveillance devices.

Logan's team slipped through the Hidden City's paths and alleys, trying to stay out of sight using buildings, structures, and objects. They saw Vaniryans walking around the city but it wasn't crowded. While Logan wanted to marvel at the sights, there was no time. They had a job to do, and their helmets were recording everything anyway, so he could watch it once they got home, *if* they got home. After five minutes, Captain Velasquez checked in with Team Strong.

"Strong, this is Velasquez… copy."

"Copy Captain, we're working through the buildings, nothing yet. No human heat signatures… no audio. Strong out." The infrared and audio surveillance devices were critical to finding Emma and the others. The infrared sensors, with a range of up to 750 feet, could search for heat signatures resembling human body temperatures, while the audio surveillance device, with a range of 1,200 feet, could hear through most walls, ice included.

After a few more minutes, Commander Strong checked back in to report something unusual. "Captain, audio surveillance is picking up a ton of vibration above the ice ceiling."

Commander Davis immediately pointed his audio device up toward the ceiling of the glacier and the device's digital screen exploded from the vibrations. "Captain, look at this."

Captain Velasquez looked at the device's orange and red bars going crazy and responded, "Could be the air assault ships we witnessed through the portal amassing for their attack. We may not have cleared the battle by as much time as we thought. Let's move fast, people. Velasquez out."

Through a gap between buildings, Logan saw a low hill with a large structure on it that looked more elaborate than the rest. It also had a wall around it. "Captain, there's a large structure on a hill straight ahead, enclosed in a wall. It stands out to me... could be significant."

"Good eyes, West. Let's head that way," said Velasquez.

While the teams searched the city, Bryan and Allysa surveilled their assigned side of the extraction point's perimeter area, relaying intel back to the others. As they climbed a short hill behind a building, struggling on the icy footing, Bryan asked Allysa, "Still glad we volunteered for this?"

"Honestly, yes. I've never felt more a part of something."

"Me, too. It's the superhero code: you never abandon your friends."

"You know, Bryan, if we were to hang out when we get back, I'm pretty sure it's not going to live up to all this, no pressure."

"Hang out...? You mean, like a date?"

Allysa, embarrassed, replied, "I'm sorry, I didn't mean to assume anything. I just thought maybe you wanted to."

"I do, definitely! I just didn't realize you felt the same way."

"Really?" asked Allysa, genuinely surprised, thinking she had made her mutual interest obvious.

They came to the hill's crest and looked down over an open ice field surrounded by glowing bushes with small children – Vaniryan children – running around playing some kind of game.

"Oh, my god, look at those kids," said Bryan.

"It's so sad," whispered Allysa, distraught thinking of what was about to happen to them. Tears swelled in her eyes.

"I know," responded Bryan. "C'mon, we have to go. Are you okay?"

Allysa sniffled. "Hardly, but yeah, thanks. You're right, let's go."

They proceeded back down the hill and circled around to a different location. That's when Allysa saw them: Dokalfar walking up the streets and Vaniryans heading in the opposite direction, afraid of the Dokalfar.

"Bryan, do you see that? We have to let everyone know!" declared Allysa. She promptly activated her all teams communication channel: "Hi... this is Allysa. I'm seeing the same black and gold dressed soldier-types we saw at Electra."

"That means Supay is here!" exclaimed Logan. "Captain, the battle is coming."

Velasquez acknowledged and announced, "All teams, get ready, hostiles are in the house. Anders, Callister, return to the extraction point. We all need to get back at the 30-minute mark. I'm not sure there's going to be much left of this glacier by the time one hour rolls around. Velasquez out."

They kept heading uphill toward the walled structure. When almost there, Commander Davis announced, "Captain, I've got something on audio coming from the left side of the structure..."

"Turn on your audio feed for us to hear," instructed Captain Velasquez.

Commander Davis turned on the audio in his helmet while keeping his communications channel open, and they all heard Qelios say, "You are cunning, but not enough to save them."

Next, they heard Captain Evans reply, "Emma and Jill are no one's prisoners. I think you should worry more about who is going to save you."

"That's them!" shouted Logan.

"They're in trouble! Let's go!" shouted Captain Velasquez, sprinting uphill. Into the com system, he ordered, "Strong, get your team back to the portal. Targets located."

Commander Strong responded, "Copy that. My team's standing by, ready to assist. State your location..."

"No, you won't make it here in time. Return to the portal, that's an order Commander! Velasquez out."

They raced toward Qelios's compound, no longer concerned with anonymity. The two guards protecting Qelios's gate shouted at them to stop, but when they didn't, the guards began shooting. The combat-trained SEALS fired their semi-automatic weapons, taking out both guards. The bullets didn't kill the guards, but rather they caused some kind of chain reaction in their internal energy that knocked them out.

As the team got close to the gate, Supay's air forces outside the glacier began firing at the ice ceiling. The blasts echoed and reverberated throughout the glacier. The glacier had a protective shield around it, but Logan and the others knew it would give way soon. Each time Supay's fighter ships blasted the glacier, the glacier ice turned a bright shade of green in the area where the laser blasts struck it.

Velasquez led the team through the gate, collecting the guards' laser guns off the ground. They expected to encounter additional resistance on the interior of the structure but were surprised to find none. They hurried to the structure's entrance door. It was locked so Velasquez and Davis took their new laser guns and blew the door apart, right about the same time Supay's fighter ships broke through the outer glacier.

Inside the cold compound, they heard screaming and laser fire. They raced down the entrance hallway, following the noise. They found the cylinder-shaped tunnel of ice where the noise was coming from and ran down it. As they got to the end, they heard more yelling.

They heard a female shout, "Crap, they're all protected by some kind of shield!"

That's when they burst into the pentagonal pyramid. They saw Supay dragging Emma toward the sphere, enveloped in an energy field.

"Emma!" exclaimed Logan. "Captain, they can't reach that sphere!"

Captain Velasquez, watching as Captain Evans fired helplessly at Supay and his Dokalfar in an attempt to stop them, hazarded a hunch that Emma too was protected in the protective shielding that was absorbing Captain Evans's shots. And so, he grabbed a grenade off his belt and tossed it high in the air over the Dokalfar. It landed just beyond the sphere.

The second Captain Evans saw it flying through the air and hit the ground, she heard that familiar clink and bounce and pulled Quimbey down behind the ice statue. The grenade exploded, blowing the sphere off its base and generating enough force to knock Supay and his Dokalfar backward onto their backs. Protected within their energy fields, the shrapnel from the grenade didn't hurt any of them.

Velasquez's team ran into the pyramid firing, and Emma was free, for the moment. The energy net Supay had been using to drag her toward the sphere was gone and she leaped to her feet to run. Supay stood up as well and grabbed her arm. He released a charge of energy from his hand up her arm to incapacitate her, but to his surprise, it didn't. Just then, Logan bowled into him to jar her loose, lowering his shoulder like a football player making a hard-hitting tackle.

Logan and Supay fell to the ground, while Emma fell backward after Supay lost his grip of her arm. Logan fell face-first into the ground, cracking his helmet glass and cutting his face, but fortunately, not his eyes.

Emma saw Logan as she rolled away and cried, "Logan!" He looked back at her and their eyes locked. In just an instant, a flood of emotions—especially astonishment and love—moved through them. Unfortunately, the moment was short-lived. Supay's right arm charged with energy and he swung at Logan, striking the ground as Logan rolled away to avoid it. From the ground, Emma kicked Supay in the legs and Commander McGee crashed into him next.

McGee briefly fought with Supay, giving Logan and Emma an opening to get back up to their feet and run. Eventually, Supay released a blast of energy into McGee's body that killed him instantly. Velasquez shouted "McGee!" He began firing wildly at Supay out of anger.

Meanwhile, Commander Davis and Captain Evans kept firing at the Dokalfar, but the aliens' shielding continued to protect them. Dr. Arenot saw a different, larger weapon lying on the ground near a dead body. He raced out to grab it, and as soon as Professor Quimbey saw him do so, she screamed, "Jonas, look out!"

The Dokalfar shot at him, fortuitously missing. Davis and Evans gave him as much cover as they could, now taking to firing repeatedly at the Dokalfar's feet to blow up the ice where they stood. Since the ice wasn't protected by the Dokalfar's shielding, the blasts into the ice caused the Dokalfar to stumble and lose their footing. Dr. Arenot made it to the weapon and pulled the trigger. A red laser blast exploded from the tip of the weapon that widened into a 20-foot-wide red cone of laser fury that struck both of the Dokalfars and drove them back into the opposite wall. Dr. Arenot kept firing unrelentingly until his final shot not only broke through the Dokalfar's energy shield but also blew a hole in the wall itself, causing ice and metal to crash down on the Dokalfar.

Recognizing the unmatched strength of Dr. Arenot's weapon, Velasquez shouted, "Arenot, shoot up!" while pointing at the pyramid's ceiling above Supay. Dr. Arenot fired the powerful weapon at the top of the pyramid and after several quick blasts, the ceiling and two far walls of the pyramid came crashing down on Supay.

There was no way of knowing if Supay or his Dokalfar were dead, but the blasts and resulting debris had clearly incapacitated them, giving everyone a chance to escape. Logan and Emma trailed right behind Evans, Professor Quimbey, Dr. Arenot, Davis, and Velasquez as they hightailed it out the exit, down the tunnel, out to the outer hallway and out the front door.

Outside, the battle Logan, Dr. Arenot, and the SEALS knew was coming had arrived. Dark fighter ships, smooth and triangular in shape, were shooting away at the Hidden City's buildings with their laser cannons. Structures were falling while Remnants everywhere ran for cover, hoping to avoid the fighter ships picking them off with laser strikes. Chunks of ice crashed down from the glacial ceiling, flattening houses and buildings.

As chaos reigned and explosions echoed, Velasquez led them all downhill. They had to sidestep debris, evade falling ice, and dive out of the way of incoming laser fire. Whereas their initial trek through the city was slow and methodical, their race back to the portal was the opposite: it was a full-fledged, unabashed sprint. They had to change directions as laser fire and ice chunks destroyed or blocked routes, but they kept running, just like all the other Remnants looking to escape but with nowhere to go.

A fighter ship from above took a shot at them and blew a hole in the ice just to the left of Velasquez and Davis, with the explosion knocking them both over. They were hurt. The group rushed to their aid.

"Everyone get to the portal now! That's an order!" screamed Captain Velasquez, grabbing his broken right leg in pain.

Captain Evans refused. After all, she was the highest-ranking SEAL. "You ain't my superior, Velasquez, and we're not leaving you behind."

"Mine either," shouted Logan.

Captain Evans, strong for her size but weakened by the atmosphere, helped hoist Velasquez up onto Logan's shoulders so Logan could carry him. Emma and Professor Quimbey helped lift Davis, who appeared to have a shattered ankle, onto Dr. Arenot's shoulders. They resumed their escape, though at a slower pace.

Another one of the dark, triangular-shaped fighter ships flew their way. Because Dr. Arenot was carrying Commander Davis, Captain Evans grabbed Qelios's weapon from him and fired it at the ship. The ship fired back, hitting the building to the side of their position, but Evans's 20-foot-wide laser blast didn't miss, clipping the back of the fighter ship and causing it to change direction, although the shipped remained unharmed due to its protective shielding.

As they got closer to the extraction point, the overhead blasts of the glacier ceiling and incoming fire from fighter ships eerily stopped. The fighter ships had taken to circling around searching for something.

"They're looking for us. They've stopped shooting because they want Emma," surmised Captain Evans.

"Why?" Logan asked.

"They think she knows—" The captain stopped mid-sentence as a ship flew very close to their location.

They ducked into a nearby building, and once the ship passed, Logan said, "Hurry, this way." He and Dr. Arenot guided the group back through the buildings to the extraction point.

When they got there, there was no portal, not that they expected it. They were well beyond the 30-minute mark and presumably, hopefully, the other teams had already safely returned home. They stood on the embankment waiting desperately for another portal to reappear, hoping that those who made it back to Earth advised Covington to re-open one as soon as he could without waiting until the one-hour mark. They didn't have that much time remaining, as the fighter ships had located them and were gathering above their heads, waiting for further instructions with their laser cannons locked and ready to fire on the group. Dokalfar on foot were also starting to close in and surround them.

"Some rescue plan, huh," said Captain Velasquez, maintaining his sense of humor even as he fought unconsciousness.

"You did alright, Velasquez, you did alright…," Captain Evans assured him. Velasquez weakly smiled.

"Get close together!" screamed Emma.

"Why?" asked Dr. Arenot.

"Because if they want me, they won't shoot if I'm in the middle."

They all gathered around Emma. Captain Evans looked up and saw a ship approaching that was larger than the others. It stopped in the middle of the mass of triangular-shaped fighter ships, right above their location. It carried Supay.

"If anyone has an action hero plan, now's the time," uttered Captain Evans.

"It's like you said, Evans, we're no one's prisoners," replied Emma. She pulled a grenade off Commander Davis's weapons belt.

"You sure about this, James?" asked Captain Evans.

"I'm not going to let them kill all of you and torture me until they kill me." She lifted the grenade above her head so the enemy could see it.

Captain Evans said, "James, I told you the day I met you and I meant it: you're kick-ass, don't you ever forget it! Okay, pull out the pin but make sure to keep your finger on the safety lever until you're ready to detonate it."

Emma looked at Logan and, although more frightened than she had been in her entire life, bravely said, "I love you." He mouthed the same words back. She pulled out the pin, being sure to keep her finger on the safety lever until it was absolutely necessary.

Supay understood exactly what Emma was doing and said to his Dokalfar Commander, "They are trapped. She won't do it. The humans have too much compassion for life. Take me down to the ice."

Supay's ship lowered to the ground. Captain Evans said, "James, get ready, but don't let go of that lever until you have to!"

Supay's ship touched down, a ramp lowered and out walked Supay with six Dokalfar. Supay approached, staying about 30 or 40 feet away. He said to Emma, "What are you going to do? Do you wish all your friends to die for you? If you come, I will spare them."

Looking downhill at all the dead bodies, Emma replied, "Like you did for all the other Remnants of the Hidden City? I'd rather spare them your view of mercy."

"My view is the only one you, or anyone else on this miserable planet, have left."

"James," said Captain Evans, "It's almost time to let go…"

Emma was getting ready to do the unthinkable when a portal to Earth opened up just a few feet in front of them!

"Now!" screamed Logan.

Emma threw her grenade toward Supay and they bolted for the portal. The grenade exploded in front of Supay, prompting his Dokalfar to start firing at the humans.

"Stop!" ordered Supay, not wanting them to harm Emma. They ceased fire but the humans, like the portal, were already gone.

Supay had lost the battle but not the war. He knew there was another way to find Emma: *on Earth*. Though frustrated she had slipped through his fingers, he was calm as he spoke to his Dokalfar Commander, "The girl is the Missing Remnant. What we are looking for is on Earth."

"Should we continue with the destruction of the Hidden City and Jaannos?" asked the commander.

"Destroy the whole star system, commander."

"Sir?"

"Destroy the star and let's get all the ships back home to go through the time conduit. We have no more use for this planet or its inhabitants, as they will only rally to help her if she returns with the Leyandermál. Prepare the star fusion cannon."

"Yes, sir."

Supay's ship flew off into Vanirya's orbit, followed by the rest of his ships. A few minutes later, after his fleet had flown a safe distance away from TYC 129-75-1, Supay stood on the bridge of his ship coldly gazing out at the star that kept Vanirya warm.

"Fire," he said dispassionately, turning and walking away.

Supay's vessel fired its star fusion cannon at TYC 129-75-1. The star exploded in a powerful blast that obliterated Vanirya and its orbiting moons in seconds, a catastrophic celestial event that wouldn't be seen on Earth for another 800 years...

Chapter 31 – Reflections

"So, you're saying he's some kind of shape-shifter?" asked Dr. Christiansen, the white-bearded, white-coat scientist sitting across the table from Logan. Another female military scientist sat beside Dr. Christiansen, assisting and taking notes. Multiple cameras filmed Logan from different angles, including one directly behind the scientists.

"Yeah, it was like seeing my own reflection in the mirror," responded Logan, who was also hooked up to several different monitors. "Somehow, after touching me, Supay recalibrated his energy to look like me. It was bizarre."

"What do you mean by 'recalibrated his energy'?" questioned Dr. Christiansen.

"I mean, all matter in the galaxy, living or dead, you, me, this table, all of it… everything, everyone's made up of protons, neutrons, and electrons, right? At a subatomic level, we're all made up of the same thing: energy, and somehow, he moved his around to replicate me. Maybe he read my energy signature or something."

"So, you think these Vaniryans can change shape by manipulating their subatomic energy?"

"Yeah, maybe some of them at least, I'm not sure. Some people can wiggle their ears, maybe Vaniryans can wiggle their protons, I don't really know how it works."

"And you showed Supay where Earth is?"

"Unfortunately. At the time, I thought he could help us. I didn't know he'd turn out to be Darth Vader—"

The tape stopped. The large monitor on the wall that everyone else in the Situation Room was watching, froze.

"The details he shares in that video are pretty frightening," commented President Barrett.

General Covington responded, "Yes, Mr. President."

"And the polygraph he was hooked up to confirmed he was telling the truth, as well?"

"Yes, sir. I've spoken to them all since they returned home and watched the interviews, and all essentially say the same thing. And as expected, they all passed their polygraphs, too."

"And Supay is the one who, according to Inca mythology, controls a race of demons from the underworld, who Nordic and Inca mythology refer to as the God of Death, and who Vaniryan lore says wants to unmake the universe?" asked the president.

"Yes, sir. It appears Nordic, Incan, and Vaniryan mythology overlap,"   replied   Covington.

"Are we going to be ready for the God of Death's arrival?" the president asked the room.

NSA Director Orson chimed in, "The video feed captured by the SEAL team's helmets gave us a lot of intel about Supay and his army, Mr. President. We'll be ready, sir."

"You really think so, Sue?" questioned the president.

Director Orson responded, "Oh, yes, I do—"

The president retorted, "Yeah, well, I'm not so sure. I saw nothing on that video footage that you all played for me earlier that gives me your confidence. Unless you were watching a different

430

game tape than me, what I saw was an enemy capable of cloaking itself in an energy shield our artillery can't penetrate, ships with forcefields and better maneuverability than our best assets, and an enemy that can detonate our sun from outer space."

"Sir, respectfully, we don't know if Supay destroyed TYC 129-75-1," said Orson.

"General, can you play the last part from Ms. James's interview again?"

"Yes, Mr. President." General Covington made some quick inputs, switched over to the video of Emma sitting in the same chair Logan had been sitting in, and hit play.

Now Emma was being interviewed, and she said into the camera, "He told me if I went with him, he'd spare them."

"But you didn't believe him?" asked Dr. Christiansen.

"No. If you'd seen all the dead bodies lying on the streets, you wouldn't have either."

"And what did he say after that?"

Emma looked into the camera despondently and said, "That his view of mercy was the only option I, or anyone else on the planet, had left."

"Pause," requested the president. "General, based on the video capturing the number of reverse rotations Mr. West took Vanirya around its sun to go back in time, how far into the past did you go?"

"I'll let Dr. Ehringer answer that."

Dr. Ehringer sat at the far opposite end of the SIT-Room table, furthest away from the president. He had flown in from Nevada for the meeting. He responded, "Based on the video and our study of it, best estimate... 816.35 years, Mr. President."

"And Edgar, based on NASA's most recent calculations, how long ago did TYC 129-75-1 go supernova?"

Dr. Bowling replied, "Our most recent modeling suggests 816.41 years ago."

"Any more questions?" asked the president. No one said a word. The president looked at NSA Director Orson and continued, "Puffery will get us nowhere, Sue. Don't anyone in this room tell me again we are prepared for Supay's arrival until we actually are, is that clear?"

"Yes, Mr. President," said the SIT-Room in unison.

"Starting right now, we need to get ready, and it's going to take a hell of a lot more than watching video footage to prepare for this. I want a Readiness Preparation Proposal by the end of the week. We need faster ships. We need to be able to defend ourselves. We need better weapons. Hopefully, those weapons the team brought back with them from Vanirya will help us catch up fast to their technology. And we need help. When is the Prime Minister getting here?"

Mr. Garrison responded, "Prime Minister Menputyn's arriving this afternoon, sir."

Director Orson was incensed. "You're bringing in Menputyn after he admitted to stealing top-secret Pegasus intelligence and conducting years of surveillance and a hostile operation against U.S. citizens? Why wasn't I consulted, sir?"

"Because we knew you wouldn't approve, Sue," replied President Barrett. "This is a global problem now. None of that matters anymore. Let's remember, he lost citizens on Vanirya, too, and from all accounts, his country's ahead of us on understanding certain aspects of the z-particle technology. As Mr. West said, it's time to bring him into the fold. We need to understand everything we can before Supay gets here if he isn't here already."

432

"I still don't understand what Supay's interest is in Ms. James," commented the Commander of the Air Force Space Command, General Staley.

"Supay thinks Ms. James knows where to find the secret knowledge he's looking for, and perhaps she does, whether she knows it or not," replied the president. "Warren, flip to the part where Dr. Christensen asks Ms. James about that."

General Covington adjusted the time index, and the video switched to a different portion of Emma's interview. General Covington hit play and the video ran again.

"And you really don't know what he wants from you?" asked Dr. Christiansen.

Emma shook her head, "He thinks I know something I don't, just because I met the Vaniryans."

"Is it possible the Vaniryans told you and you just don't remember?"

Emma hesitated before responding, "Are you asking me if it's possible the Vaniryans told me where the Missing Remnant is or the Leyandermál? I have no idea. All I know is I don't remember them telling me anything like that when I visited them."

The president gestured with a nod to Covington to stop the video again. Covington obliged.

"Why'd she hesitate there?" the president asked Covington.

Staring at the frozen image of Emma's eyes, Covington replied, "The lie detector picked up nothing, probably because she was being truthful, but if I had to guess, I'd say she isn't sure about what she knows and what she doesn't know. She probably isn't sure about much of anything anymore."

"That's probably true," said the president. Looking around to address the room, he added, "We are at war with an enemy capable of ending the human race, and the moment he finds what he's looking for, I don't doubt for a second that's what he'll do."

"But you're still letting her fly to Iceland?" asked NSA Director Orson.

"We can't lock her up, Sue. There's no point. We don't know when Supay is coming. It could be 10 or 20 years from now – or 50 years from now for all we know – and what would you have us do? Chain her down in a dungeon that whole time? And let's not forget, Supay can travel back into the past, too. He may already be here, or he may already have been here, so it's entirely possible nothing we do today may have an impact. The best thing we can do right now is to protect Ms. James and provide her with any assistance we can to help her figure out who she is, what she knows, and what we can do to understand and prepare for Supay. She's the key to this whole thing. We need her help, especially now."

General Covington piped in, "And, let's not forget that in addition to West, Quimbey, and Arenot, Captain Evans and Captain Velasquez are going with her, too."

"Can't we at least send experts into the field first?" Orson asked the president.

"Experts?" replied the president with a chuckle. "You know, a few years ago, my grandchildren came to stay with me at the White House. I think it was over the holidays, but anyway, as they always do, they introduced me to something new on the internet, and that time it was something called Google Translate. An astonishing tool really, one I'm not afraid to admit I've used to help me read foreign correspondence a time or two since then."

The officials in the room laughed, humoring the president as he told his story but also trying to figure out where he was going with it.

Calmly, the president continued. "Well, last night as I was reading some of the notes you all prepared for me in advance of today's meeting, I looked up the word Leyandermál, which Ms.

James said the Vaniryans used to refer to the 'secret knowledge' Supay is looking for. I had a hunch. Took a few phonetic guesses and spelling variations, but once I got it right, turns out the Icelandic word Leyndarmál is Icelandic for the word *secret*. The words are practically identical. Does anyone think that's a coincidence?"

The president looked around waiting for an answer, but the room remained dead silent. "I didn't think so. Anyway, that's what I spent my time doing last night after dinner. What were the experts doing? I'm sure not looking that up or I would've heard about it. Sue, I'm done waiting for the so-called experts to figure this out. We've run out of time. For centuries, the world has been telling us about this 'secret,' warning us that today was coming, giving us a chance to prepare, and we didn't listen… well, everyone except for Emma James and Logan West. So, Sue, to answer your question, I *am* sending the experts into the field first. There's more in Iceland to find, and frankly, Emma and Logan are the ones I want looking at it. Any other questions?"

The president again waited for someone to speak up. No one did, and so, President Barrett stood up and said, "Alright, everybody. Get me the Readiness Preparation Proposal by the end of the week."

Yes, sir, said the room collectively as President Barrett walked out.

ΔΔΔΔΔΔΔΔΔΔΔΔ

Logan sat on Emma's bed while she packed a duffle bag with clothes, grabbing anything she could find to stuff into it. "You know, if you overpack it, you're not going to have any room left for shoes or souvenirs," he said.

Emma smiled, then began tearing up. She went to sit down next to him. She buried her head in his chest and he put his arm around her. "I want to feel safe back here in our world, in our own time, but honestly, I'm just really scared, Logan."

"Yeah, I know. Me, too," he replied, rubbing her back. "We're going to get through this."

"Why me? All I ever wanted to be was a cryptologist."

"You've always been a whole lot more than that since the day I met you."

"I'm serious."

"Me, too. Do you think I'd fall in love with just any cryptologist?"

He's succeeded in bringing a smile back to her face. Emma sat up and wiped her eyes. "You know I love you, too, right?"

"I do," replied Logan, hoping someday to hear those same two words from Emma during their wedding vows. He wanted to ask her to marry him in the worst way, but the moment just didn't feel right. It felt selfish. Emma's mind was understandably elsewhere, frightened and worried, and now more than ever, she had bigger things to deal with. They both did.

"Logan, what you and Jonas did, finding us, risking your lives to save ours, was incredible. Not a lot of people would have done that, I mean, you risked everything."

"I'd do anything for you."

Emma knew he meant it. Never had she felt more loved. "When we get back from Iceland, I promise we'll go back to Hobā for that DO-OVER, okay?"

"Sounds good," he replied.

She leaned in for a kiss and an extended embrace. Then, she stood up. "Alright, I'm going to jump in the shower, before we head out to the airport. Just give me like 20 minutes."

"Sure."

Logan stepped out of the bedroom and Emma disappeared into her bathroom to take a shower. She soaped her body and shampooed the little hair on her head which had started to grow back. After finishing, she let the hot water run on her face and head, keeping her eyes closed for a few minutes of solace. Inside her mind, she felt safe for a time, but then, Supay's wretched face crept into her thoughts. Supay glared back at her and said:

If you had just come with me, girl, I would have spared everyone... every living soul on that planet would have survived.

"That's not true!" snapped Emma angrily, fighting back against her overwhelming sense of guilt for Vanirya's destruction. She tried to shake Supay from her mind but couldn't. Instead, she imagined him saying: *I hope you make the right choice next time when I find you on Earth.*

Emma opened her eyes. Doing so was the only way to make the thoughts of Supay go away. She turned off the water, rubbed her face, grabbed a towel, stepped out of the shower, and tied it around her body. She moved to the sink and looked into a steamed-up mirror. She reached forward to wipe it off, but instead, her mind drifted again, this time to something else they were flying to Iceland to investigate. Rather than wiping off the mirror, using her index finger, she wrote into the steam, *Issor.* "I'm going to find you, I promise," she whispered. Since Vaniryans lived for thousands of years, in her heart, she had to hope Isa was still alive in Iceland or somewhere else on Earth.

With the steam slowly starting to evaporate, Emma saw in the reflection the mirror on the wall behind her, reflecting Issor's name spelled backward... *rossI.*

"Wait a second!" she uttered. Rossi, the exact reverse spelling of Issor, was her mother Mary *Rossi* James's maiden name! In near disbelief, she re-wrote the words issor and rossi into the mirror before the steam dissipated to see them one more time:

rossi
issor

Emma was floored. Was there a relationship between her mom's maiden name, Rossi, and her dear friend Issor? Was it possible Isa, stuck on Earth 816 years ago, changed her shape to fit in among humans, and maybe even started a family, flipping her name around to spell Rossi? Was Isa a long-lost ancestor, a relative of Emma's?

Emma started laughing out loud. Suddenly, the near-instantaneous bond she had forged with Isa that seemed so hard to explain and wonderful, seemed so obvious. Emma abruptly finished getting ready. She was anxious to get out the door. It was time to go find Isa.

The End...

Audiobooks

If you enjoyed THE COORDINATE (Book 1) or THE HIDDEN COORDINATE (Book 2) in book format, perhaps you would enjoy hearing it performed by the amazing audio narrator, MacLeod Andrews, produced by the amazing publisher, Podium Audio!! Available on Audible now!!

THE COORDINATE (Book 1 in *The Coordinate* Series)

THE HIDDEN COORDINATE
(Book 2 in *The Coordinate* Series)

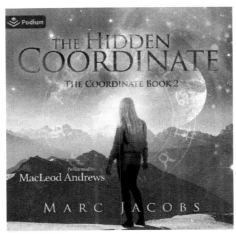

Leave A Review

Thank you for buying THE HIDDEN COORDINATE, Book 2 in THE COORDINΔTE Series. I truly hope that you enjoyed it, and if you did, please consider leaving a review for THE HIDDEN COORDINATE and/or rating it, so that others can discover THE COORDINΔTE Series and join in on the adventures of Emma James and Logan West. I would love to hear your feedback. Leaving a review anywhere would be great, but also, please considering leaving a review on Amazon or Goodreads too!

Receive Updates

Receive updates for the sequel (Book 3) and audiobook releases by signing up for Updates at www.marcjacobsauthor.com or by emailing me at marc@marcjacobsauthor.com

Contact Me

If you would like to contact me, I would love to hear from you. Please visit my website at www.marcjacobsauthor.com or shoot me an email at marc@marcjacobsauthor.com.

Thank you!

Marc

About Marc Jacobs

I have always looked to the stars as a reminder of humanity's minuscule place in the universe. I find inspiration in the science fiction genre because it feeds the imagination and keeps people believing in a greater world of possibilities. In my debut science fiction novel, THE COORDINATE, and the sequel to my first novel, THE HIDDEN COORDINATE, I continue to explore a question that I have wondered about my entire life, one that has remained unanswered throughout the history of mankind, "Are we alone in the universe?"

Once again proving that no moment in life is to be wasted, as I did with the first book in The Coordinate series, I wrote THE HIDDEN COORDINATE while driving to and from work every day, dictating the story into my iPhone Notes App. As long as the traffic on the streets of Los Angeles continues, I should have plenty of time to keep on writing!

Credits

Book Cover: Alexandre Rito / Podium Audio

Voynich Manuscript Cover and All Interior Images depicting the Voynich Manuscript - Beinecke Rare Book and Manuscript Library, Yale University

Made in the USA
Middletown, DE
29 May 2020